TALINA
IN THE TOWER
a tale of beastly tongues

Michelle Lovric

Orion
Children's Books

First published in Great Britain in 2012
by Orion Children's Books
a division of the Orion Publishing Group Ltd
Orion House 5 Upper St Martin's Lane London WC2H 9EA
An Hachette UK Company

1 3 5 7 9 10 8 6 4 2

The Orion Publishing Group's policy is to use papers that
are natural, renewable and recyclable products and made from
wood grown in sustainable forests. The logging and
manufacturing processes are expected to conform to
the environmental regulations of the country of origin.

A catalogue record for this book
is available from the British Library.

ISBN 978 1 4440 0338 3

Typeset by Input Data Services Ltd, Bridgwater, Somerset

Printed in Great Britain by Clays Ltd, St Ives plc

CONTENTS

PROLOGUE

Venice, November 30th, 1866, Saint Andrea's Day

A S THE MOON rose, so they came.

Eyes cast down, the water-rats rowed their fearsome passengers, easing the boats through ink-dark canals without so much as a creak of an oar. Those rats knew it would be death to make a noise: instant death by blow and claw, with a clean skeleton floating on the morning tide like a white flute-shell surrendered to the battering ocean.

Their passengers disembarked without a backward glance. The rats kept their heads bowed. The creatures' claws rasped on mossy wooden steps and clicked on Istrian marble, a stink of old meat and wine sauce floating behind them. They padded along narrow streets where the windows were tightly shuttered against the ferocious cold.

The only sounds, apart from the click of claws, came from fretful children and their lullabying mothers. Hearing a little girl's cry, the creatures paused a moment, looking up. They scratched a sign on the door. Then they moved on, stopping

I

only if they noticed a cat cowering in the shadows.

'Ze Venetian cats are too thin,' they complained. But they took them anyway.

When each slope-backed creature reached the bell-tower of its assigned church, it began to climb. From lintel to sill, they swung their darkly furred limbs. From stone to brick to wood they moved, too self-assured to hurry and yet too powerful to be slow.

It was exactly one minute before two in the morning when each beast finally mounted the spire of its tower. The moon hung low in the sky like an over-ripe apricot, illuminating a sudden, terrifying change to the silhouettes of one hundred and seventeen Venetian bell-towers from Santa Maria Valverde to Santa Chiara. Instead of pretty finials and angels, the tops of those towers now bore the shapes of shaggy creatures with long jaws and pale opal eyes aglow above the matted darkness of their muzzles.

The bells tolled. As the two rich, sad notes faded, each creature pointed its snout to the moon and howled in a strange language. It sounded like Venetian distorted by an exaggerated and quite unconvincing French accent.

'GIVE EET BACK!'

The howls echoed down the Grand Canal, across to Giudecca, and then rolled off into the lagoon.

'Give eet back!' demanded the echo, 'Give eet back! Give eet b ... a ... c ... k!'

On top of the magnificent onion-domed bell-tower of the church of the Madonna dell'Orto, the greatest of the creatures drew his jaws back in a ghastly grin, spat out his sage-leaf cigar and shook a huge clenched paw.

'GIVE EET BACK!' he howled, louder than all the others.

Then the Lord of the creatures added, with the strongest and worst French accent of all, 'OR WE SHALL COME AND GET EET.'

2

On the morning of December 1st, 1866, the Venetians woke with a terrible sense of something wrong. It was not just that their cats did not come home for breakfast. The Venetians felt guilty, as if they had forgotten their mothers' birthdays. No one talked of seeing or hearing the creatures on the bell-towers. Or at least, if they did remember some howling in the night, they put it down to the habitual groans of the pipes in their ancient houses, or to the shrieking *bora* wind that haunted the city in winter.

'*Tempo da lupi*,' people called it. 'Wolf weather.'

But every night after that, the creatures would mount the bell-towers and howl their demand. And their threats. And shortly afterwards, they began to act on them.

Now it was not just the cats. Each night, another Venetian disappeared: men, women, children. A curfew was imposed.

Of course, there were whispered rumours of wild, shaggy creatures rowed in gondolas by rats. The street-cleaners complained that in the early hours a dreadful smell permeated the air: something that stank like meaty, rotten dog-breath. One man even claimed to have heard the creatures talking in rasping voices under his window. In *French*, he said.

But Gianni Nanon, pale and wild from lack of sleep, was dismissed as a fantasist by the editor of the newspaper, who printed the story simply as a joke:

'FRENCH GHOST-CREATURES' OVERHEARD BY 'IMAGINATIVE' VENETIAN. PLAGUE OF KIDNAPPINGS CONTINUES. MORE CATS MISSING. NEW RAIDS ON VENICE SWEET SHOPS. CHIEF SUSPECTS: PASTRY-BANDITS FROM ROVIGO. RANSOM NOTES AWAITED.

Rovigo was a shabby town on the mainland. Her unruly citizens were famous (and much mocked) because every single one of them was cursed with an incurable sweet tooth. Why cursed? Because every single bakery in Rovigo was afflicted with an inability to cook a cake that would rise or a cream pie that didn't curdle. Of course, this might be explained by the rats who infested every flour sack and butter churn: no town ever needed cats like Rovigo did. The cake-starved Rovigans had earned their nickname 'Pastry-Bandits' from greedy raids on nearby Venice, famous for the genius of her bakers. Blaming Rovigo for the kidnappings of humans and cats suited most Venetians, even though it hardly explained why the raiders were also stripping the bakeries of every single pan, fork, knife and ladle.

Yes, people said, it was all Rovigo's fault. But that did not get the crimes solved or the lost Venetians back. Despite the complete lack of ransom notes from Rovigo, the alternative explanation for the kidnappings and catnappings was simply too terrible: no one wanted to believe a bespectacled, curly-haired boy called Ambrogio Gasperin, who had crept out in the night in his dressing-gown to sketch the silhouette of a savage creature on the very top of the dangerously leaning bell-tower of Santo Stefano.

Ambrogio Gasperin labelled his picture 'French Monster on the Crooked *Campanile*' and brought it to school next day.

Ambrogio's French mistress, Mademoiselle Chouette, shuddered when she saw it. '*Français*! Neverrr! *Des navets*! Turnips! *Non*!'

With a toss of her neat head, she gave Ambrogio one hundred lines: '*I shall not make things up. I shall do my proper French homework, not drawings. And I shall not argue with my teacher.*'

Using a hand still sore from those hundred lines, Ambrogio defiantly nailed his drawing to a tree in the playground before he went home. But by next morning, it had been ripped away, violently. A shred of paper dangled from the loosened nail.

The howling continued in the night.

And Venetians, their cakes and their cats, continued to disappear without trace. After Ambrogio Gasperin's drawing, more boys were taken than girls.

It was some weeks before people began to notice that the doors of those who vanished were always defaced by a scratch of five long, sharp nails.

1
On the night of the full moon

Venice, January 30th, 1867, Saint Martina's Day

ON THE NIGHT of the full moon, Talina's father did not come home from work. Well after dusk, when everyone else had gone, he sat frowning at a piece of paper on his rosewood desk behind the panelled door that bore the sign,

Marco Molin,
Keeper of Most Ancient Manuscripts,
Department of Malignant Spells,
Invoked Pestilences and Abominable Rites

'It cannot be true,' he said over and over again. 'No! Such an unfair, frightful thing!'

But his disbelief failed to make the piece of paper any less real.

The door to his office rattled.

'Who's there?' he called into the empty air. 'I can smell you.'

He screamed once, before he was silenced.

'Your papà must have forgotten the time!' Talina's mother said affectionately. 'I'd best go and remind him. No, you can't come, too. Remember the curfew!'

She added darkly, 'And remember why we have it.'

Lucia Molin smoothed her daughter's wild dark-gold hair, which tumbled from her head like a curtain of tangled corn husks, too full of life to ever be confined in a plait.

'Go to bed, kitten,' she urged. 'We'll be back before you fall asleep.'

When her mamma failed to return by midnight, Talina lit a lantern and threaded her way carefully through the dark streets to the Venetian Archives. The city breathed its night sighs into her ears. Her cat Drusilla trotted alongside, casting suspicious looks into every dark corner.

At the Archives everything was dark and locked. Talina inched her way around the building, checking for scratches on the door and the smell of rotten meat. She threw stones at a certain high window, shouting 'Mamma!' and 'Papà!' Finally she sat down on the marble steps, tucking herself, cross-legged, into the shadow of the lintel.

Talina was just thinking about bursting into tears when Drusilla climbed into her lap, thrusting her soft black muzzle into her mistress's face.

'I've tried everything, Drusilla,' protested Talina, stroking the cat. She was now only one prickly sneeze away from those tears.

'Indeed, and all in vain, of course.' A man's voice fell like the winter's night itself: bitter, cold and quiet. Talina looked up into a familiar face clad in skin as thin and grey as a dusty cobweb in a dark room.

'What are *you* doing here?' she whispered. 'Breaking the curfew? Were you lying in lurk for me?'

'Since I'm your Guardian, obviously, I've come to take you home with me.'

'I am going to wait for Mamma and Papà. Not. Going. With. You.'

He sighed, a small gush of cold air without the warmth of compassion. 'In spite of your reputation as the most impudent girl in Venice, Talina Molin, that is exactly what you are going to do.'

On days when Talina had achieved the very pinnacle of naughtiness, on days when her French mistress Mademoiselle Chouette, the neighbour Signora Cassian and the local policeman complained in outraged terms about her behaviour and what they described as her 'beastly tongue' – those were the days when Talina's father had threatened, with a catch in his voice, 'If you don't behave better, kitten,' – her parents always called her 'kitten' – 'then we'll be forced to send you to live with your great uncle Uberto in his lonely stone tower on the edge of Castello. He is your Guardian, remember. You know the way it works. One more little flouncy and ...'

The thought of going to live with her great uncle Uberto had been enough to make Talina rewrite her wickedly rude French essay and clean up the pool of fake egret blood outside Signora Cassian's house. She'd even written a 'sorry' letter to Signora Cassian, with no 'buts' in it at all.

Now, in the dim light of her lantern, her Guardian poked at Talina disparagingly with his pointed black shoe, as if she was something unpleasant he'd nearly trodden in.

'Get up.'

'No.' Loyal Drusilla hissed in agreement.

The Guardian bent over Talina. Their eyes met: his, small,

pale and expressionless; hers, large, brown and glittering with rebellious tears.

'Wilful, is it? I do not tolerate indiscipline. Neither in children nor cats. In fact I don't tolerate cats at all. Vile, thieving beasts, without a conscience.'

Drusilla leapt off Talina's lap, erected her right back leg like a spear and showed just what she thought of the Guardian's words.

'I'm waiting for my parents,' insisted Talina. 'I'll wait all night if I need to.'

The Guardian's hard fingers sought her shoulder, wrenching her out of the doorway and into the moonlight. He tugged her long hair until she moaned with pain and straightened up. Drusilla leapt into Talina's arms, her teeth bared.

'Evidently you do not have parents any more.'

'Liar! Liar! You're a forty-faced liar, each one of them ugly!' Talina finally succumbed to the tears that so badly wanted to come out.

'All writers are liars. And you shall soon become accustomed to the sight of this face, girl. It's a matter of indifference to me whether it appeals to you. Or not. But let me have a look at you, quickly. I may find those tears useful.'

'*Useful*?' sobbed Talina. 'You are a monster! And I *hate* all your stories, particularly *The Orphan-Eaters* and *The Rack & Ruin of Raffaele Rasa*, *The Dire Deaths of Daniele Dario* and *The Miseries of Maria Montin*. And worst of all *Talina in the Tower*. How dare you use my name? I can't imagine why anyone would want to read all those dreadful stories. Why do you always kill off the children or the parents in them?'

'I notice you've *read* all those stories. Good little girls usually die. They must do, as one so rarely hears of them in real life. And parents generally disappear . . .' His voice was

9

chill and light as mist, '. . . one way or another.'

'Mine are coming *back*, I tell you,' sobbed Talina.

'I don't believe so. If they *would* insist on going out at full moon, what could they expect? And I must have my dues, of course.'

He pulled a notebook from the pocket of his long black coat and turned Talina's face from side to side, swiftly noting down how her tears shone dimly like moonstones in the lamplight and how her shoulders trembled when she sobbed.

'Now come,' he snapped the notebook shut. 'Quickly. We've tarried long enough.'

Talina said, 'If I can't wait here, then I'm going back to my own home.'

'You don't own your home. You are a child. You own nothing in the whole world.'

As he spoke, a dense, jagged shadow traced the ground in front of them, and a sudden look of terror contorted his features. Above, large wings flapped.

'What bird could be so big?' wondered Talina.

The Guardian seized Talina by the elbow and dragged her through the dark streets, over the Rialto Bridge, through San Marco and all the way to his tower at Quintavalle at the far end of Castello. Talina struggled in the Guardian's bony grip. Drusilla followed at a wary distance on silent paws. The flapping shadow was never far away, swooping across buildings in their path.

Suddenly the tower lurched out of the water in front of them, slapped by shafts of moonlight, which revealed tall pocked walls studded with sparrows' nests. The shadow swooped up the wall, and a cloud of sparrows skittered upwards, shrill with fear.

Her Guardian unlocked the door and pushed Talina inside. Drusilla slunk in too, before he had time to slam the door in her face.

'Enter at your own risk, cat,' Great Uncle Uberto hissed. From behind him came a cacophony of growls and snapping jaws. 'May I present my wolfhounds, Razin, Futfallo and Gierch-it.'

Drusilla leapt up to the mantelpiece, where she stood with her tail plumed and her eyes narrowed. The dogs scrabbled on their back legs, baying at her.

'Accredited cat-killers each and every one.' The Guardian's pleasure was chilled by bitterness. 'Otherwise, I wouldn't have bought them.'

'Just one night! That's absolutely all we're spending here,' shouted Talina.

2
Rune-ish and rumpled

the tower at Quintavalle, three months later:
April 29th,1867, Saint Caterina's Day

TALINA SAT BOLT upright in bed, woken by the
howling. She cried out, 'Mamma! Papà!'

But somewhere at the back of her sleep-muzzy
mind lurked the sad awareness that no one had seen a trace
of her parents in the last three months. And behind that lay
the knowledge that the howling happened every night at two
o'clock. She reassured herself that no paws had left scratches
on the door of the tower. She was scrupulous about checking
every evening before going to bed, just as the chittering of
the sparrows grew drowsy and soft.

None of the other stolen Venetians had come back. But
this didn't mean that Talina was going to give up on her
parents. Giving up was not in her nature. She had written
out a hundred 'WANTED' notes with sketched likenesses
of her parents. She had pinned them on street walls, sent
them off on home-made kites on windy days and launched
them down the Grand Canal in bottles. She pushed them into

the hands of tourists in San Marco and into the handbags of old ladies waiting for trains. But there had been not one single reply. So all these weeks later, Talina was still waking up every morning in the twittering tower at Quintavalle, longing for the touch of her mother's hand and the sound of her father's voice.

Drowsiness tugged at Talina's eyelids. She settled back under the fraying quilt, rearranging her tangle of corn-husk hair like a sleeping-cap.

Talina's huge bed was nothing more than a straw pallet supported on four piles of encyclopaedias. The counterpane was covered with books three layers deep. This left just a narrow channel in the middle, into which Talina inserted herself and Drusilla, like two letters in an envelope. Spring was running desperately late that year, and the tower seemed to soak up the cold of the lagoon through its walls. The Guardian, however, had not provided anything more than a thin, hairy blanket, and the ancient patchwork quilt. Drusilla could lie against only one side of Talina at a time, comforting her with body heat, a soft, fast heartbeat and a sensation of being still at home. So Talina had to keep the other side warm with books.

Interestingly, some books were warmer than others. She'd banished the chilly binding of the thrilling *Adventures on Snow-Capped Peaks* from the bed, in favour of a cosy old cookbook called *Warm from the Oven* and Professor Marìn's latest volume, *Midsummer Sprites*, which was just like a hot-water bottle.

Much as she despised her Guardian's books, Talina was determined to be a writer too. She'd been writing stories since she was five. She'd been sending them off to book publishers and magazines since she was eight. She had written more than five dozen stories about ghosts, cats, castles, monsters and extremely clever children. She was

13

always halfway through one, with three others simmering, and new ideas thickly scribbled on the flyleaves of old books.

Some of her most vivid ideas came from her dreams, especially since her parents had disappeared. She was so afraid to lose a brilliant thought in the night that she'd hung hundreds of pencils and pieces of paper from the roof's beams on lengths of string. So, without even lighting a candle, she could always find a pencil with her fingers and make notes on the nearest scrap of paper. Some mornings, she woke up to find all the pieces of paper covered with scribbles. Sometimes she'd written ten different things one over the other on the same piece of paper, which was very irritating. Talina was an exceptionally tidy little dancer but her handwriting was not neat, even in daylight, even on lined paper, even when done under the teacher's nose. Done blind, in the middle of the night and half-asleep, Talina's handwriting was frankly rune-ish and rumpled.

Despite all her brilliant ideas, Talina had not managed to sell any of her stories to *The Wonderful World of Girls* or *The Young Ladies' Literary Gazette* or any of the other publications that so frequently printed her Guardian's terrible tales.

Whenever Talina received a rejection letter, she always sent one right back, rejecting it: '*Your lack of imagination staggered me sideways till I realized that a person of your limited sensitivity could not possibly understand work as complex and subtle as mine. So go and boil your boots in ginger beer and stop using them to stamp on budding talent.*'

She'd received so many rejection letters that she used them to wrap her snack for school every day – after she'd used the backs of them for writing her own ideas in the night.

But in the last month, Talina had finally found secret employment and a small income as a writer. By pretending to be a noblewoman of thirty-five with a 'nervous debility', she'd secured a job writing testimonials for a patent medicine known as Manitoba Gargling Oil. Talina's letters were printed in advertisements in the paper, just as if they came from a real woman.

Dear Sir, – Forgive my humble missive but nothing could stop me from expressing my gratitude. I was racked by a sick-headache: such a grip did it get upon me that I was obliged to take to my bed. This was my shipwrecked state when I first sampled your excellent preparation, Manitoba Gargling Oil. Not only did it cure me of the pain in my head, but also of warts, eye-strain and toothache. In short, I should long since have been dead but for your life-saving product. I shall, at all opportunities, recommend Manitoba Gargling Oil, which I believe to be of general benefit to mankind.

Talina signed herself 'Principessa Paulina Pessel'.

'Principessa Paulina Pessel' received 100 lire for every letter that was published, and a free sample of the oil. She used it to clean her boots.

She didn't want her Guardian to know about her job, so for all correspondence with the Manitoba Gargling Oil Company, Talina used what she still considered her 'home' address in the Calle del Teatro. She went there whenever she could to check for letters stuck into the grates of the oval windows on the ground floor. She couldn't get inside any more: lately, her Guardian had ordered the front door sealed with a chain, 'to prevent looting'. But who, Talina thought scornfully, would want to loot her tiny, shabby home, which had more books than silver forks?

Now the morning light was seeping under her eyelids; the wet wrestling of the waves below washed into her ears.

Drusilla licked her nose. There was no point in putting off the unspeakable moment. Talina was famished and no one was going to bring her breakfast in bed. No one was going to bring her breakfast at all, in fact. And she'd woken up with a better idea than breakfast anyway.

She leapt out of bed, planting her feet on the icy floor with a little shriek. She poured cold water out of her jug into a chipped basin and hurriedly washed all the important places, while hopping up and down to keep warm. Drusilla conducted her own more thorough grooming on the patchwork quilt. Talina cast a quick eye out of the window – another sunny, frosty day. The last few black-stalked apples glowed in the trees down in the Calle dei Pomeri. Across the lagoon, Talina could see a fresh fall of snow on the hills of the mainland. Immediately below her, in Quintavalle's single V-shaped street, people's shadows were growing blackly out of their feet, and even the pigeons had their dark twins. The orchards on the north side of the island glittered with frost. Snow and frost in late April! That was an unwelcome rarity in Venice. Everyone was complaining about it, especially Talina.

Now she wriggled into five layers of clothing – starting with cotton cami-knickers, continuing with two flannel petticoats, followed by a linen dress, and then a thick woollen one, finally covering the whole bulk with a pinafore. She slid into woollen stockings and laced her boots, still a little sticky with Manitoba Gargling Oil.

Then she hurried downstairs to the kitchen of her Guardian's tower. She did not need to worry that he would be there. She seldom saw him, unless he required her to model as some wretched child in its death throes for one of his books. Great Uncle Uberto inhabited the upper storeys, where Talina was forbidden to go. Just occasionally, late at night, her door creaked open and she caught a glimpse of the thin silhouette of her Guardian, and felt his pale eyes staring at her.

'No doubt hoping to find me weeping or foaming at the mouth in a fit brought on by awful impudence!' Talina harrumphed silently to herself. She posted signs saying 'Keep out!' and 'PRIVATE' on her door, and always pretended to be soundly asleep, breathing deeply. Eventually, his light footsteps could be heard climbing to the remote heights of the tower.

Every child in Venice knew the fairytale tower where Talina now lived. Yet no one knew exactly when it had been made, though it must have been at least a thousand years before. And no one had ever taken care of it since. It was built of brick and pierced with arched windows on each floor until the belfry, which was topped by a pinecone spire. There was a risky-looking lean to the east, which partly accounted for the disappearance of the old bell – swept through the arches and down into the lagoon in a storm many centuries past. Missing bricks had made a honeycomb of its outer walls, in which thousands of sparrows built their nests, so the tower twittered quietly to itself from dawn to dusk.

The tower perched uneasily in the lagoon on the north-eastern edge of the city. It was planted in the water, its base furrily mossed between the low- and high-tide marks. A cast-iron bridge, narrow and rickety, connected it to the land and its former church, Our Lady of the Sparrows, now ivy-clad and derelict. Just above the bridge's rusted guard-rail was a loose brick, where the key to the tower was hidden.

From a distance, the tower looked cold and achingly lonely: inside it was colder and lonelier still. After three months' residence, Talina felt a sharp pang every time she saw other girls holding their mothers' hands. She hated to see fathers rowing their daughters to school. Even though the Guardian was famously rich, there was no jolly housekeeper, no maid, no valet, no butler and no cook. Instead, the three savage dogs, beaten into cravenness, fetched and carried. Drusilla catnapped in the kitchen at her peril.

However, Talina only had to step across the drawbridge if she wanted kind and gentle company. Talina may have been deprived of parents, but she was not deprived of grannies. Quintavalle was an island of elderly widows and their cats. No one knew why there were so many of them. Granny baking smells permeated the Quintavalle air. Granny-shaped underwear hung from cross-hatched clothes lines between the houses on the south side of the street. Grannies with baskets sat knitting while they waited for windfalls from the apple trees on the north side. And just as there were hundreds of old ladies on the island, so there was a complete absence of children, apart from Talina. She'd been joyfully adopted as an honorary grand-daughter by all the old ladies of Quintavalle.

Walking home from school took a great deal of time, as she stopped to have her cheeks pinched, her nose kissed, an almond comfit pushed into her mouth, or she was asked to wind wool, or hold a naughty cat for its nails to be clipped while listening to a story told by a granny with a face as soft and lined as a bunched-up silk handkerchief. The grannies taught her the dances of their girlhoods: the *Furlana*, the *Fancyman Jig* and the *Fascinating Stoat*, accompanying her on the country bagpipes. Nonna Meghin giggled, 'You know how a stoat mesmerizes its prey by dancing? Well, the *Fascinating Stoat* will *confuzzle* any male!' Talina didn't really know what confuzzling was, but she loved the rippling, frenetic dance. In church on Sunday mornings, Talina's sure treble mingled with the sweet warbles of the grannies.

Afterwards, she'd come home with one granny or another for milk and cake.

'Dear, dear,' the old ladies clucked, as Talina, petted to pieces, finally left for the lonely tower. 'That little girl is too thin, and too wild, and too lonely. I hope there's a good hot Sunday lunch waiting for her.'

Talina didn't have the heart to tell them the truth. There was never a hot meal waiting for her. She assembled her own meals from the ingredients that were provided without her ever asking for anything. Every morning, food appeared in a spotted swag on the doorstep. The dog called Futfallo stood on his back legs, nudged open the door bolt, picked up the swag and dumped it, snarling, on the table. Gierch-it delivered the post. If either dog even hinted at usurping the other's role, there were bared teeth and lunges. Talina was most afraid of the dog named Razin. He always came unnecessarily close, and breathed on her for an unnecessarily long time when he delivered her pocket-money in a yellow leather pouch. Everything, from *The Young Ladies' Literary Gazette* to onions for the stew, arrived at the tower with a thin coating of dog saliva.

Talina never saw her Guardian eat. Even on Easter Sunday, Talina and Drusilla had shared a tearful supper alone in the kitchen, remembering her parents and festive feasts past.

She wondered what her Guardian dined on.

'Small children, probably,' she muttered to Drusilla as she clattered pots and bowls onto the kitchen table. 'That's what *he* eats. He certainly enjoys killing 'em off in his stories, so he must do something with all those corpses. Or perhaps he feeds them to the dogs.'

'*Too much imagination and <u>not enough</u> discipline*,' the French mistress, Mademoiselle Chouette, had scribbled on Talina's essay on the subject of creatures who howled in the night, their pedigree in literature, and in Venice, to which she had added an eye-watering account of the evil doings of an old man who lived in a lonely tower. Many were the French mistress's underlinings and capitals. '*Ravenous reading without discrimination is NOT advisable*, particularly *in a child with FLOUNCING tendencies*.'

'Poor style, exaggerated and ineffective,' commented Talina, correcting the corrections at the kitchen table while she ate. She could just imagine Mademoiselle Chouette shaking her surprisingly pretty turquoise earrings in horror as she scribbled out the red wiggly lines under some colourful words and reinstated the exciting adjectives that had been crossed out. In Talina's opinion, the woman misguidedly thought it her duty to correct every child who ever opened her mouth.

The French teacher had insisted, '*As if it wasn't* tragique *enough trying to make sense of your appalling handwriting*, petite *Talina, but you also insist on these ridiculous fantasies! You must try to confine your stories to things that might* actually *happen. Dogs do* NOT *deliver dinners. Nasty old men do* NOT *eat children*.'

There was an extra line, scribbled out, at the end of these comments. Talina, surrounded by cooking ingredients in the kitchen, held her essay up to the lamplight, and read the words Mademoiselle Chouette had written but then tried to hide beneath slashes of ink, '*By the way, those vile creatures are* NOT *French. They have the most appalling mockery of a French accent that I have ever heard*. C'est abominable!'

Talina marvelled, 'Oh my! So Mademoiselle Chouette *has* seen them. Or at least heard them. *She* knows it's not Pastry-Bandits from Rovigo taking the people and the cats.'

Drusilla nudged Talina's hand towards the mixing bowl. Breakfast's pancakes had been a disaster rejected even by Razin. This evening Talina had a much more ambitious plan. She didn't fancy the lamb chops Razin had brought her, so she'd laid them out as peace offerings on the floor. She felt like something warm and sweet for supper.

'The oven's hot?' Talina applied her wooden spoon so violently that several spoonfuls of cake mixture departed the bowl in the direction of the walls, the sugar basin, the coal scuttle, the recipe books and Drusilla's nose. 'Nearly ready. We don't want lumps, do we? I do so hate it when cakes go wrong. Now where was I?'

She lifted a floury hand to turn two batter-splattered pages simultaneously.

It never occurred to her that such a simple thing might change her life.

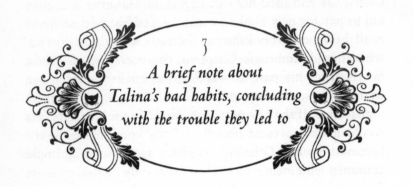

3

*A brief note about
Talina's bad habits, concluding
with the trouble they led to*

ONE THING WAS true about her French teacher's criticism. Talina was a ravenous reader, and did not much care what she read. The problem was getting *enough* to read. For Talina had a very special skill. She could read two books at once: one with each eye. So she needed twice as many books as even an ordinary bookworm.

Only Signorina Tatti, the school librarian, suspected something was afoot, though she'd never actually caught Talina in the act. Talina had scraped the shelves of the library to the very furthest reaches, taking home even *Analytical Chemistry of Venetian Drains 1832* and the Library Catalogue when all else had been consumed by those avid eyes of hers. When Talina had read the library dry, Signorina Tatti was obliged to ask the School Board for an increased budget for book acquisitions. The librarian grumbled to Talina, 'They threatened to take it from my wages next time!'

Talina had kept her two-books-at-a-time talent a secret from her parents, knowing that her appetite for reading would quickly outstrip her father's earnings at the Archives.

She did not want them to go without just to keep her in books. She found other ways of feeding her reading habit. Lately, she had used her earnings from Manitoba Gargling Oil to pay for new books by instalments. She had accounts at all the Venetian bookshops. Discreetly, with the help of her schoolfriend Ambrogio Gasperin, she borrowed the latest novels from his parents' fashionable bookshop near San Marco. Those she kept out of the kitchen, returning them immaculate. If she saw notice of a death in the *Gazzetta*, she would always present herself and her condolences at the bereaved house. Grieving relatives, faced with a house crammed with memories to clear, were only too happy to let Talina take away an armful of heavy books.

Talina would read anything: encyclopaedias, veterinary manuals, romantic novels and children's fairytales. The only exception was anything written by her Guardian. She had no need to re-read such horrors as *How Rodrigo Lost his Legs* or *Whatever Happened to Enrico?* Unfortunately, every household in Venice seemed to have several of them. For generations, Talina thought sadly, so many lively Venetian children had been terrorized into dull good behaviour by those dense little volumes.

Talina was not one of them. Her parents were too kind to mention her Guardian very often, so most of the time Talina was indeed the most impudent girl in Venice, and sometimes referred to as 'The Terror of the Neighbourhood'.

It wasn't just what her parents described affectionately as 'Talina's having a little flouncy' – when she lost her temper and spoke 'in beastly tongues'. Talina went in for a lot of campaigns. For example there was the one against killing egrets for their feathers. Fashionable women liked to wear the delicate white plumes in their hats, not caring that the beautiful birds had to die in order to provide them. Talina had climbed in through a window to 'borrow' the egret-

23

feather hat of her modish neighbour, Signora Cassian. She dipped the feathers in red paint. Then she put the hat on, with a carving knife added at a rakish angle, and danced around Venice, letting the egret 'blood' drip behind her. The *Gazzetta* had published a picture of Talina, standing on one leg to perform her scintillating egret dance in a pool of fake blood, with a sign on her pinafore that read,

EGRET FEATHERS ONLY LOOK BEAUTIFUL ON EGRETS. STOP THE SENSELESS SLAUGHTER.

Talina's famous egret dance was in fact rather similar to the *Fascinating Stoat*, those looping, weaving and 'confuzzling' steps she would soon be taught by the grannies of Quintavalle – which perhaps explained how well she took to it. But the egret dance had led to trouble: Signora Cassian recognized her missing hat in that picture, and there'd been a note on Talina's report card from her French mistress Mademoiselle Chouette that asked, '*Why must the most intelligent girl in my class also be the most bad, the most nearly mad, and the most impudent?*'

'This is exactly the sort of thing that will make Great Uncle Uberto say it's time to take you to the tower, kitten,' her papà warned, his face pale and his eyes almost wild. 'Just one more bad report from your school ... that's all he needs.' Her mother had uttered a faint protesting cry, hugging Talina tight to her chest.

'She's just a little fractious, Marco!'

When Talina was a baby, Great Uncle Uberto had offered to pay for her education. Her parents could not afford to refuse. There was no one else to help: their own families had been carried off by a cholera epidemic. Uberto Flangini already owned the lease on their tiny house in the Calle del Teatro near Santo Stefano. So, reluctantly, they'd signed a contract which stated that Talina would be 'taken in hand' if she proved dull-witted or failed to take advantage of her schooling or 'fell into bad, mad or impudent habits, as certified by her educational institution'.

'As if a child of ours could ever fail to be clever!' the Molins had reassured themselves. And indeed, Talina had proved a remarkably clever baby, and an even cleverer little girl. But her parents had not bargained for her being quite so impudent. Or being quite such a mistress of the 'little flouncy'.

The contract also specified that Talina must be 'made available for studying' whenever the Guardian wished to observe a real child for descriptive purposes in his books. So at least once every six weeks, Talina was required to attend Great Uncle Uberto's tower, where she had to submit to his commands to 'sag against the door as if you've just heard your best friend is dead' or 'lie down and look mortally ill with a wasting disease'. Worst of all, she hated climbing the stairs between the parlour and the best parlour, where she was obliged to perform her tragic enactments. Because as she rounded the last stair she always came face to face with a huge stuffed animal, something like a hyena, with a lot of wolf in it as well. Its fur was riddled with dust, and the stitching was gruesomely visible. She'd nicknamed it 'The Child-Mauling Thingy'. The sight of it never failed to make the hairs rise on the back of her neck.

And in the fine print at the end of the contract, Talina's parents had pretended not to notice – because it was quite unthinkable that it should ever happen – there was a clause that appointed Great Uncle Uberto as Talina's Guardian in the event of their own deaths. Both Talina's mother and father were decades younger than the Guardian, who was already an old man when Talina was born. In fact, he was so old that it was never fully established just how he was related to them. If the truth were known, each parent had thought that he belonged to an outer branch of the other's family tree. (In fact, Venice being tiny Venice, he was distantly related to both.)

When Talina first found out about her Guardian, she'd shuddered. But then she asked hopefully, 'Shouldn't my education include all the books I can read?'

Her parents had politely put that suggestion to the Guardian. His reply had been curt. 'Certainly I shall pay for the child's books. The ones I choose, that is. The ones least likely to encourage impudence.'

And so a boat had arrived stacked with all his own grisly tales in their expensive morocco bindings and with their horrid illustrations of wretched and ailing children. Talina raked through the crates, but all she found were multiple editions of *A Fatality in the Family*, *The Ruin of Rosato*, and *The Downfall of Davide*.

There was not a single book on magic, which was fast becoming Talina's favourite subject. For each birthday and Christmas, she begged another volume by the young Professor Marìn, a friend of her parents', who was causing such a stir in Venice with titles such as *Magical Means on a Budget*, *Beastly Tongues* and *Enchanted Eggs*.

Her parents worried about Talina's attraction to magic. Magic also seemed attracted to Talina. It even came off on her fingers.

'Show me your hands, dear,' Talina's mother would say at bedtime. 'Look, there's another bit of spell on your thumb! Where's the book?'

And Talina's mother would patiently find the smudged page, and press her daughter's thumb down upon it until the full text of the spell was restored to the paper.

'My goodness,' she would say. 'I worry about you, kitten. What if you got mixed up in the wrong kind of magic?'

'Is there a wrong kind?' wondered Talina.

At the memory of her mother's gentle hand on hers, Talina's eyes filled. She wiped them with a wrist coated in flour.

Apart from magic books, Talina loved recipe books. She adored to cook, favouring sugary dainties rather than savoury and wholesome dishes like Cream of Lima Bean Soup or Pressed Chicken. She also had a tendency to make terrible messes, spoil her clothes and burn her fingers.

She'd insisted on bringing her books to the tower of Quintavalle when she was forced to go and live there. The Guardian had allowed her just one official visit to her old home in the Calle del Teatro. In her parents' empty bedroom, Talina had climbed inside a wardrobe and shut the door, so she could breathe in the perfume of her mother's dresses. She'd pushed her hands inside her father's gloves. She'd laid her head on her mother's dressing table. But eventually, as the sun set in a blaze of red wine poured into orange juice, and the house grew dark, she'd gathered a few clothes and many books – mostly on cooking and magic – and dragged them in a trolley through the streets and over the bridges back to the twittering tower.

'Don't even think about it!' At Quintavalle, Talina shook her fist at the circling sparrows. She took off her coat and spread it over the books. She didn't care if they spattered her corn-husk hair. The evening light threw the tower's sharp shadow over the ruins of the church beside it in a menacing manner, making the tendrils of ivy seem to twitch and slither. But back inside her circular bedroom, the books made her feel very slightly more at home, as did the framed photograph of her parents that she'd hung above her bed.

Her tower bedroom being without even a fireplace, Talina spent as much time as possible in the kitchen. Cooking kept her warm. Although she still burnt her fingers and spoilt her dresses, Futfallo, Gierch-it and Razin nearly always devoured the messes these days. They'd have preferred to eat Drusilla, but they seemed to like burnt tarts and blackened toffee too.

That evening, Talina was unable to sleep. She'd been reading *Magical Means on a Budget* with one eye, and *Substantial Cakes for the Working Classes* with the other. Lying on her book bed, an idea came to her. She worked out that she could magically stretch two eggs, half a cup of slightly weevilly flour, a handful of sugar and a chocolate bar with dog tooth-marks in it into a 'Delicious Family-Sized Triple Layer Chocolate Sponge Cake'. She leapt out of bed as the bells of San Pietro struck midnight, and padded down to the kitchen with her lamp, Drusilla yawning and complaining behind her.

She'd closed the door to keep out the dogs, and lit the gilt-brass three-light chandelier that hung from the kitchen ceiling. The last of the flour had been emptied from the *Farina Fellina* sack with a little picture of a cat on it. The wood-burning oven was blazing, the cake-tin already buttered. Talina's dark-gold hair, eyelashes and mouth were ghostly with flour. And she was chatting nineteen to the dozen to Drusilla, whose fur too was bedecked with egg and sugar. Perhaps this was how Talina came to mix up the words of the two books she was reading at once.

Instead of 'fold in the *Farina Fellina*', Talina murmured abstractedly, *'fammi felina'* – 'make me feline'.

In other words, 'make me a cat'.

As she uttered the final syllable, she felt herself simultaneously shrinking, yowling and arching her back.

'Miaow,' said Talina. And no one could have been more surprised than Talina herself to hear it.

She tried to say, 'What the . . . !' But all that came out was another 'Miaow!'

She clapped her hand over her mouth. Or she would have done, if it had not turned into a little furry paw.

The top of the table disappeared. The floor was suddenly closer.

'I'm shrinking!' thought Talina as the two books clattered on to the floor beside her, along with the wooden spoon. Her clothes tumbled off her like the leaves of an over-ripe artichoke.

'Miaowwww!' screeched Talina, struggling out of a tangle of linen and wool, to find herself face to face with Drusilla.

'I warned you,' said Drusilla.

'You can talk?' Strangely, when she addressed her cat, Talina found that she could speak in words as well as miaows. 'Drusilla, why did you never talk before?'

'I talk Felish,' said the cat. 'Now so do you, apparently. I whispered warnings to you in your sleep! I told you not to read two books at once when you were playing with spells. But would you listen or understand? No. It was bound to get us into trouble. And it has. Your parents always used to call you "kitten". Now look what's happened.'

In the mirror over the mantelpiece, Talina caught a glimpse of the kitchen. The room was as she'd last seen it: chairs, oven, buttered cake-tin, cake drippings and eggshells on the table.

But where, before, there had been a girl and a cat in the room, now it was occupied only by two cats: one small, stunned-looking tabby and the majestic black creature who was Drusilla.

4
Cats in a sack

the tower kitchen, a few minutes after midnight,
April 30th, 1867, Saint Pio's Day

D RUSILLA'S EYES ROUNDED with alarm. Talina felt
something jab painfully at her rear. She spun around,
to face the toe of the Guardian's pointed black shoe.
Behind him, Futfallo, Razin and Gierch-it strained and
gagged on their triple leash. Talina and Drusilla cowered by
the oven, their tails intertwined for comfort.

'Owning a tail is the strangest feeling!' thought Talina,
twitching it experimentally. And, under almost any other
circumstance, she was sure it would have been rather nice.

The Guardian was glaring down at her. 'A vile, thieving
stray cat in my kitchen at midnight! Shall I feed it to the
hounds?'

Futfallo, Razin and Gierch-it leapt into the air, baying
with joy.

'Why did *he* come in here right now?' wondered Talina
aloud. 'He *never* comes into the kitchen. And why is
everything such a strange colour?'

Drusilla whispered, 'Remember, cats see differently. We are colour-blind to red and green, for example.'

The Guardian asked the dogs, 'When did you last taste cat flesh?'

Talina tried to shout, 'Can't you guess what's happened? Look at the magic book and the recipe! This is exactly the kind of thing that happens to children in your horrible stories.'

But when she opened her mouth, all that came out was a whining mew.

The Guardian, smiling horribly, dropped the leash that restrained the three dogs. Futfallo, Razin and Gierch-it stampeded across the room towards the cats, slavering with delighted bloodlust.

'Jump!' screamed Drusilla, sailing smoothly up to the mantelpiece.

'I can't. I'm not a—' but somehow Talina too was flying through the air, impelled by her strangely powerful back legs. As the dogs leapt after her, one strut of the triple leash snagged on a corner of the table. Futfallo's huge head struck the solid oak leg and he rolled over, whimpering, dragging his companions with him.

'Idiot hounds! But I suppose,' mused the Guardian, 'there's not much eating on a cat. And you dogs would only make a mess.'

He gave the dogs a look that made them put their tails between their legs. Then he glanced at the table. 'Even more of a mess. Filthy child. Where is she?'

'Here!' yowled Talina.

The Guardian grabbed her mid-yowl by the scruff of her neck, so she had to swallow hard. He thrust her into the empty *Farina Fellina* flour-sack.

Talina choked and sneezed on the flour dust. Through the mesh, she saw the Guardian turn towards Drusilla. He

31

hissed, 'She loves you more than anything, doesn't she, cat? You worthless beast! Who deserves no love at all.'

The mouth of the sack was tugged open. Drusilla was thrown in on top of Talina. The two of them grappled for a way not to bump noses or claws, ending up wrapped around one another, each with a head over the other's shoulder and each throbbing to the heartbeats of the other. Then they felt themselves lifted and swung over the Guardian's back.

'How can my heart beat so fast?' Talina panted to Drusilla.

'Didn't your books tell you that we smaller mammals have faster heartbeats than humans?'

'Of course! That,' Talina recalled, 'must be why cats have shorter life spans. They live faster.'

'In other words, we die sooner,' observed Drusilla grimly.

The door creaked open. The cats felt a shiver of the *bora* wind through the mesh. They were in the street. The Guardian strode forward. The door slammed behind him and the sound of waves filled the air.

The Guardian cursed, '*Incoming* tide. Damnably inconvenient. I'll just have to go where the tide will work for me.'

It had been another cold and humid day, a combination possible only in waterbound Venice. The stones had sighed their salty breaths, which had dried into tiny crystals. Talina heard the salt crunching like splinters of glass under the Guardian's shoes. All the Venetians were inside, tucked up by their fires. There were no footsteps other than the Guardian's. Not a single one of Talina's honorary grannies poked her head out of her door to bid good evening. Not a single granny's cat left its fireside cushion to come outside and mew in sympathy.

At first, Talina had tried to follow where the Guardian was taking them. She consulted the map of the city's winding streets that all Venetians kept in their head.

The echoes told them that the streets were narrowing. The Guardian must have walked southwards, into the most densely inhabited parts of the city. They heard the crunchy flap of washing on lines overhead. Drusilla and Talina howled with every footfall but still no one poked their head out of a window or a door to demand, 'Where are you going with those cats?'

Only the sparrows seemed alert to what was happening. They twittered urgently, and sang loudly, despite the dark hour.

'What's he planning to do with us?' quavered Talina.

'Why,' asked Drusilla gloomily, 'do humans generally put cats in sacks?'

After the Guardian's eighth shift to the left and the ninth turn to the right, Talina could no longer tell if they were near la Fenice or the square of San Zaccaria. He turned again, and again. Eventually, the quiet gurgling of small canals turned into the insistent whispering of waves.

'I think we're near the Grand Canal,' she told Drusilla.

'And I think that is not good news,' Drusilla replied tersely.

That was when the Guardian paused, lifted the sack off his thin shoulders and tied the neck in a double knot. He spun it around his head once before he sent it flying into the air.

They travelled through the emptiness for five long seconds, Drusilla and Talina tumbling around in a painful tangle of claw, tooth and fur.

They landed with a splash.

The cats scrambled towards the nose of the sack, desperately gnawing and tearing at the fabric. The water had already soaked through, immersing them in its iciness up to their muzzles. Talina's legs hung limply, too cold even to kick. There was no time, no breath, no energy to cry out.

Their teeth had no effect on the sturdy hessian. Inside the *Farina Fellina* sack, the canal was closing over their heads, and both of them were mumbling on mouthfuls of salt water.

Talina cried, 'Drusilla, can you do one last thing for me? Please can you call me "kitten" like Mamma and Papà used to?'

'Kitten,' gasped Drusilla. She put a tender paw on Talina's ear.

Talina felt her eyes shutting. Her limbs had already given up. Now her brain and heart had stopped believing that they could survive. Beside her, Drusilla's lithe body fell limp. Talina felt the air rushing out of her lungs, and salt water rolling in instead.

A wave pushed the sack over and the two cats, deeply unconscious, floated inside like specimens in a bottle at a natural history museum.

5

The Company of Christ and the Good Death

the canals of Venice, the early hours of April 30th, 1867,
Saint Pio's Day

THE SADDEST WORK of the members of the
Company was to retrieve unknown drowned bodies
from the water: that's why its full name was 'The
Company of Christ and the Good Death'.

Venetians were prone to drowning: it was an ancient
superstition among them that it was better not to learn to swim.

'The sea must have what the sea wants,' they were fond
of quoting.

And, every so often, the sea took. When the stones sweated
slippery danger, there were always drunken, clumsy – or just
plain unlucky – Venetians who slipped and fell into the
canals. Some time later, the kind, quiet men of the Company
of Christ and the Good Death would pull their corpses out
of the water and take them to the cemetery island of San
Michele for a decent burial.

But on the chilly night of April 30th, the men of the
Company were set to a most unusual job: rescuing not the

waterlogged bodies of young and old Venetians, but the skulls, mummified fingers and shrivelled arms of saints who had been dead for a thousand years or more. Balled fists of waves punched the fragile bones to and fro, breaking them into even tinier fragments, all gently glowing with centuries of goodness. They floated in the slipstream of the moonlight.

Inside the churches, terrible damage had been wrought on the glass cases and reliquaries that once held the saints' remains. There were teeth-marks on the golden casings and paw prints in the shattered glass.

Saintly relics had been plundered from all over the town: the head of Saint Ulderico and the thigh of Saint Eliseo from the Carmini, the finger of Saint John the Baptist from Sant'Alvise, the rib of Mary Magdalene and the arm of Saint Bartholomew from San Geremia, the bones of Saint Trifone from San Felice, the finger of Saint Hermagoras from San Marcuola, the arm of Saint Ametisto from Santi Apostoli.

And their splintered bones now floated out of the city on icy waves that were every shade of black: pigeon, panther, jet, coal and unlucky cat.

A proclamation was spiked on the door of each looted church.

> *Venetians, your so-called history*
> *and your so-called faith*
> *have gone out with the tide.*
> *This town shall henceforward be called*
> *by its true name:* LUPRIO.

The kind, quiet men of the Company of Christ and the Good Death read the words with startled eyes.

'Luprio?' said one of them. 'It sounds like something to do with wolves.'

36

6

Ostello delle Gattemiagole

on a different stretch of the Grand Canal,
at about the same time

'WHAT ARE ALL these bony bits in the water tonight?'

The woman leant over the edge of her *sandolo*, raking her hooked pole through the shattered saintly tibulas and fibulas until she snagged the sack that floated among them.

'Tsk tsk tsk. More pretties left to drown! This town has no heart, no heart at all.'

Although she was more than seventy years old, the woman deftly drew the *Farina Fellina* sack towards her with a strong and practised hand.

'More than one in here, I believe. Not moving, not moving at all. 'Tis dead and gone that they are, the poor pretties,' she muttered. 'No heart, no heart. Every night the same. The poor beasts murdered without a thought. And if they don't drown them in sacks, they leave them out in the streets to starve. Or freeze to death. Or get taken.'

She lifted the sack into the boat. Tutting, she slit the double knot with a fish-gutting knife she drew from her belt. Two lifeless cats tumbled out, joining the half-dozen feline corpses already lying on the damp floor of the *sandolo*.

The old woman looked sharply at the small tabby and the large black cat.

'Not in the water long, I'd judge. Mayhap only minutes. Mayhap there's hope.' And she picked up the tabby, laid it on the bench beside her, bent over, opened its slack little jaws, and breathed into its mouth, gently pumping its chest with her fists.

She was rewarded with a voluminous sneeze straight into her face.

'I thought so, thought so indeed, little pretty! You'll be living another day. Now what about your beautiful friend?'

A minute later Drusilla was also spluttering and spitting salt water.

Ostello delle Gattemiagole

The sign above the door in the Rio Terra Farsetti was painted in untidy blue letters on a plank of pine.

The woman paused underneath. She was dragging the sack of dead cats behind her, cradling Drusilla and Talina in her other arm. They were too weak and dazed to protest, or even to exchange a miaow.

The woman lowered them gently to the ground and produced a large black key from her pocket. The stone was cold under their paws. As the woman opened the door of the Ostello delle Gattemiagole, a smell of cat urine rushed out, sharp as a knife in Talina's nose.

Although she was a cat now, the smell was horrible to her. Even Drusilla flinched. She mentioned, 'Of course a cat's sense of smell is twelve times better than a human's. Sometimes this is not an advantage.'

The woman appeared not to notice the stink. She stroked Talina's damp head, saying, 'There, my pretty ones, in you go.'

Drusilla mewed, 'I've heard about this place. Not good things.'

'What choice do we have?' Talina shivered.

The woman shooed them in, closing the door behind them. She busied herself with lighting a pair of gas-lamps and adding coal to the embers of a cosy fire.

The soft yellow glow of the lamps revealed at least three dozen pairs of green, orange and yellow eyes staring unblinking from corners, platforms and a sagging bed. An elegant white cat detached herself from the shadows and walked languidly towards the newcomers.

Drusilla whispered, 'Oh no, that's the Contessa! The word on the street is that she runs all kinds of scams and she's got some ripe old bully-boys working for her.'

As Drusilla spoke, two knock-kneed tom-cats swaggered off their mouldy cushions and stood behind the Contessa. To Talina's new way of seeing, the red rims of the bully-boys' eyes were simply black, and simply terrifying.

'That's right, that's right,' said the woman, who was ladling fish-heads and vegetable peelings from a barrel into troughs on the ground. 'Welcome the new ones. Show them the ropes.'

'Welcome' did not quite describe the expression in the slanted eyes of the Contessa or the battered faces of her retainers.

'You 'eard wot da missis sayed,' miaowed one of the toms, a big ginger. 'You's one of us now, see, and you's gotta know da rules.'

'Da rules! Da rules!' agreed a grey cat with orange eyes, fawningly. 'Dat Albicocco, he speak da *troof*!'

'Yer not wrong, Bestard-Belou,' replied Albicocco. 'And da rules is, "what *she* sez goes", all right?' The ginger pointed his tail at the Contessa, who apparently felt it unnecessary to utter a word.

'Why?' asked Talina, despite Drusilla's discreet nip to her tail.

'Cos dis is wot 'appens when ye don't do what she sez,' Bestard-Belou demonstrated a clout in the air with his ragged paw. 'Dog-bite-my-ear! Is yew stoopid or something?'

The woman saw none of this. She was already leaving, a spade tucked under her arm and the sack of drowned cats bumping along behind her.

'Play nice, my pretties,' she urged, as she shut the door. 'And remember to groom. There's a family of humans,' – she snarled the word 'humans' – 'coming tomorrow, in need of a nice cat.'

'A noice cat! Heh heh heh!' sneered Bestard-Belou.

The door slammed and the key turned in the lock.

A young black-and-white cat approached timidly, nudging Talina with his nose. 'This way,' he said, in a friendly voice, showing Talina and Drusilla to a cardboard box in a corner. 'Don't sit there annoying the Contessa and her boys. Not healthy for you, that. I'm Brolo. Whom do I have the pleasure of ... ? And how did you end up here?'

'How did *you*?' asked Talina.

The black-and-white's eyes moistened. 'My dear mistress grew sick. I stayed with her till the last, even when she was too ill to find food for me, or herself. No more boned turkey, pâté or Charlotte Russe, my particular favourite – just water and tinned sardines for months on end. Eventually,' he sobbed, 'my darling mistress succumbed to a sardine bone stuck in her throat. I followed the funeral cortège to the church. When I came home, the doors were bolted and there was a "For Sale" sign on the house. Her family didn't want me. Or at least they didn't want to feed me. So they left me on the streets to be eaten by those ... beasts that howl in the night. Fortunately Signorina Tiozzo found me first. Now, how did you two come to be floating down the Grand Canal in a sack? Bad luck or what?'

In whispers, Talina and Drusilla told him.

Brolo's sympathy enfolded them like a cashmere blanket. 'Dogs, eh? Wicked Guardian, eh? A cat-hater? Mixed-up magic? What a down-in-the-dumper! Well, let me tell you how things are around here. Oh! Well, well, look at that rat on the window-sill. They're such eavesdroppers, those creatures. Shoo!' he called. 'There's cats in here who wouldn't scruple to eat you raw, you know.'

Bestard-Belou and Albicocco were already creeping up to the sill. Albicocco slavered, 'What looxury! A rat wot serves hisself fresh! Butter upon bacon! I got the hungries on me summat *fierce* tonight.'

The rat hesitated and then slipped out of sight. Brolo continued with his story.

Signorina Tiozzo loved cats and despised people, Brolo told them, while he generously groomed their wet fur and shared a piece of liver with Drusilla. Talina gnawed hungrily on a withered Brussels sprout, a vegetable which, in better circumstances, she despised.

'But Signorina Tiozzo loves us in an "I-know-what's-good-for-you" sort of way,' Brolo explained. 'She doesn't hold with cuddling or indulging us. She provides this *magazzino* for us to live in. She had a man build those shelves up there so we'd have somewhere to go when the high water comes in. She keeps a fire for us when it's cold. And she trawls the Rialto market for fish-heads and bits of veg. And begs liver and kidneys from the butchers. Heart of gold, she's got!'

Every night, Brolo explained, Signorina Tiozzo went out in her boat, looking for drowned or drowning cats. To the ones who had not survived, she gave a decent burial among the most beautiful flowers in the Botanical Gardens at San Giobbe.

'What was she saying about the humans tomorrow?' asked Talina.

'Anyone in Venice who wants a cat can come to the Ostello delle Gattemiagole and choose one of us. You'll see how it works in the morning. Look, you're dry now. Let's get some beauty sleep. It might be our lucky day tomorrow.'

Drusilla nodded, settling down to her accustomed sleeping position, which resembled a roast chicken. Brolo lay on Drusilla's left side; Talina settled against her right. In moments, both Drusilla and Brolo were asleep. But Talina lay awake, re-living all the panic and fear she'd not had time to feel properly since she turned into a cat.

'How utterly foolish I was,' she lamented, 'to mix the spell and the recipe! But more to the point, why did Great Uncle Uberto decide to drown us? The brute!'

The snoring of cats filled the air. Drusilla vibrated gently beside her. Talina fought a desire to jab her in the ribs. She wondered, 'How can she sleep? Doesn't she realize what trouble we're in?'

She reminded herself, 'Well, I guess Drusilla is used to being a cat. And napping most of the time.'

Talina thought she would never get to sleep in that cold,

stinking place. Normally, she could never fall asleep without reading first. Even in her bookbed in the tower, even lulled by the sleepy chirruping of sparrows, she could not sleep without first reading until her eyelids drooped.

'Can I still read now that I'm a cat?' she wondered. 'Can I write? Can I hold a pencil, even? How can I become a girl again? Mamma and Papà,' she broke into a sob, 'used to say I was a naughty kitten.'

Sad and frightened thoughts chased each other round in circles until she felt dizzy and exhausted. But the warmth of Drusilla's body was soothing, and so was Brolo's deep breathing.

The next thing Talina knew, spring sunlight was warming the cardboard box, Drusilla was licking her vigorously, and Brolo was urging, 'That's it, look your best, both of you. The humans have arrived. They have children too. Hurry! You want to get to the litter tray before the bully-boys. Oh, too late. Look at them!'

The evil looks of the big ginger cat had dissolved into sweetness. Bestard-Belou had shed his tough expression, rounded his eyes, fluffed up his fur. With their heads slightly on one side, the bully-boys were licking their paws and running them over their ears and giving winsome little purrs, soft as a mother's kiss.

Brolo whispered, 'Humans think that's ever so endearing.'

Signorina Tiozzo bustled in, urging, 'Come in, do, and see my pretties! In desperate need of love, they are.' In a quieter voice, she mumbled, 'I wonder, are you people capable?'

From their cardboard box, Talina and Drusilla could see four pairs of shoes, all of different sizes. The shoes were expensive, polished to a shine. A father, a mother, a boy and a girl, Talina guessed. Looking at their feet, she put the children at around her own age – in human years anyway. Cat years were faster, of course, she remembered.

'Look at them fancy cloves wot dey's wearing,' laughed Albicocco, 'velvet-trimmed coats 'n' all. That's silk and linen damask with watered ground on da woman. Dey's in the money. I bet dere's veal and sausages and all sorts at dere 'ouse.'

'Eugh!' squealed the little girl. 'What an utterly repulsive smell. I really cannot be expected to bear it without sickening and dying on the spot.'

'Wash yer mouth – we is *spotlessly* clean, girlie,' growled Albicocco.

'Clarissa, we'll give you a dose of Manitoba Gargling Oil when we get home,' soothed the mother.

Talina, with a good view of the girl's petticoats, saw that everything was ribboned, ruched and starched. She was momentarily grateful for the comfortable simplicity of her fur.

'Hold your nose, darling,' advised the girl's papà. His voice softened, 'Look at the dear little fellows!'

Both bully-boys were practically turning themselves inside out with enthusiastic purring. The father leant over to stroke them and the newspaper fell from under his arm. Talina looked at the headline.

'I can read!' she thought with relief. But her joy was quickly dampened as she scanned the story about the smashed saints and the strange proclamation about Venice being renamed 'Luprio'.

The girl Clarissa whimpered, 'Mamma, you promised me a *kitten*. I don't want these big grown-up dirty cats.'

For a second, Albicocco's face slipped into its habitual sneer. He looked as if he was about to take a bite out of Clarissa's ankle, which was perilously close to his jaws. But he remembered himself and began to rub up against the skirt of the human mother. The Contessa stretched herself languorously in front of the father. Then she turned her back and looked at him over her shoulder.

'She winked, the flirt!' noticed Talina. The father bent to stroke the Contessa's immaculate white fur.

'Aren't there any kittens?' whined Clarissa. 'I'm sure kittens don't reek like these old cats. Peugh, peugh and *peugh*!' She fanned herself with her hand.

'I'll have that hand off at the wrist, girlie,' snarled Bestard-Belou.

'These cats don't even look very friendly,' said the mother, holding her skirts daintily off the flagstones. 'Perhaps we should go to the pet shop at San Luca after all. I heard they have some dear little Persian kittens in.'

'Dear they shall cost too,' observed her husband.

Signorina Tiozzo grunted with disgust.

The girl's brother said, 'But these cats *need* a home much more than some spoilt pedigree kitten.'

With a start, Talina thought, 'Oh my! I think I *know* that voice!'

'Oh, just stop talking!' Clarissa squealed at her brother. 'We all know *you* can talk the hind leg off a donkey!'

The cats of the Ostello delle Gattemiagole united in pleading purring. Several rolled over on their backs and showed their bellies, invitingly. Bestard-Belou miaowed and winked, 'A dear little boy and girl! I likes a little girl to sit on, if she has a plump lap and the key to the larder, both.'

But the little girl pointed at Bestard-Belou. 'And that one is plainly mad. Winking and twitching like that!'

Brolo stood on his back legs and begged like a dog. 'Me?' he miaowed, 'Me? Me?'

The boy knelt to caress Brolo's head. Talina, crouching in the box, caught sight of the boy's face through a cascade of brown curls parted strictly in the middle of a high, pale forehead. A pair of round spectacles balanced precariously on his lightly freckled nose.

'I *knew* it!' thought Talina. 'Even though he looks a funny colour, that's definitely Ambrogio Gasperin.'

She whispered to Drusilla, 'He's in my class at school. He's very clever, even though he's a bit odd sometimes. Argues like you wouldn't believe. Perhaps I can make him understand . . . ?'

Ignoring Drusilla's doubtful look, Talina crept out of the box. But the human family had already stepped back into the street. She could hear them sighing loudly with relief in the fresh air. As Talina reached the door, she was sent flying by the boy rushing back in. He pressed a coin into Signorina Tiozzo's grimy hand. 'To help feed the poor cats,' he said. 'It's all I've got. But I'll come back, I promise, and I'll bring some more.'

'Ambrogio!' called his mamma. 'Come here at once! We are to take luncheon at the Cappello Nero. I don't want them thinking you don't wash.'

'You'd better be off, young sir,' said Signorina Tiozzo. 'Bless you for your good heart.'

As Ambrogio hurtled out, he stopped for one second to caress Talina's head.

'It's me! Talina! From Mademoiselle Chouette's class,' she cried, but all that emerged from her mouth was a desperate miaow.

Signorina Tiozzo closed the door with a curdled expression. 'That family no more deserves that kind young gentleman than Venice deserves you, my pretties.'

Talina leapt to the window ledge – 'I could never jump like that as a human!' she thought – and gazed after Ambrogio. He turned back and waved, mouthing the words, 'I promise!'

She smiled and nodded back. She believed him. She trusted him. Her whole body vibrated with hope and pleasure.

'I'm purring,' she realized.

'There's a rat arrived for you, Talina,' Brolo announced in a whisper. 'He's badly hurt.'

It was after midnight. Drusilla and Talina were half-dozing in the box, paws and tails entwined. A triangle of moonlight fell on the floor of the Ostello delle Gattemiagole. In the window, the silhouette of a large rat twitched. Where the moonlight touched it, the rat's fur was visibly slicked down with water and blood.

'Poor chap,' Brolo whispered, 'he's almost done for. Bad luck or what? You'd better see what he wants, quick-like, Talina. The other cats have noticed.'

Talina was wide awake now. 'Why would a rat want *me*?'

Even as she spoke, Bestard-Belou had snatched the rat in his jaws. Through his full mouth, he mumbled, 'I likes a rat, ye know. I likes a little bit o bone to crunch. I doan hold wid that soft pap da missis give us. I am fond of a pigeon too, if 'tis fat and bony both.'

Albicocco cuffed the rat out of his friend's mouth, 'Yer mistaking me for someone who cares 'bout what yew puts down yer ugly froat, Bestardo.'

The rat lay on its back on the reeking flagstones. Three dozen cats drew around it in a tight circle. It opened its eyes, and spoke perfect Felish in an educated tone. 'Before you eat me, gentle cats, do me the honour of hearing my story.'

'Do yew see any gentle cats 'ere?' Albicocco asked.

'Not a one,' growled Bestard-Belou.

The rat interrupted, 'It's about those beasts that roam our streets at night. The beasts who take Venetians. And cats.'

Talina felt her fur tighten.

'My cousin Glauco were et by one o' them monsters,' confided Albicocco.

'And my sister Annamaria, and my uncle Giorgio!' whispered Brolo. 'What a down-in-the-dumper, that night.'

The Contessa keened, 'My last litter, all taken.'

'And me own dear mother, Dog-bite-my-ear!' howled Bestard-Belou. 'So make wid da talking, rat! Make it good and make it fast. Remembering my ma always makes me hungry.'

7
Whys & wherefores

just after midnight, May 2nd, 1867,
Saint Atanasio's Day

THE RAT'S WOUNDS were dreadful to behold. The grooves of five claws were thick with blood all the way down his belly. Bestard-Belou observed, 'Somebody had a go at eatin' this one already. I doan generally help meself to someone else's leavings. Dey always takes da liver and kidneys, both.'

The Contessa glared at him. 'Let the rat speak.'

The cats drew closer. Talina, Brolo and Drusilla quietly made their way through the taut furry bodies to reach the inner circle around the wounded creature.

'Allow me to present myself. I am Doctor ... Raruso ...' The rat's voice was proud, though torn with pain. 'I had hoped for a private interview with her, but ... circumstances ... Two nights ago, a rumour started, strange new rumour ... that a ... not-quite-cat ... has appeared in Venice. And now they're saying ... that she's *here*. At your esteemed Ostello delle Gattemiagole. We, that is, *Venice*, needs ... her help. Because of the song, you know. The one that started the rumour. The one that the birds are singing without cease.'

'A not-quite-cat, ho ho ho didgever 'ear the like!' sneered Albicocco.

'Nothing like that here,' said the Contessa dismissively.

'We's all cats froo-n-froo,' agreed Bestard-Belou.

Drusilla looked hard at Talina. She asked the rat, 'What song?'

In a single rush of ragged breath, the rat warbled,

There shall be a little cat
A cat who wasn't always that
A cat who's lost what she loves best,
whose tongue is fierce; whose heart no less.
It is her quest
to find the truth, the light, the right
and save this city from her plight –
from threats and howls and nightly frights.
Talina who was in the tower
Talina who —

''Scuse me, but 'as we got a cat called Talina 'ere?' asked Albicocco. 'I is not aware of a cat o' that name in our presence, savin' 'er grace.'

Brolo bravely interrupted, 'Let the rat finish his song. Poor beast and all, you know.'

'Sez who? Yew shrew-struck or sumpin? You want some?' Bestard-Belou menaced.

Doctor Raruso's sigh ended with a rattle in his throat. 'Don't you cats wish to know ... what's happening in Venice? The ... whys and wherefores of this terrible situation? In my learned opinion ...'

Then a long shudder ran through his whole body and he fell silent, breathing fast and shallowly.

50

'Ye want to be pulling yersself together, rat,' Albicocco licked his lips.

Suddenly Doctor Raruso opened his eyes and began to speak again. 'Do you know the history of Venice, cats?'

'Course we do. Yew think we is hignorant?' blustered Bestard-Belou.

There was a short silence while the cats licked various parts of themselves and batted some potato peelings around the floor in an embarrassed fashion.

Talina said quietly, 'The first settlers came here in the fifth century. The founding date of Venice is AD 421.'

'The first *human* settlers,' corrected the rat. 'What nobody realizes is this: someone else was here before them. '

'Nah!' chorused the cats complacently.

The rat seemed to rally a little. He propped himself up on one paw, and spoke clearly.

'I must begin further back, in a deep part of time ... in another place, thousands of human miles away from Venice ... a time and a place where wolves and humans lived in harmony.'

'Wolves? Wot's *dey* got to do wid anyfing?' scoffed Albicocco. 'Least of all, wid a nice rat dinner.'

'Wolves,' Doctor Raruso continued stubbornly, 'are ancient creatures. And they were pleasantly flattered when the first humans chose to imitate them by living in family groups and pairs, by hunting in packs and so on. But then the humans decided that wolves were in competition with them for all the goods of the earth. They began to kill wolves, not even to eat them, but just to try to stamp out their race. They killed defenceless baby wolves if they could find them. And pregnant females as well. Soon the human atrocities against the wolves destroyed the respect between the species. The wolves hid away in dark places of the world – where rich pockets of magic seethe – particularly in those Siberian plains that lie in the shadows of mountains. After some centuries, one race of wolves changed. After so much crouching, slinking and hiding, their backs developed a natural slope, or so they say. The magic they breathed changed their natures, too. They became wilder and more daring. They even dared to ravage the sheep flocks of the humans, and the henhouses and also the kitchens. They ravaged so much of the land around them that they became known not as wolves but as "Ravageurs".'

'Ravageurs,' repeated Talina, tasting the word on her tongue, finding it bitter and dreadful. She shivered.

The rat nodded. 'It got worse. Eventually, they say, it led to war. The Ravageurs have always claimed that they were driven south from the Siberian plains in the great Lupine Wars. They say that the few survivors made their way here, taking refuge on an island in this lagoon … in the quarter that Venetians now call Santa Croce. The Ravageurs called it "Luprio".'

'Luprio!' said Talina. 'Like the proclamations at the churches where the saints' relics were smashed. They said "Luprio" was the new name of Venice!'

Doctor Raruso nodded wearily. 'The old name, in fact. The Lords of Luprio were the Ravageurs. That's what they say, anyway.'

'And that's why those Ravageurs are so snobbish and arrogant,' said the Contessa, with the air of one who knew what she was talking about. 'That's why they think they are so entitled.'

'Indeed,' confirmed the rat. 'For centuries … as their legends have it, the Ravageurs ruled not just Venice but the lagoon, easily gaining mastery over all the other creatures. All of us – rats, ducks, egrets – we bowed to their will. If we did not serve them … they simply ate us in sauce. In fact, there's one important thing about Ravageurs that we have learnt to our cost – they must keep eating constantly and in enormous quantities, or they quickly die. They have two breakfasts, four luncheons and five suppers, and they feed in between, too.'

He subsided in a new fit of coughing.

'Yew'll 'ave to do better than dat, rat. We *cats* dint niver agree to bow to the will of no Ravidgers!' sniffed Albicocco. 'No matter 'ow many suppers dey eat.'

'*The Compleat History of the Venetian Empire* says that cats arrived in Venice in the ninth century,' Talina put in quietly. 'The Venetian merchants brought them back from Syria then. Hundreds of years after the Ravageurs, in other words.'

'Hoo sayed dat?' demanded Bestard-Belou suspiciously. Albicocco was counting on his claws, cross-eyed with concentration. Brolo covered his mouth with his paw and stared at Talina significantly. She took his point, bending down to lick her tail as innocently as possible.

Doctor Raruso drew a long, trembling breath, and continued: 'By the time humans arrived here, the Ravageurs had become semi-enchanted creatures ... they had left Siberia with rich northern magic in their blood. Here in Venice they soaked up into their fur some of the antique magic that flows through our waterways. So they became invisible – to adult humans at least. Only human children up to the age of thirteen or fourteen can see them. But most adult humans can still hear them. Or feel them through the extra senses, the ones they don't much use. Especially the sixth sense, they say.'

'Dere's too much saying goin' on round 'ere,' lamented Albicocco. 'Too much sayin' and not nuff chewin'.'

'When the time comes,' Doctor Raruso said with dignity, 'you are welcome to partake of my mortal remains, felines. Better and more hygienic than leaving me to rot. As the old proverb goes, *superbo in vita, spuzzolente in morte* – proud in life, stinking in death. My mission ... is almost accomplished. Pray let me finish ... The adult Venetians have always chosen not to believe in the Ravageurs. In the old days, the adult humans insisted that the Ravageurs were monsters of the fearful imagination, and nothing more. And now their descendants prefer to maintain a fiction that some "Pastry-Bandits" from Rovigo are kidnapping their loved ones ... along with all the cats and cakes and cooking equipment. They pretend ... ransom notes will arrive from Rovigo at any minute. Even though not a single one has ever been received. The human capacity for self-deception is ... truly more terrifying than a Ravageur, if you ask me.'

'*Ambrogio* says the creatures are real. He saw one!' Talina whispered to Drusilla. 'You know, the boy from school who came here. He drew it. And my *awful* French mistress, Mademoiselle Chouette – she's an adult but *she* knows they exist too. She's heard them, and she hates them because—'

Albicocco demanded suspiciously, 'Wait a griddle-grabbing moment there, Mister Rat! So zackly how did dem humans from hunnerds of year ago get dem Ravidgers rid? If dey couldn't even see 'em?'

Doctor Raruso whispered, 'The first Venetians simply did not know there were Ravageurs on the island of Luprio. The Ravageurs never built anything, just mud-heaps for sleeping in, which the humans used as building blocks or to shore up canals.'

'But. But. But. Given how very beastly they hevidently is, why dint them Ravidgers fight back?' Bestard-Belou demanded.

'And if they did, why isn't there anything in the history books about it?' Talina dared to ask. 'The Ravageur Wars would have been very important and—'

Bestard-Belou's look closed Talina's mouth. Doctor

Raruso replied, 'For some reason, the Ravageurs did not mount an attack ... until now. It is something we rats have never understood. The Ravageurs ...'

Everyone waited out the rat's next cough. Frailer than ever, he continued, 'As the old proverb goes: *l'amor, la tosse, la mossa de corpo, xe tre cose che no pol star sconte* – love, a cough and, excuse me, diarrhoea, are three things you can't hide. Where was I? The Ravageurs retreated ... to one of the furthest and most deserted islands of the lagoon. They've surrounded it with a private cloud of impenetrable fog. Why, if your boat enters it, you can sit at the bow and not be able to see the prow! A few rats know how to steer through it, of course. It is our job. We rats have traditionally served as the Ravageurs' slaves, their gondoliers, and also ... their meals. That's if they can't get their paws on ... the kind of food they really like: *Timballes de queues d'Ecrevisses Mantua, Terrine de foie gras avec sa gelée* and *Faisan à la Financière*.

'Not humans?' Talina's voice was thick with hope. 'So they are not actually eating the humans they take?'

But before Doctor Raruso, shaken by another ferocious cough, could answer, Bestard-Belou interrupted, 'And if dey was drove out of Venice – or Luprio, or whatever dey called it – fourteen hunnerd oomin years ago, so why in da name of lamb chops did dem Ravidgers wait until *roight now* to start saying that dey want it back?'

'It may have something to do with the new Lord of the Ravageurs, who is an ugly specimen in every way. It is he ... who has ordered the tallest human chimneys to be filled with gunpowder.'

'Gunpowder!' wailed Talina. 'What kind of ...?'

The rat ran a shaking paw down the welts on his belly. 'The kind of creature who did this to me. And this,' he pointed to a burn on his paw, 'with his sage-leaf cigar. Until

I told him the words of the song. Then he laughed and fell on his food like a mad thing ... so I was able to escape. That Grignan's the worst Ravageur that ever lived. As the old proverb goes, *in casa vècia no manca mai sorzi* – the old house never lacks a rat – every family has its black sheep, its low-life evil-doer ... But in fact ... *all* the Ravageurs seem ... maddened, baddened ... in the last few months. Something has changed in them – the Ravageurs are ... not as they once were. They are wild, strange ... perhaps ... unwell.' He shuddered.

Drusilla bent over him with concern, licking his paw.

''Ere, me first!' growled Albicocco.

The bully-boys drew closer. Drusilla put a protective paw on the rat's belly, and stared defiantly at the other cats. 'Let him *finish*,' she hissed.

'So *that's why* ... Venice needs the not-quite-cat ...' the rat gasped. '*Urgently*. The Ravageurs are on the move. Tomorrow could—'

Then he wheezed and his jaw fell slack.

'Oho, he bust of his own accord, wivout us havin' to do nothin'! Shame,' observed Bestard-Belou. 'I could of stood to watch 'im sufferin' nobly for a bit longer. Has a tenderizing effect, all dat noble suffering.'

'Heh heh heh,' sniggered Albicocco. 'Excuse me while I break me own heart.'

'You grisly, greedy beasts!' yowled Talina.

'You didn't ought to have said that, Talina,' cried Brolo, as a spitting blur of orange fur wrapped itself around her, growling, 'Wash yore mouf! Where yew from? Rovigo or somefing?'

8

So close

a few minutes later

A KEY TURNED IN the door, and a familiar voice inquired, 'How are all my pretties this dark night?'
Albicocco removed his jaws from Talina's throat and sauntered back to Doctor Raruso, only to find Bestard-Belou standing proprietorially over the rat's body.

Signorina Tiozzo swiftly resolved the argument that was brewing as to who was going to eat Doctor Raruso. She picked him up and threw him in the sack with the drowned cats she had collected from the canals.

'No good ever came from eating a rat,' she observed tartly.

Side by side, so their ribs touched through their fur, Talina, Drusilla and Brolo wept shocked and silent tears for Doctor Raruso.

Signorina Tiozzo, meanwhile, emptied a stack of glistening fish-heads and crabs into the feeding trough. Not a cat moved.

Talina whispered to Drusilla, 'They were all hoping for a bite of Doctor Raruso, the ghouls!'

Drusilla answered, 'And perhaps they're also thinking about what he told us.'

'What's this? No appetite this evening, my pretties?' asked Signorina Tiozzo.

Thirty-eight cats sat silently on their haunches, thoughts of fish-heads and crab-legs apparently far from their minds.

'Well, there's no accounting for cats,' observed Signorina Tiozzo, picking up her spade and key. 'That's why I love them so.'

Before she was even out of the room, the Contessa drawled, 'I gather the late rat's so-called "not-quite-cat" is one of our two recent arrivals? No doubt, it is the one who is so well-versed in human history. Step forward.'

Drusilla and Brolo flanked Talina as she skittered into the centre of the room.

'I want you to know,' said the Contessa, barely glancing at Talina, 'that in our opinion, a not-quite-cat is a cat who is not-quite-good-enough. We'll have no more showing off. I assume that is understood.'

Talina nodded. Nor were the Contessa's words lost on Albicocco and Bestard-Belou. 'Ye heared what she sayed?' demanded Albicocco.

Bestard-Belou added, 'And you unnerstand you'll be gettin' da fish-heads only *after* we've sucked dem now?'

'Yer not wrong, Bestardo,' growled Albicocco. ''Ceptin' insofar as sucked head is too good for the likes of *her.*'

Talina nodded humbly and went to make herself as small and insignificant as possible in the deepest corner of the cardboard box, where she was joined by Drusilla and Brolo. They conferred in whispers.

Drusilla warned, 'Talina, please don't get too hopeful. You mustn't break your heart a second time. This news does not mean that your parents are alive. How can we trust a rat? Even an educated rat?'

'The humans must be hostages, not food. Listen,' Talina insisted. 'We know the Ravageurs always arrive in gondolas. So it must be true they are still living on an island, as Doctor Raruso said. There are hundreds of islands in the lagoon. They haven't even mapped them all.'

'And this one's hidden in a fog that never lifts,' remembered Drusilla.

'Someone must tell the humans about what Doctor Raruso said, and all. How can we do that?' Brolo wondered.

'We'll have to get ourselves adopted by someone,' Drusilla said.

'I can still read. So perhaps I can still write?' added Talina, hopefully. 'I have to get hold of a pencil.'

The morning brought more humans looking for cats.

Signorina Tiozzo appeared somewhat awed by her new visitors, curtseying over and over again to a plump gentleman of about forty years with a goatee beard, extremely elegant in his round black-rimmed spectacles, despite the truffle sauce stains on his waistcoat. He was accompanied by a lively-looking overgrown boy of a man with a battered hat crammed over tousled red hair and what looked suspiciously like a dressing-gown cord around his trousers instead of a belt.

Sleepily, Talina looked out of the box. Then she leapt to her feet. 'Look! That's Giuseppe Tassini, the famous lawyer, historian and gourmand! And look who's beside him: Professor Marìn!'

Drusilla explained to Brolo, 'They are Talina's heroes. She adores their books and the professor's a friend of her parents.'

'Dear Professor Marìn!' Talina craned her neck towards the man with red hair.

Joyfully, she took in his inquisitive eyes, full of fun and wisdom at the same time. He had a way of looking at people that made them talk to him. Signorina Tiozzo, normally laconic with humans, had melted into gushes and giggles.

'Looks a most pleasant chappie,' said Brolo approvingly.

Albicocco growled, 'Generous wid da fat of the milk and plates of sliced steak, both, I'd wager.'

Professor Marìn was saying to Signorina Tiozzo, 'I'd like one to train up as a writer's cat. A female, I suppose. Must be clever and affectionate, supportive, you know the sort of thing? A lap-sitter and an encouraging purrer.'

'The professor could help me!' whispered Talina. 'In fact, he's probably the only person in the world who can help me. It was *his* magic book that got me turned into a cat,' she explained to Brolo. 'We've got to get adopted by him, Drusilla. You too, Brolo.'

But all the cats of the Ostello delle Gattemiagole had the same idea. They had already taken to their winning ways. None more so than the Contessa, who minced backwards and forwards in front of the professor, pluming her tail in curlicues and purring tunefully.

Talina took a deep breath and leapt from the box. But Bestard-Belou was too quick for her. He tripped her with his paw, rolled her over on her side and sat on her. 'No ye don't, not-quite-cat. I'm fly to *your* game and I ain't 'avin' none of it. Wot makes ye think it's *your* turn for a looxurious 'ome? There's many cats wot has been here months. And many cats wot is far more deserving than yew.'

Under his hefty haunches, Talina struggled to breathe. The musty fragrance of Bestard's coat flooded into her nose. She nipped his flank till he squawked and shifted. But he did not let her go.

'This one is a graceful creature,' said Professor Marìn, picking up the Contessa, who snuggled into the crook of his arm and licked his hand.

From under Bestard's haunch, Talina watched helplessly.

Giuseppe Tassini looked dubious. 'There's something not quite honest about that cat.'

'And there's generally something not quite honest about writers,' laughed Professor Marìn. 'At least, the interesting ones. It would be nice to have something beautiful in my house.'

'And clean,' agreed his friend, stroking his goatee. 'And not crooked. Or scribbled on. You really should get a housekeeper, Ridolfo.'

'Someone to disturb all my papers in the name of dusting? I don't think so.'

Signorina Tiozzo was chattering, 'Why don't you take another one or two, Professor? You know how it is with cats. You get one, and you really love it. Then you want another one. And mayhap another. And they could be company for one another when you are off in the Archives, researching. And three cats is a nice round number, I always think ... and as for *four*, well, I—'

'This one will be quite enough,' said Professor Marìn firmly. 'But here's a little something for the other furry fellows.'

He handed Signorina Tiozzo a banknote. It must have been a large one, as she gasped, curtseyed and held it to her chest.

'Are you sure, Professor? This'll keep my pretties in milk and kidneys and Manitoba Gargling Oil for a month!'

'Do cats gargle?' wondered Talina, while the professor shook Signorina Tiozzo's hand warmly, saying, 'You do a great thing for Venice, dear madam. Where would Venice be without her cats?'

Choked with emotion, Signorina Tiozzo lifted the Contessa into a basket and handed it to the professor.

Then he and Tassini were gone.

Bestard-Belou rose unceremoniously, leaving Talina flattened on the floor. Her spirits were even flatter.

'My one chance,' she moaned. 'So close.'

9

A strange one

'I'D JUST LIKE to visit them,' the boy was pleading outside the door. 'You know my mother won't let us take one of these poor cats home. We've got a stupid fat Persian kitten now, with a punched-in face and no sense of humour.'

'As I suspected,' said Signorina Tiozzo with crisp disapproval.

Ambrogio persisted, 'But *you* said these cats need love. I can give them that. And my pocket-money.'

Signorina Tiozzo's silhouette blocked the light of the doorway. She stood with her arms folded over her chest.

'And I have an idea,' continued the boy's voice, nervously. 'You see, I am really quite good at drawing. I could draw pictures of your cats and we could—'

'We?'

'You could sell them to raise more money for their food.'

'You're a strange one, laddie. Why aren't you out kicking

over rubbish bins and throwing sticks to dogs, and teasing girls – all the things that boys normally do?'

'Actually, everyone says I am a strange one. But they also say that there's no harm in me,' Ambrogio Gasperin said truthfully. 'And they also say I could argue the legs off a millipede.'

Talina thought, 'That's very true. He definitely could. Two millipedes, even.'

'I'm going to be a barrister, you see,' explained Ambrogio. 'I have to hone my skills.'

'So I've noticed,' said Signorina Tiozzo crustily. 'You're a mighty boy for the words. And I see you've brought a drawing block. Come in and let's see what you can do.'

Ambrogio crouched eagerly on the floor. 'Now where's that little tabby?'

It was agony for Talina to stay still while Ambrogio sketched her portrait. But Bestard-Belou had fixed his orange eyes on her. And Albicocco stood behind his friend, miming a good cuffing.

So Talina sat like an Egyptian statue of a cat, listening to the scratch of Ambrogio's pencil on paper.

'Is Ambrogio drawing me like myself, but in cat form?' Talina wondered. 'Might he recognize me, somehow?'

The two children had been friends. Not close friends, because at their school boys and girls did not do such a thing in public, for fear of teasing. But there had been a quiet understanding between them, a tendency to sit together in the classroom and to pass notes to one another that always ended 'Private, mind!' There had also been a few discreet exchanges of books on magic, and of course Ambrogio had secretly lent Talina volumes from his parents' shop. And once, just once, he had defended her from the scorn of the whole classroom. She felt herself blushing through her fur just remembering that day.

Mademoiselle Chouette, provoked by some impudence of Talina's, had sent her to stand in the corner.

'But that's how you punish *tiny little children*!' Talina had erupted.

'It is as a *tiny little child* you behave,' answered Mademoiselle grimly, shaking the pale head around which a gleaming chestnut plait was wrapped three times. And the whole class had burst into giggles and guffaws as Talina slowly made her way to the corner, where she stood, barely holding back tears of humiliation. It was then that Ambrogio had leapt from his seat and thrust himself into the opposite corner.

'But *you* are not naughty, Ambrogio!' Mademoiselle had protested. 'Not today, anyway.'

'He's not naughty, he's touched in the head!' sniggered one of the boys.

And the malicious whisperers of the class had completely forgotten about Talina in their rush to taunt Ambrogio. She'd never really thanked him properly, she was sorry to admit.

'Do you know, kitty,' Ambrogio smiled at Talina now, 'you remind me of someone? There was this lovely girl at our school. She was brilliant. She *looked* all soft and dreamy-sweet like a cream-fed kitten, but she was the Terror of the Neighbourhood! She was a girl everyone took notice of. I really was very keen on her. I couldn't tell her so, of course – *she*'d never look at a dolt like me.'

'I liked you very well!' Talina ached to tell him. 'Even though you *would* keep staring at me. That was a bit disconcerting.'

Ambrogio continued sadly, 'I'm only good at drawing.

And arguing. But that special girl—' he gulped back a sob, 'was taken by those ... those *things* that come in the night. Even though all the grown-ups pretend that the monsters don't exist.'

Talina could not stop a little mew from rushing out of her mouth.

'That's it, kitty, *you* know they exist, don't you? If what they say about Pastry-Bandits from Rovigo is true, that they're also taking humans and cats, then *where are the ransom notes*? I've seen one of the monsters. On a tower. I am sure they took Talina, and her parents too.'

Talina shook her head violently. She nuzzled his hand, making his pencil drop. She seized the pencil in her mouth. The wood and lead were bitter on her tongue.

'Kitty, you don't want to eat a pencil,' said Ambrogio gently. 'I'll get you some food.'

He rose and went to the sack where Signorina Tiozzo kept a mixture of grain and fish-powder for skinny days when there was nothing better.

The pencil was hard to hold. Twice, Talina dropped it. It hurt, stabbing into the inside of her cheek as she tried to guide it over the paper.

'Eh? Wot you at, not-quite-cat?' Bestard-Belou rose from his mouldy cushion and trotted towards her.

But she managed an approximation of 'I AM Talina' at the bottom of Ambrogio's sketch before Bestard-Belou pounced, knocking the pencil out of her mouth.

Ambrogio came back to her, carrying a smelly handful of fishmeal.

Then he dropped fishmeal all over the floor.

'Did you write that, kitty?'

'Miiiiaaaaaooooow!' agreed Talina.

'Go away, Ambrogio, there's a good laddie. Don't be coming back. I said that you were a strange one.'

'Are you not a little strange yourself, Signorina Tiozzo? Therefore, does it not stand to reason that—'

'Stop using that courtroom language on me! Never heard the like. You're saying that poor little tabby is a human girl? My pretties are not safe around a madman, be he ever such a small one. Now shoo. You may have a kind heart but you're touched in the head.' She tapped her wrinkled forehead.

Ambrogio pleaded, 'At least let me take Talina.'

'She's not Talina. She's a poor stray cat someone tried to drown.'

Talina stood up on her back legs and snatched the pencil from Ambrogio's pocket. She took it in her mouth. There was no paper, so she hurriedly scratched in the dust of the floor. 'I AM A GRIL.'

'Look! She can write with her mouth!' Ambrogio gestured at the marks on the floor.

But Signorina Tiozzo's eyesight was not good. And Talina's mouthwriting was even more rune-ish and rumpled than her handwriting. And anyway the desperate scrawl was that minute obliterated by Bestard-Belou coming to thump his large hindquarters down on it. 'That's enough from yew,' he glared at Talina. 'I knew yew was trouble. Yew's goin' to be on litter-box duty tonight, innit, scrubbin' out da trays wid dat Mannytobby Gagging Oil, innit.'

'Excuse me,' a man's voice called through the door. 'Signorina Tiozzo?'

Professor Marìn entered, carrying a basket in which crouched the Contessa, spitting and arching her back.

'I am sorry,' he said, 'but this cat is not acceptable. Why, hello there, Ambrogio! How are your parents? The bookshop? Is my latest selling well?'

Ambrogio nodded enthusiastically while Signorina Tiozzo protested, 'The Contessa is the most beautiful cat we've ever had. The most feminine. You said—'

'She has appalling manners and stole my dinner. She appears to have friends among the lowest of the catfolk of this town. There were six gentleman-callers on the window-sill from dusk till dawn, serenading her. No, thank you, Signorina Tiozzo. This fair temptress is the opposite of what a writer wants. I haven't written a page since madam arrived. We writers crave tranquillity. I'll have this one, dark and quiet and dignified as the night. And a real loner, I hope.'

He was pointing at Drusilla.

10

'If in doubt'

a few moments later

AMBROGIO TUGGED THE professor's sleeve. 'Professor Marìn. I agree that the black cat's a beauty, and you should definitely take her. But this little tabby is a perfect writer's cat. She can even write a bit herself with a pencil in her mouth. Look!'

He held out the sketching block on which Talina had written 'I AM Talina'.

Professor Marìn started. 'I'll be—'

Signorina Tiozzo interrupted, 'Don't be listening to the boy. He's not quite the thing.' She tapped her head. 'Yes, the black beauty is a good cat; she'll not give you any trouble. Tch tch tch, here, little one.'

She emptied the Contessa unceremoniously out of the basket and held the door open invitingly for Drusilla. The Contessa strutted off to her bully-boys, her aristocratic nose in the air.

But Drusilla just stared. Then she looked at Brolo and Talina. And she nudged Talina, and pushed her, until she

69

was in the basket. She did the same with Brolo, and then finally stepped inside herself, settling conclusively into her roast-chicken position in front of them, despite the lack of space.

'Err, I wasn't planning on *three* cats.' But Professor Marìn was smiling. 'But friendship is a beautiful thing among the beasts,' he murmured. 'Magical, even. I must write about it.' He pulled out a notebook and scribbled a few lines.

'But *Talina*!' Ambrogio hopped up and down in frustration. 'You don't understand!'

'I shall call the tabby Talina if you like, young chap,' said the professor kindly. 'My friends Marco and Lucia Molin had a daughter called Talina. She was very fond of my own magic books, as I recall. Such a tragedy – all three have—'

'Been taken! I know that's what people said. But it's not true! I think Talina got turned into a cat.'

Signorina Tiozzo raised her eyebrows. 'That Ambrogio's talking shoeshine again!'

'Ambrogio,' said Professor Marìn, looking at him with sudden comprehension, 'would you care to come to my home for tea? Your parents won't mind. Perhaps we can discuss this further.'

'I'll carry the cats!' Ambrogio offered eagerly. 'Santa Croce, isn't it?'

Professor Marìn's house was a lanky disreputable-looking confection of peeling Gothic and Renaissance windows, crooked chimneys, ten different kinds of rotting bricks from five diverse centuries and three sorts of plaster, all falling off. You would never have guessed that this ramshackle establishment hosted one of the best private libraries in Venice.

Inside, everything was crooked but cosy.

In his cavernous library, Professor Marìn drew the crimson and green velvet curtains and set the basket on the desk. The gas-lamps by the fireplace were already lit, and a fire glowed in the cast-iron grate, illuminating thousands of gilded volumes, many of which bore the professor's own name on their spines.

When the professor opened the lid of the basket, the three cats emerged, gazing at him hopefully. Ambrogio clenched his fists, whispering, 'Now's your chance. Don't let me down, Talina.'

'Well then,' said Professor Marìn, 'where's my book *Speaking Creatures: How to Loosen Beastly Tongues*? Been a long time since I wrote that one. Must refresh my memory. Otherwise ... well, otherwise we'd need to wait till the Epiphany, on January 6th, when all beasts may speak for one day only.'

'January 6th!' wailed Ambrogio. 'You mean we'll have to wait nearly a year to see if this cat really is Talina?'

'Let us hope not, dear boy. Now, in that spirit, see if you can find the kitchen – careful! The stairs lurch! And bring me a bowl of milk, an onion, a knife and the little black bottle that says 'If in doubt'.

Twenty minutes later, Professor Marìn had diced the onion and mixed it with a few drops of the black liquid so that a pungent greenish vapour filled the room. He'd read out a long paragraph from the 'Feline Foibles' chapter in *How to Loosen Beastly Tongues*. And Talina – her tongue fully loosened – was already halfway through her account of her misadventures.

'... so there I was, a *cat*, in a terrible fix, all because I'd mixed up a spell and a recipe. I guess I wasn't concentrating properly.' Talina paused for breath and another sip of milk, bedewing her whiskers with white droplets.

Brolo piped up, 'Bad luck, or what? What a down-in-the-dumper!'

Professor Marìn said reprovingly, 'Bad practice, actually. One of the first rules of magic is to concentrate, Talina. Terrible things have happened even to grown magicians who got distracted mid-spell.'

Drusilla sniffed, 'It is not such a terrible thing to be a cat, actually.'

'Sorry. Of course it isn't,' apologized Talina. 'It's been an honour. It is just that the rest of the story hasn't been so good.'

'Threatened by dogs, thrown in the canal to drown, then bullied by the Contessa and her gang! No, not really,' agreed Professor Marìn. 'Now what's the matter with *you*, Ambrogio? Not like you to let a conversation go by without joining in with a bit of cross-examination! You look as if you've seen a ghost.'

'The ... cats ... are talking,' sputtered Ambrogio. 'And ... I *can understand them*.'

'Ah, so you breathed in the If in doubt vapour too and the spell has worked both ways,' said Professor Marìn. 'I've got pretty good Felish myself, but it seems that the spell has given you that ability too, young man. It's always been one of my theories that magic can be eavesdropped. I daresay you'll be able to speak Egrete and Bearish, even Ratsch now, should it come to that. All cats, of course, speak human tongue. They just disdain to. I must write something about the Contagious Diffusion of Spell Steam ...' He rummaged unsuccessfully in his desk for an unscribbled-on piece of paper, and finally settled on a parchment lampshade, upon which he wrote a few swift notes in Latin.

'And next time,' he added, 'I must hand out some of these, to avoid side-effects and accidental contagions.' He rattled a jar labelled 'artificial noses – iron, velvet-lined'.

'Talking cats!' mumbled Ambrogio, still dazed. 'Like spelling bees?'

'And talking rats, too!' Talina remembered. Now she told them about the ill-fated visit of Dr Raruso, even reciting by heart the words of the song that named her. Next she explained the origin of the Ravageurs and their arrival in Venice. Ambrogio and the professor sat on the edge of their chairs, listening in shocked silence.

'"Ravageurs"?' said Professor Marìn finally. 'So that's what they're called. That's not a name I've come across. But if they come from so deep in the past – perhaps that's not surprising? Surely there's a book, or a manuscript in my attic ...'

He was already heading for the door. Talina bounded in front of him and put her paw on his foot.

'But first you can turn me back into myself, can't you, Professor Marìn?' entreated Talina. Without realizing it, she began licking her paw and washing behind her ears in a supplicating way.

'Actually, you are rather sweet as a cat,' teased the professor. 'From what I can recall, you were remarkably impudent when you were a human girl. Don't I remember that you were known as "The Terror of the Neighbourhood"?'

'If in doubt can't turn me back into a girl?' asked Talina.

'No, we need something stronger,' the professor murmured distractedly, running his fingers along the spines of volumes on his shelves. 'Something, frankly, that I haven't tried before. It hasn't come up. Something a bit riskier, I'm afraid. Side-effects, you know ...'

Talina blurted, 'And even if you can turn me back into a girl, what will happen to me?'

'I suppose I'll have to take you back to your Guardian. Legally speaking.'

'My Guardian who tried to drown me?'

'But can you be sure that he knew who you were? Really, really sure?'

'No,' Talina mumbled defensively, 'but he certainly likes dead children better than live ones.'

'Well,' said the professor, 'those are just his stories. All that's certain is that Uberto Flangini, like a few misguided souls, simply dislikes cats.'

'Loathes us,' said Drusilla bitterly.

'I don't know your Guardian, Talina. I don't believe anyone truly does. I certainly find his books disturbing. But I'm more worried that they sell so well, which means that people *want* to terrorize their own children with such horrors. But truly, I sometimes wonder whether Uberto Flangini is not evil, but in fact dreadfully unhappy.'

'You're *sorry* for him?' spat Talina, arching her back and sticking her tail up in a straight line.

Ambrogio growled, 'That nasty old man *should* be unhappy, or at least ashamed of himself!'

'Make me into a girl again anyway, please, Professor Marìn,' Talina begged. 'And then, won't you let me stay with you? *He* must think I'm dead or run away to sea, or something. He wouldn't want me back anyway. So I don't need to go back to his tower, ever, do I? Do I? And please don't say, "Wait and see", Professor. Show me that you are better than that.'

'I'm afraid,' said Professor Marìn regretfully, 'that "wait and see" appears to be the optimum and only answer to that question at this moment.'

It was deep in the middle of the night, in the professor's cosy, crooked kitchen. Outside, thick coils of fog wound

74

themselves around the bell-towers of Venice, wrapping the whole town in softness. Even the howls of the Ravageurs were muffled. Ambrogio had gone home hours before, promising to return before school in the morning. The three cats sat in a semi-circle at the professor's feet, nibbling on a Golosi's Potato Pie with Anchovies. (Except Talina, who tore the anchovies out of her portion and laid them in a line for Drusilla, who particularly relished them.)

Professor Marìn leant over an iron saucepan, folding flour and some fur gently snipped from Talina's tail into a mixture of vanilla essence, milk, water and a drop of something from a bottle labelled 'Desperate Measures'. He muttered to himself, adding drops of liquid from various small bottles in his pockets. The reversal spell was clearly much more complicated than the tongue-loosener.

Professor Marìn's kitchen was more of a laboratory than a place to make supper. Instead of sacks of flour and canisters of tea, coffee and biscuits, there were shelves lined with bottles bearing labels inscribed in copperplate with such names as Hedgehog Gall, Lockspittle, Birds' Tears Amber and Bat Brains. Everything was just a little askew. Even the teapot and the sugar basin lurched on their metal stands. There was a bottle of Manitoba Gargling Oil upended in the sink.

'Good stuff, this! It cleans the drains famously,' said the professor, removing it so he could fill a jug with water. Enjoying her human voice, Talina was reading aloud more labels. 'Foul Philtre, Middling Sprite ("More Mischief than Malice"), Parboiled Brigand Toes ... Oh dear! How do you use Vampire Vomit?'

'Sparingly,' said the professor, smiling. 'Far too many people overuse vampire matter.'

On the range, three small cauldrons boiled merrily, emitting steam of rainbow hues into some very large tea towels draped over a rack suspended from the ceiling. From time to time, the professor sniffed, adding drops of Birds' Tears Amber. He checked the tea towels, turning them to make sure they absorbed the rainbow vapour into every stitch. Then he returned to the saucepan, frowning at its bubbling contents.

'It's not working,' he whispered, his mouth pulled down at the corners. 'I begin to suspect that to reverse the spell we may need to re-stage the whole accident using the *actual* books that turned you into a cat, Talina.'

'But they're at the tower,' mourned Drusilla, 'guarded by three unspeakably vicious dogs.'

'Wouldn't copies of the same books do just as a well?' asked Talina.

'Worth a try. *Magical Means on a Budget*? I must have ten editions of that. Can you remember which one it was?'

'The first edition, of course,' said Talina proudly. 'But what about *Substantial Cakes for the Working Classes*?'

Professor Marìn shook his head. 'I'm not your man for cooking – more for concocting, you know.'

'Ambrogio's parents have a bookshop,' said Drusilla, jumping to the window-sill. 'Let me out, Professor.'

When Drusilla reappeared at the window-sill an hour later, her tail was bushed up like a birch-broom.

'Ravageurs,' she hissed to Talina and Brolo. 'All over the place. Thank goodness for the mist. Being moonlit-night-coloured has its advantages, too. Then I used an old rat escape tunnel. Peugh!' Drusilla wrinkled her nose fastidiously. 'Now I know what fear smells like, and it isn't pretty.'

'But does Ambrogio know he's to bring *Substantial Cakes*?' Talina asked anxiously.

'Of course. Can't say I'm impressed with his sister's Persian kitten, by the way. It caught us whispering, and I was obliged to ... oh dear. I'd hate to think I was turning into a bully-girl.'

'Never!' Brolo and Talina welcomed her into a basket Professor Marìn had thoughtfully set in front of the embers of a cosy fire. They groomed Drusilla until she stopped trembling. Then all three wrapped their paws around one another and fell into a deep-breathing sleep.

At dawn, they were roused by Ambrogio beating on the door with *Substantial Cakes* clumsily wrapped in brown paper under his arm and a pair of his sister's boots looped over his elbow by the laces.

'Wonderful!' Talina purred and went to weave around his legs. 'I knew you'd bring the book.'

Then she looked up and saw that Ambrogio's smile was in fact a twisted grin of pain. His cheeks were chalky white. His right ear was in the custody of Mademoiselle Chouette, their martinet of a French mistress.

Her mouth was set in an angry grimace.

Two transformations

a misty dawn, May 4th, 1867, Saint Ada's Day

'A GARÇON WHO steals from 'is own parents' shop is a criminal in the bud,' Mademoiselle Chouette announced, her turquoise earrings quivering. 'As for a *garçon* who robs 'is sister's boots! I was on my early morning *promenade*, for my 'ealth, and I caught 'im in the act. *Mon Dieu*! Then 'e argued and argued with me and promised that 'e would explain everything if I would only come with 'im. In the end, I was so *fatiguée* that I said, '*Ah! Zut, alors! Bien!*' Then we 'ad to hurry because we thought we heard growling behind us. And suddenly, *voila!* We are at *your* door, *mon cher* Professor Marìn! *Quele surprise!*'

Her face suddenly softened into an unexpected smile.

Professor Marìn, in his dressing-gown, gently extracted Ambrogio from the French mistress's grip. 'What a pleasure to see you, Emilie! Come in out of that fog! Careful of the step – mind the lurch! *Pardonne mon pyjama!*' Using the lighted candle in his hand, he indicated his shabby paisley

78

robe – tied with an old curtain cord. Mademoiselle Chouette blushed and cast down eyelashes that were surprisingly long.

Talina thought, 'It must be the candlelight. She almost looks ... pretty! Who'd have thought it possible?'

Even in sepia cat sight, Talina had to admit, there was something undeniably attractive about Mademoiselle Chouette's silk dress, her jacket of velvet and the soft, glossy curls escaping from two tortoiseshell combs.

The professor too turned scarlet, and stammered, 'B-b-but as you are here, dear Emilie, why not come in for breakfast? And to see a most interesting experiment involving two of your livelier pupils?'

'No! No! No!' whispered Ambrogio. 'Get rid of her, Professor! She's a fire-breathing dragon! A horrible hag!'

Talina nudged the professor's ankle in agreement.

Professor Marìn laughed, 'Emilie? A hag? Then you can't ever have seen a real hag, my boy. Actually – and I don't mind who hears it – the fact is that Emilie's a bit of a sweetheart. She's been giving me private French lessons for years. I still can't seem to get the hang of French magic. It might be something to do with Emilie's face. Makes it hard for a chap to concentrate.'

And indeed Mademoiselle's face had shed all the stony sternness of the classroom. She looked like a young girl, as she said eagerly, '*Two* pupils, you say? Can you mean that you 'ave the Terror of the Neighbourhood in safe custody! I 'ave been so worried for 'er. I miss 'er! I thought I would die laughing about 'er egret dance! *Pure magie*, it was. Though I could never tell 'er that, of course. *Mais bon*, can we persuade *la charmante* Talina to come back to school? It is so very boring without 'er.'

'She's at your feet,' said Professor Marìn.

'Zis little cat is Talina?'

'*Mais oui*,' miaowed Talina.

'I'd recognize that Venetian accent anywhere,' laughed Mademoiselle. She swept Talina up in her arms, scratching her deliciously behind her ears and under her chin. 'To what 'ave you been up, *ma petite fille*?'

In the kitchen, Mademoiselle made exquisite coffee in a special French way while Professor Marìn reheated his magic mixture, adding an extra drop of **Desperate Measures** to liquefy it. A plume of smoke curled out of it, forming the words 'More **Hedgehog Gall** please!' which the professor obediently added before spooning a small quantity into Talina's mouth. She forced herself not to spit the bitter mixture out.

Propping up the books against two saucepans, Professor Marìn quickly taught Talina to say – backwards – the words of the spell she'd tried to perform with such disastrous results. Slowly, she recited the unfamiliar sounds, finally whispering, '*anilef anu immaf*'.

Immediately Talina felt her tail twitch and begin to retract inside her body like a fishing line being rewound. Her insides churned horribly.

'Wait!' she blurted. 'When I turned into a cat, all my clothes fell off me. So if, I mean *when* I turn back into a girl—'

Ambrogio blushed a ferocious shade of red.

Professor Marìn lifted a painted screen away from the fire. 'Stand behind that, dear girl.'

Mademoiselle Chouette whipped one of the tea towels from the rack above the range, saying, 'You can use this, if ze medicine works.'

'Be careful!' sputtered the professor. 'There's marinated magic in that towel! I've been infusing them with Thaumaturgic Steam for another experim—'

'*If* the medicine works?' Talina mewed. Then she couldn't speak any more because her pointed cat's teeth were pushing up painfully inside her jaw, which was rounding and turning bald. She held her paw against her head for comfort, only to see her pretty furry cat toes bloom into five human fingers, still with scimitar nails attached. Then her back legs began to shoot up. She fell and rolled onto her side, overcome with agony. The moist tea towel wrapped itself around her like a pair of large hands.

'Are you all right, Talina?' Professor Marìn called over the fire-screen. 'Oh, you poor little thing. Of course that's going to be excruciating. Ambrogio, get a stool and go to the shelf above the sink. Find the Venetian Treacle.'

'Venetian Treacle really exists? I thought it was a myth. But where would you get the vipers?'

Talina screamed, 'Stop arguing!' in strangulated Felish. Ambrogio hastened up the stool. Professor Marìn, stirring furiously, called, 'In the old days, we called Venetian Treacle by its original name, theriaca ...'

Ambrogio lifted down the heavy majolica pot and raised the lid. A beautiful perfume wafted out, along with a quiff of violet-coloured smoke.

'Put your hand in and scoop up a portion.'

Ambrogio looked into the jar. 'It's all black and gooey. Are the vipers ... ?'

'Not in a state to bite any more. They've been ground to bits with sixty-four other ingredients.'

Talina cried out again, in no language but that of pure pain. Mademoiselle Chouette clasped her hands in despair while Ambrogio thrust his fingers into the jar. They came up coated in a thick syrup that smelt of caramel-chocolate-lime-strawberry. Holding his hand carefully aloft, he rushed over to the screen. Keeping his back to whatever was happening to Talina, he reached around, his hand questing for a piece of her to which he might apply the ointment. His hand met with tufts of writhing fur, and he groaned, 'It's not working,

Professor. She's suffering so much, and she's still a cat.'

As he spoke, he rubbed his hand clean of Treacle against whatever parts of Talina he could reach behind the screen. 'There, there,' he said awkwardly.

'Is she well basted with Treacle?' asked the professor.

'Hmm.' Ambrogio moved away from the screen and then turned around anxiously.

Talina stopped sobbing and shrieking. There came the sound of a tongue rasping and a little burp, followed by, 'That's delicious!' and an 'Oh my goodness! My mother always said magic rubbed off on me.'

Then Talina's head emerged from behind the screen: Talina's *human* head, followed by her human shoulders clad in a large tea towel, which she clutched with her human hands. She stretched her human legs, smiling broadly.

'Oh!' she said, 'all the colours have come back! How good you all look! Nice and pink and healthy-looking!'

She managed to stop herself from saying 'Even you!' to Mademoiselle Chouette.

'Welcome back, Terror,' said Professor Marìn.

Ambrogio couldn't speak. He was too busy staring and pointing.

Mademoiselle Chouette rushed over to hug Talina, keening, '*Quel dommage!* Poor leetle thing!'

'Oh dear,' sighed Professor Marìn.

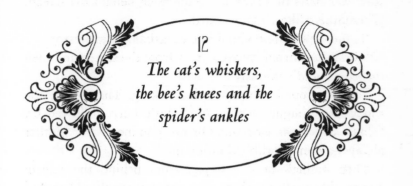

12

The cat's whiskers, the bee's knees and the spider's ankles

a tense moment later

'SO?' ASKED DRUSILLA, shooting Ambrogio a disparaging look. 'Why are you so horrified? Those are beautiful whiskers. Any cat would be proud to have them. And *you* try running through a narrow space in the dark without them!'

Talina's hands flew to her face. The spell had failed to transform one part of her. She still had long white whiskers sprouting from beneath her human nose. She buried her face in her hands and gave way to long, luxurious sobs. Damp, the wiry whiskers tickled even more.

Professor Marìn said, 'There's been too much magic swilling around my kitchen today. I'm beginning to feel a bit bilious myself from the fumes. Your mother always told me, Talina, that magic was attracted to you. I think you may have somehow intensified the dose I gave you. And of course you've absorbed the magic I was infusing into the Thaumaturgic Tea Towel as well ... so, child, I suppose you may be permeable now to the spirits of many beasts, not just cats. There may even be ... other side-effects. Your state is restored – but I am afraid it is not quite fixed. You must stay sweet and serene and reasonable at all times. Anger is particularly risky.'

'*Talina*? Sweet and serene and reasonable?' Mademoiselle Chouette asked in disbelief.

'Someone who is especially permeable to magic really runs a risk every time she departs from a calm sensible state,' said the professor sternly.

'But *whiskers*!' Talina moaned.

'There, there, child,' said the professor. 'Men have to deal with this issue on a daily basis. Ambrogio, please go up to my bathroom and fetch my razor, shaving brush and soap.'

Talina's tears mixed with scented foam as Mademoiselle carefully shaved the whiskers off. The professor said optimistically, 'In fact, I doubt if they'll re-grow. Your brain is no longer sending whisker-lengthening messages to your face. Perhaps they'll grow back only were you to get into an emotional state, if a cat had provoked you.'

'Which is unlikely,' said Drusilla.

'Do you 'ave a needle and thread, Ridolfo? And scissors?'

Mademoiselle Chouette unceremoniously shimmied out of one of her petticoats. She snipped it in half, made a few more cuts and sewed some rapid seams. Suddenly, she was holding out an undershirt for Talina. Then she seized a paisley shawl from the sagging kitchen sofa and busied herself fashioning a dress. Two non-Thaumaturgic tea towels were deftly transformed into a pinafore with a generous bib pocket. Socks were whisked out of the clean laundry basket. The boots Ambrogio had borrowed from his sister were a near-perfect fit.

Talina quickly donned her new outfit. She came out from behind the screen and curtseyed, '*Merci, Mademoiselle.*'

'*C'est chic*,' responded the French mistress, 'though your

accent remains *atroce, ma petite.* Now, a bonnet. Do you mind, professor? *Bien!*' She seized the crimson velvet tea cosy from the kitchen table and began to remodel it.

'Did you hear that?' Brolo cocked an ear.

'A sound ... like growling outside the door,' said Talina. Mademoiselle Chouette's face stiffened into its teacher-like mask.

Professor Marìn put his hands on her shoulders. 'Emilie, what do you know about those creatures who come in the night? Ravageurs, they're called. You've seen them?'

'I can 'ear them,' said Mademoiselle Chouette, 'but not see. Ravageurs? *Un nom français? Non! Des navets!* Turnips!'

The professor mused, 'Talina tells us it is the usual story – that children and animals can see them, and adults cannot. But we grown-ups can hear them sometimes. I haven't yet seen one – despite a spell to make myself childlike in perception.'

'I can help with that!' Ambrogio seized a pencil and did a swift drawing in a white space between the jam stains on the tablecloth. He made much of the jagged teeth protruding from the muzzle, the pale eyes, the matted mane and the sloping back. He added a gondola, altered the Ravageur to a sitting position and showed a team of rats poling the boat through the water as if it was a slave galley.

'Good lord! I am not entirely sorry not to have seen one in person,' said Professor Marìn. 'All the worst elements of a werewolf, a hyena and a Tasmanian devil, if I'm not mistaken. But don't worry. There are no scratches on my door – they're not coming for any of us this time.'

Trembling, Mademoiselle Chouette edged closer to him. Only the sharpest eye would have seen their little fingers linked for a moment. Then the French mistress picked up the tea cosy and her needle again.

Talina said, 'Doctor Raruso said that the Ravageurs have a good reason for what they're doing. They were here *first*. They claim that Venice is *their* ancestral land. Now they're stuck on some forsaken fogbound island in the lagoon.'

'That's why they keep howling "Give eet back",' explained Ambrogio. 'They mean "Give Venice back".'

Talina said, 'But Dr Raruso said they originally came from Siberia, so who knows why they have the French accent and the arrogance?' She added, 'Oh, sorry, Mademoiselle!'

'*Mais c'est exactement le problème!* No one understands!' Mademoiselle Chouette burst into tears of frustration. 'Those Ravageurs 'ave no French accent at all. It is a butchery of *un bon accent français*! It is a disgrace. It breaks *mon coeur*!'

The professor shyly offered her his pocket handkerchief. But he looked as if what he really wanted to do was dab the tears from those big blue eyes himself.

Ambrogio asked, 'So why should wolfy, hyena-like, devilish pretending-to-be French things think that they own Venice?'

Professor Marìn looked thoughtful. 'I was about to tell you about this when our guests arrived – about what I found in my attic last night. There's a gap in the chronicles of Venice – just before the founding of the city, traditionally in AD 421. My historian friend Giuseppe Tassini often talks of it. The trouble is, from those times, there are no documents. There was not even any paper. Just the odd bit of goat parchment. Very few people could read or write. Giuseppe has always supposed we'd never know the exact truth.'

'Are you saying that this story could be true, Professor?' asked Talina.

'That the Ravageurs really could have a right to Venice?'

'Just because it is strange and awful and there is no written proof – at the moment – does not mean it cannot be true,' the professor said gravely.

'My father,' said Talina, 'always says that all the truly important historical documents about Venice aren't even *filed* yet at the Archives. And if they were ...'

'That's preposterous!' Ambrogio paced around the kitchen like a barrister in a courtroom. 'Those vile creatures could never have ruled Venice! They're no better than bullies and cowards, trying to trick Venice into giving herself up! It is outrageous.'

'Now, now, Ambrogio. We do not know the truth of the situation. It needs investigating. Perhaps we can come to some understanding with the Ravageurs before they take' – he glanced compassionately at Talina – 'any more Venetians.'

'But what can we do, a couple of children and some cats ... and one man who is more studious than ferocious?' Drusilla's anxious face took in the professor's lanky frame.

'And a teacher of French,' cried Mademoiselle Chouette, snipping a final thread with her teeth, 'with her country's honour to defend!'

She handed Talina a handsome bonnet that now bore only the faintest resemblance to a tea cosy.

'Well,' the professor scratched his head, 'it seems to me that the Ravageurs must have baddened magic on their side. Which means that we shall need to call on the forces of good magic, like the mermaids.'

'Mermaids!' exclaimed Talina and Ambrogio in a single voice.

'You mean you've never seen one? You're young enough. But of course they are presently abroad fighting the ghosts of an old Turkish fleet sunk at the Battle of Famagosta. The ghosts of the ancient galleons arose from the seabed in a storm and immediately set course for Venice, resuming their mission to destroy her. The mermaids have their hands full.'

'Fighting mermaids! What's all this about good and baddened magic?' asked Ambrogio.

'All magic is born good. But like everything else, it can become corrupted. It seems to me likely that the Ravageurs were once just ordinary wolves who have somehow been transformed over the centuries by magic – and more recently by baddened magic. Yet even baddened magic has its reasons—'

'For taking my parents?' Talina asked. 'After all, my father is the Venetian expert when it comes to Malignant Spells and Abominable Rites. So the Ravageurs probably wanted to know what he knows. So ... I'll go and find them and demand an explanation. And get my parents back.'

Professor Marìn said, 'Admirable courage, Talina, but from what I have heard, these Ravageurs are too rude and arrogant to let anyone finish a sentence.'

'I always finish my sentences,' said Talina proudly. 'The point is that it *has* to be a child who does this. If adults can't even see the Ravageurs, how can they possibly negotiate with them?'

'That cat,' Brolo said, 'I mean girl, is quite something, I declare. I always thought human girls were namby-pamby little articles. But this one is the bee's knees and the spider's ankles, as my old pa used to say.'

'And the cat's whiskers,' smiled Ambrogio, staring at Talina.

Brolo winked at Drusilla, murmuring, 'Too-too darling, or what?'

'Talina, you truly are a terror,' said the professor. 'I never met anyone – or anything – as fearless as you. But just how do you propose to get to the Ravageurs – on their secret island enfolded in fog – and make them do exactly what you want? And I repeat, you'll need to stay sweet, serene and reasonable – or you might start changing again.'

'Into a cat?'

'Into whoever or whatever is provoking you. You and magic have a very strong relationship, Talina. You seem to intensify whatever magic comes your way. If you lose control of your emotions, goodness knows what might happen. So you of all people must be careful.'

'Yes, yes,' said Talina, barely listening. 'What if ... what if ... I could find out which child the Ravageurs are going to kidnap next? Then I could take his or her place!'

'By finding the fresh scratches they make on the door! Smart!' said Ambrogio. 'We'll just give them two children for the price of one.'

Talina's lips set in a line. If Ambrogio had been less absorbed in admiring her brave plan, he would have worried about that line.

Brolo said, 'I'll alert the cats – I know decent chaps in every parish. We'll find that door for you, Signorino Ambrogio and Signorina Talina.'

'*Mais mes enfants*,' protested Mademoiselle Chouette, 'You've 'ad as much experience of Ravageurs as a rabbit 'as of mathematics – you can't just go and get yourselves taken by those *bêtes monstrueuses*!'

'And even if ... well, I don't think we need to ... *sacrifice* two of you,' intervened the professor. 'Think of your parents, Ambrogio. I am their best customer, and their best-selling author. Even so, they would never forgive me.'

'And,' announced Talina conclusively, 'the song didn't mention you, Ambrogio. It just talked about the not-quite-cat, Talina. Me. Stop staring at me like that.'

Ambrogio reddened as if she'd slapped both sides of his face. He protested, 'The rat didn't get to finish his song. Maybe he was about to say something about a boy, who could draw and argue well—'

'But the rat died,' said Talina baldly.

'Because of what the Ravageurs did to him,' mewed Drusilla.

The silence that followed was broken by a violent battering at the door.

'Let me in, Ridolfo!' shouted Giuseppe Tassini. 'There's something you have to see.'

13

Off with their heads!

Professor Marìn's crooked kitchen, seconds later

CHOKING FOR BREATH, the historian waved a rag of crudely printed cloth in their faces. Ambrogio took it gently from Tassini's shaking hand and read:

FOR ARROGANCE AND POMPOSITY,
the bell-towers of Luprio have been put on trial.
The case: how dare they poke
their arrogant spires at Heaven?
How dare they fill the air
with the hateful clanging of their bells?
Bell-towers? No! They are lying signposts,
falsely claiming their so-called Venice is a great city.

LOOK AT THEIR BOASTFULNESS!
Santa Maria Formosa in Castello – 40 metres high
Santi Apostoli in Cannaregio – 54 metres
San Barnaba in Dorsoduro – 33 metres

San Giacomo dell'Orio in Santa Croce – 32 metres
To all these —

immediate sentence of death by decapitation.

OFF WITH THEIR HEADS!

They shall be topped and tailed,
brought low and humbled.

SIGNED Grignan, Lord of Luprio

'And do you know the worst thing? The Venetians have gone to the churches to pray for their towers,' Tassini cried.

'But that's the most *dangereux* place for them to be!' whispered Mademoiselle Chouette. 'We must divide and run to warn them. I'll take Santi Apostoli. Professor, you do San Giacomo; Giuseppe – Santa Maria Formosa. *Mes enfants* – San Barnaba for you. *Dépêchez-vous!*'

'We're too late!' cried Talina.

The spire and belfry of the bell-tower – by a canal, just to the west of the church of San Barnaba – were beginning to spin. The bells jangled in alarm. The tower groaned dustily. A small palace in front of it simply crumbled. In the misty background, the spire of San Samuele shuddered in sympathy on the other side of the Grand Canal.

'That spire's coming off,' said Ambrogio. 'Any moment. If it doesn't fall in the canal, it will crash through the church roof on top of the people.'

'That's probably just what the Ravageurs intend.'

Talina and Ambrogio ran into the church, crying, 'You must get out! Quick! The bell-tower's coming down!'

Most of the parishioners rushed out into the little square in front of the church, from where they could see the swirling head of the tower.

But a few stayed inside, grumbling, 'It's cold out there! Anyway, it's that mad girl Talina. She is always raising alarms. She'll do anything to attract attention.'

'Yes, last I heard, she'd staged a disappearance.'

'No, no!' protested Talina and Ambrogio in unison. 'Come out! This is a real threat.'

But then the shriek of twisting masonry silenced everyone. Talina and Ambrogio joined the last few parishioners running out of the church.

All eyes were drawn to the bell-tower. The ground beneath it turned swampy, then soupy. The marble and brick simply melted away. The bell-tower began to slither into the mud.

'This is baddened magic that Professor Marìn told us about,' cried Talina, but her voice was drowned by the frantic clash of bells, the grinding of stone and inhuman screams in the air. Attracted by the commotion, a flock of birds ringed the descending tower in ever lower circles.

'The seagulls are laughing!' cried Talina.

'At least *they're* enjoying it,' said Ambrogio bitterly. 'And those birds are not seagulls. Look at those bald heads! They're *vultures*!'

At the word 'vulture', a shudder spread through Talina's body, as if the big grey birds were hovering at her back, brushing her with their wings.

'Vultures in Venice? Never heard—'

The cone of the spire and the belfry suddenly skittered around like a wind-up toy. And then a deep black fissure appeared below the belfry as though an invisible giant had hacked the tower with an unimaginably vast and ferocious axe.

The parishioners of San Barnaba groaned, as if they had received the body blow themselves.

The reverberations churned the canal into a whirlpool, ejecting a gondola into the middle of the crowd. The sharp silver prow embedded itself in the soft zinc of a newsstand's wall. Meanwhile a wave rolled over a nearby fruit boat. A few moments later, a salad of tomatoes, lemons and apples was bobbing in the water, along with two angry and shaken fruit-sellers. One spat a small potato out of his mouth; the other pulled a dripping leek from his pocket.

Another invisible blow, and the upper part of the tower leant over, like a vast bird's beak pointing towards the canal. Finally, the belfry separated from the stump of the tower and crashed spire-first into the canal, disappearing except for the upside-down hollow of the belfry. A row of bells poked up out of the water with the clappers lolling like tongues in dead men's mouths.

With its top struck off, the blunted body of the tower began to sink. It was swiftly consumed by the mud as if it were a filament of spaghetti sucked up by a greedy mouth.

Then there was silence, followed by the weeping and terrified cries of the crowd.

'That's it,' said Talina, quietly. 'I've had enough. The creatures who are mutilating Venice are also holding my parents.'

Ambrogio nodded silently.

Talina looked around her at the darkening sky, feeling the stars impatiently waiting to come out.

'I'm going to find those Ravageurs,' she said. 'And I'm going to do it tonight.'

14
Frimousse and Rouquin

Cannaregio, the night of May 4th and 5th, 1867,
Saint Pellegrino's Day

TALINA SQUIRTED A little oilcan of Professor
Marìn's 'Lockspittle' into the keyhole, which yielded
instantly. She let herself in, closing the door behind
her.

The first thing she heard was a long, fruity snore.

'Good,' she muttered. 'Louder, please, if possible.'

The snorer obliged with a window-shaking masterpiece,
composed of a deep snarl, a trilling whistle and a throaty
roar.

One of Brolo's cousins had delivered the information that
the home of the Ravageurs' next intended victim was in
Cannaregio, a humble two-storey house near the abattoirs
and the Botanical Gardens. A single rushlight burnt in its
hall. Talina picked it up, took off her shoes and padded
silently up the stairs and down a narrow corridor until she
found the room she wanted. She crept to the bed of the
sleeping child, a boy about eight years old. Gazing down at

his peaceful face, she thought, 'I don't have to do this. I could just leave him here.'

The boy stirred and opened his eyes. At the sight of the strange girl with the rushlight in her hand, he sat bolt upright, pointing an accusing finger.

'Who are you?' he said. 'A thief? I shall just about fix your giblets if you've come for my toy train, you brute!'

'I,' intoned Talina, standing up to her full height, only slightly taller than the sitting boy. 'I am the Terror of the Neighbourhood. You'd better do what I say.'

'Well I ain't very terrified of a flea like you. A *girl* flea. Anyway, my pa's gonna come and git you any second,' threatened the boy. 'And he's gonna dose you *good* with Manitoba Gargling Oil, and then ... he'll march you off to the police—'

He was interrupted by another terrifically loud snore.

'Your pa, I presume? The one who is "gonna come and git" me?' Talina mimicked the boy's accent. Then she remembered there was no time for teasing.

'Get under the bed,' she hissed. 'The Ravageurs are coming for you tonight.'

'The what? I ain't never heard of no such thing as a Ravidger.'

'So you never heard any howling in the night? Or heard of anyone in Venice being taken away and never seen again?'

'Yes, but—' His shoulders had begun to shake.

'Well, let me tell you. Those poor people have been taken away – by creatures called Ravageurs, who are like wolves, only much bigger, much nastier and much more hungry. They have teeth as long as lizards and claws like sabres, and ... they mark the house of their next victim with five scratches on the door. Short ones for a child; long ones for an adult.'

The boy's lip was trembling now.

'Do you know what's on your front door right this minute?'

The bedcovers were still warm from the boy's body when Talina slipped inside, setting the rushlight on the table beside her. He sobbed quietly to himself underneath the bed, 'Why me? Why me? Why me?'

'You'd better be quiet, milksop,' Talina had to instruct only once. 'If they hear you snivelling, they'll take you too.'

When they came, it was two of them.

Talina heard the front door hinges give under a quick, skilful wrench. The snores of the boy's father never faltered.

Heavy paws with long nails clopped swiftly up the stairs.

The bedroom door creaked wide open. Talina saw, for the first time, the silhouette of a Ravageur head, black against the dimly lit wall of the room. Its lips were drawn back. A thick brush of erect fur ran along its sloping spine, making it look much more like a hyena than a wolf. It carried an embroidered canvas swag tied across its torso with leather strips.

The moon, coming out from behind a cloud, suddenly brought the thick muzzle to life and colour. An intensely red tongue drew itself over jagged yellowy fangs, each of which was *longer* than a lizard – some as long as Talina's fingers. An eye glinted the palest green. A ruby dangled from a tattered ear.

Talina could distinctly feel the hairs rise on the nape of her neck.

'It's just the moonlight making it look so big,' she told herself. But she was wrong. As he proceeded into the room she saw that the Ravageur was – impossibly – bigger than his shadow.

'Baddened magic,' she thought, 'must be doing that. But he reminds me of something ...'

The creature moved towards her, his bitter breath preceding him. She hastened to lower her eyelids and to feign a deep, even breathing. A second set of paws clopped into the room.

'Frimousse,' grumbled the first creature, 'where is ze *petit garçon*? The *hommelette* what we 'as come for to get? I don't lak zis *maison*. Eet's *poor*. Eet stink of cabbage.'

'Shut your meat-trap, Rouquin, or I shall kick you in ze *schafflouse*!' snarled Frimousse, lifting the counterpane. '*Voila! Une petite fille.*'

Talina thought, 'I can understand them! It must be the Spell Steam.'

But even Talina – Mademoiselle Chouette would have been surprised to hear – was disgusted by the creatures' exaggerated and yet incompetent French accents. She risked a quick look from under her lashes, and saw the red-furred Rouquin use his teeth to draw a list out of his swag. Close up, his fur was rippled through with nasty mange scabs. Scratching his right leg with his left one, he complained, 'But eet says 'ere that we should get *un garçon* at thees *maison*. Tommaso d'Este.'

'Boy, girl – all look ze same to me,' said Frimousse. '*C'est chic*, not big, not 'eavy. Sleepin' lak a baby. No trouble. Tie 'er up.' He leant towards Talina so she struggled not to choke on his corrupt breath. With enormous effort, she kept her eyelashes lowered and her face motionless.

'*La peine!* I am *allergique* to ze females,' Frimousse sneezed wetly and then wiped his nose on Talina's hair.

Rouquin poked his head into his swag, producing a sack with thick handles. Frimousse flipped Talina into it, pulling it up to her neck so that only her head jutted out. Then Rouquin nudged the sack so its handle looped over

Frimousse's neck and tossed Talina onto his friend's back. The Ravageur, Talina aboard, loped towards the door.

'I am riding a Ravageur!' Talina thought of her parents. Were they too taken like this, from the Archives? Strapped to stinking Ravageurs, slipping through the streets in the dark?

An unpleasant sweetish smell too close to her nose made her wonder, 'Is mange contagious?'

'I still smell *garçon*,' mumbled Rouquin. Talina heard the boy under the bed breathe in as if preparing to scream. To distract the beasts, she extracted one hand from her sack, reached down and pulled Frimousse's tail, hard.

'Aggh!' screamed the Ravageur. 'You do that again, *ma fille*, and I shall chew off your hand right up to your leg.'

Rouquin lashed his wiry tail at Talina's shoulder so hard that it winded her. She sobbed with pain, curling up inside the rough hessian.

The Ravageurs trotted downstairs and out into the street. Through the coarse weave, Talina could see a gondola waiting in the canal at the end of the *calle*. The Ravageurs lowered themselves in, and the rower-rats set themselves to pull at their miniature oars without any instructions, their paws clenched over the wood. From her position on Frimousse's back, Talina could see a complicated mechanism of tiny oar-holes just above the water level. The rats bent over their work with their eyes lowered. A sour grainy smell of rat sweat flowed back over the deck.

'Now, to the Ravageur palace!' hoped Talina, nursing her aching shoulder.

But Frimousse and Rouquin had other errands: looting errands. The gondola moored by the poles of various jetties snugly clad in vivid green stockings of moss. They stopped at butchers', fishmongers' and fruit shops. The rats were despatched inside, returning with swags dragged in their teeth. They emptied the contents on the paving stones. The Ravageurs pawed disdainfully through the loot. At each place, only one or two things proved good enough: a single peach or a handsome sausage. The rats stowed the chosen goods carefully in the boat.

'Now, ze sweeties!' snarled Rouquin. 'Rats – row!'

'Which confectioner do you desire?' a rat asked humbly, eyes still downcast.

'Golosi's, of course, imbecile!'

The rat nodded to his companions. At Rialto, eight of them leapt out of the gondola and disappeared. They returned, dragging a sack from which floated the delicious perfume of lemon peel and candied violet. The Ravageurs poked the bottles and packets, settling on Barberry Drops, Pistachio Pralines, Marsh Mallow Syrup, Angelica Comfits, Neapolitan Wafers and Jujube Paste.

'Zat'll keep 'em quiet for a while anyways,' Frimousse laughed coarsely.

'Keep *whom* quiet?' wondered Talina. 'The humans they've kidnapped? But why give them treats?'

Finally, the gondola departed from its last mooring and nosed into the Grand Canal, following the path of a silvery moon into the lagoon. As they left the island of San Giorgio behind them, Frimousse tipped Talina from her sack. He reached into his swag and brought out a red scarf.

'We don't want ze *petite fille* to see where we are going,' he told Rouquin.

'*C'est vrai*. Blindfold the prisoner,' Rouquin ordered a pair of rats, who hastened to take one end of the scarf each. They ran around Talina's shoulders with the ends until her head was bandaged like a mummy's. The rats were careful, however, to leave holes for her nose and mouth.

The last thing she saw before the rats covered her eyes

was Frimousse scratching himself furiously, while Rouquin gnawed at a large scab on his leg.

'You revolting mangy murdering monsters!' she screamed. At the back of her mind, she heard Professor Marìn's voice warning her, 'You must stay sweet, serene and reasonable or—'

Rouquin said, surprised, '*Mais* zis one speak lak us! But is not good what she say.'

He cuffed her head so hard that it fell back against the planks.

Frimousse shouted, 'Too hard, Rouquin! "Alive," *he* always says. "*Alive.*" You know he likes to play with zem first.'

Talina heard nothing more, and felt nothing more.

15

At the court of the Ravageur Lord

an unknown corner of the Venetian lagoon,
an unknown number of hours later, as far as Talina
is concerned. For all she knows, it could be days.
But in fact, it is the morning of May 5th, 1867

'WE'RE 'ERE.'
Frimousse tore the scarf off Talina's head,
cuffing her ear for good measure.

'Ouch!' she cried.

'I told you she was still breathing,' Rouquin said
triumphantly. 'She was just 'aving a leetle sleep.'

Talina kept silent, contemplating the approaching shore:
a wild, seemingly barren place with a few tousled shrubs.
When she looked behind, she could see nothing but a ring
of glowering grey fog.

The island of the Ravageurs, Talina thought, looked just
the way Venice – or Luprio – must have looked when the
original creatures fled there thousands of years before: just
a few clumps of land, cut through by channels of swift water,
and covered with heaps of muddy clay. As the rats rowed

her closer, she saw that the clay was crudely decorated with five-stroked swirls.

The jetty's wooden legs were like totem poles. At the top of each pole were pairs of wolf paws holding severed human heads, all carved from oak and wearing horrified expressions. The rickety wooden path to the shore was lined with what at first glance appeared to be lamp-posts. But Talina soon realized that the iron poles held gibbet-cages full of protesting, hungry-looking cats. Frimousse and Rouquin climbed out, dragging their sacks of food, leaving Talina and the rats in the boat. The rats set to scrubbing the oar-locks with Manitoba Gargling Oil.

'Stay,' warned Frimousse, his mouth full of sacking. 'No, better to *make* 'er.'

He dropped his sack, leapt up to open an empty gibbet-cage and yanked Talina out of the boat by the scruff of her pinafore. Then Frimousse knelt, and Rouquin nudged Talina onto his back and up to the gibbet-cage.

'It's too small,' she protested.

'Shall I bite off a leg and an arm?' offered Frimousse. 'Then you'll fit naissly.'

Talina hastily folded herself into a sitting position, her arms wrapped around her knees.

'*Voilà!*' Rouquin clanged the door behind her and nosed a bolt through a black latch behind her head.

'That'll teach 'er!' muttered Frimousse. 'Tail-puller! Which reminds me ...'

He leapt up to Talina's head, wrenching out a clump of corn-husk hair through the slats of the cage.

'Stop it!' spluttered Talina, tears sprouting from her eyes. A drop of blood fell on her pinafore. The side of her head burned as if someone were holding a torch to it.

'Why my hair, you brute?' she wept.

'Grignan's instructions,' he said mysteriously, trotting off with the thick hank trailing from between his teeth.

Struts of cold metal pressed against Talina's forehead, legs and knees. The piteous mewing of the gibbeted cats broke her heart. She felt like mewing herself.

'Why do they keep the poor things out here?' she mused.

Down in the boat, a rat mumbled to his companions, 'Foolish human maid. Don't she know as how they'll snack on a cat if there ain't nothing else to hand?'

Another chimed in, 'And they jest loves cat bacon.'

'You can speak?' exclaimed Talina.

'And you can understand Ratsch?' squeaked the first rat in alarm.

'I ... am under a spell,' explained Talina. 'I was briefly a kind of cat. Then—'

'Not,' trembled a third rat, 'the not-quite-cat? In person! Her very self?'

'Yes! That's me. Talina. From the song.'

'Ssssh,' urged his companion. 'We don't want the Ravageurs hearing that.'

The third rat whispered, 'Then Doctor Raruso found you!'

'Yes, he came to the Ostello delle Gattemiagole in San Marcuola—'

The first rat began to chant the song that Talina had heard at the *ostello*:

There shall be a little cat
A cat who wasn't always that
A cat who's lost what she loves best,
whose tongue is fierce; whose heart no less ...
Talina who was in the tower
Talina who—

'Dear Doctor Raruso!' he stopped to smile. 'No braver nor wiser fellow to be found in all the rat-runs of Venice—'

'I am very sorry to tell you that Doctor Raruso is dead,' said Talina. 'He seemed a very pleasant gentleman. I am afraid he was tortured before he died. So the song may not be a secret any more.'

Each of the rats put a single paw across his breast, and then saluted, whispering, 'Rest his rodent soul.'

'So,' Talina felt rude dragging their attention back to the problem in hand. 'I came here deliberately, because it's obvious that's no nursery rhyme. I am meant to be something to do with putting an end to all this bullying and kidnapping.'

'Oh you are, are you, *ma petite*?' Frimousse had crept back to the jetty unseen.

'Yes,' said Talina stoutly, though her whole body trembled. 'So what have you done with the Venetians? The men, women and babies? Did you ... eat them?'

'We tried a few,' answered Frimousse, wrinkling his nose. 'But there are no good recipes for correct saucing and spicing of 'uman beings, at least none zat we could find. So in the end eet was better to give zem something to do.'

'What something to do? And how many was that few,' Talina quavered, 'that you ... tried?'

Grinning horribly, Frimousse nudged the gibbet-cage lock with his nose till Talina tumbled down onto the jetty. For just a moment, the Ravageur seized Talina's leg in his jaws, letting his fangs graze her flesh through her wool stockings. Then he shook himself, shouting, 'Échalas! Croquemort! Escort 'er.'

Two more Ravageurs stepped up.

'You too,' Frimousse growled at the rats. 'You're needed in the Great Hall and the *Sala del Sangue*. You know what for.'

The rats scampered off.

'The *Sala del Sangue* ... The *Blood* Chamber?' thought Talina.

Talina was astonished to discover that those swarthy lumps of mud enclosed a palatial building, like a jewel inside a grubby fist. The interior walls were lined with tapestries of hunting scenes – but not the usual ones. Ravageurs were shown hunting humans. In tiny, precise stitches, captured humans were seen tied to stakes or being carried towards steaming black cauldrons.

There were no windows. Daylight faded as they walked deeper into the building. Golden sconces smoked with beefy tallow candles at every corner. Talina descended a dozen massive stairs, a Ravageur at either side of her. The last step opened into a Great Hall.

A fireplace yawned at the far end, belching black smoke and blue flame. Dangling from the ceiling were awkward chandeliers made of bones tied in bunches with leather strips. They dripped wax onto the thick fur of the beasts below.

Ravageurs stood in ranks, their red tongues lolling out of their mouths. Many wore emerald or ruby earrings, or golden rings around their tails. Some were liveried in striped scarves or diamond-patterned capes. Many were guzzling a dark liquid from great bowls strapped to iron stakes anchored on big stones.

'What's that?' Talina worried aloud. 'Blood?'

'Devilsdrench,' whispered a rat, rushing past her towards a tiered stool. '*They* say it's made from boiled baby blood but actually that's rather disagreeable in taste, so they just pretend. Really, Devilsdrench is just jujube juice and molasses.'

The rat scampered up the five-tiered stool, beside which stood a harp. Ten rats stood in pairs on their back legs and began to play the high and low notes according to the height of their tier. Their nails were enamelled a shimmering blue. Behind them, a mirror doubled the whole scene. The effect, musically and visually, was delicately pretty.

Some Ravageurs growled along with the rats' careful tune. Others wiggled their heads appreciatively in time to the music. A few stared curiously at Talina. She stared right back, defiantly, with her arms crossed over her chest.

Her eye fell on a tank hewn from sparkling rock crystal. It was set into the wall like a jewel. Something was moving inside it; rather, dozens of somethings were scuttling along the floor and all over the crystal walls of the tank.

'Not scorpions! Anything but that!' Talina recoiled. She hated insects. She would even admit to being afraid of spiders. And scorpions, with their arched tails full of poison, were the worst kind of creeping beast. She watched with fascinated repulsion as lines of the scorpions swung up curtains of silky threads in gold, black and brown. Then she recognized a hank of dark-gold hair beset with black, wriggling forms. She gasped, 'That's *mine*! They gave my hair to the scorpions!'

That, she recalled, had been on the instructions of Grignan. 'So where is the Ravageur Lord?' wondered Talina. 'None of these look one bit lordly. Except perhaps *him*.'

She was gazing at a tall and unusually well-groomed Ravageur. Frimousse bowed to him, and kicked her forward, murmuring, 'Magisterulus, Sir Vizier, I present ze prisoner, Tommaso d'Este, as ordered.'

'Does not look like a "Tommaso" to me,' said the Vizier. 'The human males have short fur. You donkeys! We are looking for boys because of that drawing. Boys! Boys who might be friends with the perpetrator of . . . Boys!'

He pointed to Talina's long corn-husk hair in disgust.

Talina interrupted, 'Of course I'm not Tommaso d'Este.

I am Talina Molin, daughter of Marco and Lucia Molin – you took them already– '

A trumpet squawked. All eyes were drawn to a door that opened directly onto a dais at the end of the Great Hall.

'Behold!' intoned the Vizier, 'Lord Grignan forsakes his Growlery to come among us!'

Rouquin and Frimousse cowered.

The door swung open. First the tail, and then the hindquarters of a huge Ravageur became visible. The creature walked backwards onto the stage, his looped tail sweeping the floor. As his head became visible, he was seen to be smoking a large cigar, the fumes of which rolled across the room and made Talina cough. The sound she made was drowned by all the rats clapping loudly and cheering, though their faces were tense. The Ravageurs bayed approval at the appearance of their leader.

Two monstrous fellows in red capes approached the back end of their ruler. Reverently, they lowered their muzzles and kissed the air above his tail.

Magisterulus announced, 'Is there any other who today deserves the honour of saluting Lord Grignan's hindparts?'

There ensued some whispering among the Ravageurs. Croquemort and Échalas were pushed forward by their friends. Bashfully, they mounted the dais and kissed the air above the rear end of their Lord, their heads lowered and their tails tucked in between their legs.

'Oh my! How very, very rude and silly,' thought Talina. 'But then, these Ravageurs are all boys! So I suppose that they must have these stupid games. No wonder they took my father from the Archives – he's researched much better Abominable Rites than that! *But where is he*? Where are all the Venetians?'

There was not a human being to be seen in the Great Hall.

Unless, Talina shuddered, those were human bones in the grisly chandeliers.

Finally, when all the kissing and grovelling was done, the Ravageur Lord swung round and glared the length of the Great Hall. As his eyes slid over the rats, they prostrated themselves, trembling. Finally his eye found Talina. At the sight of her, he spat out his cigar and drawled, 'So what does this little Venetian have to say for itself? A little begging in its quaint little language? Some screaming? Are you going to offer me your favourite toy? I do so love it when they weep!'

Talina felt a knot in her throat. The skin thrummed at the back of her knees. She opened her mouth but nothing came out.

'Nothing to say? Not even your name?' taunted the Ravageur Lord, strutting backwards and forwards across his stage. 'I shall give you a name. *Voilà!* Your name is Ratfood, as you're obviously too scrawny for *me* to eat.'

'Ha, ha, ha, Ratfood!' the Ravageurs grinned and guffawed.

Grignan glowered at Talina. 'If you're not going to entertain us, why shouldn't I kill you immediately?'

'Because I have questions.'

The Ravageurs whistled and growled, while their Lord stared at Talina. 'But this one can speak like—'

Now that Talina had started to talk, the words tumbled out so fast and furious that she could scarcely believe her own ears. She declared, 'Yes, I have *interesting* questions. Such as – such as ... Who gave you the right to kidnap Venetians and cats? And by the way, why don't *you* even bother to *pretend* a French accent like all your minions? Not very well either, I may say. But most of all I want to know what you've done with my parents. Because ...' She quailed into silence and confusion. Her vision was changing alarmingly. All the yellow bones in the chandeliers glowed but the brown fur of the Ravageurs had grown dull and misty.

'Oh no!' she thought. 'I must keep calm somehow. Sweet, serene and reasonable, as the professor said.'

Grignan wasn't even looking at her. She followed his eyes to a piece of paper nailed to the wall near his altar. It was a highly accurate drawing labelled 'French Monster on the Crooked *Campanile*'. And it was signed 'Ambrogio Gasperin'.

'Oh!' escaped from Talina's mouth.

Grignan's eyes narrowed. 'So do you happen to know this Ambrogio Gasperin?' he drawled. 'Perpetrator of this insulting drawing? We intend to get him. We'll take all the boys in Venice until we find him. And when we do, he's for the pot.'

'Oh my ... I mean, no, never heard of him,' gabbled Talina. 'Or her. Funny name, Ambrogio, don't you think? Um—'

She breathed deeply, whispering urgently to herself, 'Sweet, serene and reasonable. At all times.'

The Ravageur Lord inspected his claws. Something red clung between two of them. He sucked it out loudly.

'Vile,' muttered Talina under her breath.

'Delicious, actually. But how would you know? What a gristleless untasty life you humans live. Why so silent now, Ratfood? Speak up!'

'You make me ... nervous,' she faltered. 'Don't you know how that feels?'

'Can't say that I do.'

It was his casual disdain that did it. A wave of heat suffused Talina's face and her head suddenly emptied of 'serene and peaceful' and filled with fire. 'Give them *back*!' she shouted. 'Give them back, all the fathers and mothers, and grandfathers and grandmothers and children and aunts and cats you have taken!'

'Oi, what's that growing on 'er nasty little face?' called Rouquin.

'Oh no,' thought Talina, 'whiskers! And my heart is beating fit to burst, and I bet my eyes are turning green and round.' She dared not touch her nose.

Her voice sounded husky. The reds and greens had drained from the Ravageurs' capes and jewels – again, the blue of the fire and the yellow of the tallow candles were the only colours she saw clearly. 'I'm turning into a cat again,' Talina wailed. She found herself squatting on all fours.

'But this isn't like before,' she thought. 'I'm not a cat. My hair's sticking up like a mane – just like the mane of a Ravageur! My collar is so tight! And why do I feel so much like fastening my teeth into something meaty?'

She repeated to herself, 'Sweet, serene and reasonable. I must stay—'

Grignan bounded off the stage and gripped Talina by the back of the dress that now strained across her back. He shook her hard, throttling the breath out of her. The fumes of smoked sage-leaf made her dizzy.

'Who do you think you are?' Grignan bayed. 'One of us?'

'One of *you*?' cried Talina. 'That's the last thing in the world I want to be.' She held up her hand, screaming, 'Stop!'

But that hand was now a paw, thickly furred with grey. Yet her legs were still her own and her arms and body were human.

Grignan slammed his own massive paw down on hers, pinioning her to the floor. 'What *are* you?' he roared.

16
Sweeter with dessert

one intake of breath later

BEFORE TALINA COULD collect enough wits to answer, a Ravageur trotted in from the next room and whispered something to Magisterulus.

'Second Breakfast is served in the *Sala del Sangue*,' announced the Vizier.

Two hundred dripping red tongues lolled out of two hundred black muzzles.

The Ravageur Lord stroked his nose. 'It's always fun to play with the little ones – but more amusing, of course, when one's appetite's already slaked.'

The Vizier simpered, 'And, Lord, this girl – or whatever she's turning into – is very thin and no doubt particularly bitter in flavour. We should fill our bellies with something more appetizing first.'

Fear and rage battled inside Talina. Rage won. She stuck out her tongue. She was appalled to see that it flopped out so far of her mouth that she could see it, twice its normal length and much redder than she ever remembered it from the bathroom mirror. She felt the left side-seam of her dress give way from armpit to waist.

A door slammed in the distance. A rich smell of meat wafted into the room. In spite of herself, Talina's mouth filled with water, and she sniffed greedily at the air. Some of the Ravageurs moaned with pleasure, and a long filament of saliva dropped from Grignan's jaws. He told the Vizier, 'You're right. Tie the prisoner up. Whatever she is, dealing with her will be sweeter with ... dessert!'

Frimousse knocked Talina to the ground and dragged her across the hall until her head collided painfully with the corner of a table. She sprawled on the floor, her legs splayed in front of her, her back against a table leg. At a nod from Magisterulus, some of the rats ran around Talina with ropes, fastening her to the table leg. One of the rats from the boat winked at her as he scampered off. Another tucked one end of the rope into her left hand, which he had just tied behind her.

'It's a bow, not a knot,' he hissed. 'Wait till they start eating. They'll forget everything else in the world. Then just pull.'

She thanked him with her eyes.

The rat nodded. 'Good luck, not-quite-cat. No one told us you'd also be a not-quite-Ravageur.'

'Things happen to me when I get angry,' she whispered. 'I'm beginning to think that what happens is that I start to look like whatever or whomever I'm angry with.'

'Tricky, that,' the rat sympathized. 'Plenty to raise anyone's hackles round here.'

From across the room boomed Grignan's stern voice: 'Is it done properly? Rat-work can be so shoddy.'

The rat froze. Talina could see his heart pumping in his chest.

'Oh no,' thought Talina. 'If they see what he's done, we'll all be killed! They won't wait for dessert.'

Reluctantly she let go of the trailing end of the rope. The rat's face suffused with relief. 'Pretend you've fainted,' he whispered.

Talina closed her eyes and let her head loll forward. Frimousse inspected the coils, but his eyes were glazed and his mouth open, releasing a long spool of dribble onto Talina's shoulder.

'She's out!' Frimousse reported. 'Dead to ze world!'

Then he forgot her entirely. Three wide doors swung open. Frimousse joined the other Ravageurs swarming through the opening, nipping and snarling at each other in their haste to get what were evidently considered the best seats on the far side of the room. Talina felt the breeze of two hundred Ravageurs rushing past. Against her will, she breathed in the rancid cloud of fur and skin flakes they left behind.

Despite their hurry, each Ravageur paused for a second in front of a niche just inside the *Sala del Sangue*, where he spat with deadly accuracy at a crude portrait of a man in antique costume etched into a ragged piece of parchment. The portrait was ringed by a rope of living blue fire, which snarled and pranced around it. Talina thought she could see tiny malicious faces and little punching arms in those flames. She wondered who the man could be, but his features were all frayed and blistered with violent applications of Ravageur saliva.

Grignan strolled after the Ravageurs, accompanied by the Vizier. They too paused to spit at the portrait, hitting it precisely in the middle of the sticky face. They did not cast a look backwards to where Talina slumped, doing her best to look unconscious. Breathing through her nose, she stared under semi-closed lids through the open doors.

The *Sala del Sangue* was dominated by a long, narrow

table in a U shape, at human-knee height. Bloodstained leather skins were laid over it. On those the rats swarmed, setting out hundreds of black spoons, glistening with a dark liquid. The Ravageurs perched on leather cushions, little growls of hunger escaping from their jaws. Talina was disgusted to see that some lapped from bleached human skulls, cut in half and mounted on black stones. Others scratched themselves, raising more puffs of skin and fur, or snapped at their neighbours.

'First,' commanded the Vizier, 'your medicine!'

The Ravageurs screwed up their muzzles with distaste. But they lowered their heads and lapped the black spoons clean.

Talina was puzzled. 'Gripe Cordial? Worm syrup? Whatever it is, it's not working. Those Ravageurs are horribly mangy. Some have more bald patches than fur!'

A dozen doors opened simultaneously on the far side of the *sala*, where the favoured seats were. As if kicked from behind, a large sheep rushed in from every door, each wearing a kind of harness with an elaborate saddle strapped to its back. On the saddles sat silver salvers heaped with food. As the sheep trotted around the U-shaped table, Ravageurs turned and dragged whatever they fancied from the nearest salver onto the filthy leather tablecloths.

'Well, I can see why they don't bother with plates,' thought Talina, watching the Ravageurs tearing at their meat and guzzling the sauces. Between courses, they impatiently sucked the spilt juices that had soaked into the leather tablecloths.

One course appeared to be delayed. Howls of frustrated hunger rang through the *Sala del Sangue*. Talina watched in horror as a Ravageur's jaws closed around a woolly waiter's neck. His companions turned on him in fury.

'Lay off, Nochin Quinchou! You barbarian!' the two

Ravageurs on either side of him shouted, nipping him until he let go of the sheep.

'I forgot myself, Croquemort. Sorry, Fildefer,' muttered Nochin Quinchou, hanging his mange-ridden head, while Croquemort slapped him repeatedly on one side of it. 'Ouch, ouch, you'll have my ear off!'

Evidently this was the only form of table manners that the Ravageurs observed: not to eat the waiters.

The Vizier announced each new dish as it arrived on sheepback from the kitchen. In spite of her disgust, Talina leant forward with interest. Years of poring over French cookbooks made nearly all these dishes familiar to her – though she'd never had the luxury of tasting them.

Timballes de queues d'Ecrevisses Mantua

Prawn-tail mousse

*

Terrine de foie gras avec sa gelée

Goose livers with jelly

*

Faisan à la Financière

Bankers' Pheasant

*

Tournedos de Rat Mort

(one Talina had not seen before)

*

Canard Pompéien

Pompey Duck turned out to be a cold duck stuffed with *foie gras*, its flesh decorated with spices painted on in a design of red and black on a white background.

*

This was wriggling with live lobsters, which the Ravageurs picked off with terrible relish, smashing the crustaceans on the table and tearing their tails off.

For dessert there was:

Le Soufflé aux taupes caramélisées, ses Macarons et Chantilly

Souffé of Caramelized Moles with macaroons and whipped cream

The Ravageur Lord was the only one to eat off a kind of plate. He was seated at the ruins of an altar above the open ends of the U-shaped table. Talina was horrified to see that a beautiful old illustrated book served as his place setting. A sage-leaf cigar lay smouldering perilously close to one corner of it.

'No doubt stolen from the Archives at the same time as my father!' thought Talina.

A butler Ravageur clamped a tarnished silver ladle in his jaw to serve Lord Grignan reverent helpings of every delicacy – straight onto the book. Occasionally, when the page became so saturated with bloody sauce that the food slipped off it, the butler deftly spread a new chapter open with his claw. Beside the book was a large glass jar of Spiced Mostarda from Golosi's. Grignan picked up the pot with his jaws and emptied a splash of the orange fruit mustard onto his food.

The final course was announced as *La Corbeille de 'Fruits'*. In this fruit basket, instead of apples and peaches, however, there were squirming frogs and toads. This was accompanied by a foaming red liquid in buckets placed at intervals around the table. The Ravageurs plunged their heads into them with gusto.

The rat's voice came from beside Talina. 'Thank you for covering for us. You've got a cool head, not-quite-girl. Now don't move. That Rouquin is still keeping an eye on you.'

'Thank you for looking out for *me*,' she whispered. 'What are they drinking?'

'Hot raw rabbit juice,' the rat wrinkled his nose.

'Don't they know that you can get *tapeworms* from raw meat?'

'Tell me about it! No, I'll tell *you*. See that one over there, next to Lèche-bottes, him – Crassiceps?' The rat pointed a shaking paw towards a scrawny Ravageur whose head was all but buried in a haunch of lamb. Crassiceps raised a bloodied muzzle, and seemed to stare straight at Talina. She dropped her eyelids. The rat whispered, 'They made us pull a seven-metre tapeworm out of his rear end! That's why they call him Crassiceps – after the *Taenia crassiceps*, that fearful tapeworm, which had got wrapped round his insides. They're all infested, the Ravageurs, and with the mange too. Except Grignan, of course.'

'Ugh!' Talina hurriedly changed the subject. 'And another thing – aren't there any girl or lady Ravageurs?'

The rat said, 'Yes. They keep them . . . aside.'

'Whatever for?' asked Talina. 'Are they even more vicious than the males? Or uglier, even?'

'Not at all. But the he-Ravageurs don't think much of them.'

Talina felt sorry to have insulted the females. She asked, 'Don't they even eat with the males?'

'They feed in their quarters. The Ravageurs send them their leftovers, if there are any. Look to your right.'

Talina observed Croquemort and Échalas leaving the room with buckets of leftovers in their jaws.

'Off to feed the females,' said the rat.

'With buckets? Where are their silver platters?'

'Oh no, when they remember – which isn't always – they just empty the food into the females' trough, or throw the cakes through the bars. They enjoy watching the females scuffle for morsels.'

'How horrible. But troughs? Bars? They treat them like prisoners? They leave them hungry?'

'As far as the Ravageurs are concerned, the females are worthless except for breeding. They give them a lot of sweets, because it keeps them giggly and stupid. That's how they like them.'

Talina was feeling far from giggly or stupid. An idea was surging through her brain like an electric shock. She demanded, 'Speaking of slavery, who prepared all this food? Ravageurs could not possibly pluck those tiny little birds, or stuff the *foie gras* into the duck, or roll the butter into those garlic-and-parsley breadcrumbs! Only *humans* have hands clever enough to do that.'

'Oi, we're plenty clever,' the rat bristled. 'But hey, you are starting to look like—'

Talina barely heard him. 'I knew it! So now the kidnapped humans are forced to work in the Ravageur kitchens?'

At the thought of her studious father toiling at a stove, instead of at his old rosewood desk in the Archives, Talina felt an immense pity, mixed with anger. How dare they reduce him to this! How could they enslave and humiliate that quiet, dignified man!

She turned her head to rub her nose, which was itching badly, against the table leg, too upset to notice that it was distinctly longer and bristlier than normal.

Talina calmed herself. 'But they're not actually killing the humans. As long as the humans are useful to the Ravageurs, they will keep them alive.'

She took a deep breath and looked longingly towards the nearest sheep passage. That place where the sheep came from – her parents were almost certain to be there.

But now it was not just Rouquin who kept staring at her. Nochin Quinchou could not take his eyes off Talina: pale and crazed, they swept over her again and again, while their owner feverishly scratched at his ear, which really did seem to be hanging by a thread since Croquemort's beating. Some of the other Ravageurs were still worrying the leather tablecloths with their teeth, or scratching at their mange.

The meal was drawing to a close. The Vizier rose and trotted to the stage where Grignan sat, wiping a shaggy paw over a mouth greasy with Golosi's Mostarda. Magisterulus announced, 'Lord Grignan's speech!'

The Ravageur Lord rose.

'Soon,' he told his creatures, 'we shall have the pleasure of making an example of a Venetian brat. This prompts me to speak to you once more of the greatness of the Ravageurs and the blind folly of the humans. The Venetians are such fools! They refuse to find out why we Ravageurs are punishing them: they prefer to pretend we do not exist! They put their heads in the sand like stupid ostriches.'

'Big brainless birdies, zat's what zey is!' shouted Rouquin.

Grignan silenced him with a look and continued. 'We Ravageurs have a worthy grievance. The humans stole our ancestral land and forced us into exile. They are low, dirty thieves. It is *their* kind who are the *beasts*.'

'Huh, beasts!' sneered the Ravageurs.

'This,' thought Talina scornfully, 'sounds like a rehearsed speech. From a script.'

Grignan's voice rose to a roar. 'Our humiliation was just a stepping stone for the Venetians. Our beautiful lagoon nourished their greedy empire. Our green fields were turned into stone. They paved our hunting glades for squares. The humans built only poverty and death for the noble peace-loving creatures of the lagoon. Since the humans invaded, we—'

Talina felt her hands prickle with fury. She thought, 'All this self-pity! These Ravageurs are hardly peace-lovers. They don't live in harmony with their fellow creatures! Look what they do to rats and cats!'

Hundreds of little stabs of pain pierced Talina's skin. She glanced down at her arms and held in a scream. Coarse black hairs were breaking through her flesh. Her nails were growing at a visible speed, curling into talons. Her shoulders, too, had swelled. Her dress split all the way down the left side now. The ropes were straining.

'I must keep sweet, serene and reasonable,' she told herself. 'I mustn't rise to this. I *know* it's all lies. But my goodness, that meat smells good.'

Grignan's roar grew even louder and more furious: 'Since the Venetians robbed us of our rights and our home, we have been condemned to wretched roaming in desolate wildernesses, ever excluded from what's rightfully ours.'

The two Ravageurs nearest to the fire-ringed portrait spat at it again, careful to avoid the blue flames. Now Talina noticed an inscription above it: '*May the Flame of Shame Torment our Enemy Forever.*'

'Shame!' called out some of the Ravageurs. 'What poor ones we are!'

'They seem pretty comfortable to me,' thought Talina angrily. 'Not very wretched at all. And one does not find a lot of *Soufflé aux taupes* in desolate wildernesses I'd have thought.'

'Since the humans stole our ancestral land ...'

Talina raged silently, 'So he keeps saying. But how do we know that they *did* steal it? Says who? Oh!'

She'd just caught sight of her own nose – now a hand's breadth in front of her face, pointed and covered with fur.

Her dress and pinafore were hanging off one – furry – shoulder. The rope was fraying where it stretched.

Grignan strode about the stage as he warmed to his theme. 'The humans exterminated my ancestors and carried off our cubs, subduing their spirits and turning them into that half-wolf breed, the domestic dog, the biggest insult to ferocity ever to grovel in front of an inferior species.'

The Ravageurs screamed, 'Gnaw zem to bits!' 'Tear out their intestines!' Talina pictured Futfallo, Razin and Gierchit, who'd have loved to do exactly that to her and Drusilla. She thought, 'Not *all* dogs are an insult to ferocity.'

And this made her think of the Guardian, who terrified even the dogs. If she didn't find her parents, she might have to go back to *him*.

She trembled with fury.

Looking down, she saw dark hairs poking out of the tops of her socks and her hands had thickened. More black hairs sprouted from the joints of her fingers. She flinched at the smell of her own breath – meaty and rotten.

Over in the *Sala del Sangue*, Grignan seemed to be thinking about Talina's parents too. He had paused in his rant while the Vizier whispered something in his ear. Now he stiffened, and looked around warily. Talina strained to catch what they said.

'The surprisingly hairy prisoner said *what*?' Grignan asked Magisterulus. 'You say this *Ratfood* thing claims we already have its parents?'

His eyes were narrowed with suspicion.

'I expect they're peeling or washing something up at this point, if we didn't eat them,' the Vizier said casually.

'Where did we claim them, and when?'

Talina raged silently, 'You have no *claim* to *anyone*! You *kidnapped* them three months ago.'

Magisterulus consulted some runes roughly hacked into

the wall behind the platform. 'Told us itself, name of Molin.'

With his back to his Lord, the Vizier did not see Grignan drop down on his hindquarters or his eyes open with displeased surprise. Nor did Magisterulus notice the look of hate his master now shot at the fire-ringed portrait. The Vizier chattered, 'Yes, here we are. January 30th, from the Archives. The male, let me see – ah yes, Marco Molin, Keeper of Most Ancient Manuscripts, Department of Malignant Spells, Invoked Pestilences and Abominable Rites.'

The Vizier turned and saw Grignan's expression at last. He closed his jaws with a snap and lowered his head.

'The girl is of absolutely no import then,' Grignan pronounced, emphatically, after a short silence. He changed his tone to nonchalant. 'Did you get her hair, by the way?'

The Ravageur Lord appeared not to care one way or the other when Rouquin grovelled, 'Yes, sir! A great clump came out nice 'n' easy. Put it straight in the scorpion tank, lak I was s'posed for to do, sir.'

'Hmmm,' said Grignan, dismissively.

But there was something furtive in Grignan's eyes as he said it. Something that made the Vizier step forward with concern. Something that made the butler turn a fresh page and ladle an extra helping of *Tournedos de Rat Mort* onto Grignan's book, topping it with a glistening mound of Golosi's Mostarda.

As the Ravageur Lord loudly – with exaggerated slurping and gnashing – savoured the *tournedos*, the eyes of his creatures were fastened in fascination on his working jaws, watching their master's feat of greed with respect.

'This is my chance,' Talina thought. Her fingers inched backwards until they found the end of the painfully tight rope. She tugged. As the rat had promised it would, the bow slid undone. Her bonds loosened. With relief, she shrugged off the ropes and stood up, surprised to find that 'up' meant on all fours. Hastily, she picked up the corner of her damaged dress in her teeth.

'The kitchen,' she whispered to herself. 'I must get to the kitchen.'

To get to the kitchen she had to cross the *Sala del Sangue*, passing through the middle of the Ravageurs. It was then that she caught sight of herself in a smeary mirror behind the rat harp. She suppressed a howl.

She was no longer herself, nor even recognizably human. Only the torn dress she held up with her teeth identified her as anything different from ... a Ravageur.

Her instinct was to lie down and weep, but Talina forced herself to think rationally. 'Being a cat was reversible. Being one of these horrors must be too. Professor Marìn will have something for it. And just now it's useful. They won't notice me if I cross that room now – now that I look almost exactly like one of them.'

Still, it was a terrifying thing to enter the portals of the *Sala del Sangue*, to walk past the ranks of Ravageurs still sucking their tablecloths on the U-shaped table while staring with rapt envy at Grignan on the stage.

She passed the first cluster of Ravageurs. As she rounded the curve of the 'U', Nochin Quinchou's eyes bulged for a second at the sight of her. She trotted on as casually as she could, joining two other Ravageurs who were gathering empty rabbit-juice buckets. Between them, she felt almost safe.

The sheep doors were metres away now. All she had to do was make it past the section of the table where Frimousse and Rouquin sat. Frimousse sneezed loudly as she passed, but did not take his eyes off his master. Talina was staring so hard at their backs that she did not notice Fildefer fling a stripped lamb bone on the floor – but she felt herself trip on it. Her flailing elbow sent a rabbit-juice bucket flying from the mouth of the Ravageur beside her. It landed on the floor, spinning.

Half a dozen heads turned in her direction.

'Who's zat?' cried Croquemort. 'A female? In the *Sala del Sangue*? Kill 'er!'

Frimousse looked closely at Talina, trembling by the door. 'No, it's ze human girl thing woken up. Ze human females always make me sneeze. But zis one's . . . not so much human now. How 'ard did you hit 'er, Rouquin?'

'Whatever she is, now she's awake, we can play wiz 'er!' rejoiced Rouquin. 'I know lots of nasty games. Is so funny when zey squeal! "Sweeter with dessert", Lord Grignan said.' He frowned. 'But she looks a *leetle* bit too much lak . . .'

Grignan slammed the book closed on top of his *tournedos*, which squelched loudly. Rouquin cowered, his head down.

'Let her go and join the other slaves, you imbecile,' mumbled Grignan. 'We have the hair. I'll deal with her later. She's not very interesting. I wouldn't eat *her* if they gave her away free with a French restaurant.'

Those were the last words Talina heard as she slipped through the door.

'Or could it be,' she thought, 'that I have something rather *too* interesting to say? That he doesn't want the other Ravageurs to hear?'

She looked back and caught Grignan's eye.

Its liquid glitter told her, 'I'm not finished with you at all.'

17

In the Ravageur kitchen

a slippery second later

BEYOND THE SHEEP door Talina found herself in a
passageway blackened with smoke. The floor was
slimed with nervous droppings.

She proceeded gingerly towards a sound of clashing metal
and the darkly intense smell of roasting meat, which still
made her nose twitch greedily.

Light flooded the end of the corridor, making her hasten.
But when she arrived at the doorway, her cry of 'Mamma!
Papà!' died on her lips.

She was in a vast kitchen, peopled by slaves who toiled
like ants, some heaving loaded baking trays, others stirring
gigantic cauldrons; a dozen were elbow-deep in washing-up;
six more were plucking the feathers from a small mountain
of dead geese.

Along a central table ran a line of lecterns, lit by a
flickering forest of candelabra. On the lecterns lay spattered
cookbooks, many in French, and grandly illustrated. On

another table, dozens of cats were swiftly sorting ripe and unripe beans into neat piles with deft paws.

Talina recognized a boy from her school. Dark-haired blue-eyed Sargano Alicamoussa was weeping over a stack of onions. She noticed Gianni Nanon, the man who first eavesdropped on the Ravageurs: now he was peeling potatoes. The prettiest girl in her class, Clara Massianello, was trimming artichokes with a blunt knife. Talina's eyes skittered over the room, searching in vain for her parents.

People caught sight of her and hastily lowered their eyes, muttering to one another and looking fearfully towards the door.

Into the silence, Talina shouted, 'Has anyone seen my father? Marco Molin? The Keeper of Manuscripts at the Archives? Or his wife?'

But everyone kept his or her head bent, and redoubled the speed of work. The sounds of scraping knives, sloshing water and beating spoons were all that could be heard. The cats quietly abandoned their bean-sorting and slunk under the table.

Finally there came a terrified whisper from Sargano Alicamoussa.

'Is that really you, Talina? What's that growing out of your face? Why is your nose so long? Why are your eyes that opal colour? Is that *fur* on your back? And, excuse me for saying so, Talina, but I think you should know that your dress is split right down one side.'

It sounded lame even to her when she explained, 'It happens when I have a little flouncy ... when I lose my temper, it seems that I start to look like the animal I've got angry with ... I'm especially absorbent of magic, you see.'

Sargano's handsome face was bewildered.

'You don't understand a word I'm saying, do you?' Talina asked. 'It's too bad! *So* frustrating! Oh well, that's my solution, then, I suppose. I'll have to get all beastly with you humans. Then I'll start to look like one of you again. Pardon me while I—'

Talina took a deep breath and screamed, '*Why* won't you answer me? What's *wrong* with you? Why are you acting so frightened, you lily-livered sops? I'm just a girl looking for her mother and father. What's happened to your human decency? Has it gone to the same place as your courage?'

Three hundred brows wrinkled and three hundred mouths gasped as Talina's mane, muzzle and claws shrank away and she stood upright like an ordinary human girl, though a red-faced, loud one in a badly torn dress.

'That worked anyway!' Talina sighed with relief. 'But they obviously don't quite understand me. I may be mostly human again but I suppose I'm still speaking Ravageur or something.'

A large tortoiseshell cat strolled over to Talina and stuck out her paw. A strange mixture of Ravagish and Humantongue now actually, with a touch of Felish.'

'No!' Talina moaned. 'I am Talina, and I am one hundred percent *human*.'

'Tigger-Maria, pleased to meet you, or half-meet you,' the tortoiseshell said in Felish, looking dubiously at Talina. 'But if you keep turning Ravageur, you won't find cats pleased to meet you in general. Ravageurs don't eat a lot of humans, as they find them untasty, but they will eat a bit of cat now and then.'

'I assure you, I shall never eat a bit of cat!' cried Talina.

'I know what you're thinking: "Not much eating on a cat."'

'I wasn't—'

'But there's a particular part, round the ribs, that the Ravageurs like as a snack. They call it cat bacon. They like it smoked in strips and wrapped around grapes or baby corn cobs as a crunchy snack between meals. So, miss, what *are* you, exactly?'

Talina explained her situation breathlessly, while helping herself to a needle and thread still bloody from being used to sew up a stuffed side of mutton. She tacked her dress and pinafore into a semblance of decency, pausing sadly when the cat assured her that there were no kitchen workers by the name of Molin.

'If I were you,' added Tigger-Maria, 'I'd flee smartish, before Grignan changes his mind. He's a devil for that.'

'I bet he is,' said Talina. As she spoke, her eyes – now taking in more colour – roamed over the cats, who had climbed back up on the tables and resumed sorting beans. She noticed six pure-white kittens among them.

'Er, Tigger-Maria, do you mind if I take these? I'm a ... friend of their mother's. I'll return them to her. That's something I can do. At least someone will be getting their mother back!' She couldn't hold back a sob.

'Help yourself,' said Tigger-Maria. 'They're no use here – always giving themselves airs, the little tykes. There's a door behind the scullery,' the cat pointed, while Talina tucked the kittens into the large pocket of her pinafore. 'That door leads directly to the outside, and then it's just a few minutes to the jetty. But be careful when you pass the Stake House.'

'The Stake House?' Talina did not like the sound of it. Something clicked in her stomach, as if locking in a very disagreeable sensation.

'You'll know it when you see it. And smell it. And feel the flies biting. It's the big bird box with the raw meat on stakes all around it. It's where the Ravageurs keep their vultures.'

Talina tucked the last of the kittens into her pinafore and fled.

18
Conversation with a rat

at the shore of the Ravageur island,
one minute after that

TALINA RAN SO fast that she saw the Stake House only in a blur. She tried not to sharpen her impression of its bloody palings, or to let the image enter her memory. But she could not escape the smell.

'Pooh!' she whispered. '*Che cagnòn!* What a stink.'

She was still retching when she reached the jetty. The gondola was moored just where Frimousse and Rouquin had left it. Talina leapt in. Quickly, she buried herself under the sacks she found there.

'We'll hide here till dark, and row away,' she told the kittens, 'back to Venice.'

'We don't row,' one of the white kittens said in a superior tone. 'We are rowed.'

'I was obviously right about who your mother is,' Talina told them.

'You should curtsey when you speak to us,' came the reply, 'or Uncle Bestard will see to you.'

The sacks smelled strongly of Ravageur. After a minute or two, so did Talina and the white kittens.

'Horrible!' said Talina, trying not to breathe.

A gloomy voice answered, 'Smelling like a Ravageur is your best way of hiding from 'em. And as for rowing yesselves away, you'll never do it, be you ever so strong. The currents that flow round this island is slow and dangerous. Then when you reach that circle of fog, you'll go round and round in it, blindly, forevernever. You has to know your way – or you is a drowned thing.'

'Who's talking? Who are you? Where are you? But keep your voice down!' whispered Talina.

One of the rower-rats poked his head up from under another sack at the far end of the boat. He looked hard at the kittens, 'I sees you brung some cat-brats with you, missy. For why?'

'Why shouldn't I take these kittens home to their mother? Everyone else round here just takes what they want,' said Talina indignantly.

'Temper, temper,' sneered the rat, talking out of the side of his mouth. 'Hardly becomes some*thing* like you to criticize others.'

'Don't you work for the Ravageurs, then?' asked Talina hotly. 'You're one of their rowers. Aren't you literally one of their creatures?'

'Not me. I has me pride. This is me own vessel and I takes it when I likes. Sometimes I likes Ravageur wages. But I wouldn't niver lower mesself to go in their house and play their harp.'

'Well, you're different then. If you'd been in there, you'd know. The other rats don't serve them because they like to. They are simply terrified.'

The rat leant forward argumentatively. 'But of what? Them Ravageurs don't scare Altopone,' he pointed to his chest. 'I've seen more Ravageurs than your knees has seen linen napkins, missy, and I can tell you this: It don't take much courage for a huge Ravageur to kill a rat, do it? Does a human get a medal when it kills a mosquito? They kills only to amuse themselves. And they attacks only creatures what is weaker than they is. They is dangerous all right, but they is more hyena than wolf. Someone ought to say "boo!" to 'em once in a while. But no one does. They is all too blind. Humans is blinded by that thing wot they have, wot rats do not. Imagination. The human race is cursed with it. It makes 'em do ridiculous things. Like pretend. Pretend that them Ravageurs is Pastry-Bandits from Rovigo. Pretend that everything is all right ... As if!' he scoffed.

'But imagination means that we humans paint pictures and write books and make music ...'

'I'll bet my front teeth against your petticoat ribbons that pictures, stories and melodies aint going to help the Venetians against the Ravageurs. The only way they can save themselves is to find that inscription and show the powers that be that it's all true,' he chuckled. 'But they haven't got the slightest idea, those clowns in Venice.'

'What inscription?'

'The one what tells how the Venetians really got Venice from the Ravageurs.'

'Where is it!?'

'Ah,' said Altopone, 'well, that would be telling, missy.'

'Have you seen it?'

'Of course. It is hardly buried out of sight.'

'So have I seen it?'

'No doubt. But humans don't ever really *see* anything, I find. The inscription is hidden where any creature may see it.'

'Hidden where any creature may see? Why must you talk in riddles, you irritating creature?'

'Altopone likes a riddle.' The rat tapped his chest comfortably.

'You are the most maddening rat I ever met. You are totally infuriating! You are—' She waggled a reproving finger at him, only to see that her hands – now seeming yellowy blue in front of her – were shrinking to the dimension of a rat's paws.

'I simply mustn't have a flouncy now. I do *not* want to be a rat,' Talina told herself.

'And an impudent not-quite-Ravageur, not-quite-rat is not something what you can have a civil conversation with,' grumbled Altopone, glowering. 'Especially with a lapful of cat-brats. You can get out of my boat right now. Out, out!'

'But—!'

'No buts. Just leave.'

Talina changed her expression to a pleading one. 'If you row me to San Marcuola in Venice, I'll consider you absolutely the most charming rat of my acquaintance. And recommend you to others ... And I can pay.'

'I hope you change your underwear as often as you change your mind, missy.'

'And ... there's something you should know – I'm the not-quite-cat from the song, Talina who was in the Tower. Uberto Flangini's tower ... You should help me! I'm supposed to save the Venetians,' she added. 'And that includes the Venetian rats, of course.'

The rat whistled. 'Dr Raruso's prophecy. The not-quite-cat! Well, well, well. *That*'s starting to make sense. Flangini's tower? The one by Our Lady of the Sparrows at Quintavalle? Well, then you should know all about—'

Talina interrupted rudely, 'So will you take us or not?'

'If you'd only let me finish—'

A drumming of paws could be heard on the shore.

'Yes or no?'

'Climb in. I can see there's no telling you anything, missy.

You'll have to work it out for yourself, more's the silly pity.'

Talina scrabbled under her pinafore for some coins. But under her breath, she growled, 'Ludicrous animal!'

'Say, missy, is that your own nose?' the rat whistled.

'Of course it's mine,' blustered Talina, her good intentions forgotten.

'It's just that, well, it's a bit longish and pointy – and that tail is a bit, well, bald.'

With a cry of horror, Talina saw something pink and scaly thrash out from under her skirt.

'Welcome to the club,' smiled the rat. 'San Marcuola, you say?'

'Or Santa Croce.' Talina thought of Professor Marìn's house. 'I desperately need some **Desperate Measures** to top up my human-ness,' she whispered to herself. 'But no, first, these kittens need their mother. Even if she isn't very motherly.'

Altopone put a paw into his mouth and gave three sharp squeaks. Eleven elderly rats tottered from behind stones and bushes.

'We've got a job on,' Talina's new comrade told his friends. 'We're taking this young missy to Venice. Full fee. Get to it.'

There was some back-leg scratching, and one rat muttered, 'If you say so, Altopone, but this aint one of your better ideas. That girl-thing looks like trouble. Never heard of a human *leaving* the island.'

Grumbling, the old gentleman rats unhitched the ropes, pushed the gondola away from the jetty and set to rowing with their miniature oars.

Waves beat against the gondola. The ring of fog loomed ahead and suddenly devoured the front of the boat. Dr Raruso had been right – inside the fog, Talina could see nothing – not even the prow. But Altopone's comrades rowed in silent confidence, the large rat occasionally consulting a compass and barking an order. After twenty minutes, the

134

boat broke through the curtain of fog into bright winter sunshine. The gondola sped through a part of the lagoon Talina was sure she'd never seen, dotted with islands where a fierce wind blew the reeds into the shapes of men praying and had bent the shrubs backwards.

All the way back to Venice, Altopone tortured her with jokes and hints about the mysterious inscription. Hard as she tried, she *would* keep rising to Altopone's bait. After uncountable hours of banter, Talina had shrunk to the size of a large rat. She was the same size as the kittens, who eyed her with professional interest.

When it was clear that Altopone was not going to reveal the secret of the inscription, Talina changed the subject. She challenged him: 'So who *really* owns this boat?'

'Well, I own it now.'

'But if it was lost at sea, do you know how to build another?'

'No, of course I don't know how. I am a rat.'

'So the humans who built this boat actually own the *idea* of a boat.'

'Well . . . what about the tree what it is made of?' Altopone asked triumphantly.

'Who owns the tree?'

'Exactly! Whoever owns the land owns the tree. Speaking of which, land-ho!'

The towers of Venice were just visible in the distance, silhouetted against the setting sun.

'What . . .' Talina asked, 'should I do if I ever need to get back to the Ravageurs' island?'

The rat whistled. 'That's not a question I've ever been asked before. I seen more little girls than your nose has seen lace handkerchiefs, but I never met a one like you.'

'I haven't finished with those Ravageurs. I haven't found my parents yet. I need to make them tell me—'

'You really are something. You don't know the meaning

of fear, do you? A little thing like you! You're human, aincha? With the big imagination to match? So don't you imagine those Ravageurs seizing you by the throat, shaking you till your jugular bursts and spatters the walls with your blood, then dismembering you while you is still living and fighting over your beating heart ...'

'Absolutely not,' said Talina. 'I didn't imagine those things until you mentioned them. I thought you said they were cowards.'

'As I said, they're plenty brave with someone smaller or weaker than themselves.'

Fear had conquered anger by the time they rowed down the Cannaregio Canal. It was more as girl than rat that Talina slipped off the boat just by the Due Sirene pharmacy near the Ponte delle Guglie. She counted the coins into Altopone's hand. 'Really – I have to know how to find you if I need to come back,' she whispered.

'Just ask for a *spazzino* called "Ettore". Santa Croce's where he sweeps the streets. Tell him Altopone is wanted. And I'll be at this exact spot at midnight the same night.'

Nodding, she waved goodbye. He saluted her with a cynical grin.

'Let me know when you work it out about the inscription, why don't you, not-quite-cat? Keep your sights high, that's what I'd suggest, heh heh heh! You'll get it eventually.'

No sooner had she turned her back on him than Talina saw by her shadow that she had fully returned to her human shape and dimensions, though two rat whiskers remained, as she discovered by looking at her reflection in a shop window.

She was pulling them out, one by one, when Altopone's voice floated across the water: 'Jest had a thought. You didn't let that Grignan take any of your hair, did you?'

'Why?' called Talina.

'Oh dearie me,' came the answer, and not a word more.

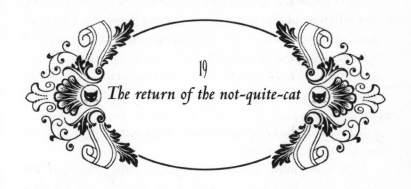

19

The return of the not-quite-cat

Venice, the evening of the same day

TALINA'S FIRST STOP was the *ostello* in the Rio Terra Farsetti. She could not wait to return the kittens of the Contessa. The arrogant little creatures nipped her thighs through her pinafore all the way, and complained loudly until Talina found herself sprouting more whiskers with frustration.

'I've got two words to say to you,' she said. 'Cat bacon.'

After that the kittens sulked and sniffed, not condescending to talk to her.

Outside the *ostello*'s window, Talina mewed loudly until a battered head appeared at the window. As she leant over towards it, the familiar stink nearly knocked her over. She managed to say 'Good evening' in a civil fashion.

Bestard-Belou hissed. 'Dog-bite-my-ear! That not-quite-cat is now a not-quite-girl wid whiskers. And she still talks Felish. And looks a bit rattish. Wass goin' on? I doan like it, I sez.'

'I'll be caterwauled!' muttered Albicocco, joining Bestard-

Belou at the sill. 'Dares to show her face round here after robbing the Contessa of what was rightfully hers – a good 'ome. Stoopendous cheek of it!'

'Actually,' whispered Talina. 'I've brought the Contessa back something that *is* in fact rightfully hers.'

She placed one white kitten on the window-sill. It mewed plaintively.

'My baby!' The Contessa's airs and graces disappeared. She rushed to the sill and licked the fluffy white bundle through the grate with unabashed tenderness. 'One survivor! My darling!'

'In fact,' said Talina, 'they're all here.' One by one, she pulled them out of her pinafore pocket. 'I think I can roll up this wire enough to let them in.'

'Do that thing, why doancha,' said Albicocco, 'Not-quite-cat.'

The Contessa said quietly, 'I owe you, Talina.'

Talina turned away, unable to watch the spectacle of the Contessa's motherly joy at the safe return of her kittens. It reminded her too painfully of what she herself had lost, and was still no closer to finding.

Albicocco sighed, 'Aw! Aint that beautiful, but, them kitty-babies? Smart and sweet, both. I'm a fool for a kitten, dat's da troof. More fun than a barrel of blind mice, a good litter.'

'I feel a cry coming on,' sniffed Bestard-Belou. 'Make wid de hankies, fastish. So what's the story, not-quite-cat?'

Quickly, gulping back tears, Talina told the cats about her visit to the Ravageur island and what she had found there.

'And 'ow eggsackly do this pertain to us?' asked Albicocco.

'I thought you would want to help,' Talina cried in frustration. 'You are Venetian cats after all. Your friends are the Ravageurs' prisoners and slaves. And ... worse. Don't you want to save them?'

A shameful tear flew from her eyelash and clung to the grate, glittering like a dewdrop. She had not meant to resort to it, but she now told the horrified inhabitants of the *ostello* about cat bacon.

Albicocco whistled through his whiskers. 'Some o dem poor cats in da gibbets is probably our uncles and nevvies. But I doan see what we kin do for 'em. Even you can't see, can you, girl?'

She shook her head, 'Not yet.'

'Yew's still lookin' remarkably rattish for a human, girlie. Yew want to get yesself sorted out,' sniffed Bestard-Belou. 'Yew want to stop being a not-quite-somefing. Otherwise yew is an orphan in all the world, ye know, not nuffink and not the other thing neither.'

Albicocco said, 'Come back when yew's got a plan, I sez.'

But the Contessa looked over her shoulder and mouthed, 'Just come back when you need us, Talina. We'll be ready.'

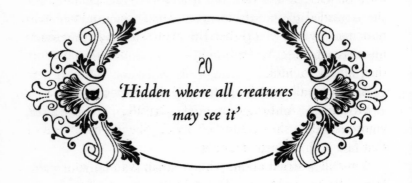

20

'Hidden where all creatures may see it'

at Professor Marìn's crooked house in Santa Croce,
nearly bedtime, that same long day

THE EMPTY SUPPER plates had been pushed aside;
new candles had been lit on the stumps of the old
ones. Over a final deep swig of **Desperate Measures**,
Talina contemplated her fingernails – fully human, at last,
but still grey with the dirt of the Ravageur palace, the *ostello*,
and a nasty fall she'd taken as she ran over the Rialto Bridge
back to the professor's house. Her bruises from the Ravageur
kicks and punches had been soothed with Venetian Treacle.
Her hair was matted with dust. At Professor Marìn's, she'd
just realized, no one was ever going to tell her to wash her
hands or brush her hair before eating. The strange thing was
that *not* being told to do these things made her long to do
both.

Hours had passed. She'd finished recounting her latest
adventures to the professor, Mademoiselle Chouette,
Ambrogio, Giuseppe Tassini, Drusilla and Brolo. She'd told
them of Grignan's rabble-rousing speech, and his absolute

certainty that the humans had stolen Venice from the Ravageurs. She'd explained about Altopone and his boat-for-hire. Her throat was stiff and sore with speaking. As she struggled to remember every detail, she couldn't help noticing how close together the professor and the French mistress sat, or how Ambrogio's eyes seemed to have lost their ability to blink.

'Yes, it's really me! Stop staring!' she snapped at him.

Mortified, Ambrogio petted Drusilla rather more vigorously than she cared to be petted. She informed him of that fact with a reproving paw.

'I'm still worried about why Grignan wanted your hair,' fretted Professor Marìn. 'And put it in a scorpion tank, you say? There are so many spells—'

'Grignan's historic claims to Venice have no basis in the record books,' Tassini fretted. 'Yet, from what you say, Talina, he is so sure.'

'What about Talina turning into a Ravageur when she got angry!' Ambrogio marvelled. 'And into a rat! Ugh!'

Mademoiselle Chouette observed, '*Très ironique.* The most impudent girl in Venice, and every time she is impudent, she turns beastly, *mais littéralement. Drôle!*'

Talina retorted, 'Not so very droll for me! Anyway, I was never fully a Ravageur or a rat. I just started to get a bit that way. Ambrogio, you absorbed the Spell Steam too. You never know. It might happen to you as well.'

'Tell us again – where did the rat say the inscription was?' Ambrogio hastily changed the subject. 'The one that says how the Venetians got Venice from the Ravageurs?'

'He said, "It's hidden where all creatures may see it". But of course he may just have been trying to annoy me at that point.'

'Where all creatures may see it,' repeated Mademoiselle Chouette softly, looking around her.

'What can everyone see in Venice?' Ambrogio mused. 'Sky. Water.'

Talina objected, 'You cannot inscribe something on air or water. Not so that it lasts.'

'Not "where all creatures *can* see it", we must note,' said Tassini, 'but "*may* see it". In other words, they may see it, *if* they do something in order to see it.'

'Humans like to write on stone,' remarked Drusilla.

'And Venice is built out of stone. So the inscription is in a building! It must be! You're a genius, Drusilla.'

Drusilla licked her paw, modestly.

'Talina,' Ambrogio murmured, carefully not looking at her, 'do you know how many buildings there are in Venice? How many walls? Hundreds of thousands. How many inscriptions? We can't get inside every palace and house in Venice! It would take a lifetime to find the right inscription. How would we know it if we saw it? We are just as badly off as before.'

'And the sea-level has risen,' said the professor despondently, 'in these last hundreds of years. What if it's below the waves now? Or covered in moss?'

'Or high up, so you'd have to be a bird to see it?' offered Tassini.

'High up,' mused Talina. 'Altopone said, "Keep your sights high."'

'Like at the top of a tower?' suggested Mademoiselle Chouette.

'Where it would always be safe from water, and prying eyes!' Ambrogio clapped his hands.

Talina jumped up. 'When I mentioned that I lived in Uberto Flangini's tower, the rat said, "*That*'s starting to make sense." Of course it does!'

'Could Flangini know?' Professor Marìn knitted his brows. 'Could he be part of this?'

'Wouldn't put anything past him!' muttered Talina. 'Ambrogio,' Talina looked at him warmly, 'do you know where we're going now?'

Blushing, he lifted his spectacles from his nose, held them up to the light with a critical expression, polished one lens on his sleeve and then answered in his most lawyerly manner – in a quite unsuccessful attempt to hide just how delighted he was to be included in Talina's plans this time. 'We shall proceed from this place to the top of your great uncle Uberto's tower. All the way to the top floor, where we can climb out of the windows and have a look.'

Then he faltered. 'But Talina, you can't just prance in and say, "Hello there, Great Uncle Uberto. I'm not dead after all."'

Talina interrupted, 'Then I'll say, "Yes, the Ravageurs took me, but they spat me out. I'm too impudent to eat. So do you mind if I have a look at the wall outside your study at the top of your tower? I don't suppose what one might see there is secret, is it? That's not the reason why you never let me, or anyone, come higher than the best parlour, obviously. Can't be. Thanks so much, Uncle Ubie ... "'

Ambrogio breathed, 'So what *are* we going to say to him?'

Talina's face split into a grin. 'We're going to say precisely nothing to him. There are forty minutes a day when my Guardian is never at home.'

Every afternoon at exactly four o'clock, Uberto Flangini took his three dogs for a walk, usually to the post office and back. He would be gone for forty minutes precisely. And the next day, at exactly 3.45 p.m., a boy and a girl were hiding in the clammy ivy-haunted shadows of the ruined Our Lady of the Sparrows next to the gently twittering tower at Quintavalle.

As soon as the Guardian's narrow back, clad in a long black coat, retreated down Quintavalle's single winding street, Ambrogio and Talina parted the curtain of ivy, sprang to the drawbridge and ran to the door. Talina snatched the spare key from its hiding place behind a loose brick. They crept into the tower.

The kitchen was clean and deserted. The next floor, chiefly devoted to a bathroom, was also shining clean.

They were not even up to the third floor when Talina heard the familiar bark of the ferocious Razin from the street. A second bark made it clear that the dog, instead of going away, was coming closer.

'The Guardian must have forgotten something!' groaned Talina. 'A manuscript to post to his publisher or something.'

'But how to get away from here?' Ambrogio despaired. 'If we run away now, we're bound to run straight into your great uncle.'

Talina looked out of the window at the dozens of clothes lines nodding with old lady underwear.

'I know how. The grannies! We just have to get to Nonna Meghin, and we'll be fine.'

Talina pointed down to a pretty cottage twenty paces from the drawbridge.

'That won't get us very far,' said Ambrogio doubtfully.

'Oh yes it will. Run!'

At Nonna Meghin's, Talina was seized in a hug. 'They said you were taken away by the Pastry-Bandits, my little mushroom!' sobbed the granny. 'But here you are, safe and sound and pretty as a wren ... though that's a nasty pasty pallor on your cheeks, child. That poor great uncle of yours must be—'

'He mustn't know I've been here! I've got to hide from

him! I can't explain yet, but will you trust me, Nonna? We need to get off Quintavalle without being seen. Can you help us? This is Ambrogio, by the way. He's my friend. Can you help us?'

'Nothing simpler, darling,' chuckled the old lady. 'Quick! Let's go out to my back garden.'

At the end of Nonna Meghin's triangular garden, the granny put her fingers in her mouth and gave a sharp ungrandmotherly wolf-whistle. Nonna Nazzarina's whiskery face appeared at her back fence.

'These children need to get off the island without being seen,' said Nonna Meghin importantly. 'The old elopement routine, understand?'

'*Si si si si si*!' laughed Nonna Nazzarina. 'Time to get out of the stable, sister – let's show this town we're not too old to horse around!'

She bent down to kiss the children. '*Ciao, Talina, mia piccolina*! And your oh-so-handsome friend! Have you done the *Fascinating Stoat* for him, *carissima*? There's not a boy who'll withstand it.'

'No,' said Talina firmly. 'Well, not intentionally.'

If she had, she'd have understood better why Ambrogio gave her all those long looks, which might well be described as 'confuzzled'. She hoped he would not understand Nonna Nazzarina's little joke. But unfortunately he was staring at the ground, blushing like a sunset.

Nonna Nazzarina gave Ambrogio's burning cheek a little pinch. 'Over you come, my little sugar-dumplings. So sweeeeeet!'

Talina and Ambrogio clambered over the wall, and Nonna Nazzarina hurried them through her dark house to the front door, where she popped out, rapped on the next-door house, exchanged a few words with Nonna Stella, and then positioned herself at the spy mirror. 'Your great uncle is just about to pass by. When I say "Go!" run next door,' she told Ambrogio and Talina, enveloping first one, then the other in a talcum-powdery embrace.

At 'Go!' the children found themselves in Nonna Stella's hall, where the atmosphere was heavy with the smell of caraway seeds and boiled pillowcases. They ran down the narrow wall to her back garden and over her fence to Nonna Massoleta's pocket-handkerchief of green, and through *her* house to the next street, where Nonna Grigianella passed them on to Nonna Spinina and so on until they were ejected from the house of Nonna Angelina right into the square in front of the church of San Pietro. They were breathless from all the hugs, blinking from the constant changes from bright gardens to dark halls, and coated from head to foot in a fine film of talcum powder.

Talina heard a faint clinking in her pinafore pocket. One of the grannies – she couldn't remember which one – had slipped two small bottles of Manitoba Gargling Oil inside it, whispering, 'For your Great Escape! In case you need to stop any hinges from creaking.'

Back at Professor Marìn's crooked kitchen, Talina and Ambrogio hung their heads, mumbling the story of their failure. Mademoiselle Chouette, the professor and Tassini fell silent. Then Tassini declared, 'Well, we'll just have to go up the *outside* of the tower.'

'It's eleven storeys high, isn't it, Talina? We'd need a magic carpet for that,' Ambrogio sighed.

Professor Marìn's face brightened. 'Why, I've been working on just such a thing. But it is not very strong – could not support the body of a fully grown adult. Remember that tea towel of mine?'

'A tea towel?' chorused Talina and Ambrogio dubiously.

'This isn't just any tea towel, however. It's a Thaumaturgic Tea Towel that I've been hoping to use to send out for cups of that delicious hot chocolate they do at Caffè Florian.'

He whipped it off the range rack and shook it out in front of them, dispersing fragranced steam.

'Isn't that the same tea towel that was hanging over the range when Talina was being turned back into a girl?' asked Ambrogio. 'That we wrapped her in?'

'It is. But now it's been infusing magic steam for several days and *can* possibly fly one small person up to the top of a tall tower.'

He busied himself lighting lanterns. 'We can talk as we walk.'

'One small person?' asked Talina.

'Yes, just one small person, standing on one leg.'

21
Just one small person, standing on one leg

at the northern reaches of Castello, after dusk,
May 6th, 1867, Saint Flavio's Day

'SO ... YOU JUST ride the thermal currents from the lagoon up to the required height,' Professor Marìn concluded. 'Nothing could be simpler.'

'Umm,' huffed Ambrogio. His face was glum in the lantern-light as they hurried back to Quintavalle. 'I suppose there's no possibility that it might be *me* who gets to fly the tea towel?'

Professor Marìn explained happily, 'Well, in fact I have *two* prototypes of my Thaumaturgic Tea Towel. So, *two* children, each standing on one leg.'

Ambrogio's glumness was replaced by incredulity. And then worry.

'Hey! Talina poked Ambrogio in the ribs. 'Remember my one-legged egret dance?'

'How could anyone forget? It was in the *Gazzetta*. And the fake egret blood coming out of your neighbour's hat! What *was* that?'

'Red ink and squashed cherries. So, this is what you have to do. Pretend that your legs are as long and black and light as liquorice shoelaces. Imagine your feet are star-shaped and yellow. Then act as if you're standing on a pole in the lagoon, and tuck one of your legs into your breast feathers. Just close your eyes and concentrate. I promise that it works.'

'I don't have star-shaped feet and I don't have feathers.'

'Don't be silly, the egret dance is easy! Or the *Fascinating Stoat* would work nearly as well. They're quite similar, actually. Almost there!'

Dusk had fallen, and the grannies of Quintavalle were tucked away by their fires with their cats. Not a soul stirred on the island; even the birds were unusually quiet. Professor Marìn led the way to the ruins of Our Lady of the Sparrows. There, he carefully laid one of the Thaumaturgic Tea Towels on the ground. Talina kicked off her shoes, stepped on it, raised her lantern aloft and assumed the one-legged egret (and *Fascinating Stoat*) position.

Nothing happened.

'So, um, is there a password for getting it into the air?' she demanded. Professor Marìn's face was strangely contorted. With a hot flush of embarrassment, Talina suspected an attempt to smother laughter. But she held her head high and tried to control her temper. She didn't want to turn into a red-haired professor.

He spluttered, 'Try ... *Volate!*'

On uttering the Venetian word for 'fly!', Talina immediately whirled into the air and over the water. The lantern flew out of her hands, plummeting into the waves. She teetered wildly on the tea towel, clinging to the edges of the fabric with the curled toes of her right foot. The other tea towel whisked out of Professor Marìn's pocket and fluttered about after her.

'Oh,' thought Talina. 'Of course I said "fly!" in the plural.'

To balance, she extended both arms, patting down the air and twisting her body this way and that as if she were swimming waves of water instead of currents of night air. In a few seconds, she was enjoying herself. She flew halfway up the tower wall, and was greeted with alarm by the roosting sparrows. They curved their wings over the eggs in their nests.

'I'd never hurt you! It's me, Talina!' she told them. They settled down quickly, though their bright eyes never left her.

'I wonder what's made them so nervous?' she thought.

A glance below showed her four anxious faces staring out of the darkness, their lanterns raised above their heads.

'*Calate!*' she ordered. And the two tea towels immediately dropped downwards.

'*Piano!*' she shouted. 'Gently as we go!'

Talina returned to earth with dignity and style, stepping lightly off the tea towel to do a self-congratulatory twirl.

'You fly like you dance,' breathed Ambrogio. 'It's so ...'

'Come on!' Talina urged Ambrogio. 'Stop staring at *me*. The *view*'s amazing. Could I have another lantern, please?'

Ambrogio's Thaumaturgic Tea Towel whisked him into the air before he had assumed the one-legged egret position. Or even the stoat. In fact, he found it better to balance on two legs tightly pressed together, steering the fabric with small motions of his feet. Soon he was swooping around the tower in circles, laughing. Talina chased him, crying 'Tag!'

'Excuse me,' the professor smiled. 'You make a fine pair of fireflies, but we have a job to do here.'

'Sshh,' hissed Mademoiselle Chouette, exactly as if they were in a class. Then she winked. 'Have you a pencil and paper, *mes enfants?*'

'*Mais oui!*' With serious faces, Talina and Ambrogio rode their towels upwards, holding their lanterns away from the windows and shading the flames with their hands. As they passed the best parlour, Ambrogio shuddered.

'What's *that*?'

'I call it "The Child-Mauling Thingy",' said Talina. 'Don't worry. It's dead and stuffed.'

They flew to the eleventh floor. Through the glass, they could see the Guardian's study, every surface heaped with close-written piles of paper. Great Uncle Uberto himself bent over a desk with his back to them. Talina's shoulders erupted with pins and needles at the sight of the back of his head silhouetted by his gas-lamp.

'Don't even breathe,' she urged Ambrogio.

But the dog Razin was at the window in a second, barking ferociously. The children edged around ninety degrees to a bricked-up window facing south.

'What is it?' fussed the Guardian's voice. 'Seen a sparrow, have you, dog, or a firefly? And look! You've gone and knocked over the Manitoba Gargling Oil! What a mess! How shall I clean my pen nibs now?'

There was the sound of boot leather meeting dog flesh, and Razin whimpered so piteously that Talina almost felt sorry for him, which was better, she thought briefly, than being angry with him – and starting to look like him.

'I can't see any inscription,' whispered Ambrogio.

'It must be on the other side, facing towards the sea.'

'But that's the way *his* desk faces. He'll see us.'

'We need to create a distraction.'

Ambrogio whipped down a couple of storeys and called to Professor Marìn, 'Ring the doorbell!'

A few moments later, the sound of chimes flew from the window near the wall where Talina hovered, followed by the voice of the Guardian, mumbling, 'Dratted nuisance – this time of night!' and the sound of footsteps descending, paw thumps and growls.

'Quick! It'll only take him a few minutes to get back up here.'

Talina and Ambrogio hovered around to the wall that faced northeast into the lagoon. They traced the bricks with their lanterns and fingers.

'There it is!' breathed Ambrogio, lifting his lamp to illuminate a lozenge of marble embedded in the brick. The words were speckled with birdlime, and several letters were missing where the marble plaque had crumbled. With difficulty, Ambrogio read aloud:

DEED OF SALE
LET IT BE KNOWN THAT
ON MARCH 25TH, OF OUR LORD 421,'

'The historical founding date of Venice!' whispered Talina.

WE, THE RAVAGEURS,
HEREBY CEDE OUR RIGHT TO OUR ANCESTRAL LANDS
NOW KNOWN AS LUPRIO,
AND ALL SURROUNDING ISLANDS,
AS FAR AS THE EYE CAN SEE,
IN EXCHANGE FOR FIVE SHEEP, SIX BRASS BUTTONS,
A DOZEN FANCY PASTRIES, A MINK JELLY AND
TEN FIRE-BUCKETS OF HUMAN WINE

Human wine? There was something about that phrase that worried Talina. But Ambrogio was pointing at the final words, much smaller than the rest:

SIGNED AND WITNESSED
UBERTO FLANGINI FOR THE VENETIANS
VERPILLION GRIGNANNE OF LUPRIO FOR THE
RAVAGEURS

'That must be your great uncle's ancestor, Talina. And that must be why the inscription's on his tower.'

'So Venice doesn't belong to the Ravageurs at all! They *sold* their stupid old Luprio to the humans!' cried Talina jubilantly. 'We can tell Grignan just what to do with his outrageous claims ... and ...'

Then, looking at Ambrogio's miserable face staring at the inscription, she fell silent.

When she eventually spoke again, it was to say, 'Oh. I see what you mean. That puts a different light on things, completely.'

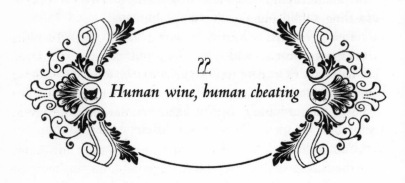

22
Human wine, human cheating

Our Lady of the Sparrows, a few dismal moments later

IN BLEAK SILENCE, Ambrogio had handed Talina his lamp so she could sketch and then make a second copy of the inscription.

As he rolled up the paper and thrust it in his pocket, the Guardian's ascending footsteps had echoed through the tower's windows. They had fled on their tea towels, spiralling around the tower to the ground, carefully avoiding the windows.

Down in Our Lady of the Sparrows, Ambrogio placed one copy each in the hands of Giuseppe Tassini and Professor Marìn. Their faces at first lit up, and then fell. They exchanged agonized looks. Tassini folded his arms. The professor handed his sheet to Mademoiselle Chouette, his fingers lingering on hers for a second.

'Look at what ze humans paid!' she exclaimed. 'Such a paltry sum for all these islands! All zis land!'

'As far as the eye can see,' said Professor Marìn in a voice almost devoid of expression.

'But you don't really own something,' said Ambrogio, 'if you've tricked a naïve creature into giving it away to you for practically nothing. That's not buying. That's a kind of stealing. Old Flangini was a scoundrel.'

Tassini sighed, 'And it's worse than that. For the Ravageurs must have been here hundreds of years – the Deed of Sale says that these were their *ancestral* lands. They gave up their history for a bit of food, some buttons and some sheep! I am ashamed. If this is the foundation of our great city ...'

Talina shouted, 'So *what* if the Venetians took advantage of the Ravageurs! It was the Ravageurs' fault for being so unintelligent and so greedy. Mink jelly – ugh! – and pastries! I'm going to take this straight to Grignan. Let's see what he thinks about it.'

'Stop, Talina,' cried Ambrogio. 'It'll only make him furious. He'll just destroy the evidence. He'll tear it up and then tear *you* limb from limb.'

'I'll tell him you've got another copy. So there'll be no point in murdering me. Anyway, as the rat said, *anyone* may see the inscription, if they care to look.'

'But remember your hair, Talina,' urged Professor Marìn. 'Grignan's got a piece of your hair. It's too risky. With that hair—'

'What can he possibly do with a bit of my hair? I've got plenty more!'

'It only takes one strand to perform any number of unpleasant spells.'

'He won't have time to do any spells! I'll have the element of surprise.'

'*Mais certainement*,' said Mademoiselle Chouette. 'It'll be *extrêmement* surprising for a start, if you can find your way back to an unknown, uncharted island in the middle of the lagoon, *ma petite*.'

Tassini added, 'One that's hidden in a ring of enchanted fog and doesn't want to be found.'

'You've forgotten about Altopone, the rat,' said Talina. 'I'm going to find the *spazzino* Ettore, and he'll get Altopone and the old gentleman rats to come for me at midnight tomorrow night. We'll row through the night. By the morning I'll be at the island.'

'Can I—'

'No, Ambrogio, *your* parents aren't missing. And *you'd* be missed if you disappeared for a day. Your family would be worried sick. Appreciate it and all, really I do. But this is something I have to do alone. Uberto Flangini is my great uncle and his shame is my family's shame too.'

'I'm good for more than free lends of books,' muttered Ambrogio.

'Don't you think I can do it on my own?'

Talina glared at the troubled faces of her friends.

'No one,' said Professor Marìn, 'doubts you can get to the Ravageurs' island, Talina.'

'We're just verr' worried about whether you'll come back,' said Mademoiselle Chouette.

The Terror of the
Neighbourhood

On the island of the Ravageurs, the morning of
May 8th, 1867, Saint Vittore's Day

TALINA AND GRIGNAN were alone together in the
Sala del Sangue. This was not, apparently, a
conversation that Grignan wanted his subjects to
overhear. Anyway, the other Ravageurs were frantically
occupied with mysterious preparations on the shore. None
of them had noticed Altopone rowing the gondola into a
clump of bulrushes. Talina had crept past a bobbing fleet
of black boats and witnessed the inexplicable sight of six
Ravageurs shouldering a grand piano onto a *peàta* barge.
Now she stood in the space at the centre of the U-shaped
table in the deserted *Sala del Sangue*, trying as hard as she
possibly could *not* to lose her temper.

'You dare to come back,' howled Grignan. 'Are you too
stupid to be terrified, Ratfood?'

'I am not Ratfood. I am Talina, the Terror of the
Neighbourhood,' Talina said bravely, through rattling teeth.

Remembering the song, Talina ventured, 'I'm also the

not-quite-cat who's going to set it all to rights – all the badness that's been done.'

'Yes, Ratfood, so I have gathered,' Grignan shouted. 'And yes, badness has been done! As you now know, old Sior Flangini cheated my ancestor out of our ancestral lands. Then Flangini proceeded to make his family rich, selling off parcels of land until it was all in tiny separate ownerships. He blurred the lines, kicked sand over the true story. So no one would trace the great big cheat back to him. Then he had my poor ancestor Verpillion Grignanne killed, stuffed and mounted!'

Talina thought, 'The Child-Mauling Thingy by the best parlour! That's what it is – a stuffed Ravageur. Grignan's great-something-or-other!'

Grignan paced to and fro, snarling, 'Shame and stinking ignominy on the humans and the name Flangini for ever!'

He glanced with fury at the fire-ringed portrait burning in its niche.

Talina realized, 'That must be the old Flangini, the ancestor of my Guardian.' She told Grignan, 'Flangini was a very poor specimen of a Venetian. As is his descendant, I might add. But all humans are not Flanginis,' countered Talina. 'My parents, for example.'

'Oh yes,' laughed Grignan. 'Your parents.'

Struggling to suppress her rage, Talina said stoutly, 'You cannot hide the fact that *your* ancestor accepted the humans' payment. Whatever the price, he *sold* your ancestral lands for something he wanted more. No one forced him.'

Grignan, seating himself heavily on his dais, laughed bitterly. 'A cheat is not a sale. Except maybe to a sneaking Venetian.'

A few hairs sprouted under Talina's fingernails.

'I shall *not* lose my temper, I *shall* not lose my temper,

I shall not *lose* my temper,' she chanted to herself. '*I shall not turn Ravageur.*'

'What's that, Ratfood?' Grignan leant over his gravy-stained book, dipping his muzzle in a large jar of Golosi's Mostarda, so that his jaws dripped large clouts of the orange jelly.

'Why not take the matter to some kind of court?' asked Talina as evenly as possible.

'Any court would give me back my land,' snapped Grignan, 'but it would not give me *revenge* for these centuries of exile. I want the Venetians to feel our pain. Then I want the Venetians to feel terror, and despair. Then I want them to know the misery of homelessness and humiliation. And if they still don't leave, then I want them to die.'

Talina found herself crouching on all fours. The reds and greens were draining from her vision. She tried to speak evenly as she protested, 'But it is not *today*'s humans who did this to you. They don't even know anything about it. I agree that Sior Flangini was ... less than honest. But modern Venetians are kind, and truthful. They would share the land with you, or come to some kind of compromise. You'd only have to talk ... and, by the way, isn't there something that you Ravageurs are not quite ... fair or honourable or upright about?'

'What do you mean, Ratfood?'

It was too much. Talina exploded in a rush of long red tongue, 'What about your own females? Is it right, the way you treat them? Locked away, kept stupefied by sweets. Food thrown in a trough, while you dine in luxury! Would you treat them any better if you owned Venice? Would they too be given the freedom of the city?'

'For why? I believe there is a swampy area in the north where we may deposit them, and build a mud wall to keep them out of sight. Quintavalle, the humans call it.'

'Oh,' said Talina, 'I happen to know that part of town quite well.'

'I daresay,' the Ravageur Lord said, 'in your fashion.'

He might as well have said, 'in your pathetic, worthless, human fashion'.

Talina sprouted a thick wad of fur around her knuckles.

'Now really, Ratfood,' he growled. 'Are you trying to tell me that human beings are kind and honest? It delights me to be the first to inform you that you personally have been betrayed by your own kind. For it is one of your own kind, your very own blood indeed, who has done away with your parents.'

'Done away with . . . ?' Talina's voice trembled.

'Uh huh.' The Ravageur's mouth was full. He was eating a little drumstick decorated with a plumy white feather.

'Wait a moment. Is that *egret* that you're eating? You eat *egrets*?'

'Believe that we do that thing,'

Talina burst into tears of frustration. 'Tell me what you've done with my parents, you . . . you . . . egret-eater! Or I'll . . . I'll . . .'

'Their exact fate, I don't actually know. It depends how long they can eke out a seed cake and an egg between them. Perhaps they found some moss to gnaw on? Certainly they could live for a short while on the bits of gristle left between their teeth from their last meal. Of course, they'll be suffering a bit without any light or heat.'

Talina screamed, 'You mean they've lived like that for the last three months? What have they ever done to deserve such a thing? It is atrociously cruel and unfair!'

'Atrociously cruel and unfair, eh? Well, you humans would know all about that! And you, Ratfood, were you never cruel or unfair to your parents? Did you ever make them worry, break their hearts with your impudence? Did you ever? Did you?'

Talina hung her head silently. Grignan continued, 'It's time for you to hear the truth of what happened the night your parents disappeared. January 30th, was it not?'

Talina nodded tensely.

'On that particular night, a certain human named Marco Molin was engaged in classifying some ancient manuscripts in a quaint old department of the Venetian Archives.'

'The department of Malignant Spells, Invoked Pestilences and Abominable Rites,' said Talina proudly.

'He was a dedicated man, and he'd been working late. But he had a wife and daughter whose company he loved. So when he glimpsed the clock, he shuffled his things together and reached for his old coat, for Marco Molin was not a rich man. The lease of his humble house in the Calle del Teatro was in the name of one Uberto Flangini, for instance. And he had to depend on the charity of others to educate his daughter.'

'How could *you* know all that?' demanded Talina.

Grignan smiled. 'I know a lot of things that would surprise you. For example – as Marco Molin straightened the papers on his desk, a document appeared from between two pieces of parchment. I imagine a sneaky, tricky piece of paper – it must have seemed almost as if it crawled on invisible slimy legs into his hands. It was a handwritten copy of a certain Deed of Sale etched on a tower wall at Quintavalle. Now this was not something that Marco Molin had ever dealt with before – his department, as you know, normally handled grimoires, books of spells, almanacs and handwritten curses. This document was something else.'

'But its meaning was quite transparent,' Talina whispered. 'My poor father must have been so shocked!'

'Indeed. Marco Molin innocently despatched a messenger

boy to fetch his kinsman Uberto Flangini from Quintavalle. The note he sent was full of horror and revulsion. Obviously, he wanted to ask Flangini if he knew anything about his ancestor's dishonourable negotiation.'

'So . . .?'

'The messenger boy ran the whole way. Uberto Flangini received that note about twenty minutes later. But Flangini did not come straight to the Archives, Ratfood. You see, I myself had been to visit him only a few nights before – because he himself had been the first human to read that inscription for fourteen hundred years. He'd been wiping the condensation from his windows and saw it in the reflection. Then he had used a mirror to write it down. He'd heard our nightly calls for justice. One of my minions, Croquemort, climbed his own tower every night. So your Guardian hoisted a note up there. 'For the Ravageur Lord', it said. He threatened to expose our claims to Venice as void. He thought he was being clever . . . but he never expected a personal visit from me.'

'And you put your case to him. So he realized that he was not so clever after all. That if he exposed your claim as empty, then he'd take down his own family's reputation with it.'

'Exactly. And then I *encouraged* him to make a another copy, which I took away, a kind of paper hostage. I gave your great uncle a few days to consider his position . . . and left him a messenger – my useful vulture Restaurant – to send to me when he was ready to do business. Restaurant waited in the church of Our Lady of the Sparrows. The sparrows, incidentally, provided snacks while he waited.'

'Poor little birds!' Talina thought. 'That night the Guardian brought me to the tower, I saw a black shadow flying in front of us – that must have been Restaurant. No wonder the sparrows were terrified when I flew up there on the tea towel. They must have thought it was Restaurant coming back.'

Grignan's rasping voice pulled her thoughts back to the present. He drawled, 'But your Guardian kept me waiting too long. Insultingly long. Unforgiveably long. I had to teach him a lesson, make him think a little harder on the consequences.'

'So you put the copy of the Deed of Sale on my father's desk where he'd be sure to find it.'

'I knew you'd work that out. When he received that urgent message, Flangini knew exactly what Marco Molin had discovered. Your father was eloquent in his disgust. So Uberto Flangini's secret was revealed – he'd had a taste of the bitter shame that would follow him for the rest of his life, dirtying his family's name for ever.'

'But,' said Talina bitterly, 'there was one way of stopping it from getting any further.'

'Indeed. Flangini finally saw sense and sent the vulture to me. So I despatched Frimousse, Rouquin, Échalas, Croquemort and Lèche-bottes to the Archives to remove—'

'My parents! Five Ravageurs against two helpless humans!'

'We'd meant only to take your father. But your mother would insist on arriving almost at the same moment as my minions. Her bad luck. And yours. Croquemort told me she cried out, "But there's a child at home alone!" And he replied, "The child will be taken care of. So you choose: Be quiet and come along. Or scream and die."'

Talina's heart hurt with imagining her parents' terrified faces, their choice that was really no choice.

'So my Ravageurs removed your parents ... and the potential scandal and problem for both Flangini and myself. Now he knew he had to guard the secret on his tower. It was already stained with the sacrifice of Marco Molin and his wife. He'd have to guard that secret now, with his very life.'

Talina growled, 'All this sacrificing! It's not just because you're afraid of your claim being shown up as empty! It's also because you were afraid of looking ridiculous, weren't you? Brass buttons and mink jelly and fancy pastries indeed! A bit of something shiny or sweet, and your whole race was suddenly homeless. *That's* why you haven't told the other Ravageurs about it – they wouldn't want you for their leader if they knew what a stupid thing your ancestor did. He betrayed your whole race! And once your friends found out about that, *you'd* be the one wretchedly roaming in desolate wildernesses or whatever you said … in a trice!'

'And you were homeless too,' retorted Grignan vindictively, 'after your parents were taken.'

Talina thought back to that wretched night.

'So that's why my Guardian was waiting for me at the Archives! Having disposed of my parents! He knew exactly where I'd be – looking for them! But that doesn't matter any more. Where *are* they now? I demand that you tell me!'

'Demand away. An island. An almost deserted island we call the Isola di Butoléta.'

'Maggot Island?'

'Indeed. Until your parents came, the entire population consisted of worms. Who will conveniently dispose of your parents' remains when they are dead, if they are not dining off them already. Meanwhile, Marco and Lucia Molin have served *me* rather well as bait! They brought *you* back to me for convenient disposal. For I must deal with you now, my flouncy little friend, you skinny not-quite-anything with a temper to burn down the house.'

'On account of that song,' Talina realized with horror.

'Precisely. You see, it's become obvious to me – if not to you – that if there's no more not-quite-cat, then there's no more prophecy, and no more threat to the Ravageurs' dominion. And when I've done with you, I've promised some particular pieces of you to my vulture, Restaurant.'

'My friends have a copy of the – oh!'

From the corner of her eye, Talina had caught a glimpse of something large, white and grey on a beam above their heads. A creamy neck rose from a ruff of grey feathers. There was a gust of cold air as the bird beat its brindled wings in a gesture of pure menace. On each foot, three talons gripped the beams.

'Those feet are the size of a human head,' thought Talina.

The vulture dipped its neck and regarded her intently, its head on one side.

Talina's courage crumpled as she met the bird's cold, inquiring eye. She suddenly knew in her heart that she would have business with this creature. She did not know how or when. She whispered aloud, 'That bird will get me, if it can; if not today, very soon.'

'Too true, too true,' crowed Grignan. 'But Restaurant won't touch you now, of course. He'll wait for the leftovers. You are currently looking a bit too much like one of us.'

Talina clapped her hand over her face, disgusted to feel the Ravageur muzzle under her fingers.

A trumpet squawked and the doors opened.

'Ah,' observed Grignan, 'time to feed. First Luncheon.'

Two hundred Ravageurs rushed in and took their places around the U-shaped table. Above them rose the usual unsavoury cloud of loose fur and skin. Nochin Quinchou headbutted Croquemort out of his place. There was a brief scuffle, a howl; then something red, blotched and jaggedly triangular lay on the leather tablecloth.

'Ooh!' cried Croquemort. 'Look at that!'

Everyone jostled to see. There was a great clatter of overturned skull-cups and medicine spoons.

'It's Nochin Quinchou's ear dropped off at last!' exclaimed

Frimousse. 'It was zat loose, was bound to 'appen.'

'It didn't drop off, it was *pushed*!' sobbed Nochin Quinchou. 'That Croquemort!'

'Cheer up, Nochin. Bits of me are dropping off all ze time,' said Échalas, the lankiest of the Ravageurs. Half his tail had been devoured by mange.

Suddenly all the Ravageurs were competing to show the ravages of mange on their bodies – infected flanks, back legs riddled with sores, a muzzle almost bald.

'What about my ear?' whined Nochin Quinchou.

A grey shadow swooped over the table. The ear disappeared in a flurry of feathers.

'Restaurant!' thought Talina.

Over the tumult, Grignan shouted, 'I don't see any reason why you should go on living now, Ratfood. I know everything you know.'

He told his subjects, 'Enough! Be quiet and take your medicine. And listen. This female has begun to bore me. What do you think we should do with her? Gather round!'

One by one, the Ravageurs were leaving their places at the table, either jumping on top of it, or crawling underneath. They closed in on Talina, like rabbits fascinated by a dancing stoat.

'Stoat!' thought Talina wildly. 'The *Fascinating Stoat* will *confuzzle* any male! The Ravageurs are as male as possible, nasty things! I suppose I'm really the rabbit in this scenario, but I can *pretend* to be the stoat.'

And she began to dance.

She danced the mesmerizing steps she'd learnt from the grannies of Quintavalle. She looped, leapt, swooped and twirled. She paused, fascinatingly, and loped backwards, then sideways. She wiggled, crouched and stretched. And while she danced, she reached into her pinafore pocket for the small bottles of Manitoba Gargling Oil that had been tucked in there by one of the grannies. She tipped them both over herself. 'Now I'll be too slippery to get a hold of, if they make a lunge for me. And I certainly won't taste very nice. Maybe they'll spit me out.'

The Ravageurs' eyes grew round and their heads began to sway in time to the unheard music of Talina's dance. Their red tongues lolled out of their mouths and they lost themselves to a state of rapt greed. Some of the Ravageurs, hypnotized, started dancing too, in a strange, vigorous yet sleepy way, as if drugged. Croquemort and Nochin Quinchou nuzzled one another affectionately, and danced in a circle together. The vulture, perching on his beam, nodded drowsily in time to the rhythm of Talina's dance.

Even Grignan's cold eyes softened, then drooped. And he too began to sway and turn around in rhythmic circles. Then he rose on his back legs and began to hop and loop like a stoat. From his mouth came not growls but a soft, singing whimper. In a moment, the whole *Sala del Sangue* was reverberating with the thud of pairs of prancing Ravageur paws and the high-pitched crooning of the oblivious dancers.

Talina waited no more. She fled through the nearest sheep exit.

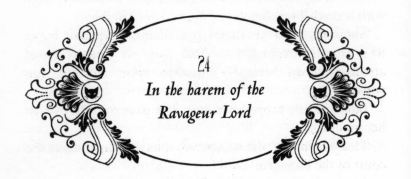

24

In the harem of the Ravageur Lord

five breathless minutes later

AFTER RUNNING THROUGH interminable mud corridors lit by stinking tallow candles, Talina was unexpectedly brought up short against an intricate screen secured with iron locks and bolts. She shivered. Her breath came in ragged gasps; her corn-husk hair, pinafore and shoes were sticky with Manitoba Gargling Oil.

No one was chasing her. She could hear no drumming pawfall, no pursuing growls. What she *could* hear – in the distance – was the continued thump of dancing paws and soused-sounding chants and moans punctuated by the odd dreamy squawk from Restaurant.

'The grannies would be so proud,' Talina thought. 'My *Fascinating Stoat* confuzzled those Ravageurs *perfectly*.'

She leant against the wooden screen, panting. A pair of soft paws closed around her face. Another pair came out from behind and held her around her waist, and a third pair covered her mouth and held her throat. But it was all done so gently, like the tickle of a kitten. And a beautiful perfume of rose petals clung to the fur on the paws that held her, the nails of which were enamelled in iridescent colours.

'Who are you, leettle sticky one?' asked a feminine voice with a gentle French accent. 'Are you een trouble?'

'Show us,' said another voice, 'that you do not mean to scream, by tapping your back paw. We cannot breeng attention down here. We need to know zat you can whisperrr.'

Talina hastily tapped her foot. The paw was lifted from her mouth.

'Please help me,' she whispered. 'I have escaped from the court of the Ravageur Lord.'

A sharp intake of breath echoed through the dark tunnel.

'No one escapes!' said a childish voice. 'Eet is not done.'

A womanly voice suggested with authority, 'Poor one. She is trembling. Let us release 'er,' and all the paws flew off Talina's body. She stood still, uncertain of what to do next.

A young voice asked, 'Does ze leetle sticky one 'ave any milk jelly?'

'Sssh!'

The older voice continued with its gentle instructions: 'Now turn around and let us see your front. What do zey call you? I am Bidet, the Mother of the Harem.'

Talina slowly turned. She peered in through the screen and suddenly drew breath. Her eyes, adjusting to the gloom, made out the massed ranks of hundreds of small, almost delicate Ravageurs, crowded into a dark cave with a low ceiling and just a single lantern near the door. It illuminated a feeding trough, from the back of which cruel spikes pointed upwards. Anyone who escaped over the trough would be immediately impaled there.

'I am Talina,' she said. 'Who are you?'

'Oh but zis one is ugly! And how she steeeenk!'

'That's not me,' said Talina hotly. 'That's the Manitoba Gargling Oil.'

'Ssssh, Bique! Do not be rude. She 'as nice whiskers at least.'

'She is not a cat, eef you look close, you see that she is a human, but also a leetle bit like us. Is a half-monster! I am afraid!'

'Me too! *Moi aussi! J'ai peur*!'

The eyes of the Ravageur females closed to slits. Their ears flattened and turned to the side. Their mouths curved to nervous grins. Their heads lowered and their fur sleeked down. Every single tail was tucked under the body of its owner. They howled softly under their breath.

Bidet urged, 'Hush, Bique, Bourrique, Bassinoire! Quiet, Ripopette! *Tais-toi*, Caboche! And the rest of you, too. Let ze little monster speak.'

Talina smiled in as friendly a manner as she could manage. 'Not a monster. I am a human girl. I had an accident with a spell and now I am a bit cat and sometimes a bit Ravageur – a bit everything, really. Depends who I'm with and how angry I am.'

'Is angry? With us!' the females backed hastily away from the screen.

Talina smiled, 'Not at all. You are the female Ravageurs?'

'*Mais oui!* And the baby girl Ravageurs and the leetle girl Ravageurs.'

'They really do keep you *in the dark* down here!' Talina could not keep the shock out of her voice, 'Do you never see the sun or the sea or the Great Hall ... ?'

'They say we are ugly and stupid and useful only to look after the cubs.'

'And you believe them?'

'No one 'as ever told us anything different,' replied, Caboche hanging her head.

'I can tell you,' Talina bristled, 'that you are living creatures, with every right to walk free. And you are fairly polite, and civilized,' she muttered, 'which is more than I can say for your husbands, brothers and fathers. Unlike them, your fur is glossy – you don't have the mange, do you? You are as lovely in your way as … as … these flowers!' She pointed to a few pots of anaemic violets straining towards the light just inside their cell. Now she noticed that the poor creatures had tried to prettify or at least alleviate the brutal gloom of their prison: the floor was neatly swept, and hundreds of empty jam pots from Golosi's had been arranged in patterns on shelves.

'You are a kind girl to say so, but 'ow can we believe what you say? Unlike our husbands, we 'ave no jewels, or fancy capes and hats.'

'That's not what makes someone beautiful!'

'We 'ave no right even to be beautiful, we are told. So we may not step abroad. We must stay 'ere, where zey can keep an eye on us, and discipline us if we misbehave. But, in exchange, we 'ave our food, and we are kept safe. And we 'ave the honour of being ze wives and mothers of ze Ravageurs. Why sometimes – though not often enough – they even bring us sweets!'

'Chantillia Baskets!' sighed one of the pups. 'Milk Jellies, Jewel Liqueur Drops and ratafia biscuits, soft and crunchy at the same time …'

'Maraschino Ice!' whimpered a small girl Ravageur. 'So cool, so elegant!'

'Neapolitan wafers …'

'Golosi's Mostarda!'

'Ah! Ah!' the lady Ravageurs almost blew Talina over with a hot collective sigh. 'Zat is the best of all.'

'I love those things too. But I wouldn't give up my freedom for them. You don't have any kind of life,' said Talina. 'You poor things. You don't even have fresh air. And look at the horrible names they gave you – "Caboche" means "blockhead"; "Ripopette" means "worthless" and "Bique" means "silly goat"! And a "bidet" is a thing that humans use to wash their ... well, never mind. You are all insulted by your very own names!'

'Is it not so for all female creatures ze world over?' asked the largest of the lady Ravageurs. 'To be treated so, and to bear ze shame of stupidity?'

'*Oui, oui*, Bourrique,' said Bidet. 'So we are always told.'

Talina sat cross-legged on the floor. She began, 'Now let me tell you a few things you ought to know.'

'... So,' concluded Talina, fully a girl again, 'you would consider the idea of *not* being so utterly submissive to your husbands and fathers and uncles? And of being kind to the poor humans who make the delicious sweets, who will then help you escape to a life of freedom? You'll help me find my parents? Good. We are agreed.'

'*Mais oui*,' said Bidet.

'*Milles bombes!*' cheered the young female cubs.

'Don't forget ze list, *chérie*,' urged Ripopette.

Talina read from the scrap of paper she'd just covered with words:

Meteors in Candy
Poppy Drops
Chantillia Baskets
Jewel Liqueur Drops
Catechu Drops
Syrup of Pinks
Quince Compote

Angelica Comfits
Neapolitan Wafers
Gimblettes
Golosi's Mostarda (lots)

'But they are *all* sweet things!' Talina chided. 'That's not good for you. How about a few nourishing vegetables, some *risi e bisi*, rice and peas? Some fresh tomatoes? Don't you want to stay healthy and strong, with clear heads . . . ?'

'We don't know how to cook,' confessed Bidet. 'We are used to being fed.'

'But cooking is wonderful fun! When this is over, I'm going to teach you all how to bake and broil and roast,' Talina promised enthusiastically. 'And perhaps some lessons in table manners too – you probably shouldn't eat in front of people, without some rehearsals, first.'

Bique called, 'And don't forget ze Orange Flower Ice and ze Maraschino Cherries.'

Talina was about to give a smart retort to this, but she could hear the unmistakeable sound of male Ravageurs – not far enough away – waking up from their state of unfocused dancing rapture. From the thudding of paws, it seemed some were still dancing, and others were groaning drowsily, 'Ooh my head! What's going on?'

Rouquin yelled, 'Frimousse, *mon ami*, get off zose back legs! Stop swaying lak dat! You look lak—'

And Frimousse retorted, 'Where is zat damnable not-quite-cat? Zis is 'er doing, *n'est-ce pas?*'

Over all their mutterings, Grignan shouted, 'You curs, there isn't time to catch her now. She can't escape us, in the end. Where would she go? There are more important things afoot, and we have wasted precious hours! We cannot be late for 'The Sad Event'! Fetch the piano! Fetch the Dark Snow Dome! The gramophone! Launch the barges!'

Ravageurs thundered from the *Sala*, through the Great Hall, towards the outside world and the shore.

'Sad Event? Dark Snow Dome?' squeaked Talina. 'What can he mean?'

'We know nossing, as usual,' sighed Bidet.

'Well,' muttered Talina, 'let's hope it's not another horrible thing to deal with before I can find Mamma and Papà.'

'So sorry,' murmured Bidet. 'How the leetle one suffers. *Malheur.*'

There was a glint of dark blue at the far end of the corridor. Dusk must have arrived, Talina realized, while she explained 'proper respect due' and 'equality' and 'freedom' to the amazed females of the Ravageur harem.

Talina bade them a hasty farewell, ran to the open window, climbed out and rushed down to the shore. As she'd hoped, Altopone still sat in his gondola, hidden in the bulrushes, glowering and cleaning his whiskers.

'You missed the big launch. Never seen such a thing. So many boats! I suppose you wants taking back to Venice?' he sighed.

'No, at least not yet! I want to go to Maggot Island, fast as you please.'

Altopone shook his head. '"I want", does it? Wants doesn't always get, missy. I've heard tell of that place. But it's not on any map. We might row about the lagoon for twenty years without finding it. You'll have to go home and find out more. Bookish, aren't you? Must be in an old book or on an antique map somewhere. So – Venice?'

'Venice then,' Talina accepted wearily.

'We'll need to go slow, to give the Ravageurs a good head-start.' Altopone pointed to a dim cluster of boats just approaching the ring of fog.

Talina had plenty of time to tell the rat of her discoveries inside the Ravageur palace while he manoeuvred through the fog, making maddeningly slow progress through the lagoon. The weak sun set. Altopone made frequent stops to pick up elderly rats stranded on rocks where the Ravageurs had left them to starve, being no more use as rowers. This reminded Talina painfully of her parents.

'It's been nearly three months since they were kidnapped,' she told Altopone. 'How long can they survive on a pound of seed cake and an egg?' she mourned. 'Surely there's something else growing on the island. Maybe ... maybe, if things got really difficult, they could try to ... eat the worms?'

'Even we rats draws the line at that,' muttered Altopone.

Talina's face was still tight with disgust as she fell asleep. She woke to see that the sun had already risen again and to hear the clocks of Venice striking ten. She sat up, rubbing her eyes as the rower-rats pulled into the mouth of the Grand Canal.

Then her jaw dropped. Suddenly, she understood what the Ravageur fleet of black boats was for, and exactly what Grignan had meant by 'The Sad Event'.

'Close that mouth or the flies'll get in, missy. Surprised, are you? You want to keep up with current affairs, my girl,' reproved the rat.

He handed her a newspaper. 'Picked up an early edition yesterday on my way to get you.'

The obituary page of the *Gazzetta* was taken over by a single sombre advertisement illustrated by a skull and cross-bones superimposed over a crude drawing of the city, blurred as if seen through tears.

The death is announced of the city briefly known
as Venice,
a city no one will miss.
The funeral will be held at 10a.m. on May 9th.
All loyal Luprians welcome to the festivities.

175

'What's the date today?' Talina asked Altopone. 'Is it . . . ?'

'Yes, May 9th,' he answered. 'Of course. And I seen more funerals than you've et chocolate éclairs, missy,' said Altopone, 'but I aint never seen one like this.'

He stared straight ahead, his tail trembling.

25
Funeral for a city

Venice, May 9th, 1867, Saint Isaia's Day

IN VENICE, MAY 9th had dawned grey and vague. On the orchard islands, the vines sagged against the poles, their tendrils tightly curled as if in private grief. Each Venetian seemed to walk around within his or her own little envelope of mist, fists thrust into coat pockets, heads down. Even the older children wanted to hold their mother's hand as they walked through town.

On his way to school, Ambrogio tapped at the door of Professor Marìn's house But there was no news of Talina: just drawn faces and clenched hands. Instead, Tassini silently showed him the newspaper announcement of the funeral and Mademoiselle Chouette held out a letter from the headmaster that read '*All pupils are excused class today so that they may attend a funeral.*'

'This is history being made,' said Tassini heavily. 'Come, boy. We must all bear witness, young and old.'

So it was that, fortified with Mademoiselle Chouette's hot chocolate and hand-rolled croissants, Ambrogio came to be perched with the professor, the historian and the French mistress at the best vantage point on the Rialto Bridge at ten o'clock that morning, watching a procession of black boats making its way along the Grand Canal.

First came a *peàta* barge painted a black so deep that it seemed like a floating hole. Even its floorboards were black as boots. On top of the *peàta* was a grand piano with a keyboard of exclusively black keys. This was visible to the adults; only Ambrogio and the other children could see the Ravageur dressed in a top-hat and a black tail-coat seated on an ebony stool to play the instrument. But everyone in Venice could hear the appalling sounds he made: crashing discordant runs and clashing chords. Behind the pianist stood another Ravageur in evening dress. The tails of his coat floated behind him like the forked tongue of a serpent. He drew a shrieking bow across an ebony violin with black strings. In front of them lay a black coffin, draped with black furs and crowned with a wreath of black roses. In white were chalked the word *Venezia, March 25th, 421 – May 19th, 1867*.

Children in the crowds pointed at the Ravageurs and screamed. But their parents could see only the coffin and the keys of the piano pressed down by invisible claws.

Ambrogio, peering from the Rialto Bridge with a telescope, saw that in the centre of the wreath sat a snow dome the size of a bucket. Inside it glittered a glass model of the entire city of Venice. But instead of silver or white powder, bat-like flakes whirled around the miniature bell-towers and palaces.

He handed the telescope to Tassini, who noted. '*Black snow, like ashes.*'

'Yes! And there's a jar of Golosi's Mostarda right next to it. And a smoking cigar. How strange!'

'You'd rather not see what is smoking that cigar,' Ambrogio assured them.

'But who's rowing the barge?' Mademoiselle Chouette asked. 'And 'ow does it move so smoothly?'

Tassini trained the telescope on the water. 'Ratpower,' he answered. The boat was surrounded by water-rats who strained to propel it through the water with their shoulders, while valiantly paddling with their free arms and legs.

As the funeral barge passed by, Ambrogio suddenly saw what it had blocked from view. Behind it, the Grand Canal was almost black with boats.

Every kind of Venetian boat was represented: the light, leaf-shaped *sandolo a la ciosòta*, the *sandolo buranèlo*, the *sàndolo sampieròto* and their cousins, *the mascaréta* and the *pupparìn*, the prawn-tailed *batèla a còa de gàmbaro*, the oriental-looking *caorlìna*, the mallet-headed *barchèta a massòche*.

All these boats were painted so solidly black that it looked as if they had been dipped in primaeval mud. All were apparently empty, apart from massive bouquets of funeral flowers in white, yellow and pink, and ranks of silent cormorants, each holding a black rose in its beak. Above them roamed a restless flock of vultures, who occasionally swooped to hook a wriggling squid in their beaks.

Next came a flock of black gondolas, each topped by a cabin with a curved roof. The cabins were heavily curtained in black velvet, but the children of Venice caught glimpses of shaggy muzzles, flashes of teeth.

Behind the gondolas swam at least three hundred water-rats, in an arrow formation.

A flag fluttered from the last boat. Painted on it were the words:

To symbolize all the fishermen,
gondoliers,
fruit-sellers,
who shall no longer be here.
Rest in peace, Venetians.
You'd be better off dead
than staying here now.

'Ambrogio!' It was Talina's voice coming from below. He craned his neck. There she was, perched in a rat-rowed gondola that had joined the other boats sculling under the bridge. Ambrogio waved frantically.

Mademoiselle Chouette mimed horror. Talina lip-read: '*Mais* Talina, what 'ave you done to the clothes I made for you?'

'I'm sure Manitoba Gargling Oil doesn't wash out,' Talina sighed.

'Stop, please, let me out,' she urged Altopone. 'Those are my friends over there.'

'And you're looking just like 'em again,' grinned the rat.

'I guess it's a long time since I was angry with you,' Talina said, smiling. 'I'm grateful, truly, Altopone. So will my friends be. And we're going to save Venice, you'll see. The Ravageurs will not have it all their own way.'

'It'll take more 'n' bigger friends than that,' observed Altopone, 'to save you and your kind and your city now.'

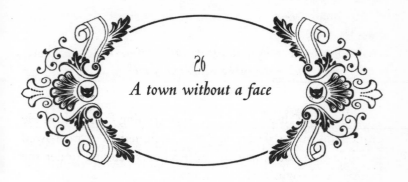

26

A town without a face

life after death in Venice, May 9th, and the following days

A FTER THE FUNERAL, a sudden fog fell on the city. On the mainland, it coated the fruit trees and wheat stalks with a hard cladding of frost that strangled and rotted at the same time. The next four nights, brutal hail fell without mercy, killing ducks in the rivers and pulping the delicate shoots of the year's crops. A bitterly cold rain flooded the dismal fields, drowning the bean and grape vines. If the sun didn't come out soon, the newspapers warned, Venice would starve to death. Or freeze. No one dared light the fires in their homes because every morning all the fireplaces were mysteriously full of gunpowder, as if it had poured down with the heavy fog.

The next onslaught was against the statues. The mist that had settled on Venice now started to eat away the features on their faces. In just a few days, their heads were plain white globes – sexless and sinister as tragic masks above their flowing robes.

'Without our statues, we are a town without a face,'

lamented Giuseppe Tassini. They were all assembled around a damp copy of the *Gazzetta* at Professor Marìn's kitchen table.

His small house now resembled a rather eccentric military barracks.

Ambrogio was spending every possible moment there, under the pretext of receiving extra Latin tutoring from the professor.

There'd been no more talk of sending Talina back to the tower. She'd been set up with a comfortable cot in a screened corner of the library, and fitted out with a luxury of improved flannel drawers and chemises by Mademoiselle Chouette, as well as a pretty sprigged dress fashioned from half a bathroom curtain. Professor Marìn had allowed Talina to hang her pencils from the library beams and he'd provided her with plentiful paper. She spent every possible minute of her time scanning the professor's collection of atlases and maps, searching for a rock, a promontory or mudflat with the name of 'Maggot Island'. That is, when she was not in the kitchen, cooking up heartening feasts for the troops.

The professor had not been falsely modest in saying he was not much of a cook. But he was an enthusiastic diner when it came to Talina's sizzled sweetcorn fritters, her artichoke goulash and, most of all, her caramel custard toffee chocolate puddings. Talina soon learnt to adapt recipes from the few volumes that approximated cookbooks in his kitchen, such as *Ancient Secrets of Marzipan Reveal'd* and *Sprites with Spatulas*. There was little in the way of proper cooking implements, so Talina improvised with the professor's Patent Amulet Amputation Saw for a bread-knife, his Fiend-Forceps as tongs and his Necromantic Insufflator for dusting cakes with icing sugar. Somewhat more reluctantly, she resorted to a fat syringe labelled 'Elf

Enemas' to baste her spicy sausages, and only after scrubbing it out first.

Tassini, now a permanent fixture, also appreciated Talina's cooking. He'd arrived with a wheelbarrow of atlases, dictionaries of Slavonic tongues, and travellers' tales from antiquity – and even a chronicling tablet from the Royal Library of Assyria at Nineveh. The historian had taken over the dining room to work and sleep. He did little of the latter, spending every waking hour trying to trace the true ancestry of the Ravageur tribes in Siberia.

Professor Marìn had gallantly offered his own bedroom to Mademoiselle Chouette, who had brought a small sewing machine with her. The professor himself slept in the snuggery off the kitchen, imposing a midnight curfew on Talina's cookie-baking.

They were all nibbling despondently on her cherry macaroons now – a great waste, Talina thought, as the fist-sized pink rounds were outstandingly delicious: fluffy inside and delicately crunchy on the outside. But there was no denying the depressive power of the *Gazzetta*'s latest report. Ambrogio pointed to an etching of one of the faceless statues. 'This is certain to be a message from Grignan, another of his threats.'

As if to confirm this, when they turned the page, they found a transcription of a poem that had been affixed to the doors of the Basilica of San Marco.

When did it start to blow cold, little city!
When did the water flow cold?
When will the cold quite enfold you, little city?
When will you start to grow old?
Where did your stone faces go, little city?
Those faces that once were so bold?

When did they bring you so low, little city?
Was it a long time ago?
Now there's no life in your soul, little city,
For all your fine memories are sold.
You think you're a sight to behold, little city,
But your end is already foretold.

'He has gifts as a poet, this Grignan,' said Professor Marìn, without pleasure, looking at the *Gazzetta*'s transcription.

'If only that was a clue as to their true origins!' Tassini crushed a cherry macaroon in his fist. 'The texts disagree. From Toulouse, one scholar says! Or from the Black Mountains of the Pyrenees. Or the swamps of Rieux.'

'I think they just came from Hell,' said Ambrogio, solemnly. 'Or some place like it.'

Listlessly, he picked up an American volume from Tassini's place. It was entitled *The Natural History of Mystical Quadrupeds*. He read aloud: 'Ravageurs are such ferocious and useless creatures that all other animals detest them, yea, they even hate each other … Perhaps of all other animals, Ravageurs are the most hateful while living and the most useless when dead.'

Tassini's biggest book of all was simply called *Parasites of Mammals*, and he kept it permanently open the section to do with sarcoptic mange. Talina shuddered at a magnified drawing of *Sarcoptes scabiei*, the mange-mite, a squat, thorny, scaly creature with a blunt head and stubby legs.

Tassini explained, '*Sarcoptes* burrows into the skin of its victims to lay eggs. The subsequent scratching leads to hairlessness, scabs, infection and sometimes death. And look at this!'

He flung open a veterinary journal to show an article

entitled 'Dumb and Furious Rabies in Wolf-and-Hyena-like Creatures.'

'Zere are *two* kinds of rabies?' asked Mademoiselle Chouette.

'Dumb Rabies – paralysis of the throat, loss of voice, slobbering, and then death. Furious Rabies is the one we have to worry about – starts with the slobbering and strange barking, followed by an aggressive period in which they will attack even inanimate objects, but, most of all, other creatures. At this stage, Ravageurs have no fear of humans. But eventually this is followed by the paralytic phase. The tongue sticks out of paralysed jaws, and then the creature dies.'

'Do you think our Ravageurs have Furious Rabies? They certainly fight one another.' Talina reminded them of the fate of Croquemort's ear, adding, 'And their tongues stick out *a lot*. It's perfectly revolting.'

'They might be in the second phase of Furious Rabies, yes. This would explain why they have taken to attacking humans after so many centuries of a retired existence in the lagoon.'

'Doctor Raruso also said that they are unwell! And that they had changed recently, since Grignan came to power. I just remembered something else! The Ravageurs take some kind of medicine before their meals. From iron spoons. Grignan orders them.' She clapped her hand over her mouth.

Ambrogio said, 'Do you mean ... What if that *isn't* medicine?'

Professor Marìn said, 'By Jove, that could be the explanation. Grignan is poisoning his own kind, to make them aggressive! Furious Rabies and mange – a very poor combination for the temper.'

'And Grignan himself doesn't have rabies, of course,' guessed Ambrogio. 'He's just naturally bad.'

'As Doctor Raruso said, "The old house never lacks a rat – every family has its black sheep, its low-life evil-doer",' quoted Talina.

'Yes, a blot, that's Grignan,' said Ambrogio. 'Is there a cure for Furious Rabies?'

'Usually only death,' said Tassini grimly, pointing to the last page of the veterinary journal. 'But not for a long time. They can wreak a powerful amount of damage in that time.'

'There is nothing for it,' said Professor Marìn, stabbing at the *Gazzetta*'s poem with his finger, 'we must capture this beast Grignan and put him on trial for crimes against his own species as well as ours. Then perhaps they will turn against him as well. Only then can we save the city.'

'And my parents,' Talina put in.

'But Grignan would never submit to a human court. He's seen just how fair humans are,' Ambrogio said bleakly. 'Why should he expect justice from us?'

'When I suggested a court case, he just sneered,' Talina told them. 'He wants to be judge and executioner himself.'

The professor's eyes lit up. 'But Grignan *could* be tried by beings who are more than human.'

Talina stared at him.

'Have you never heard of the Chamber of Conversation, child?' asked Professor Marìn. 'What do they teach you at school these days?'

Mademoiselle Chouette's eyes flashed and her turquoise earrings danced angrily.

'Be fair, Ridolfo,' Tassini rushed in before she could speak. 'The Chamber has not met for five hundred years.'

The Chamber of Conversation, he explained, was an institution named in the city's ancient charter. The members – known as Have-a-Voices – were ghosts of Doges past, figures from Venetian history and other magical beings.

'So a kind of courtroom?' Ambrogio asked eagerly.

'The Have-a-Voices are magical beings?' wondered Talina. 'Like witches and wraiths?'

'Several of each. Good Witches are in short supply, as they can be created only on Christmas Eve. But then they're born so wild that it takes another five hundred years before they are coven-ready. But yes, a few Good Witches and many Righteous Wraiths. Penitent Hags. The ghosts of three Admirals of the Fleet. Mermaids, if available. Proceedings take place in a secret room – the Chamber of Conversation, which simultaneously translates from one beastly or ghostly or human tongue to another. It is also a little different from human courts – some would say better – in that anyone with a case or information against the accused is entitled to conduct a cross-examination.'

'Even a very young person?' Ambrogio's face was shining.

'Even a child. If that child has a case and can carry an argument,' smiled Tassini. 'Boy, I think you were born for this.'

'Where is it? I never saw such a place,' said Talina.

'Ah, it floats just above the human law courts at Rialto,' replied Professor Marìn. 'A *higher authority*, as it were.'

'How do we get to it, then? A spell, I suppose.'

'Even simpler – a clearly expressed desire will do it.'

'All we have to do is get Grignan there,' said Ambrogio.

'But he's *never* going to clearly express a desire to be judged, is he? We'll have to force him to agree. So how are we going to trap him?'

There was a moment's despairing silence, and then Talina shouted, 'I know how. Not-Quite-Setting Toffee!'

187

27

Not-Quite-Setting Toffee

the kitchen-table conference continues at Santa Croce,
May 15th, 1867, Saint Sofia's Day

IT WAS ONE of Talina's favourite recipes. You didn't have
to wait for it to harden, because it never did. At least not
until you got it into your mouth, when it immediately set
in a solid glossy coating over your teeth. Then you'd have
twenty-four hours of sweetness on your gums and a
deliciously busy time licking all the remnants from the gaps
between your back molars.

'You know how Grignan always goes up the bell-tower
at the Madonna dell'Orto to howl his threats? Why don't
we fly up on the tea towels and coat the tower with my Not-
Quite-Setting Toffee? Grignan's got a sweet tooth, like all
the Ravageurs. He won't be able to resist a lick. As soon as
his tongue touches it, he'll get stuck up there.' Talina was
already ransacking the professor's cupboards for ordinary
sugar and molasses. She rejected a large roll of **Sweetened
Skylark Song** and a jar of **Blacker-than-night Treacle**.

'How shall we get him down?' asked Ambrògio. 'Will he have to lick the tower clean?'

'Or gnaw off 'is own feet? Like Monsieur Fox in a trap?' Mademoiselle Chouette looked quite cheerful at the prospect.

'Ugh. No, I don't want that,' shuddered Talina. 'In fact, I accidentally discovered, when forced to eat a salad one day, that a teaspoon of vinegar easily loosens the toffee.'

'But where will Grignan get a teaspoon of vinegar, stuck up there?'

'Exactly. And he won't know about it either. So we'll have him just where we want him. Ravageurs have to keep eating, or they quickly die. Poor Doctor Raruso told me that. So we'll tell Grignan that unless he agrees to be taken to the Chamber of Conversation, we'll leave him up there to starve.'

'Or chew 'is own leg off and die,' insisted Mademoiselle Chouette.

'Stop it!' Talina squealed. 'Don't forget he's still the only one who might be able to tell me where my parents are!'

'Will this be big enough, do you think, Talina?' Professor Marìn staggered out of the kitchen snuggery with a black concocting cauldron large enough to take a bath in.

'Absolutely. If we boil all day and all of tomorrow, it'll be ready by tomorrow night. Then we'll take it up by Thaumaturgic Tea Towel, and paint the tower with brushes. If I can use your Sprite Spatula, the one with the bone handle, for stirring, Professor ...'

Grignan tried to raise his clenched paw to shake at the moon, as he always did. But the paw would not lift.

'Strange,' he growled. He bent his head and sniffed

something sweet. Then his nose too stuck to the bricks of the onion-dome bell-tower of the church of the Madonna dell'Orto.

'Treachery!' he howled, indistinctly, for the top half of his jaw was stuck to the other. He tugged at the toffee, shaking the ancient masonry, already weakened from bearing his weight on so many previous nights.

Other Ravageurs, howling on other fog-wrapped spires, could not hear his muffled cries, or see his distress. They did not see the plaster dust and broken tiles flying from the tower as Grignan writhed and kicked in a vain effort to free himself. Instead, his minions busied themselves emptying sacks of gunpowder down Venetian chimneys, and then descended and made off in their gondolas, quite unaware that their Lord was left in a most embarrassing predicament.

Meanwhile, below Grignan in the *campo*, the professor, the historian, the French mistress, Ambrogio and Talina gathered around an enormous picnic basket.

Talina whispered, 'What now?'

'We wait,' smiled Emilie Chouette, 'until 'e get reeeelly hongry.'

'He's a Ravageur. That won't be long,' said Ambrogio. 'And he'll see the note we left in a minute. That'll make him feel like crunching a few bones.'

Grignan had already seen the note. He couldn't help it. His eyelashes were stuck to it. He crossed his eyes so that he could read it.

'Nooooooo!' he howled. 'Neverrrrrr. Everrrr.'

Down below the professor frowned. 'We'll want to deliver him to the Chamber of Conversation a bit sooner than that. Let's make the decision easier for him. Emilie, could you arrange the plate for me? In that special French way? I'll let the Thaumaturgic Tea Towel out.'

Minutes later, a plate of French delicacies was circling

the top of the tower, wafting its delicious perfume around Grignan.

He groaned, '*Assiette de choucroute et ses petits ...*'

He snapped his jaws ineffectually. The plate descended to earth, where the humans made short and pleasurable work of it.

Meanwhile the Thaumaturgic Tea Towel took up the next course, '*Filet de cervelles en jus avec ses ...*'

Droplets of moisture fell from the sky.

'What's that?' asked Talina.

'Ravageur dribble, I think you'll find,' spluttered Ambrogio, wiping the thick slime off his shoe. 'Unusually thick, isn't it?'

'So do you think he's ready to negotiate up there?' wondered Tassini.

'I'll go up and see, shall I?' offered Ambrogio.

'Be careful, young man,' urged Tassini. 'Don't let him bite you.'

Ambrogio was by now an old hand on his Thaumaturgic Tea Towel. He sped up to the top of the tower in one smooth motion.

'Grignan!' he shouted, only half-sure that he wanted the Ravageur Lord's full attention.

The Ravageur swivelled his opal eyes in the direction of Ambrogio. He could not move another muscle. All four paws, as well as his head, were stuck to the toffee. Still he tugged at the tiles, dislodging showers of dust and fragments of brick.

'Grignan,' Ambrogio said with dignity, 'if you will agree to be transferred to the Chamber of Conversation, for a fair and final judgement by the Have-a-Voices, we shall free you from the Not-Quite-Setting Toffee—'

'Who are you?' Grignan's growl came out jerkily as the dome wobbled beneath him.

'Ambrogio Gasper—' The words were halfway out of his mouth before he realized how incriminating they were.

'The boy who insulted us with that drawing! I might have guessed. You are doomed, boy. Doomed.'

Ambrogio gulped.

Grignan snarled deep in his throat, with a ferocity of foul breath and anger that rocked Ambrogio backwards on the tea towel. He teetered helplessly on the delicate fabric edge. There was nothing he could grab to steady himself. If he swung forward he would fall on the tower, and be stuck in the toffee just like Grignan. What's worse, he would be trapped *beside* the Ravageur Lord on a dome that was looking far from solid now.

Ambrogio looked down, dizzily. Far below him were the faces of the professor, Emilie Chouette and Talina, all taut and white in the moonlight.

'They'll never be able to catch me,' was his final thought as he started falling.

The last thing he heard was Grignan laughing and another sound curiously like the beating of wings.

'Restaurant!' shrieked Talina. 'You leave him alone!'

But the vulture was coasting a metre above Ambrogio's plummeting head, his beak wide open and his talons fully extended.

The second Thaumaturgic Tea Towel lay carefully folded in the picnic basket. At the sound of Grignan's laugh, it sat up to attention in swift folds. Then it arched and thrust itself out of the basket like a small sheet inhabited by a small ghost. It sped upwards.

'Grab it, Ambrogio! With your other hand!' cried Talina.

The first and second tea towels were already together, one

at each of Ambrogio's hands, which closed over them. The tea towels instantly puffed up with air, like white balloons.

Restaurant tried to clamp his talons around them, but succeeded only in getting his legs crossed and tangled. He spun into a somersault, careered into a gargoyle, hit his head on a drainpipe and flumped to the ground in a heaving heap of feathers.

Meanwhile Ambrogio floated gracefully down, landing gently on his back, where he lay quietly for a moment, looking pleased as Christmas, while his friends gathered around him, checking his bones and splashing cold water on his face.

'I'm fine,' he smiled. 'But one of the Thaumaturgic Tea Towels is in a poor state. I tore it on the way down.'

Professor Marìn picked up the damaged towel and ripped it solemnly in four. The white squares immediately repaired themselves with neat hems all round.

'Thaumaturgic Handkerchiefs, my friends,' he said, offering one section each to Talina, Mademoiselle Chouette, Tassini and Ambrogio. 'You never know when such a thing will come in handy. And the interesting thing about infused fabrics like this is that the smaller the piece, the more concentrated the magic. You'll find these little fellows even more biddable than the larger item.'

'They already do what we say,' observed Talina.

'Better than that, now they'll do what you *think*,' the professor added. 'And *I* think we must send up the *Îles flottantes* now.'

'Talina's *chef d'œuvre*!' Mademoiselle Chouette clapped her hands. 'Her masterpiece!'

With pride, Talina lifted the crystal bowl from the basket. The dessert glittered, its foamy piles of soft-poached meringue floating like islands in a sea of fragrant custard. A swirl of caramelized spun sugar encrusted each peak. Below the custard nestled sponge biscuits soaked in kirsch.

'A remarkable French culinary invention. It does rather remind one of the Venetian lagoon, doesn't it?' said Professor Marìn sentimentally. 'Sweet islands in a flowing liquid.'

'Hopefully it will remind Grignan of his empty belly and the risk of imminent death if he doesn't eat something very soon,' said Talina briskly. 'I'll take it up. No, Ambrogio, don't argue with me. You shouldn't be wasting a single word on me ... we need you to be preparing our case against the Ravageurs for the Chamber of Conversation.'

With that, she ascended on the whole tea towel, while the *Îles flottantes* were borne aloft on one of the Thaumaturgic Handkerchiefs.

The dessert made ten quick circuits of the top of the tower, each time closer to Grignan's nose and drooling muzzle.

At first, Grignan threatened Talina. 'You'll never get away with this,' he growled.

'Watch me,' she smiled, twirling on one leg.

'Don't forget I've got your hair,' he mumbled.

Talina thought, 'I really must have the professor explain properly about the hair. And the scorpions.'

But she was not going to show doubt or weakness to Grignan, not when she'd *nearly* got him where she wanted him.

'You've stolen one handful of my hair?' she said scornfully. 'So what? I'm not exactly short of it.' And she spun in graceful circles, sweeping her hair in a thick dark gold arc around her.

The fissure under Grignan's back legs opened up alarmingly.

'Grignan!' Talina shouted. 'That dome is going to break off any minute. Either you express a clear wish to go to the Chamber of Conversation – or you're going down with that tower, and getting smashed to pieces.'

A tumble of loosened bricks and a gush of dust confirmed her words.

Grignan growled, 'I shall attend the Chamber of Conversation. I shall listen to the Have-a-Voices. Just let me have these floating islands. That's all I ask.'

Even as he said the words, his body's outline was fading to a ghostly transparency. Soon he had disappeared completely, along with the bowl of *Îles flottantes*.

'We've won!' shouted Talina, descending. 'He's submitted. But the thing is ...'

The professor and Mademoiselle Chouette were dancing a triumphant minuet and Tassini was throwing his hat in the air for Ambrogio to catch. So no one heard Talina's anxious whisper: 'Don't any of you wonder if, when Grignan said "Just let me have these floating islands", he meant the meringue in the bowl ... or did he really – could he possibly – mean the one hundred and seventeen floating islands of Venice herself?'

But Professor Marìn was already speaking the incantation that began: 'O Chamber, and your wise Have-a-Voices, kindly admit us, Friend and Foe, Destroyer and Victim alike ...'

28
The Chamber of Conversation

THE CHAMBER OF Conversation was contained in curved glass walls, like a bubble. It hovered in a silver fretted fishing net high above the bridge at Rialto.

A bank of benches housed the ranks of Have-a-Voices, all seated solemnly at desks and scribbling notes with ostrich-feather pens on parchment. The frondy plumes of the pens tickled their noses, causing frequent sneezes.

'What 'ave we 'ere?' spluttered Mademoiselle Chouette.

'Good Witches, for a start,' noted Talina. They were easy to identify by their diaphanous forest-green robes and stupefying beauty. The Penitent Hags were gruesomely ugly, their dismal looks not improved by noses rendered bulbous and red by persistently flowing tears.

'Now *that*,' Professor Marìn told Ambrogio pointedly, 'is a *hag*. I don't think you'll find any resemblance to Emilie!'

'Not at all! And those must be Righteous Wraiths,'

196

Ambrogio pointed at six shimmering upright apparitions with quicksilver coursing through their transparent veins. 'What are they all scribbling?'

'Their memoirs. The sessions here can be rather long.'

The ghosts of the three former Admirals of the Venetian Fleet were the most human of the Have-a-Voices in appearance, but they too were slightly translucent, apart from their half-moon hats, which they doffed with the utmost elegance to the newly arrived company before settling down again on their benches.

There was also a tank of water – shaped like an enormous teardrop – with nothing inside. 'For the mermaids?' guessed Talina.

'Who are still away dealing with the Ghost-Turks,' boomed one of the Admirals of the Fleet. 'Unfortunately. We could do with those excellent ladies right now.'

On a golden chair at a higher level sat the ghost of a small but perfectly formed Doge, enveloped in ermine and wearing the traditional curved *corno* cap. He held a crystal gavel filled with water in which a solitary goldfish swam.

'So let's hope he doesn't have to rap it hard,' thought Talina.

'Oh my goodness, look at *them*!' said Ambrogio.

The back of the glass bubble was studded with the mounted heads of animals: zebras, squirrels, rabbits, minks, goats and even chickens. The heads were conversing about the case in animated tones, snorting and flapping their ears for emphasis.

Talina caught disturbing shreds of chatter: 'They say the humans will have to leave the city!' and 'The rats predict the worst' and 'It's all up for ...'

The front benches of the public area were occupied by rows of rats wearing bandages and aggrieved expressions.

'Victims of the Ravageurs,' thought Talina.

With so much to look at, and listen to, Talina had not at first noticed the change in her own appearance. So she was surprised when she caught sight of her reflection in the empty mermaid tank. She'd left the *campo* of Madonna dell'Orto in an apron well spattered with Not-Quite-Setting Toffee, with her hair still wild from shaking it at Grignan. Yet she had arrived in court with her hair neatly brushed and wearing a clean starched pinafore over her best pink dimity dress – which she'd last seen in the armoire at the tower at Quintavalle.

Ambrogio had somehow changed into his Sunday suit, complete with checked waistcoat and green cravat. His shoes shone like liquorice. He was scribbling notes onto his spotless white cuffs with a stub of a pencil, and quietly mouthing words to himself.

'His very first case,' Talina thought proudly. 'Most barristers start with something simple, like a bank robbery. Not the theft of a whole town, kidnapping, enslavement and potential mass murder.'

Mademoiselle Chouette was dressed in an elegant sky-blue dress that transfixed the professor, who wore an uncharacteristically pure-white cravat, with no ink stains on it at all. His red hair was neatly slicked down on his head. Tassini sported a dinner jacket unusually deprived of gravy. His goatee beard was carefully combed and his glasses shone.

'But there's one person, or creature, missing,' thought Talina. 'Did Grignan not honour his promise?'

With a clatter, Grignan now appeared in the room inside a cage. One back leg was shackled to the bars. He was devouring the *Îles flottantes* with an abomination of table manners.

Looking at the faces of Professor Marìn, Tassini and Mademoiselle Chouette – all three rigid with fear and distaste – Talina realized that the Chamber of Conversation not only translated all beastly languages but made magical creatures visible even to adult humans.

'Zis is what zey look like? *Les Ravageurs?*' whispered Mademoiselle. 'Zey don't look French at all!'

The Chamber sat silent while Grignan guzzled and slurped, spraying the ushers, a pair of solemn herons, with custard and sharp shards of caramelized spun sugar. The birds groomed themselves with their long black beaks, spitting out bits of toffee. But they remained resolutely at their posts beside the cage.

The little Doge averted his eyes from the unpleasant spectacle. He pointed to an empty seat beside his own, beckoning to Professor Marìn. 'For your contributions to aeromancy, hydromancy, astragolomancy and assorted other mancies, you, Ridolfo Marìn, are hereby raised to a place on this jury.'

'But, my goodness . . . I never thought to be so honoured!' The professor was pink with pleasure and embarrassment.

'Your place on the jury means, however, that you cannot speak for your side,' the Doge told him severely.

Professor Marìn said bravely, 'It matters not, for I have a young friend of surpassing eloquence with me.' He smiled at Ambrogio, encouragingly.

He was interrupted by a complex and elongated burp.

Grignan licked the last remnant of *Îles flottantes* from the bowl and then sent it spinning through the bars onto the floor at the centre of the room.

'For shame!' reproved a Righteous Wraith.

'Yes, Mr Grignan, you have the Chamber's attention,' sighed the small Doge.

Grignan drew himself to his full height, snapping, '*Lord* Grignan. And I am quite ready to speak. In fact, these dull-witted humans have given me just the opportunity I've wanted for centuries.'

'He's lying,' thought Talina. 'Lying like a snake!'

'Well, Lord Grignan, you may have your say,' said the Doge mildly. 'But first perhaps you would care for the use of a napkin.'

Grignan shook the slobber off his jaws so vehemently that no one in the Chamber remained completely dry, except for the Good Witches, who intercepted the debris with their wands and sent it flying back into Grignan's fur. Shaking himself like a wet cat, Grignan began.

'Never in the whole history ... of *history* ... has there been so foul a crime as that which the Venetians have perpetrated on us Ravageurs in stealing our land and casting us out. Yet, instead of being punished, the Venetians have prospered on their ill-gotten gains, concealing their crime by building palaces on top of it. And even churches. They have made a mask of magnificence to hide the evil within. But Venice herself is a crime!'

'Now it starts!' thought Talina, raising her eyebrows.

Ambrogio leapt to his feet, his mouth open, but one look from the small Doge silenced him.

Grignan shouted, 'The Venetians pretend that they were the first on this land, and that it has always belonged to them. But the meshes of Truth's net have at last fallen over those criminals. My ancestor Verpillion Grignanne was the true master of this place ... and I now reclaim it for my race, as his direct and true descendant.'

'Who here speaks for the Venetians?' boomed the Doge.

Talina, Tassini and Mademoiselle Chouette pointed to Ambrogio. He cleared his throat, rose and stepped forward.

'I may address the prisoner directly?' he requested. The Doge nodded.

Ambrogio removed his spectacles, inspected them and dusted them lightly on his waistcoat before replacing them on his nose. Then he spun around dramatically to face

Grignan. Unfortunately he'd put too much into his turn and ended up facing the Doge again. Blushing, he inched his way back round. But his voice hardly trembled as he looked Grignan in the eye. 'Verpillion is a nickname, I understand. I also understand that the "Verpillion" is a small species of green weevil – or parasite – that preys greedily on grape vines. Will the prisoner inform me if that is correct?'

'And so what if it is?'

'It is just that greed shall be central to our case,' Ambrogio replied gravely.

'*Greed* is indeed the issue here. Venetian greed—'

'No,' said Ambrogio. 'Ravageur greed. We have reason to believe – and evidence to present to this court – that your ancestor's fondness for luxurious food and wine led him to renounce his rights to this town fourteen hundred years ago. Willingly. He was not forced. Have you ever seen anything like the marks that are represented on this piece of paper, Mr Grignan?'

Ambrogio held up to the Chamber an exact copy of the inscription on the tower at Quintavalle.

'Is it not the case that in AD 421 your ancestor Verpillion Grignanne simply *sold* the lands of Venice to a human known as Uberto Flangini?'

'A robbery!' shrieked Grignan. 'Not a sale!'

The Righteous Wraiths frowned.

'But the transaction was recorded in a Deed of Sale,' said Ambrogio. 'And the price was ... as you can see here, Ten Fire-buckets of Human Wine, Five Sheep, Six Brass Buttons, a Mink Jelly and a Dozen Fancy Pastries.'

'*Mink* Jelly!' cried an outraged mink.

Grignan shouted, 'Flangini deceived my ancestor! How could the Venetians exploit a vulnerable creature so shamelessly, tricking him out of his inheritance with a few humble objects? Of all things Venice should be ashamed of, this is the worst.'

Talina met Ambrogio's eyes across the Chamber. So Grignan had changed plan. He was not going to try to deny that the sale took place, as they had hoped he would. He was going to rest his case on the terrible injustice of it. This was what they had hardly dared to fear. The faces of the Have-a-Voices hardened. The mounted animals uttered low grunts of disapproval.

'Another thing you fail to mention,' sneered Grignan, 'is that the original Flangini paid his pittance, in full knowledge of something that he hid from my ancestor. Old Flangini consciously deceived my kin.'

'What is this secret?' demanded Ambrogio. Talina sat forward in her seat.

'The original Sior Uberto Flangini had a gift of sight. He had a vision in which the island of Luprio would one day be the richest city in the world, and but a few years thence. So when he paid his paltry price, he *knew* he was swindling my race.'

'Oh no!' wept the Penitent Hags. The mounted heads murmured among themselves, their whiskers and noses twitching with doubt.

'Wait! How can that be proved after all this time? A secret sight?' demanded Ambrogio. 'In a man who must have died fourteen hundred years ago? Jolly convenient for the Ravageurs' case, I must say—'

'Session concluded,' called the Doge, pointing to a grandfather clock. 'Take the prisoner back to his cell. The Have-a-Voices shall reconvene tomorrow. Meanwhile the witnesses and defendants will be transported to a safe house – Professor Marìn's, where they must wait under curfew until the next session.'

'That could not have gone worse, could it?' lamented

Talina. 'Did you see the looks on the Righteous Wraiths' faces?'

'And the Penitent Hags obviously don't think we have a ghost of a chance,' said Tassini. 'Boy, why did you ...?'

'I was just *getting* to my point when the session was stopped,' Ambrogio stamped his foot.

'What point?' asked Talina scornfully.

Then everything in her sight crumbled into mist, and the next thing she knew she was in her bed behind the screen in the professor's library with her pencils dangling above her. She could hear scribbling and bunching up of sheets of paper, and balls of paper flying across the room.

'Ambrogio!' she said, peering over the top of the screen. 'What are you doing here?'

'Preparing our counter-argument,' he said, pointing to a stack of densely written sheets. 'Go to sleep.'

Surprising even herself, Talina obeyed.

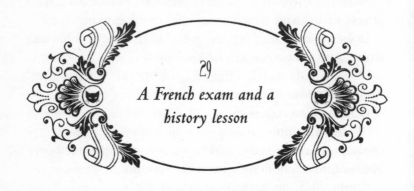

29

A French exam and a history lesson

the Chamber of Conversation, May 17th, 1867,
Saint Pasquale's Day

'THE CHAMBER CALLS Mademoiselle Emilie Chouette!'

The Mademoiselle Chouette who strode up to the witness stand bore absolutely no resemblance to the merry young woman that Talina and Ambrogio had come to know in the past few days. In fact, she was exactly like the martinet they'd dreaded in the classroom at school. The turquoise earrings hung straight down on their gold chains with not a hint of dancing about them. A velvet ribbon around her neck was fastened with a sober black cameo brooch. Her hair was dressed in severely regimented ringlets.

'So,' she snapped, 'Monsieur Grignan. You *claim* to be French.'

He snarled, 'It is *Lord* Grignan to you.'

'Boh! Your accent is melting my ears! Now, can the Chamber supply a blackboard?' asked Mademoiselle Chouette. Before she finished speaking, a handsome board appeared on a mahogany easel with an ornate ledge, upon which rested a long stick of chalk.

'*Merci!* So, Monsieur Grignan, what are ze past participles of zese verbs, with which you are so familiar in practice?'

In her strong looping cursive, Mademoiselle Chouette wrote '*mentir et voler*' on the blackboard.

'"To lie and steal!"' called one of the rats. 'Very clever! And what about "to wound and kill"?'

Grignan lowered his eyes.

'If these simple words defeat you, 'ow about the expression commonly used in French to signify...' Mademoiselle Chouette busied herself with the chalk again.

'Umm. Ahh,' stuttered Grignan.

'Really? Then ze French dictionary must be wrong,' laughed the French mistress.

Grignan recovered himself enough to snarl, 'Why should I answer to *you*?'

'The Chamber will observe that zis defendant cannot answer the most basic questions on *la grammaire française*,' announced Mademoiselle Chouette. 'A truly French creature would not need even to think about zese words. Zey would be on the tip of Monsieur Frenchman's tongue, like the name of 'is own sister.' She turned back to Grignan, 'I 'ave listened to you. Your pronunciation is a disgrace. Your grammar is a massacre. Your phrasing is a shipwreck. That goes for all your kind! You are imposters, poor imposters at that. You attempt to disgrace the French nation with these appalling accents, unforgiveable grammar and unspeakable deeds. Your reputation, *mes amis*, is *de l'histoire*.'

Mademoiselle Chouette stared straight into Grignan's eyes across the room.

'She doesn't flinch!' marvelled Talina. But she felt suddenly afraid for the French mistress.

'Well said, sister!' enthused a witch.

'*Brava*!' called the mounted heads.

'Hear, hear,' called the Righteous Wraiths.

Mademoiselle Chouette turned to face the Doge and Have-a-Voices with a magnificent sweep of her silk glacé skirt. 'I leave the next interrogator to shed more light.'

It was now Giuseppe Tassini's turn to cross-examine Grignan. Waving a roll of parchment, the historian explained how – in the middle of the preceding night – he'd finally succeeded in tracing the true ancestry of the Ravageurs.

'And it turns out,' Tassini told the Chamber, 'that these creatures are nothing more than humble – if ravening – wolves from the Siberian wastes, who fled south from an exceptionally cold winter in around AD 400. They arrived in Venice just a few years before the humans. There were no heroic Lupine Wars. There are no ancestral lands.'

'I just knew it!' squeaked a mink. 'But why don't they look zackly like wolves any more?'

Tassini smiled. 'Passing through France, they were joined by a band of African hyenas who'd escaped from a circus in Marseilles. The resultant interbreeding explains the sloping backs and teeth formation of the Ravageur.'

'So what about the French food?' asked a plump squirrel. 'The *tournedos*, the *jus*-es, the sauces? They picked that up on their travels too?'

'Just so!' Tassini flourished a large, dusty tome. 'The pretensions of the Ravageurs are unmasked: their desire for fancy French food is revealed as another travesty!'

The Righteous Wraiths stroked their chins and then nodded emphatically.

A dignified zebra accused Grignan, 'You are not even animals any more, you Ravageurs. *Proper* animals don't carry on as you do. They do not have lords. Or slaves. They do not make plots. They just get on with—'

Tassini explained, 'The Ravageurs are afflicted with

mange and may well be rabid now, poor creatures. Which would explain their recent aggression.'

'Ugh! Can you get rabies from particles in the air?' cried a squirrel. 'Are we breathing it now? Oh! Oh! Oh!'

'A little self-control, please!' The small Doge rapped his crystal gavel, causing the goldfish inside it to swish around in a worried manner. The squirrel clapped a paw over his mouth with embarrassment.

Tassini concluded, 'But the hard fact remains – the Ravageurs' so-called ancient claims to Venice are just as false as their French accents!' Tassini turned to Grignan. 'Do you deny it, sir?'

The Ravageur Lord growled deep in his throat.

'Call Counsel Ambrogio Gasperin once more,' Tassini requested, 'to finally settle our case.'

Ambrogio stood up smartly with a thick file under his arm. He looked terrible, with dark circles under his eyes, as if he'd been up all night: which, of course, he had.

Grignan's brooding silence now had a definite smoulder of brimstone about it. He rose menacingly on his back legs, causing all the mounted animal heads to suck in their breath. Ambrogio kept his eyes fixed on the terrified Have-a-Voices. 'Now I ask the Chamber to re-examine the primary evidence.'

From his file, he produced copies of the document that he had made outside the tower.

'No no no no no!' hissed Talina. She wanted to run over to him and rip it out of his hands. Why was Ambrogio reminding the Chamber of the Ravageurs' best case again? Was *this* what he spent all night preparing? She saw the professor and the historian exchange worried glances.

Grignan leant forward in his cage.

Ambrogio began, 'My Lords, we do absolutely acknowledge that the Venetian Uberto Flangini bought the land from the Ravageurs at an exceedingly low price.'

The mounted heads chattered and twittered excitedly.

'*What* are you up to, Ambrogio?' whispered Talina.

Ambrogio winked at her, continuing, 'But let us now consider exactly *what* old Verpillion Grignanne sold the Venetians in this contract. What was here in AD 421? Not a single house, let alone a palace. Not a church, nor a tower. No bridges. Nothing but isolated islands, barren marshes – a humid wasteland that flooded with every tide. Nothing but that dark and smelly substance so uniquely suited to the Ravageur tribe – mud.'

The Ravageur Lord battered his head against the bars of his cage.

'Grignan, I refute your claim that you *ever* owned Venice. Even if the Ravageurs *were* here first, just *slightly* ahead of the humans, your so-called Kingdom of Luprio was a fiction. In the time you spent as "lords" of this land, you Ravageurs cared for nothing, built nothing, made nothing, planted nothing.'

'Not a carrot, not a cabbage!' blurted a mounted rabbit head, only to be shushed by its companions.

Ambrogio continued, 'And who has the right to a city anyway – those who *dishonestly* claim *ancient* land rights ... or those who actually *build* its wonders?'

Ambrogio gestured expansively at the beautiful city below the floating room. 'Wonders that reach up into the sky! Lovelier than any other city's, past or present! Famed throughout the world! Who built these exquisite palaces, these graceful bridges, these lofty churches? Who brought trade here from all over the Mediterranean? Who created all the beautiful paintings and wrote all the learned books? And then made the elegant galleries and libraries to house them?'

The small Doge commented, 'Yes, I suppose a lived-in

landscape has its biography, like a family. It is a point well made, Counsel.'

Ambrogio blushed with pleasure. Talina clapped her hands.

The mounted heads all swivelled approvingly in Ambrogio's direction. A rabbit chittered excitedly, 'Tell us more, little sir!'

'It is the *Venetians* who made Venice what it is now. *They* dredged the canals and reclaimed the land. They put down the waterproof Istrian stone. They dug the wells for sweet water. They brought the railway right into the city—'

Grignan muttered under his breath, 'Wonders? The Venetians starved the natural canals. They stole the fish. They drove stakes into the heart of the soft mud—'

'Since when did the Ravageurs care about the natural world?' Ambrogio demanded. 'I put it to you that the Ravageurs have a right only to the crude piles of mud that they sold Uberto Flangini.'

'They were not crude,' interrupted Grignan. 'The detailing of our architecture is . . . ambiguous.'

'Ambiguous! Murky, more like!' Ambrogio's voice rose. His stature seemed to grow. There was a strange angular cast to his shadow as he strode across the Chamber and his curly hair seemed even bushier than usual. 'I put it to you that mud is all you Ravageurs are entitled to. May you live on, and in mud! Mud, dark and dirty, is all you deserve. And who are you, you Ravageurs? Were you in Noah's Ark? Are you noble beasts? You are not creatures who have made your way in the world, except by exploiting and killing others. You, with your mange and tapeworms, are just mange and tapeworms yourselves.'

Professor Marìn muttered, 'Ambrogio, this is not good law. This isn't even good argument.'

Tassini whispered, 'The boy damages our case with these crude insults.'

Grignan sat in his cage, his mane growing bigger and bigger, his eyes glinting.

Ambrogio's voice became unnaturally deep and he tugged at his cravat which seemed to have grown suddenly too tight. A few black hairs sprouted on the backs of his palms. 'You Ravageurs are offensive wild animals. Ravening beasts, stenchy savages, creatures of murder. Venice is a great civilization. What right have *you* to even approach it?'

'Ambrogio!' protested Tassini. 'One can go too far!'

Talina cried, 'You're letting yourself down, Ambrogio. You mustn't lose your temper like this. And remember, you absorbed the Spell Steam from the **If in doubt** too. If you get angry – well, you start to look like what's making you angry. I told you this would happen. Open your collar, or you'll choke.'

As Ambrogio struggled with his cravat, a blush descended like a red velvet curtain. His Ravageurish features subsided quickly back to those of a spectacularly embarrassed boy.

'I rest my case,' he muttered, sitting down hard. 'Talina, your turn.'

By the time Talina had forced Grignan to admit to the Chamber how he'd kidnapped and enslaved the humans in the Ravageur kitchens, and had moved the Chamber to tears with her account of how he'd left her parents to starve to death on a remote island of worms, Grignan's mane had inflated alarmingly.

The Righteous Wraiths were convulsed with outrage. The witches had taken several turns around the room on their brooms, just to relieve their tension. Proceedings had briefly halted while the Doge had lectured them on their indiscipline. And the Penitent Hags had almost dissolved in tears of pity for the poor mistreated humans.

Then Talina started on the Ravageur treatment of their own kind.

'You have enfeebled your females with sugar and darkness ...'

'Oh no!' wept the Penitent Hags. 'Oh, 'tis too bad, too bad!'

The witches listened stony-faced. But the drumming of their long black fingernails on the benches revealed their anger.

Outside, dusk was falling. The Chamber of Conversation darkened. Winged cats flew about with tapers in their mouths, lighting the sconces on the walls, each fitted with a little bottle of Manitoba Gargling Oil with a wick inside.

As the full moon began to rise in the sky, Grignan made low baying noises. His head swayed from side to side. His growls took on the rhythm of an incantation. His pitch rose higher to a screech painful on the ear.

'What's happening down there in the city?' shrieked a mink.

Below them, all the wooden poles along the Grand Canal burst into blue flame as if they were gigantic matches struck by an invisible hand.

'It's baddened magic!' Talina's voice was thin with horror.

Grignan broke his chains and rolled round and round in a blur until he upturned his cage. He smashed his way through the wooden planks of its floor, and bounded to the centre of the Chamber, where he shouted, 'Let's save this court the travesty of a deliberation, and a false judgement. If the city is destroyed, then that's the end of all controversy. If all the things built by the Venetians are gone ... then the empty, wasted land will belong once more to the Ravageurs. Even the boy Ambrogio cannot deny that.

'And lest anyone say that Luprio was but a single island, while Venice is a city sewn together by her three hundred bridges ... well, I shall destroy every one of them. All two hundred and twenty-two arches of your railway bridge too! Without her bridges, Venice will no longer be a city. Just a clutch of smoking outcrops in the lagoon!'

Laughing and roaring, Grignan leapt against the glass bubble, creating a clean circular opening. As the air rushed into the Chamber, he flew out into a soft starless night illuminated only by the fire-swept poles burning down to stumps in the dark, tumultuous water.

30

The Great Fire of Venice

the broken Chamber, the night of May 17th, 1867

'THIS IS WHAT the Dark Snow Dome meant!' cried
Talina. 'The Dark Snow Dome at the Sad Event!'

She ran to the fractured edge of the bubble,
pointing down. 'They were ashes, those black flakes in the
snow dome at the funeral procession. The ashes are real
now. Grignan never meant for this case to be decided in a
proper court. He planned to burn the city to the ground,
right from the start.'

Below them, the city was succumbing to the blue flames.
Like a curtain caught by a careless candle, old palaces swiftly
lit up with garlands of azure fire. Shimmering in the infernal
heat, bridges were crumbling, buildings smouldering. The
flames devoured all before them with a greedy relish,
mumbling and growling as if with delight. The gloating
of the fire was accompanied by triumphant howls echoing
nightmarishly through the city.

Ambrogio shouted, 'Look at the gas-lamps! They're

exploding! And the wind's a *scirocco*. That'll just fan the flames.'

'If the town heats up enough,' Talina said, 'then the gunpowder in all the chimneys will explode too.'

The Penitent Hags laid themselves down on the floor and wept hysterically until the tears flowed into their shaggy ears. The witches screamed curses. The mounted heads whistled and shouted.

'Order! Order!' shouted the small Doge. 'This is a Chamber of Civilized Conversation, not a Chamber of Chittering, Weeping and Screaming. You are Have-a-*Voice*s, not Have-a-Fits or Have-a-Yowls!'

The Doge banged his gavel so hard that the crystal smashed. Liberated, the goldfish made a heroic leap through the hole Grignan had made and plunged towards the Grand Canal below.

From the Chamber, they could see Venetians fleeing as fast as they could in boats, looking over their shoulders to see the strange blue flames against which their fire pumps were utterly useless. Their faces were blue with the reflections of the fire. Old Rialto fishermen pushed wheelbarrows with their fishwives in them; women hurried children through the smoke to jetties where men loaded them into workboats. Soon the streets were all but empty.

'The cats!' Ambrogio cried. 'The cats at the *ostello* can't flee. They're locked in.'

'And what about the grannies of Quintavalle?' Talina moaned. Then she thought, 'At least Maggot Island must be far enough that the fire won't spread there.'

The small Doge raised his hand. 'Professor and colleagues, I wish you where you need most to be, which is not presently in this place.'

Talina felt a milky haze envelop her. Ambrogio and the others shimmered in her sight. When she opened her eyes again, they were standing, or swaying, in front of the Ostello delle Gattemiagole. Flames were creeping all around her. Perhaps Talina was imagining it, but each of those flames seemed to have its own vicious little face hissing and spitting with malice.

Signorina Tiozzo was at the door, bent over the lock.

'You had the same idea, young man?' she smiled weakly at Ambrogio, her eyes streaming with smoky tears as she struggled with the key. She looked sharply at Talina. 'Do I know you, girl?'

The lock surrendered. Inside, the Contessa, Albicocco, Bestard-Belou and their companions lay panting on the ground.

'My pretties are poisoned by smoke!' wailed Signorina Tiozzo, rushing to administer teaspoons of water. 'Look at them! Dying!'

'Yer not wrong, missis,' croaked Albicocco. 'Get our pulses took. Yew'll find none.'

'Make wid da wreaths and weeping,' gasped Bestard-Belou. 'Reckon it's all up with us.'

The Contessa lay with her kittens around her. She opened her green eyes and uttered one piteous miaow.

Professor Marìn put one arm around Signorina Tiozzo and started picking up limp cats with the other. He said, 'I'm taking you all to my house. I've put an Incombustible Incantation around it to fend off the flames. And I've got a portable one to get us there.'

'What about the prisoners in the jails?' Ambrogio said. 'Who's saving them?'

'I'll send the cats to pick the locks when they are revived,' said Professor Marìn. 'They can run faster than fire when they are fit.'

Albicocco opened one eye. 'We'll want feeding up proper before you send us to work.'

'In my present state I couldn't eat a butterfly,' moaned Bestard.

The professor turned to Talina and Ambrogio. 'You two – to Quintavalle! The fire will not have reached it yet. I hope.'

'*How* can we get there?' asked Talina, looking out of the window at the flames leaping from roof to roof.

'You'll have to "liberate" a boat, I'm afraid. Surely the most impudent girl in Venice can untie someone's rope?'

'Of course!'

'Race the wind! You'll get there before the fire if you turn off the Grand Canal at the Rio di San Giovanni Crisostomo. Make for the Rio di San Giovanni in Laterano and wiggle your way south and east down the small canals till you cross the pools of the Arsenale.'

Ambrogio nodded. 'And then out and right to San Pietro.'

'And when we get to Quintavalle?' asked Talina.

'First, put the grannies into boats. And then make for the tower. It is where you'll find Grignan. You must stop whatever murderous plans he has. Delay him, distract him. Just for a short while, I hope. I'll join you as soon as the cats and humans are safe.'

Professor Marìn began to chant his Incombustible Incantation. He, Tassini, Mademoiselle Chouette and Signorina Tiozzo wove a clear path through the flames, their silhouettes – black against the glowing blue of fire – distorted by the armfuls of cats they carried.

Ambrogio and Talina ran to the Grand Canal and selected a sleek little *topo*. Each seized an oar, splashing themselves thoroughly in their enthusiasm. The coldness of the water was a relief amid the painful heat. They set off at a great pace, dodging falling debris and showers of sparks, and the tongues of flame that kept thrusting out at them from the alleys that they passed.

'Why,' panted Ambrogio, 'is the professor so sure that Grignan's at the tower?'

'Grignan will want to kill my Guardian,' Talina realized. 'He knows too much and he's no use to the Ravageurs now.'

'Do you care, Talina?' asked Ambrogio.

'I don't care about Great Uncle Uberto at all. But I care to make sure we frustrate every single plan that Grignan might have. And I need to know everything my Guardian knows. Everything. He might even know where my parents are. I wouldn't put it past him.'

They fell silent, saving their breath to row as fast as they could along the Rio di San Giovanni Crisostomo, which soon turned into the Rio di Santa Marina.

After San Giovanni in Laterano, they took the Rio del Fonte and then the Rio di San Francesco. A thick slice of flaming roof beam dropped into the boat as they rowed into the Corte delle Gorne. The boat filled with smoke and the terrifying roar of fire. Again, the greedy little faces of the flames struck Talina with fear – they seemed to be pounding with angry fists at the wooden planks that stood between her and the water.

'Got to kick it out!' choked Ambrogio. But Talina's bootlaces had caught fire, and she was fully occupied in stopping an angry slit-eyed flame from catching hold of her petticoats. So Ambrogio wrenched off his jacket, plunged it into the water and then used it to scoop the burning beam from the boat.

'I'll stamp on the rest of the embers,' coughed Talina, 'if you keep rowing. We're nearly at the old Arsenale now.'

She wriggled out of her jacket, immersed it in the canal and dabbed the wooden deck wherever the embers glowed. But it was too late. The fire had scorched through the wooden planks in several places, and water was pooling in the bottom of the boat.

'I'm sorry,' said Talina. 'I just couldn't get all the sparks. But I can swim – can you?'

'If I have to. Perhaps the boat will last long enough.'

The boat slid through the Canal delle Seghe. Halfway across the larger pool of the new Arsenale, it began to sink beneath them, while merciless flames were taking hold of the prow.

'It's burn or drown,' cried Talina. 'At least the water doesn't *want* to kill us.'

'Abandon ship!' Ambrogio took Talina's hand. 'Let's jump. And head towards the Porta Nuova. We just need to turn right there ... we're nearly at Quintavalle.'

The cold water took their breath away, closing briefly over their heads.

Ambrogio proved the stronger swimmer. He took the lead. As they turned into the Canal di San Pietro, Talina faltered, gripped by an agonizing stitch in her side. Treading water, she could see Ambrogio splashing a few metres ahead of her, in the shadow of a great brick wall.

'Ambrogio, wait!' she called, but her voice was swallowed by the sound of bricks being wrenched from their grouting, as painful as teeth being pulled from a mouth. The great wall beside them swayed. A whole row of bricks rippled off the top, landing in the water like cannon balls. One of them grazed Talina's shoulder as it spun into the canal.

'I think we need to go back and come the long way round,' called Talina.

'No,' Ambrogio panted, treading water. 'Come on. We just need to swim faster. We can get to the end of this stretch before the wall comes down.'

'It's far too risky,' Talina argued.

An immense shadow flickered over them, blocking out the sky.

Ambrogio and Talina turned fearful faces upwards, just

in time to see the bell-tower of San Pietro – in flames – crashing down towards them. Twin crests of water burst from beneath the tower as it hit the canal.

'Talina!' screamed Ambrogio. He could see nothing – the entire channel was blocked by the vast corpse of the fallen tower. Nor could he hear anything but the roaring flames at the uprooted base of the half-submerged tower and the distant howling of Ravageurs. He swam up to the tower and tried to scramble over it. He could not raise himself out of the water. 'Talina!' he cried desperately. 'Say something!'

Only a crackle of burning roof-beam answered him.

'It must have taken her,' gulped Ambrogio. 'The tower must have taken her down. She was exactly where it fell. I should never have let her get so far behind.'

He howled as loud as a Ravageur.

'Whatever is going on at the tower, Talina would want me to find out. And then I'll save the grannies. That's what Talina would want.'

The salt water whipped the tears from his eyes as fast as he could weep them.

The water cackled like witches in his wake. The poles in the lagoon seemed to be clasped in prayer.

Behind him, the city continued to burn. Plumes of pale blue smoke rose over it, lightening the black sky.

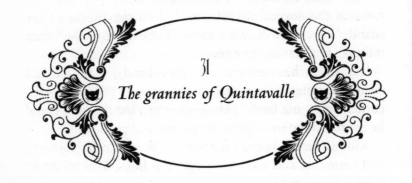

31

The grannies of Quintavalle

the Canal di San Pietro, a minute later

TALINA CAME BACK to consciousness to find herself floating on her back in the water, with an aching bump on her forehead.

'Ambrogio!' she cried. There was no answer except the roiling of the waves and the snarl of the flames on either side.

'He must be under the tower,' she wept. 'He was ahead of me, just where it fell. I should never have let him go ahead on his own. He was too brave.'

For a few minutes she abandoned herself to grief, her tears mixing with the water of the canal.

Then she thought, 'The grannies! If the fire has reached San Pietro, they'll be in danger already.'

She rolled onto her belly and began to swim as fast as she could towards the stump of the church tower. Pulling herself ashore, she ran to the first house and battered on the door. 'Nonna! Nonna!' she screamed.

Blinking and coughing, Nonna Angelina emerged. 'Talina, child, what is it?'

'You must all make for the boats!' Talina pointed back towards the dozens of craft moored on the fringes of the island. 'This fire will sweep through the orchards and then it'll take Quintavalle in minutes.'

'I'll start the message off immediately,' said Nonna Angelina, fastening a scarf around her neck. It'll be over the garden gates in a flash.' She disappeared indoors and could be heard calling over her fence to the next granny.

'Good!' called Talina after her – 'Oh, and bring lanterns and your cats and your knitting. And buns. You might be gone a good while!'

Talina saw the first lick of flame catch the granny underwear drying on the clothes line above her. The sound of grannies calling to one another rose above the roar of the fire. And in minutes a stream of old ladies was to be seen pouring out of Nonna Angelina's door, clutching their cats, their knitting, lanterns and paper bags full of buns. They made their way in a single file to the boats and climbed in, with a surprising amount of dexterity.

Talina ran to and fro anxiously, making sure that everyone was accounted for. When she was satisfied, she shouted, 'Weigh anchors and lift ropes! Let the boats float to the lagoon on the tide. I'll send help as soon as I can.'

'We cannot lift the anchors,' Nonna Meghin panted, struggling with the ropes.

Talina shouted, 'Anyone thought to bring a knife?'

'I've got scissors,' said one of the grannies, burrowing into her knitting bag.

'That'll have to do.' Talina held them above her head as she leapt into the water. As she snipped its rope, she gave each boat a sharp kick towards open water.

When the last was floating free, she set off in a steady

dogpaddle towards the tower. She dared not walk. There were too many beams falling. Too many apple trees lurching down. Too much granny underwear flaming above the street. Too many roof tiles crashing onto the pavement.

As Talina waved goodbye to the last granny, the loss of Ambrogio hit her hard. She sobbed into the dark-green water. All the time she'd been saving grannies, she'd almost managed not to think about Ambrogio, or her parents, at all.

32

Dead dogs and dreadful doings

the tower at Quintavalle,
deeper into the night of May 17th, 1867

JUST AS AMBROGIO swam his last sad and solitary strokes to the Guardian's tower, he saw a haze of sparrows hovering over a mound of foam approaching the drawbridge from the opposite direction.

'Ambrogio!' screamed Talina.

At the same moment, each of them cried out in confusion and delight, 'But I thought you were dead!'

Then Ambrogio turned away and cast his eyes down.

Paddling up to the guardrail, panting, Talina explained, 'I couldn't get past the fallen bell-tower, so I just turned around and swam in the opposite direction – you know that the island of Quintavalle is olive-shaped. So after I got the grannies into boats, when I still couldn't get past the tower that fell, well, I just turned around and came the other way ... Oh Ambrogio, it's all right, you *can* look at me sometimes. Actually—'

A howl above them silenced her.

They clambered up the bank, across the drawbridge and hurtled through the gaping doorway. The door had been torn off its hinges. Bitter wisps of sage-leaf smoke hung in the air. The tower was brightly lit, yet there was no sign or sound of life apart from the faint hissing of the gas-lamps.

'Gierch-it!' shouted Talina, tripping over the dead dog.

His throat had been gouged by five long scratches.

'Your pet dog?' Ambrogio asked sympathetically.

'Hardly a pet. He'd have eaten me and Drusilla on toast, given half a chance. But even I wouldn't wish *this* on him.'

Gierch-it must have been taken by surprise. Apart from the pool of blood around him, the kitchen was tidy.

'Too tidy,' thought Talina. 'Where are my cookbooks? Where are my special cake tins? Where's *A Wizard in the Kitchen – Thirty Second Banquets*? Where's *Magical Means on a Budget*?'

A curl of suspicion began to wind itself around her spine.

'Look!' pointed Ambrogio. Bloodied paw prints led to the stairs, and then up them. Everywhere on the next floor were signs of a violent struggle. Pictures hung awry. Bookshelves were toppled. Murano glass lamps lay in glittering fragments.

'The other dogs put up a fight,' said Talina.

'Let's hope they won,' said Ambrogio without much hope in his voice. 'Ooops!'

He tripped over a broken jar and slid across the floor, colliding with a table leg. Licking a finger, he asked, 'Golosi's Mostarda?'

'You know who loves *that*?'

'I can guess.'

On the next floor, they found Futfallo, or what was left of him. Talina turned away. Then she caught sight of the empty walls.

'This is my bedroom,' Talina told Ambrogio. 'I mean, it used to be.'

224

Her voice was as hollow as the loneliness she used to feel in that room.

'But there's nothing here. Nothing. Just dust.' Ambrogio was quiet with shock.

Talina herself could barely recognize it. The circular room had been stripped of everything that had been hers.

'He didn't waste any time disposing of me and my things!'

She wrenched open the wardrobe door. A solitary empty coat hanger jangled inside.

'All my books, my bed, my hanging pencils, my pictures, my clothes ... all gone. The photograph of my parents. All gone. It is as if I never lived here. As if I never lived. I suppose he thought I was dead, and good riddance. But this – this is *cruel*,' Talina whispered. 'There is no place in the whole world that belongs to me. And now it is as if he's obliterated even the memory of me. It *is* as if I am dead,' she sniffed. 'I suppose it makes him happy to think I am.'

Ambrogio put his hand on her shoulder. 'You're more alive than six ordinary people,' he ventured.

She shook him off. 'Don't be nice to me. Even non-existent girls can cry, you know,' she said gruffly. 'Let's go up again. The next floor is the parlour. And the floor after that is the best parlour. After that, I don't know. I've never been allowed that high.'

'Whooah!' The colour drained from Ambrogio's face as he rounded the last stair and came face to face with the Child-Mauling Thingy looming above him, mouldy sawdust spilling out of its gruesome stitching.

Talina said, 'And now we know who the Thingy really is! Or was. Meet Verpillion Grignanne – what's left of him! Do you know, I think he does really look quite a lot like Grignan, stuffed and mounted. Something about the eyes.'

'Verpillion's well dead – so what's that moaning?' asked Ambrogio.

In the best parlour, Razin was rolling on the floor in agony, his eyes white and his muzzle foamy. A smouldering sage-leaf cigar lay beside him.

'Rabies!' cried Talina. 'Grignan's infected him.'

Razin had just enough strength to lunge before collapsing in pain.

'That cigar is warm,' said Ambrogio. 'Grignan's still here. Come on!'

The Guardian's private apartments commenced on the next floor. Backed up against the wall, Talina stopped dead. This was the last thing she expected to see. All around the walls were pictures of two laughing babies. Not only were there old brown daguerreotypes and sketches, but also locks of hair, little knitted booties, and two old-fashioned blue bonnets.

'Not such a child-hater after all?' Ambrogio was puzzled.

'Perhaps,' suggested Talina darkly, 'these poor little babies are the victims in his next book. Without me to model for him, he's having to resort to pictures of real children and the poor things' toys.'

Above the fireplace hung an oil painting of a beautiful young woman with shining, happy eyes. She wore the fashion of fifty or sixty years earlier – a dress gathered high above the waist and bonnetless hair dressed in a simple classical style.

'Who's she?' asked Ambrogio.

'Another victim, no doubt. Just a bit older than usual.'

The next floor contained a narrow iron bed, and a lamp on a stool. Their feet raised puffs of dust from the threadbare rug. The remains of a frugal meal lay on a tray by the window. Great Uncle Uberto, it seemed, dined on bread and water.

'This must be where your Guardian sleeps. It's rather empty, isn't it? He lives like a prisoner. Rather pathetic, if you ask me,' said Ambrogio.

Talina was about to reply when a low growl and a weak moan could be heard from the floor above.

'We have to keep going,' said Talina, hesitating with her hand on the banister.

Another growl, and a heart-rending scream.

'Now!' Holding hands, they raced up together.

At the top of the tower, they found Grignan at the Guardian's throat.

A seething mixture of feelings flooded into Talina's heart, none of them pleasant, and each worse than the last. Uberto Flangini was her enemy. There was no doubt about that. He had tried to kill her and Drusilla. He had betrayed her parents. But he was a human being, and a Venetian. And the Ravageur Lord was a creature fuelled by baddened magic and set on murder.

She felt the prickle of whiskers under her nose and the reds dissolved from her vision again. Her heartbeat quickened.

'Talina, you look ...' quavered Ambrogio.

'The least I can do is make a distraction,' she thought. 'I cannot watch the Ravageur tear out a man's throat.'

Talina screamed at the top of her voice, 'STOP!'

Grignan stopped growling and turned his massive head. With a sinking heart, Talina faced the Ravageur Lord himself.

'Just what do you think you are doing?' she asked in her most fierce and impudent voice.

'What,' snarled Grignan, 'does it look like, not-quite-girl?' He turned back to Great Uncle Uberto.

'Talina!' gulped Ambrogio. 'You are starting to look like *him*!'

'Speak for yourself!' she retorted.

Ambrogio glanced over to a mirror on the mantelpiece and howled at the sight of his new opal eyes, black pointed ears and lolling red tongue.

'Where have all the colours gone?' he cried.

'They'll come back, when you're calm again,' Talina

growled, 'but we need to stay as angry as possible now. If we are Ravageurs, partly anyway, then we can fight like Ravageurs!' She pointed her hairy hand at Grignan.

Grignan turned again, holding the unconscious Guardian by the neck. Now he tossed the man aside and prepared to attack. Then he took a second look, and hesitated.

Ambrogio and Talina crouched on the floor, manes of fur growing at a furious pace from their sloping backs, their teeth lengthening and sharpening in their mouths. Grignan, outnumbered, took a step back towards the stairs – and screamed in surprise and pain.

His back leg was clamped in the jaws of Razin, who had not been completely destroyed, but had roused himself to take revenge on the creature who had murdered his companions and might well have killed his master.

Faced with three of them, Grignan made a sudden jump over the banister and tore down the stairs, with Razin in valiant pursuit.

'Your great uncle!' cried Ambrogio. 'Is he dead?'

'No.' The voice was feeble but audible. There was fear in his eyes as they flickered over the Ravageurish features of the children.

'Where are my parents?' screamed Talina.

'I cannot . . .' The Guardian buried his head in his hands. 'I cannot tell you because Grignan never gave me the information. I begged.'

'I'd like to have seen that,' growled Talina.

Uberto Flangini was bleeding profusely from the jagged wound to his neck. But with one final throat-tearing effort, he rasped, 'Get Signorina Tiozzo.'

Then his head fell limp against the floorboards.

'*The cat woman?*' Talina yelled at her unconscious Guardian. 'Why? You *hate* cats!'

33
The Guardian's secret

the top of the tower, dawn of May 18th, 1867,
Saint Giovanni's Day

'YOU STAY WITH him,' Ambrogio said, ripping a strip
off the curtain to staunch the blood. 'Hold this down
on the wound, hard. I'll go to fetch Signorina Tiozzo,
and Professor Marìn. And some Venetian Treacle.'

'You'll have to swim ...'

'No – look!' Ambrogio pointed to the view below them.
The fire had already burned everything that was flammable.
Quintavalle's one street was clear of blue flames.

'And Ambrogio, can you find someone to fetch the
grannies? They'll have floated to Malamocco by now. Their
lanterns will be running out of oil.' She glanced up at the
sky, 'Though dawn is on its way.'

She pictured the grannies bobbing tranquilly in their
boats, busily clicking away at their knitting with their cats
on their laps.

'First fisherman I see,' promised Ambrogio, racing down
the stairs.

Watching him from the window, Talina saw that Ambrogio had already returned to completely human form by the time he reached the bottom of the tower. He galloped down the street, palely lit by the first rays of the sun, and was lost to her view at the first corner.

She turned back to the injured man, and resumed the pressure on his wound with a hand that was restored to its normal, hairless dimensions. The bleeding was less, but his agony was evidently greater now that the shock was wearing off. Talina knew she should feel pity for her Guardian, but Ravageurish brutality still seemed to have the upper hand in her nature, even though she was rapidly returning to human form. She snarled, 'You could always regard this pain as research! You can pretend it is a *child* wounded like this. You can call it *How Uberto got his Jugular Unplugged*'.

The Guardian flinched. He stared at her in fear and astonishment.

She demanded – shocked at herself even as she uttered the words – 'Surprised to see me? I guess you hoped that I was dead – like all the other children you write about. Tell me, why do you hate children so much? Do you suppose it's because you never had any of your own?'

Tears trickled from his eyes. He moaned. He tried to shake his head, but the movement caused a fresh flow of blood.

The Guardian's tears roused Talina's fury more than his pathetic silence. 'Tears!' she raged. 'Tears! For yourself. You, who never spared any compassion for anyone else! Certainly not for those children destroyed in your books. And what about me? You never showed a drop of pity for what had happened to me, or a speck of interest in what had happened to my parents! But then again – of course, you knew what had happened to them all along.'

Her outburst only made her angrier. Talina treated him to the full extent of her 'beastly tongue', all of which the

Guardian accepted in passive silence, though tears continued to course down his pale cheeks. 'Where are my parents! Tell me! Or you *deserve* to die!' she screamed at him.

Talina burst into tears.

She had suddenly seen herself, as if she was a stranger witnessing this scene.

She fumbled in her pinafore for her Thaumaturgic Handkerchief, which was already twitching.

Then she saw that Professor Marìn had been right about the little square of fabric. She had no sooner thought, 'I must wipe those tears from his eyes', than the handkerchief flew out of her hand and gently dabbed the streaming face of her Guardian. Then it wrung itself out, and hovered up to her face to dry her own.

Downstairs at the drawbridge, the cat woman's face was tortured. She trembled as she stood on the rickety bridge that led to the tower. A canopy of sparrows wheeled overhead. Albicocco and Bestard-Belou wound their tails around her legs sympathetically. But Brolo and Drusilla nudged her sternly towards the door.

'Hurry up,' urged Brolo. 'The wind is wheeling round and all. Those flames are getting up again. What a downer!'

'I never thought I would come back here again,' Signorina Tiozzo whispered. 'This place is the scene of a terrible crime. The poor, poor man.'

'*What?*' demanded Ambrogio. 'You're *sorry* for Talina's Great Uncle Uberto? The writer who kills children in his books? Who betrayed his own kin? Who hates cats, I may add.'

'Well, *of course* he hates cats,' mumbled Signorina Tiozzo mysteriously.

'Huh?' snorted Albicocco. 'There's no "of course"s about it when it comes to cat-hating.'

But Signorina Tiozzo clamped her mouth shut, threw her shoulders back and walked through the door.

Professor Marìn and Giuseppe Tassini each took one of her arms and helped her up the steps. They passed the dead dogs in silence, broken only by Signorina Tiozzo's sobs when she reached the office with the pictures of the babies.

'My little darlings!' she wept. Albicocco and Bestard-Belou nudged her knees hard.

When they reached the room where the Guardian lay bleeding, it was to find a Talina silent with her eyes downcast, her hand carefully but gently fixed on the wound to his throat.

'Signor Flangini!' gasped Signorina Tiozzo. 'What have they done to you?'

'You two know each other?' said Talina amazed.

'This is the cat hater?' asked Albicocco. 'Not much left of him. He'll be going out with the ebb tide, that one. Call the florist. Where's me black gloves? Shame there's no good eatin' on him, but.'

'Stringy and skinny both, anyways,' said Bestard-Belou.

Ambrogio swiftly applied a handful of Venetian Treacle to the Guardian's bloodied neck. The blood evaporated, the torn flesh hissed and fizzled and invisibly reknitted itself in a moment. It was as if he had never been hurt, physically at least. But his pallor was still deathly and his face distorted with misery. He opened bloodshot, tear-swollen eyes, and whispered, 'Tell them about my wife, Signorina Tiozzo. About my babies. For I cannot bear to say their names.'

'You had a *wife*?' cried Talina.

Signorina Tiozzo began at the beginning.

'That would be,' she sobbed, 'when Uberto Flangini's young bride, whom he adored, died in childbirth.

'Twins, she had, two boys. The babies both survived, though they were weak. I thought Signor Flangini's heart would mayhap be broken by the loss of his darling Annamaria. But it wasn't like that at all. It might have been broken, but his heart was still full of love for their babies. How he worshipped them! He was forever cradling them in his arms, kissing the tops of their little heads. But then he got a fever and he resolved to keep himself away from the babies until he was better. He could not bear to lose the boys too. So he took to his bed, which was damp with his fever, and the weight dropped off him in lumps. Mayhap—'

'What about the babies?' asked Talina.

'He'd no choice but to entrust them to a flighty young maid from Chioggia, just fifteen years old. She had been a favourite of his wife, without ever deserving to be, I'll add. You know the kind of girl – always doing three things at once, all of them badly. That's how it happened.

'It was a dreadfully parched, cruel summer that year. There was no relief from the heat anywhere, particularly not in the kitchen, where the maid was obliged to look after the babies while she did all her other chores at once. In those days the kitchen was up on the eighth floor of the tower. There was a huge cooking range in there, and a stone sink ... and baskets of vegetables. And always a nice warm jam sponge – that was the one thing the maid was good at – jam sponge. And – that day only – the cat was there too. The family cat was a very mischievous creature – a terror to the poor sparrows – and he was usually banned from the kitchen. But on that day, everything was in a muddle, with the master sick, and the maid was trying to cook a lovely pot-roast with gravy to tempt his appetite ... and the babies were fretting for their dead mother. They didn't understand, poor angels. Their little faces were red with crying and they were burning up with the heat.

'So the maid put the babies in a basket, and tied a rope to it and lowered it down into the water, just enough to fill the basket with cool—'

'She did *what?*' Ambrogio cried.

Professor Marìn interrupted, 'Ah, but where she came from, Chioggia, sometimes mothers would do this, if their babies were very, very hot. The water was cleaner in those days, and it gave the babies a bit of relief.'

'Yes, sir. So the maid dipped the little babies in the water two or three times. Such perfect little boys,' wept Signorina Tiozzo, 'identical twins with dear little strawberry birthmarks on their wrists. Even those birthmarks were identical! They loved to dangle in the water, kicking their fat little legs and grabbing at the fish. The maid always said that they would grow up to be fishermen one day. That's when she thought they *would* grow up.' Signorina Tiozzo's tears flowed again. 'If only . . .'

'Please continue,' urged Talina. 'Don't leave those poor babies in the water!'

'*Magari!* If only she hadn't. The maid was just about to pull the basket back up to the kitchen when she saw what the cat was up to. He had knocked the lid off the stockpot and had got his head deep inside, taking a great, long drink of your great uncle Uberto's pot-roast gravy.'

'Had dat stoopid maid forgot to feed da pore cat?' asked Albicocco defensively.

Talina quickly asked the same question in somewhat more polite Humantongue.

'Mayhap. It was *so* hot and she was in *such* a muddle that day. Well, truth be told, she was the kind to be in a muddle pretty much most days. The cat, of course, was just following

234

his nature. When the muddled maid saw that cat doing its greedy business, she was so distressed that she forgot what she was doing. She accidentally let go of the rope, and the babies' basket dropped back into the canal with the rope following it straight down into the water.'

'No!' whistled Talina and Ambrogio simultaneously.

'*Non*!' cried Mademoiselle Chouette.

'Dear God, no!' whispered Professor Marìn.

'I'll be guttersniped!' said Albicocco.

'Of course the maid gave one of those screams that starts in your toes and throws your whole soul out of your body. Then she ran right down the stairs, still screaming. But by the time she'd climbed down the one hundred and ninety-eight steps, the basket and the babies had disappeared. She called for boatmen, for fishermen, for gondoliers. But there was no one about who could help – you know what it's like on Quintavalle. There were just widowed grannies, and what could *they* do but wring their poor old wrinkly hands? Eventually the maid found a fisherman who scrambled around looking for the babies, running his nets through the water. It was no use. The tide was fierce that day and it was on its way out. The poor mites had gone.'

'So what did she do?'

'What *could* she do? The poor brainless girl had killed two innocent children by her negligence. She went to face the music. She walked slowly back up the one hundred ninety-eight steps, sobbing all the way. Your great uncle Uberto was sleeping heavily: his fever had drained him of energy. She did not dare go and rouse him. But soon enough he rang for her, and she had to go and tell him what had happened.'

'I don't imagine 'e spared that maid a tongue-lash,' said Mademoiselle Chouette.

'In fact, he was silent as the tomb as she told him the

whole story. Of course, *she* was gibbering like a monkey, hardly making sense. But he understood, when she got to the part about dunking the babies in the water ... and the cat. Then he just made a quiet noise, like a draught in a chimney, and he ran to the kitchen, the maid following closely behind him.

'The cat, poor creature, had his muzzle in the gravy again. The pot and the roast were nearly licked clean. Signor Flangini grabbed the cat and flung him out of the window.'

'Bloody murder, that's wot dat was!' snarled Bestard-Belou.

'True. But at least now we know why Talina's great uncle Uberto hates cats,' noted Drusilla.

'Loik poison ivy,' said Albicocco.

'But why does he hate children?' wondered Talina.

'I always supposed,' said Signorina Tiozzo, 'he took to writing those horrible stories after his babies died. He was so bitter. His heart was riddled with it. Mayhap his feeling was ... if he could not have a living child, then he didn't want anyone else to have one either.'

Talina flinched with guilt. Her barbed remark to the Guardian, when he lay in agony, had been too close to the truth – and yet so far from it.

'How do you know all of this, Signorina Tiozzo?' asked Professor Marìn, gently.

'I think I know,' said Talina and Ambrogio in one voice.

'Yes, I was that maid. And after that, I knew I was not fit to look after human babies any more. And I had to make it up to that cat your Guardian killed – it was not the cat's fault that I was inattentive. The cat was only following his nature.'

'She speak da troof,' concurred Bestard-Belou.

'So you've devoted your life to looking after us.' Drusilla licked Signorina Tiozzo's hand.

'Well, that's that sorted now, and all very fine and good. But can you smell burning?' interrupted Albicocco.

'Burning and roasting, both,' said Bestard-Belou.

34

Burning and roasting, both

in the flaming tower, every moment hotter and bluer

THE LOWER PART of the tower had caught fire. Blue flames were sidling up the stairs, gnawing at the banisters, raising violent blue fists against the furniture.

'The tower's built of brick and stone, isn't it?' asked Ambrogio. 'We're safe for a while?'

'But every ceiling is made of wood,' Talina replied. 'Anyway, this *blue* fire seems to eat even stone. It seems to hate Venice as much as the Ravageurs do.'

The Guardian's face was still milk-white with his tragic memories. But now he sat up, explaining in deep shuddering breaths, 'Blue fire – this is what the Ravageurs always threatened. That fire has been made by baddened magic. It cannot be doused by water. Only the Ravageurs know how to extinguish it.'

'You seem to know plenty of things about your friends, the Ravageurs,' said Talina sarcastically. Her moment of sympathy was over. 'How odd that you do not know how to put out their blue fire. Odd to the point of suspicious, perhaps?'

'He's still a cat-hater and all,' said Albicocco with slitted eyes.

'The Ravageurs are not my friends,' the old man pleaded. 'I hate them as much as you do. I *had* to do business with them. I could not afford to have Venice know what my ancestor had done, tricking the Ravageurs out of their land. The Venetians would have run me out of town ... I needed time to find a solution, that was all.'

'So you sacrificed my parents?' cried Talina, 'to save your precious reputation?'

'No, I just agreed to let them be taken away somewhere so that I could find a way to solve the problem with the Ravageurs quietly, without publicity. Grignan promised me that your mother and father would not be killed.'

'But he did not promise you that they would not be left to starve on an island, did he?' Talina asked sternly. 'An island of maggots!'

'Every day that has passed, I have wondered about where they were, and how they fared.'

'Wondering didn't cost you anything. If they are dead, their deaths are on your conscience.'

'Talina!' reproved Professor Marìn. 'Don't you think your great uncle is suffering enough?'

But Uberto Flangini stopped the professor. 'I deserve all the impudence in the world from this girl. Oh Talina ... I am sorry. I have cost you so much.'

Down in the stairwell, the flames roared and another gas-lamp exploded.

'I'll have to go to the Ravageurs again,' said Talina slowly, 'and bargain with them, or trick them into telling me how to quench those blue flames before the gunpowder in the chimneys catches alight. Maybe the lady Ravageurs know?

They'd help me if they could. So ... how am I to get a message to Altopone and the rower-rats?'

'Aren't we forgetting something? Isn't there something here in the tower that Grignan wants?' Tassini reminded them. 'Something we could bargain with, or pretend to.'

He turned to the Guardian. 'Way back in AD 421 – according to Grignan – your ancestor had a vision of Venice as the richest city in the world. Grignan insists that old Flangini concealed this vision from Verpillion Grignanne during his negotiations to buy the city. Do you have some evidence of it? Isn't that why Grignan came here – to get it? Isn't that why he was torturing you? Trying to make you tell him where it was?'

Uberto Flangini's lips moved but no words came out.

'Whatever it is, we shouldn't be using it to bribe Grignan!' said Ambrogio. 'It should be brought as evidence at the Chamber of Conversation.'

'Even if it damages our case?' asked Talina. 'Even if it ruins it?'

'The Chamber of Conversation? The case is being held there?' The Guardian's voice was broken, his thin face suffused with shame. 'Evidence? You must mean this thing.'

He walked unsteadily to his desk and lifted a small marble figurine. Under it glittered a paperweight made of rock crystal. 'Look inside,' he said.

Everyone gathered around the fist-sized object. A perfect miniature Venice was somehow carved inside it, complete with magnificent churches and bell-towers, merchant galleons and fairytale palaces.

'No wonder Grignan wants this!' said Tassini. 'No doubt he was planning to present it as absolute proof of his case.'

The Guardian said, 'But you don't understand. My ancestor had no second sight. No vision of a magnificent Venice. It was *not* my ancestor who found this thing. My own father picked it up when he was digging in the mud to set a mooring for the boat. It's less than a hundred years old. A tourist souvenir! Grignan saw it on my desk when he first came here to see me. I remember that he was fascinated by it. I knew his interest could mean no good. That's why I hid it inside the figurine. And that's why I refused to tell him where it was, even with his teeth in my throat. I shall take it to the Chamber of Conversation and give a full explanation.'

'But we need bait for Grignan!' said Talina.

'Those Have-a-Voices are so easily distracted! If Grignan turns up with this beautiful glittering thing in his paw, he'll be sure to convince them,' said Ambrogio. 'Is it worth the risk of letting it fall into his hands?'

'I have to try,' said Talina. 'The paperweight will be my passport into his presence. The only thing I don't know is ... how do I make Grignan tell me the last thing he wants me to know – the way to put out the blue fire?'

Professor Marìn pulled a purple vial from his trousers and tucked it into Talina's pinafore pocket, alongside her Thaumaturgic Handkerchief. 'It's my **Liquid Lullaby Infusion to induce Drowsiness and Stimulate Truth-Telling**. I brought some with me, in case we needed to subdue Grignan. And I've added some **Intensified Essence of Cruelly Killed Meat**, which I hate to handle, but it will make it quite irresistible to any Ravageur. And here's another little bottle of **Dandelion & Daisy** for the mange. Wouldn't hurt to see if we can at least cure that. The poor creatures—'

But his voice was lost in a sound of beating wings and the urgent twittering of a thousand terrified sparrows.

Restaurant swept into the tower. With his beak, he grabbed the paperweight, while his talons closed around Talina's shoulders.

'That wasn't the kind of bait we meant!' screamed Ambrogio. 'Give her back!'

Talina felt herself lifted into the air, and dragged out of the window.

One minute later, there was nothing but lagoon beneath her feet, a dizzying distance below. She could no longer feel the warmth of Ambrogio's eyes on her. She felt strangely cold without it. She was buffeted by the wind that blurred the sea into innumerable tiny wrinkles below. The silhouette of Venice's remaining bell-towers dwindled in the distance.

Ever since she'd first heard Restaurant's name, Talina had somehow known, deep inside, that she would end up at his Stake House. She had no doubt of the bird's plans for her.

It was not a priority in Restaurant's bird brain to deliver her safely into Grignan's presence. His mission was the paperweight, not a living girl. No, Restaurant would drop her from a height, so she would die on one of the bloodstained palings outside the Stake House. Then he would dine on her at his leisure, while the flies joined the feast, saving his favourite parts till last.

'Perhaps Grignan has ordered my execution?' she wondered miserably. 'He said he would.'

Should she keep clinging to Restaurant's claws, helping him carry her to a drawn-out, grisly end? Or should she wriggle loose and plummet into the sea? She imagined herself down where the eels nestled and the plate-sized crabs scuttled. Then she realized, 'No, the impact will rip me in half as I hit the water.'

Death would at least be quick and clean that way.

Talina did not know how many hours they'd been flying, but finally they were circling over the Ravageurs' island. Restaurant cawed with delight as he caught sight of his Stake House.

But what Restaurant did not realize was the effect on Talina of spending all those hours in his close company. She was nothing if not fearfully angry. This great stinking bird had stolen the evidence, kidnapped her, planned to kill her cruelly, devour her slowly. What was worse, the vulture was crawling with fleas, many of whom had been delighted at the prospect of fresh meat – just as much as their current host – though *they* were happy to feed on it while it was still alive. They had swarmed down Restaurant's feathery thighs and onto Talina's head, neck and shoulders, which they proceeded to bite with great appetite. Enclosed in the bird's talons, she was not even able to scratch.

Somewhere over the island of Sant'Erasmo, Talina had started to sprout lopsided grey feathers from her shoulders. Her neck lengthened. Her bones felt lighter, as if hollowed out. And her feet had been transformed into two perfectly formed clusters of three claws. By the time they flew over the island of San Francesco del Deserto, she had a respectable pair of wings. She flapped them, feeling their power. She looked up anxiously, but Restaurant flew on, oblivious, his eyes fixed on the horizon. Only her hands and her face remained human as, many hours later, they approached the Ravageurs' island, surrounded by its grey doughnut of fog.

Now Talina saw the Stake House. The red-tipped poles pointed to the sky like sharpened pencils. Looking down on them, Talina felt shooting pains around her heart, as if rehearsing her own impalement. Restaurant made one swift pass over his territory, evidently to select his stake before moving in for the kill.

As they crested out to sea again, preparing for the final swoop, the bird quivered with pleasure. The quivering motion dislodged the smooth rock crystal paperweight in his beak. Glittering like a falling star, it dropped through the rays of the setting sun straight into the dark-blue sea.

'Lost for ever!' Talina taunted Restaurant. 'The one article that Grignan *might* have used to prove his case – even if he was going to lie about its age. You're going to be in dreadful trouble, bird-face! I wouldn't want to be in your beak for anything.'

And with that she shook her shoulders free from the claw that had opened with shock and flew with the wings her anger had grown, right down to the island and straight into the Ravageur palace. She hoped her wings would last long enough to get her to the kitchen, so that she could add the **Liquid Lullaby** to the Ravageurs' next meal, which would surely take place quite soon, given that they must eat constantly or die.

Unfortunately, her pleasure at parting company from Restaurant meant that she started shedding feathers almost immediately. Her wings were already quite threadbare by the time she entered the portals of the palace. She tried to glide down the stairs but careered out of control, colliding with the door of the Great Hall, and landing in an undignified and painful crumple at the edge of the altar, where Grignan sat brooding over a skull of Devilsdrench.

Grignan rose and stood over her, his hot breath on her face.

'My changeable friend!' he sneered. 'I see Restaurant ruffled your feathers! Now where's my evidence?'

'It wasn't yours. And it wasn't evidence of your case,' she said, struggling to her feet. 'It was just another lie. And now it's at the bottom of the sea.'

She kicked aside the pile of feathers that had fallen from her, and crossed her arms resolutely over the bib of her pinafore, where she was relieved to feel that the bottles of **Liquid Lullaby** and **Dandelion & Daisy** were still intact, wrapped in the Thaumaturgic Handkerchief.

She didn't see Grignan's paw coming, but she felt it send her spinning across the room.

When she awoke, the first thing she saw was Grignan's pale eye. He was crouching next to her, pinioning her in a corner of the Great Hall.

'Pleasant sleep? Your last. Restaurant says that you deliberately destroyed my evidence. Can you imagine how I plan to punish you?'

'Restaurant lied. He dropped it by accident. He's too cowardly to tell you the truth.'

Grignan blew sage-leaf cigar smoke straight into her eyes so that they stung and watered.

The Vizier entered the Great Hall, looking nervous. 'I hate to interrupt, Master, but this interrogation is taking some time, and our fellows are a little restless this evening. You know what happens if they do not eat! Yet they await your presence before they partake of Third Supper, naturally. And, sir, you are looking a little peckish yourself.'

A smell of meat wafted into the room, rich and perfumed with spices.

The first sheep were already waiting in the corridor when Talina, Grignan and the Vizier arrived at the *Sala del Sangue*.

'Sit there,' Grignan kicked Talina towards a chair, 'where I can keep an eye on you.'

Talina's Thaumaturgic Handkerchief twitched inside her pinafore and the bottle of **Liquid Lullaby** clinked gently against the **Dandelion & Daisy**.

'This isn't going to work,' she despaired. 'I'll never be able to sneak around the table and doctor the food. The **Lullaby** must be poured on the food *before* the sheep bring it in …'

The handkerchief, wrapped around the bottles, flew out

of her bib pocket like an arrow, up to the rough beams of the *Sala del Sangue*. It swooped through the darker areas, avoiding the glowing chandeliers.

'Yes!' thought Talina. 'Now go to the sheep corridor!'

The handkerchief bent itself in half, as if to say, 'Of course, my pleasure!'

'What was that?' called Frimousse. 'Did you see something white up in ze beams?'

'You're so 'ungry you're seeing things,' laughed Rouquin.

Out in the corridor, sconces burned with tallow candles, providing enough light to cast shadows. Talina watched the silhouette of the handkerchief twist the lids off the **Liquid Lullaby**, the **Essence** and the **Dandelion & Daisy**. She saw the drops falling onto the heaped platters on the sheep's backs as they waited for their orders.

'Service!' thundered Grignan.

Worried as ever, the sheep trotted into the dining room with trays on their backs. They looked particularly squeamish, understandably, about the *Carré d'Agneau persillé*, lamb ribs with garlic and parsley breadcrumbs, the *Soupe à la Reine*, with mutton and rosemary, in miniature buckets hooked over their ears.

The Ravageurs moaned with almost painful delight at the aroma of the food.

Talina guessed, 'It must be the **Intensified Essence of Cruelly Killed Meat**. That must be more luscious than anything they've ever smelt.'

'Wait for it!' roared Grignan. 'Medicine first!'

'Medicine!' thought Talina. 'If only they knew.'

But the black spoons were licked dry in a moment. Then the Ravageurs dragged the lamb ribs onto the tablecloths, tipping the *Soupe à la Reine* in splashes over the hunks of meat.

'Did I say "feed" yet?' growled Grignan.

The Ravageurs paused fearfully above the food, drooling into it.

Just as Talina was thinking, 'I cannot bear the suspense!' the Ravageur saliva started to fall in long columns into the *Soupe à la Reine*, which began to hiss and foam.

'Oi! Why should our drool make it bubble like zat?' asked Frimousse.

'What will it do to our insides?' demanded Croquemort.

'Stop! Don't touch it,' hissed Magisterulus. 'Look at that slick on the *Soupe à la Reine*! It's a dirty little human trick! The kitchen slaves are trying to poison us.'

'It's the girl!' shouted Grignan. He seized Talina by the scruff of the neck and forced her face into a bucket of soup. She clamped her lips shut but her nose filled up with the rich liquid, stinking of the **Intensified Essence of Cruelly Killed Meat**. She thought she would drown in it.

She felt the tips of his teeth through her dress as Grignan wrenched her out of the soup. 'That's the death warrant of every Venetian, floating in the food, right there, girl. If you've contrived something here, you'll own their deaths – they will all be on your head!'

'How could I have done anything?' spluttered Talina, *Soupe à la Reine* streaming from her nose. 'You've had me in your clutches ever since I arrived.'

'That's true. I own you. I own your life and death, now.'

'How wise, how true,' fawned the Vizier.

'Just another lie,' said Talina, without hesitation, for what had she to lose now? 'My parents own me. Because they love me.'

The strange thing was that she wasn't angry at all. In talking about her parents, Talina felt sweet and reasonable. Perhaps it was the likelihood of imminent death, but she also felt a strange sense of peace and rightness. There was no hair sprouting on her hands, no pressure on the neckline of her dress, even when Grignan drawled, 'Don't see them owning you now. Your mother? Do you see any mothers around here? Your father? Pffft. A here-and-gone man! No one's stopping me from doing this!' Grignan shook her until her teeth rattled. One of his fangs tore through her dress and embedded itself in her skin. A line of blood fell down her pinafore.

'There are all kinds of owning,' she managed with dignity, despite the pain. 'Just like there's more than one way of being a slave. You have custody of my body at this moment, it's true, but I still own my spirit.'

'That can be quenched,' raved the Ravageur Lord. 'Or eaten.'

'But even you cannot eat that part of me that was here, that defied you until the last minute,' Talina responded coolly. 'Just as you can't own or eat the world's loving memory of a city like Venice, even if she were burned to the ground. And you can't kill the fact that I am born and shall die a Venetian.'

A door slammed shut somewhere in the palace. A new and powerful waft of meaty steam rose from the food on the U-shaped table. Grignan's eyes suddenly glazed with greed. His grip slackened. Then he looked up and howled with anger at what he saw.

For some of the Ravageurs had been unable to resist the rich scent. Despite Magisterulus' warning, they had quietly tasted the food. Once they had ingested a morsel, they were powerless to stop eating. Their snouts burrowed deep into the meat.

Grignan's own jaws dropped onto a rib of lamb as if drawn there by a magnet. He shouldered two smaller Ravageurs out of their places. Suddenly he too was eating as if his life depended on it. There followed a savage spectacle of huge excesses of greed, and terrific lapses of manners, and rivalry over lamb ribs, that Talina – now wiping the soup out of her eyes, having been careful to swallow not a drop – would remember for the rest of her life with both triumph and repugnance. All through the night and into the early hours, the Ravageurs guzzled and snorted and chomped and burped. The sheep kept coming from the kitchen, their saddles laden with food onto which the Thaumaturgic Handkerchief had sprinkled the professor's concoctions.

'But why aren't they going to sleep?' wondered Talina. 'The handkerchief must have been too sparing with the **Liquid Lullaby**. Professor Marìn judged it for wolf or hyena portions, of course. The Ravageurs are so big they probably need a double dose.'

Grignan ate with more desperation and less refinement than anyone – tunnelling his way through hills of food, as if searching for something, the one savour or texture that would satisfy him.

After many hours of ceaseless feeding, the Ravageurs began to giggle and hiccough. They grew very sentimental, putting their paws around one another's shoulders between mouthfuls, and remembering old feasts, old friends and creatures bullied and creatures eaten with sauce. Grignan, his eyes distant, kept eating.

Finally, as dawn began to send rays of light down the stairwell, Talina had the courage to ask, 'By the way, Masters, how do you put out the blue fire in Venice? The city is ruined but it might be useful to save a few pastry shops and butchers for your pleasure.'

'Indeed! We should have thought of zat!' Croquemort clapped a paw over his mouth.

'Ravageur dribble's ze best way,' sniggered Rouquin. He lurched to his feet and spat at the blue fire around the portrait of old Uberto Flangini. The part where his saliva landed immediately sizzled, smoked and died down.

Talina thought, 'No wonder they are careful to spit only on the face!'

Frimousse slurred, 'Did you like ze mean leettle faces in ze blue flames, girl thing? Grignan made zem specially to frighten ze poor silly humans!'

Rouquin laughed, 'But we're 'ardly going to slobber on our own plans, are we?'

He glanced up nervously at Grignan. Seeing him oblivious, making short work of a kidney *en-croûte*, Rouquin refilled his own mouth with lark cutlets in cream sauce, crunching loudly on the bones.

'Ravageur dribble!' thought Talina. 'The female Ravageurs would help save Venice – they promised they would. But how do I get them there? It's impossible!'

She persisted, 'Rouquin, is Ravageur dribble the *only* thing that puts it out?'

'Well,' hiccoughed the Ravageur, 'zey do say zat Runic Rain can stop it.'

'Runic Rain?' asked Talina. 'Is that something that happens in Venice?'

'Not wizzout someone knows 'ow to make it,' laughed Rouquin, spitting out the lark bones.

'By the way,' ventured Talina, 'does anyone here know where Maggot Island is?'

'The poor orphaned girlie wants to know how to find the Isola di Butoléta ...' slurred Magisterulus. 'Aaah. How sweet! How these humans dote on their mothers and fathers! Shame, isn't it?'

That was the last thing he said, before his head fell on the stained leather tablecloth. One by one, the Ravageurs dropped where they sat, some resting their heads on ribs of lamb, others sliding to the floor and snuffling in puddles of spilt gravy. Grignan fell like a tree struck by lightning,

crashing to the floor so he landed on top of his unconscious
Vizier.

'No!' wailed Talina. 'I didn't find where the island is.'

Her shoulders tight with grief and frustration, she made
her way to the kitchen.

'Talina!' smiled Sargano Alicamoussa. 'You came back!
But why are you crying?'

He wiped her eyes gently with his apron while Talina
urged him, 'Gather everyone together, and come with me.'

'But the Ravageurs ... ?'

'Will be asleep for some time. I gave them some ...
medicine.'

Sargano Alicamoussa whistled, 'You poisoned them?'

'No, not exactly. Anyway, they're already ill with Furious
Rabies and mange.'

'Have you come to take us back to Venice?' asked the
adults and children crowded around Talina.

'I don't at this moment know exactly how, but I hope so.
You must prepare yourselves, though. I have to tell you that
the Ravageurs have set fire to the city. When I last saw
Venice, she was burning, in strange blue flames with faces
full of hate – flames that water cannot put out.'

'Oh!' the Venetians clutched their hearts and hugged one
another, tears pooling in the corners of their eyes.

'Come!' said Talina. 'At least we can try to escape.'

She led the humans and the cats out of the kitchen and
past the Stake House. At the first sight of it, they fell silent,
but they squealed as their heels sank into the sand made
spongy by blood that dripped from the stakes. A cloud of
flies swarmed around them so thickly that they could hear
the insects' wings clicking together. They were still trembling
when they reached the jetty on the island's shoreline, where
the waves nosed gently at the sand.

The Venetians, too long deprived of the sight of water,

stood silent with radiant joy for a moment. Then, blinking and grinning at the unaccustomed light, some waded right in. Others danced and sang. Children did somersaults, and two tall women rushed to free the cats in the gibbet-cages. There were tender reunions between cats and their human owners; and between cats and their own feline relatives.

The tortoiseshell cat Tigger-Maria was especially delighted to find a first cousin in one of the cages. She told Talina, 'We thought Luigi was lost for ever. It was a good day for us when you first took an interest in the case, girl.'

'I'm sorry,' Talina pointed to the horizon, 'the news isn't all good. Look. We have to find our way out through *that*.'

'No!' the humans shouted, gazing at the black fog that ringed the island. One boy crashed to the ground, mid-somersault.

'How do we even know Venice is out there?' cried Tigger-Maria.

'She is, I promise.'

'If she's not burnt to the ground, from what you told us,' said one man, 'with that blue fire which cannot be put out.'

'Not by water-pumps or human firemen, it's true,' mused Talina. 'But I know who could help us. We have to liberate the female Ravageurs. Anyway, we can't leave them here imprisoned and possibly starving. I don't know when the males will wake up.'

'We don't want *any* Ravageurs! No! No!' chorused the humans and the cats, their screams and miaows intertwining rather melodiously.

'And you said they have rabies!'

'No! The female Ravageurs have been just as much prisoners and slaves as you have,' Talina admonished them. 'Isolated too. So they could not contract Furious Rabies from their captors. They are *victims*, don't you understand? They have been treated like dirt, told they *are* dirt – and shut up in darkness. Just like you. Would you begrudge them their freedom?'

'Yes!' shouted one large man, his hands all wrinkled from washing up. 'We don't want to escape from the kitchen just to be eaten. Who cares if it's a male or a female Ravageur who eats us? They're all the same at core. Vile.'

'The females have been fed on sugar. They have never tasted meat,' Talina told them. 'And remember, you adults won't be able to see them anyway, so they won't be very frightening at all.'

'They just haven't had an opportunity to eat people. It's in their nature to kill and eat flesh.'

'Well,' Talina shouted right back. 'We may *need* the female Ravageurs in Venice. According to the Vizier, Ravageur dribble is one of the few things that will put out the blue fire they started.'

A short silence fell. A couple of children giggled. Gianni Nanon asked, 'What are the other things that stop blue fire?'

'There's only one. Runic Rain. Any of you got any Runic Rain, or know how to make it?'

More silence, broken only by a small girl sobbing and the waxy seaweed jostling around the legs of the jetty.

'And anyone got any ideas about how to get two hundred of us, and at least ten dozen cats, across a whole lagoon?' Talina pointed to the jetty. 'With just two gondolas and only twenty-four miniature oars? No? I thought not. Wait here, and behave yourselves until I come back! And have a good think.'

She stormed off towards the harem enclosures.

'Told you so. That Talina Molin always was the most impudent girl in Venice,' complained the washer-up. 'Known for it, she is.'

'What a flouncer!' muttered his wife, pointing at Talina's stiff retreating back.

A sweet salivant

outside the harem, the Ravageur island,
May 19th, 1867, Saint Ivo's Day

LIKE THE HUMANS before them, the female Ravageurs
blinked at the unaccustomed light. Talina had prised
open the lock to their enclosure with a fork and opened
the door, first dragging down a tapestry to cover the spikes
that edged the feeding trough.

The creatures' eyes sparkled with excitement as they took
their first steps into the world.

'It eez so beautiful!' breathed Bidet. 'Is zat what zey call
a . . . tree?'

Talina hugged her. 'Yes, it is.'

'Verr' naiss. I should like to meet anozzer one some time,'
smiled Bidet.

'There are lots of nice things for you to meet from now
on. First of all, some cats and some humans. Mind, be
very gentle with them, as they are absolutely terrified of
you.'

'Of *moi!*' laughed Bidet and all her sisters. 'As if anyone could be frightened of *us*! Pathetic and dim-witted as we are!'

'And ugly to die for!' added Ripopette.

Talina said, 'Remember what I told you – you are *not* to think of yourselves in that way. You are *marvellous*. Well, I think so.'

The female Ravageurs dipped their heads shyly at the sight of the humans, who stood sternly with their arms folded. The adults could hear but not see the Ravageurs. The children, who could both see and hear, were struck silent with fear. Clara Massaniello cried, 'They are *huge*! Look at those claws! Those teeth!'

'Be amicable!' urged Bidet, marshalling her girls behind her. 'Smile, look pleasing.'

The female Ravageurs approached the unseeing human adults with their fronts lowered, as if bowing. Their tails were raised and wagging. Bidet nuzzled Talina's knee affectionately. The children took a step backwards, dragging their parents with them. But Sargano Alicamoussa held out his hand to Ripopette, who licked it enthusiastically.

Then Sargano cried, 'Well, actually, they're just like great big friendly dogs, really.'

The washer-up said, 'So there's even *more* weight to drag to Venice.'

'But I 'ave an idea for you,' said Bidet. 'I understand, though it has not been tried, that our species is good at swimming. We 'ave ze webs between our toes, lak ze ducks!'

Talina clapped her hands as Bidet flexed a huge paw up towards the light, revealing translucent flaps of fur-less flesh between her claws.

'*Et moi*! *Et moi*!' chorused the other female Ravageurs, holding up their paws.

'*À l'eau, mes enfants*!' Bidet urged.

A dozen of the female Ravageurs splashed into the azure

water, howling and giggling. They soon settled into a brisk and powerful dogpaddle. Sargano Alicamoussa plunged into the water to join them. Ripopette squatted down in the water so he could climb on her back. He whooped for joy as she carried him through the waves.

'*Voilà!* I reckon,' said Bidet, 'that each of us grown females could carry three humans to Venice. And even the girl cubs could handle one human and a cat.'

'Yes!' cried Talina and all the children, watching Sargano enjoying himself with more than a touch of envy.

But the faces of the adult Venetians contorted with fear and disbelief.

'So, Talina Molin,' said the washer-up, 'you want us to climb on the backs of monsters we can't see and swim off into a deep black fog?'

'Come on!' Talina urged, splashing over to Bidet, and climbing on her back. Bidet's fur was as rough as it looked – it felt rather like sitting in a dense field of arrows.

'Very comfortable up here!' she lied to the humans, who were slowly making their way through the shallows, led by the children, towards the waiting Ravageur females. The adults' faces bore a curious mixture of fear and excitement as they reached out blindly and felt the wet fur under their fingers.

Talina's head lolled backwards, and she woke with a start. Anxiously, she scanned the horizon. Venice seemed as far away as ever.

The female Ravageurs had taken on the fog with courage. It was Bidet's idea to form a chain like a pendulum, and to let the head of the line – led by Bique and Ripopette – swing backwards and forwards until the opening was finally found.

Then it took many hours of patient dogpaddle to cross the lagoon.

All day, they had swum through the shining water, and yet the horizon seemed further than ever. The waves rolled around them like marbles in a jar, jostling the tired, waterlogged humans. But the female Ravageurs never faltered.

'Are you not exhausted?' Talina asked Bidet.

'We shall never tire of freedom, and light, and high skies above us,' replied Bidet. 'Even ze water is beautiful.'

'I thought Ravageurs need to eat constantly, or they die?' worried Talina.

'Not us! The males 'ave frequently forgot to feed us. We are used to doing wizzout food.'

'But I'd *kill* for a *soufflé au chocolat* right now,' muttered Gonzesse, causing the young woman on her back to faint.

'How do we even know we're going the right way?' demanded the washer-up. 'There's no sign of Venice.'

'Except the smoke,' said Talina, pointing to the blue-tinged smudge on the distant horizon.

Still they swam, the paws of the lady Ravageurs dipping tirelessly in and out of the water. But cold, hunger and fear gnawed at the spirits of the Venetians.

'We're never going to make it,' muttered the washer-up. Children started whining; women wept quietly.

Talina shouted, 'Anyone got a birthday coming up?'

A small boy sniffed, 'Yes, me. Tomorrow.'

'If there is a tomorrow,' said the washer-up, at which the boy muffled a sob.

'What's your name?' Talina asked the boy.

'Riccardo.'

'Right. We're all going to sing Happy Birthday to Riccardo!' insisted Talina. And so they did. Then Sargano

Alicamoussa admitted to a birthday the next week. So they sang again.

It was as evening fell that a Ravageur cub cried excitedly, 'I see land!'

It was one of the outer islands of the lagoon. From there, they threaded their way back via Malamocco, Poveglia, Santo Spirito, San Clemente and San Servolo.

But their first sight of Venice herself was far from joyful. The blue flames rose higher and higher, as if a volcano made of copper sulphate was erupting under the city.

The washer-up murmured, 'That would put fear in the hearts of grown men, that would.'

'The trouble is, we had no grown men in Venice, did we?' his wife answered bitterly. 'If we'd had grown men to defend us, we'd never have got into this mess. If *anyone* in Venice had had any gumption – apart from this poor brave child Talina – we would never have come to this. Admit it, Giovanni – we were just like everyone else until we got took. We pretended there were no such things as Ravageurs. Only she would admit there was something wrong. And only she saw the difference between wanting something to stop, and doing something to stop it.'

Another woman took up where she left off. 'We blamed those poor cake-cursed fellows in Rovigo for our troubles.'

A fourth voice added sorrowfully, 'We called all this on ourselves. This is our judgement.'

Bidet asked Talina, 'What are zey saying, the humans? Why do zey cry so? They are going home.'

'They are being grown-up,' said Talina. 'They are judging themselves. They are admitting that they were wrong. And now they are looking at what they have lost.' She pointed to the blazing horizon.

'Ah, but zey 'ave not lost it yet! We shall 'elp zem!' cried Bique.

'In more ways than you might guess,' said Talina. 'I need to explain something to you. It's about your dribble . . .'

After Talina's explanation, the female Ravageurs paddled in thoughtful silence for half an hour.

Finally, Talina reassured them, 'Professor Marìn will cook up something that will help you.'

As they drew closer to Venice, the tops of the bell-towers became visible through the smoke. Most had been decapitated. And the chimneys of the houses and palaces glowed like blue roses with torches inside them. As they approached, a series of chimneys in Castello burst into flames, as if in a relay race. Then another set of chimneys exploded on the other side of town.

'Why?' screamed Gianni Nanon. 'How?'

'It's the gunpowder,' said Talina, 'that Grignan kept pouring down them.'

'We won't have anything left to go home to,' wept the Venetians.

They made landfall at the Riva degli Schiavoni, empty of humans but swirling with black ashes. The grown-up Venetians leapt off the backs of the Ravageurs, without so much as a 'thank you' or a 'goodbye'.

Sargano Alicamoussa shouted at them, 'And what do you say to these lovely creatures who have helped you so much?'

The humans turned, shamefaced, and trudged back to the shore. Grudging thanks were given from under downcast eyelids.

'You're very welcome, I'm sure,' said Bidet graciously.

The children hugged the Ravageurs and accepted friendly licks with pleasure.

The humans then dispersed to find what was left of their

homes, making their way, coughing, through the smoke and flames that continually drew back, only to puff themselves up like dragons again. Talina herded her tribe of female Ravageurs to Professor Marìn's lurching house. It was quicker to ride on Bidet's back as they pounded over burning bridges and across smouldering squares. All the way to Santa Croce, the blue fire clawed at Talina's ankles, strained to leap into her hair and sent shattered glass from burst window panes whistling into her path.

At his crooked door, Talina greeted the professor with a breathless 'Can you make Runic Rain? And where's Ambrogio?'

'Talina! You are safe ... ! Come in, come in! We'll soon have you dry. Why are you looking behind you? Have you been followed?'

'You won't be able to see them, but I have about two hundred female Ravageurs with me. Yes, I'm quite sure they're not rabid. They want to help. Now ... Runic Rain! Can you make it?

'Of course I can, nothing simpler. Though it's not a quick process. Why do you ask?'

'It puts out blue fire,' she panted. 'The Ravageurs told me, when they were under the influence of the Liquid Lullaby. And where's Ambrogio?'

'Well, well, well, I never knew that. But I am afraid it takes three hours to conjure even a light fall of Runic Rain. The town is burning fast. Even my own Incombustible Incantation needs renewing every half-hour. We need to do something in the meantime.'

'I was coming to that. Professor, can you concoct something that will make these lady Ravageurs ... well, slobber? A lot! You see, Ravageur dribble is the best cure for blue fire.'

'A salivant? Of course. A mixture of liquid extract of

cinnamon, fenugreek, black pepper, ginger. And we'll need some jaborandi leaves from Brazil, which, fortunately, I have in quantity . . .'

'What will it taste like? 'orribly bitter?' worried Bidet.

Talina urged, 'Professor, can you make it very sweet? They'll drink it faster and dribble more if it's delicious.'

'Well, yes, I can add plentiful honey and sugar. We must make great quantities – they will need to drink continuously, both to manufacture the saliva and to keep themselves hydrated. Fortunately, everyone's here to help.'

He called over his shoulder, 'Amazingly good news! Emilie! Ambrogio! Giuseppe!'

'Hello, Talina,' said Ambrogio quietly, looking past her left shoulder. 'Pleased to meet you, ladies!' he smiled at the female Ravageurs.

Soon the humans were busy adding honey, sugar and pomegranate syrup to barrels of cinnamon, fenugreek, black pepper and ginger juice that the female Ravageurs were downing as fast as they could before leaping out into the streets and spreading themselves to every quarter of the city.

For hours, deep into the smoke-choked night, they ran, squatted, dribbled, drank some more salivant from the hot-water bottles strapped to their backs, and dribbled some more. Everywhere they went, the blue flames subsided in savage hisses, their faces and fists vicious to the last. In Cannaregio, Santa Croce, Dorsoduro, Castello, female Ravageurs patiently plodded and irrigated the angry flames with steady streams of drool. At Quintavalle, the grannies surprised everyone by being able to see the lady Ravageurs, and by feeling no fear of them at all.

'We're all old girls together,' chuckled Nonna Meghin.

An immediate bond was formed over cups (and buckets) of sweet tea. The cubs even made friends with the grannies' cats. But outside the grannies' houses, the blue flames continued to raise their jagged heads and thrusting arms. The female Ravageurs were exhausted, their jaws aching, their heads throbbing.

'We can do no more,' cried Bidet, fainting.

And it was then that a subtle, soft rain began to fall. At first no one exactly noticed it. All they felt was a sense of well-being and happiness.

Mademoiselle Chouette, smothering the spitting flames at the schoolhouse with sacks soaked in dribble, thought, 'But it is my favourite jasmine perfume from Houbigant in the Faubourg Saint-Honoré, Paris!'

She spun around to see who might be wearing it. But all she saw was Signorina Tatti, valiantly beating the nasty tongues of fire climbing the steps to the library door. The librarian's face, however, suddenly lit up with a smile. Gripped by some private, happy memory, she paused in her work, not noticing that the flames were slinking back into the ground.

Nearby, in the *stazione* of the Carabinieri, Bestard-Belou stopped worrying the lock to the cell that held six choking prisoners. The cat rolled about on the dirty floor, purring as raindrops leaked through the ceiling.

'Carry me out and bury me decent! Two-day-old liver 'n' kidney,' he said. 'Can't you smell it?'

Albicocco, at the next cell door, answered, 'Your nose is cracked. I can snoof somefing all right. It's chicken hearts, fresh and warm.'

Talina, dampening a sack with a flask of dribble in the prison yard, wiped the tears from her cheeks. 'Why am I crying like this?' she sobbed. The scent of her mother's freshly ironed linen apron wafted around her. She ran out into the middle of the square, trying to absorb as much of the delicious rain as she could into her already-drenched clothes. Almost without realizing it, and for pure joy, she started dancing the *Fascinating Stoat*.

'I don't understand,' she wept happily as she rippled and wove around the yard.

'Doan fret yer gizzard so, not-quite-girlie,' urged Bestard-Belou, skirting between her dancing feet. 'There's good wet and bad wet. I reckon this is the best wet I ever smelt.'

It was Ambrogio, his nose full of the scent of courtroom beeswax, who first realized, 'This is Professor Marìn's Runic Rain. And it's putting out the fires for us!'

'You can look at me if you like, now, Ambrogio,' thought Talina, still caught up in her best-ever rendition of the *Fascinating Stoat*.

But Ambrogio was gazing up at the sky with the adoring look he used to reserve for Talina.

With gentle determination, the rain took possession of the city as fast as the fire had done before it. Once the rain had gently smothered all the flames, it began to restore the buildings back to their former state, if not better. By morning, collapsed roofs were growing back as if they were living things. Fallen walls were reconstructed, brick by brick. Even the towers folded themselves up like fans and sprang back into shape. The glass reappeared in shattered windows. The rain painted the walls and the window-sills and sculpted the heads of the statues that Grignan had cursed to facelessness. Eyes, noses and mouths reappeared, some with the hint of a grateful smile. The painted poles – their blackened stubs poking out of the water like the remains of a forest devastated by fire – grew back to their full height and glory, with their little acorns freshly gilded at the top. The Runic Rain sent a breeze to pick up the bones of the saints from the Company of Christ and the Good Death. It gently carried them back to their smashed reliquaries in their own churches.

Then the rain mended the glass of those containers, giving it a final polish too.

'It's like a great big mother cat's tongue, licking her kittens!' observed Drusilla. They were all back at Professor Marìn's house, including Bidet and her harem, for whom Talina had just baked six trays of her excellent cherry macaroons.

'Venice is 'erself again,' said Mademoiselle Chouette, '*la plus belle ville.*'

'We haven't yet put right what is wrong,' Talina objected. 'So Grignan still wants to destroy the city, and thinks he has a right to do so.'

'Do you think the Chamber of Conversation is still in session?' asked Ambrogio longingly.

'It never stops while there is injustice in Venice,' said Tassini. 'That is what is recorded in the Archives.'

'Come, ladies,' said Talina to the female Ravageurs. 'Let us see if we can end this, once and for all. Bidet, please can you express a clear desire to enter the Chamber?'

'I clearly desire . . .' Bidet began.

'Is there a confectioner's on the way?' interrupted Ripopette.

Bique added, 'Somewhere with Maraschino Cherry Ices, perhaps? Oh, oh, oh, what's happening? Everything's going crumbly . . .'

'And misty!' cried Ripopette.

36
A final ruling

the Chamber of Conversation, May 20th, 1867,
Saint Bernardino's Day

THE SMALL DOGE, the Good Witches and the Righteous Wraiths sat just where they had been when Grignan escaped. Albeit damp and singed, all had smiles fixed on their faces – full of pleasant memories inspired by the Runic Rain that continued to fall lightly inside the Chamber. A wet layer of black ash lay over all the documents, the desks, the chairs and the heads of the mounted animals.

But the Chamber had resumed its deliberations.

The female Ravageurs, slightly sticky with ice-cream, quietly filled the empty seats, and sat attentively, each with a cub on her lap. Tassini escorted a round-eyed Signorina Tiozzo to a bench. The professor settled the French mistress on a nearby chair before resuming his own seat next to the small Doge.

'We've come back,' said Ambrogio, 'for a final ruling in the case of Venice versus the Ravageurs. We have brought with us additional witnesses,' he pointed to the females and their babies.

'In fact, Counsel, the judgement has just become a matter of the utmost simplicity,' said the Doge. 'Certain new facts have come to light in the last few hours.'

'Not to us,' said Talina. 'Oh my!'

She had glimpsed her Great Uncle Uberto in the dock. He looked pale and weak, but he stood upright with a determined expression on his face.

The Doge rapped his broken gavel reprovingly. 'Let us recap on proceedings in your absence. We have examined the witness Flangini and have come to our conclusions. Yes, the mud-heaps of Luprio were sold by the Ravageurs to the humans. But the sale was unjust. So we rule that the Ravageurs shall repay the exact price paid by the human Flangini. The mud under the city will again belong to the Ravageurs. But *the city they* build will belong to the Venetians again.'

Professor Marìn leant over to shake hands with Uberto Flangini. 'Well done, sir.'

Talina's Guardian hung his head, and murmured, 'Don't thank me; no one is as guilty in this matter as me and my family.'

'No doubt!' shouted Talina. 'Now someone must tell us, *where are my parents?*'

'Child,' said the small Doge, 'this is something that no one yet knows. I have despatched butterflies and flying cats to survey the outer reaches of the lagoon. Meanwhile, there are matters to arrange. Young Counsel, please instruct your colleagues.'

Then Ambrogio explained to the female Ravageurs, 'So we need you to give the Venetians Five Sheep, a Mink Jelly, a Dozen Fancy Pastries, Six Brass Buttons and Ten Fire-buckets of Human Wine.'

'Absolutely,' said Bidet.

Bique keened, 'You can 'ave the Mink Jelly *et tout* wiz our compliments. But must we really give back the Fancy Pastries?'

The Doge held up a warning finger, and Bidet hastily said, 'Of course, we agree with joy.' She glared at Bique, who lowered her head and her tail with shame.

Now the Doge inclined his small chin towards Bidet. 'Are you empowered to make this agreement on behalf of your species, madam?'

'The female Ravageurs are more populous than the males, and we also carry with us, and represent, the young of the coming generation.' Bidet held up her twin cubs. 'And we 'ave showed our good will already, by putting out the fire.'

Talina cried, 'But Grignan will never agree. He is still at war with Venice!'

The Doge replied, 'Then he is an outlaw, and shall be pursued and stopped. Now, madam,' he turned back to Bidet, 'what do you say?'

Bidet smiled, 'We say, "Of course!". All we ask is an island of our own, with a flower garden and a sugar-beet plantation. So we can make our own crystallized violets and rose-petal jelly.'

Talina frowned and opened her mouth. Bidet added hastily, 'And peas, and rice and tomatoes, too. We shall be learning to cook *risi e bisi*, rice and peas, properly, you know, with one *chicco* of *riso* for every *biso*.'

Talina explained, 'The grannies of Quintavalle have offered to teach them to cook proper healthy food for themselves. It is all agreed. In exchange for having their gardens dug each autumn.'

'Turns out we're excellent at digging holes.' Bidet showed her paws.

'Then it shall be done,' pronounced the small Doge. 'The

267

relevant goods are to be deposited with the Chamber by tomorrow. And the stolen *batteries de cuisine* are to be returned to the Venetian bakeries, every single knife and spatula.'

'But,' said Talina, 'we don't quite know what is meant by—'

'While you are at it, sir, dispensing judgements and all,' Ambrogio interrupted boldly, 'do you think you could lift the Cake Curse from Rovigo? So that their sponges rise and their cream-pies don't curdle? Then they won't need to be Pastry-Bandits any more. If they ever were.'

The Doge turned wearily to a particularly mischievous-looking witch.

'You've had your fun with that rather tedious prank, Griseldina, I think? Six centuries of fun, I believe. Just for one small ducking in a pond! Remember, you are supposed to be a *Good* Witch. Off you go and disenchant the ovens in Rovigo, dear.'

The witch pouted, mounted her singed broomstick and whistled up her black cat, who took his position on the brush with great dignity.

'It shall be done,' ordered the Doge, with a twitch of a smile at his lips, 'between midnight and cockcrow.'

'Yes, yes, I'm on my way,' snapped Griseldina moodily. 'I'll even give them my recipe for Ensorcelled Butter Buns. They'll be flocking in from Chioggia and Padova to buy *those*.'

Griseldina departed in a shower of wet black ash.

'Excuse me,' asked Talina, 'but can you tell us what Human Wine is, Your Honour? How can the lady Ravageurs pay it back if we don't know what it is?'

'I believe,' intoned the Doge, 'that we may trace this confusion back to some scribal errors in the original inscription. These things happen when the stonemason fails to concentrate, you know. For example, I believe that the '"Mink Jelly"' was in fact '*Milk* Jelly' – far more palatable.'

'Yes please!' called Ripopette. '*Love* milk jelly.'

'Well, bless my stars!' rejoiced a mink.

The Doge continued, 'And in the same way, the words following on from "Mink Jelly" should read "Human Whine" – with an "h" – not "Human Wine".'

Silence fell on the Chamber.

'I'm sorry,' said Talina, pacing to and fro in her frustration. 'But we're not really any the wiser.'

Ambrogio guessed, 'Could it mean "whine"' as in "tears"? Grignan's ancestor wanted ten buckets of human tears!'

'Tears,' observed a Penitent Hag, 'are an excellent sauce for revenge.'

'But where?' asked Ambrogio. 'Where would old Flangini have got ten buckets full of them?'

'If he was anything like his descendant, my Guardian, I suppose he could have locked children up with his storybooks and given them a bucket to cry into. You'd soon get ten bucketfuls that way,' suggested Talina. She looked at Ambrogio, hoping that he would agree. But Ambrogio was gazing at Great Uncle Uberto.

The Guardian flinched in the dock, but he was staring over her shoulder towards the back of the Chamber.

'What about tears of happiness?' asked an unfamiliar male voice, a pleasant low one with an accent from the islands.

'Happy tears flow twice as fast,' agreed another warm voice, strikingly similar to the first.

A smell of fresh fish wafted into the Chamber.

37

Strawberry birthmarks

a few moments later

UNTIL THAT MOMENT, no one had noticed the two identical middle-aged men arrive at the back of the glass room. At their side were two thin Venetians whose faces shone with eager hope.

Talina, still pacing up and down, had not noticed them. Signorina Tiozzo, caressing the eight cats piled on her lap, had not noticed them either.

Ambrogio, scribbling copious notes in an exercise book, did not notice them.

Emilie Chouette, staring tenderly at Professor Marìn, did not notice them.

But Professor Marìn, briefly removing his own gaze from hers, now cried out, 'Marco! Lucia! You're safe!'

And then Talina was in their arms. And Marco Molin was saying, over and over again, 'Our little kitten! We have you back!'

The presiding Doge tolerated a certain amount of hugging and crying – at least one bucketful – and kissing, before he said, 'The Chamber of Conversation will now hear an explanation of these new developments. The two fishy gentlemen at the back of the room will approach the bench and explain their appearance here.'

Shyly, the two men shuffled through the room, pausing to shake Marco Molin's hand heartily.

'Thank you,' Talina's father mouthed at them.

'Well?' demanded the small Doge.

It tumbled out in fits and starts as the twin brothers interrupted each other frequently. But the story that emerged was this: only that very morning, the two fishermen had been digging for bait at their secret source – 'Maggot Island – none of the other fishermen know about it!' – when they heard faint cries from a cave quite freshly sealed up with rocks. They'd dug out the rock, and released the captives.

'This poor lady and gent had survived by licking the damp walls and eating little green shoots they'd grown from the seeds in the seed cake – who'd believe it? But they would talk of nothing but getting back to Venice and finding their daughter who must be with some evil old chap who goes by the name of Uberto Flangini and hangs his hat at some strange tower over on the edge of Quintavalle.'

The other fisherman concluded, 'And then this here Marco Molin, who is keeper of Ancient Manuscripts and suchlike, and knows a thing or two, well, he insisted that this here Chamber of Conversation must be in session, and that we must state a desire to be here ... then suddenly—'

'Here we are!'

'And you, sir!' the first fisherman threatened the Guardian, who cowered in the dock. 'We've heard what you did. You betrayed your own kin! You are nearly guilty of a terrible crime. What if these good people had died? Look how thin they are! Like maggots themselves! Seen more fat on a butcher's knife! And what of their tiny helpless little daughter?'

'Not so tiny,' protested Talina.

'Or helpless,' smiled Ambrogio.

Talina felt hotly happy to hear him say so. She just wished he would look at her when he said it.

The brothers advanced on the Guardian, their fists raised.

Signorina Tiozzo rose to her feet, swaying slightly. The mounted animal heads chattered, chirped and barked with alarm.

Then Signorina Tiozzo cried out, 'Those strawberry marks on your wrists ... are they *birthmarks*?'

'Where were you born, and when, and who were your parents, gentlemen?' demanded the Doge. 'Account for yourselves before the Chamber.'

'Now there's a thing. Until very recently we would have told you that we were born on the island of Pescatoria,' answered one of the men. 'That's certainly where we grew up. As for our birth, we are told that it was nearly sixty years ago.'

His brother's face was wrinkled with anxiety. 'But we didn't know the whole truth. Sixty years ago, we have just discovered, we were adopted as infants. Our parents had been unable to have children of their own. So they took us in, and grew us up. They never told a soul about how they got us – they pretended that we were orphaned nephews from the mainland.'

His brother took up the tale. 'But, when our mother died, I found a letter from her in the little strongbox she kept in her room. She asked us to forgive her for keeping the secret all those years. The letter explained how she found us floating in a basket on the hottest day of the summer at the fullest ebb of the tide.'

'In a basket?' gabbled Signorina Tiozzo. 'A basket?'

The Doge spoke, 'Professor Marìn, will you quickly recount the story of Uberto Flangini and his two lost babies.'

As Professor Marìn's measured tones told the story of the maid and the greedy cat, the two brothers began to tremble. Then they began to weep. One of them implored, 'Anyone got any Manitoba Gargling Oil? I believe I'm going to faint.'

The professor concluded, 'I believe that if you do the arithmetic . . .'

'We are doing the arithmetic.'

'Then we must deduce that those lost babies who floated away . . .'

'Were us,' sobbed the fishermen.

'*Are* us, Papà!' They wiped their eyes and beamed at Uberto Flangini.

'Such a happy conclusion!' the Doge smiled.

'But what about Grignan?' cried Talina. 'What about his plans to destroy Venice? He will never give them up.'

'The outlaw Grignan shall be hunted down by the keenest-eyed of our creatures,' said the Doge. 'Owls shall search for him by night. By day, he shall be hunted by the hawks and the falcons. Even on the sea, he shall not be safe, for the calamari shall be on his trail. Meanwhile, the Chamber shall continue its deliberations on his sentencing – deliberations to which all living humans are extraneous. You shall return to your safe place and wait.'

'Wait?' wailed Talina in agony.

38

The Ravageur Lord's bargain

the crooked house at Santa Croce, May 20th–27th, 1867,
Saint Agostino's Day

TALINA'S PARENTS HAD moved into the professor's house – the Guardian had, it turned out, sold the lease on the little house in the Calle del Teatro. Now it stood bolted and empty, though the sills of the oval windows and the entrance hall were piled up with letters, Lucia Molin mentioned wonderingly, addressed to a 'Principessa Paulina Pessel'. And so Talina had finally told her parents about her work for the Manitoba Gargling Oil Company.

'Though I haven't had much time,' she added, 'for literary productions in the last few weeks.'

Now Talina's parents were cosily installed in Professor Marin's light-filled airy attic, among a thousand distinguished manuscripts of the professor's, so Marco Molin felt quite at home.

Or as cosy and at home as anyone could feel, with the knowledge that Grignan might strike at any moment.

Grignan tormented them with silence. Days of it.

Days in which the professor worked in miserable fits and wretched starts on his latest volume of magic, and Tassini scribbled down the events of the last few weeks for a new book of his own, frequently consulting his volumes on Furious Rabies and mange-mites.

Every so often a whir came from Mademoiselle Chouette's room – but it was just the French mistress listlessly turning the wheel of her sewing machine. Otherwise the house was melancholy and silent.

Talina had experience of silence too. It was like when she sent off a wonderful story to an editor and did not receive so much as a 'thank you'.

But this time she was not angry. There wasn't a whisper of a flounce in her now. As the third week of May turned into the fourth and the fourth slumped into the next, Talina quite forgot to be impudent. She had no spirit for it.

She was deeply, deeply worried.

Late one afternoon, someone beat lightly at the door of the crooked house in Santa Croce. But when Talina flung it open (perhaps a little too violently, she would realize later), there was nobody there.

'Hello?' she called. 'Has someone got news for us at last?'

The street was empty. Disappointed, Talina closed the door and returned to the cheerless little tea party that was taking place in the kitchen.

'Must have been the wind,' she told the tense faces. 'Oh, there it is again!'

But again there was nothing.

It was only the third time that Talina thought to look in the little pane of glass in the top of the door.

And there she saw the somewhat flattened face of an unhappy winged cat – one of the attendants from the Chamber of Conversation.

'My wing got stuck in the knocker,' the cat complained. 'Now I am deaf and mad from being slammed against the wall all those times. I suppose you want me to remember the very important message I brought you? Well, you're going to have to wait till I stop seeing stars.'

'Wait' was not the word that Talina or her friends, now crowding around the door, were able to digest easily. But soothed with stroking, mollified with milk, and flattered with grovelling apologies, the cat eventually remembered what she'd come to say.

'You are summoned to the Chamber of Conversation. The Ravageur Lord has been found and now faces the Chamber. One of the owls had the clever idea of checking on the glassblowers of Murano. Sure enough, Grignan was holding hostage the Master of Salviati's glasswork, trying to force him to make a new fake "vision" in glass. Aaah!'

Something slender and silver flashed through the window.

The cat fell to the ground, a fork impaled in its wing.

While Talina gently extracted the fork, and the professor applied Sanitary Spider Web to the wound, everyone else ran to the window. The screams of humans and animals pierced the air.

Hundreds of forks and knifes pelted through the streets, followed by hurtling pots, baking trays and mixing bowls.

'That's Grignan returning the *batteries de cuisine* to the bakeries he stole them from!' said Ambrogio. 'So he really must be in custody. The Chamber must have ordered him to do that.'

'Meanwhile, he's still battering as many Venetians as he can.' Tassini shook his fist at the sky.

Professor Marìn rushed to the shelves for his stock of Venetian Treacle.

'The Chamber will wait on us a short time, while we attend to the wounded,' he said, distributing bottles.

Grignan stood defiantly on his back legs, rattling at the bars of a newly constructed cage, this one reinforced with silver wires threaded through the slats. The witches were chanting a Retention Spell.

'To contain his spirit, too, this time,' Professor Marìn explained. 'They're regretting not doing that the first time.'

The Doge pronounced, 'We shall hear the prisoner's words at least.'

'They are these,' snarled Grignan. 'If I am to renounce my claim on Venice, I want three human babies and a recipe book every year.'

'Your savagery and effrontery astonish the Chamber,' gasped the Doge.

Below them in the city, the bells of San Giacometo struck two o'clock.

Talina suddenly swayed in her chair. Her breath snagged in her chest. She rose unsteadily to her feet and gasped, 'You are mad, Grignan! What court in the world would give you children to cook and eat?'

'You are not looking in the best of health, Ratfood, are you?' taunted Grignan, winking at her as if they shared some kind of secret. 'In your *weakened state*, your imagination runs away with you. We do not plan to eat them. Our tastes are more refined. No, they are to work in our kitchens.'

At the words '*weakened state*', Professor Marìn glanced sharply at Talina. She steadied herself and took a deep breath.

Ambrogio raged, 'As slaves? Always slaves. Even your own kind are your slaves. You *deliberately* spread the mange and Furious Rabies among your Ravageurs to make them savage, didn't you? To make them hurt and menace other creatures!'

'What if I did?' drawled Grignan, rolling over on his back playfully, and licking the tip of his tail.

'It's not a game!' shouted Ambrogio. 'Show respect to this court!'

Talina wanted to put a warning hand on Ambrogio's arm – already swelling visibly and sprouting black hairs. She wanted to say, 'Keep your temper, Ambrogio. Don't turn Ravageur!' But her own hand burned with pins and needles, and felt too heavy to lift.

'The defendant confesses to a crime against his own species. Record this detail,' the Doge ordered the court clerk, a solemn badger. He turned to the professor. 'The most ancient charter of the Chamber holds that Venetians cannot be enslaved, not for any reason. It would be eminently improper to agree to such a thing.'

The Ravageur Lord insisted, 'I reject your piffling judgement. Paying back the dishonest price – that's not enough retribution, not by a long way. The deal is still dirty. The humans must pay for what they did to my race.'

The Doge said quietly, 'In such a case, there can be no resolution that is stainless or perfect. We have found the least worst way to settle it. The Chamber shall now commence the sentencing of the defendant for his acts of terror against Venice, and to prevent him from menacing the innocent in future.'

Talina sagged down into her seat, green spots forming in front of her eyes.

'What on earth,' she wondered desperately, 'is happening to me?'

278

The Ravageur Lord stood up on his back legs again. 'Well?' he shouted. 'What pathetic punishments have you dreamt up for me, you cowards?'

'Grignan, for your demerits, you deserve to be shaved, hanged on a common gallows, and then burnt, with your ashes strewn to the wind,' pronounced the Doge.

Grignan's sneer wobbled, but no words came out of his mouth.

'Yes, that's what he deserves, and worse!' screamed a squirrel. 'The Devil's busy diggin' his grave right now.'

'Silence!' called the Doge. 'I have not finished.'

The mounted heads drew in a collective breath.

'But the opinion of this Chamber is that violence begets violence. But shame begets reform. We do not wish to murder you, Grignan, but we want to show your fellow beasts that you are not a worthy leader. So you shall live, but you shall be shaved.'

A rabbit chittered, 'He gave his friends the mange – of *course* Grignan should have his own hair cut off!'

'He should get a willow-wand whipping while they're about it,' mumbled a witch, 'treating his own womenfolk like that!'

'*Shaved!*' Grignan screamed at last.

Then the Ravageur Lord lamented not in words but in long, rhythmic howls. The fact that his life was spared appeared to be no consolation at all. The Penitent Hags cried too, tears of compassion.

'We know what it is to have done wrong,' one cried. 'Desperate sad, it is, oooh!'

The Doge rapped the broken stem of his gavel. 'The sentencing is not yet complete! Once the prisoner is shaved, then he and his cohorts shall be despatched. Back to Siberia. It is there that you shall find your true ancestral lands, Grignan.'

279

'How they gonna *make* him?' whispered a squirrel.

Talina wanted to say, 'Yes, how?' but her tongue was swollen and furry inside her mouth.

'On the way,' said the Doge, 'your course shall be supervised by German witches from the Hartz Mountains and Swedish witches from Blocken. Let us hope that your wolfish brethren welcome you back with open arms.'

'Or open jaws,' muttered Ambrogio. 'Especially given the disease you bring with you.'

'What is more,' the Doge continued sternly, 'the Ravageurs will cease to be magical creatures. Your magic shall be confiscated and distributed to good causes. You will become visible to adult humans.'

'Humans with shotguns and hunting dogs!' mouthed a rabbit on the wall, with an air of someone who knew something about such a tricky situation.

Grignan demanded in a shaking voice, 'Our rat-slaves shall attend us on our journey.'

'Demand denied. They are free Venetian creatures. If any choose to accompany you of their free will and out of love for you, then they shall also have safe conduct to Siberia. Rodents, how say you?'

The rats in the Chamber chittered excitedly. Then they stood up on their back legs and stuck their noses in the air. They lifted their tails and waggled them rudely at Grignan.

'You can kiss our—'

The Doge summarized swiftly, 'The rats refuse.'

Grignan stood frozen with anger, unable to speak. Then his head suddenly dropped, his tail curled between his legs.

'How and when?' he muttered.

'The members of the Company of Christ and the Good Death will carry you and your kind in their boats to the mainland,' continued the Doge. 'They will conquer their fear of you for they are men of faith, who will know that they are lifting a great weight of vileness and pestilence from Venice.'

'What about the vultures, sir?' asked Ambrogio. 'They are also extremely vile and pestilent.'

'Yes,' said Talina, with feeling, 'and riddled with fleas.' But no one heard her words, which emerged in tiny whispered gasps from her constricted throat.

'There shall be a roost roast in the Stake House on the island of the Ravageurs. With nowhere to live and no one to feed them, the vultures too shall then be obliged to fly away and follow their masters.'

'He looks humble now, but I just cannot believe that Grignan will simply give up and leave Venice,' said Ambrogio slowly.

A Righteous Wraith murmured, 'This is correct, I fear.'

'And indeed you are right,' replied Grignan, still towering on his back legs. 'For my parting gift is a curse. It is not a curse that will destroy the city at once. It is a curse of baddened magic as yet but in bud. But it will gradually wax large and lustrous, like a pearl in an oyster, enfolding itself in more and more layers of evil. It shall lie here, hidden, quiet, unwritten, unknown, until the moment that it shall burst forth. And with it shall come the worst enemy Venice has ever known.'

The Chamber fell silent, mesmerized by Grignan's words.

'There shall be no words or mystic runes that shall stop it,' the Ravageur Lord hissed. 'No enchantment will gainsay my curse. The Venetians may live happy for a generation, two generations even. But there will come a time when this curse will ally itself with ancient powers and take living form, destroying this place and laying to waste the souls and bodies of all who inhabit it.'

Drops of perspiration trickled from Talina's forehead as Grignan snarled, 'Until that moment, when I shall return in triumph, I am happy to pursue my destiny far away from this accursed place. Farewell, Venice! And good riddance.'

He lowered his voice, as below them the bells of San Giacometo tolled the half-hour. 'One last thing. At the moment of my capture, my vulture Restaurant took a message to my minions Rouquin and Frimousse, who awaited me in ... a certain place ... in Venice. At two o'clock, exactly, they will have put the scorpion in the pot, with the hairs of the girl-thing's head. And hidden it where you'll never find it. That was thirty minutes ago. Neither the scorpion nor the girl have much longer to live.'

With that, Grignan disappeared.

'Come back!' yelled the Righteous Wraiths. 'Come back for your just deserts!'

'No!' screamed Professor Marìn. 'Come back and tell us where the scorpion is! Now!'

'What about the Retention Spell?' cried Ambrogio.

The small Doge said, 'The Ravageur Lord is still here inside his cage. Retention Spell has taken care of that. He may not leave the Chamber without our express permission. He has simply made himself invisible.'

'But he may as well be a thousand miles away,' murmured Professor Marìn, 'if he will not give us the information we need.'

'What's that about my hairs?' gasped Talina. 'Why does everyone keep talking about my hairs?'

'I've been trying to warn you, child,' said the professor. 'It is an ancient Venetian belief that if you bind a scorpion with the hairs of a person, and then bury it in a pot of sand, and hide it ... then that person is doomed.'

'Doomed?' asked Talina faintly. Her parents put their arms around her, their lips tense.

'As the scorpion slowly suffocates, so does the person,' the professor explained sadly.

And Talina clutched her throat.

'Does it hurt, kitten?' soothed her mother.

'We must find the pot and release the scorpion,' cried Ambrogio.

'Easier said than done, without Grignan to tell us where it is,' said a squirrel.

One of the Penitent Hags moaned, 'If only we'd thought about this possibility! We could have got the witches to reinforce the Retention Spell with a Material Presence Binding. And an Open-Tongue Lock. Oh, why didn't we do that? Woe is me! It's too bad . . .'

To Talina, the hag's sobbing seemed to come from far away. There was a roaring in her ears and green spots seemed to float in front of her eyes. She swayed.

'Talina,' urged her father, 'lie down and conserve your energy. Move as little as possible. Breathe slowly.'

It was a painful struggle for Talina to snatch any breath at all.

Tassini said, 'We must think like Grignan now. Ambrogio, ladies, everyone . . . think hard. Where would Grignan hide a deadly pot? Where would he think we'd never find it?'

'Or at least not find it in time to save Talina,' said Ambrogio, in despair.

'We've only just got our little girl back,' wept Talina's mother. 'Don't let her be taken from us for ever.'

She pressed a little mirror against Talina's lips and held it up for everyone to see. Only the faintest tracery of breath could be seen, like a shadow of a spider web.

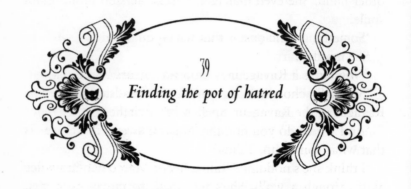

39

Finding the pot of hatred

chaos in the Chamber of Conversation

EVERYONE SPOKE AT once, including the mounted animal heads.

'How can we make the villain tell us where the pot is?' a squirrel despaired. 'We are clueless. And Grignan *wants* the girl to die.'

'We could starve him until he tells us,' suggested a sheep. 'Ravageurs have to keep eating or they perish.'

'Starving him would take too long. We don't even have minutes. Look at the girl! She's halfway dead already,' mourned a hag.

'Does he have any favourite places in Venice?' asked a fox.

'He just hates the whole place,' sighed a mink. 'Clearly.'

'What kind of pot? A flower pot?'

'A cooking pot?'

'A chamber pot?'

Talina struggled to raise herself on her elbow. She had an idea, but she could no longer talk. How to make them all

284

understand? She tugged at Ambrogio's wrists, and pointed to her numb mouth, rubbing her churning stomach with the other hand. She even managed a weak version of a blissful smile.

'Something delicious, is that what you mean?'

She nodded.

'Grignan is a Ravageur ... and Ravageurs love to eat—'

'Sweets!' chorused the mounted heads, the female Ravageurs, the Ravageur cubs and the witches.

'And where do you find the sweetest sweets in Venice? Is that what you mean, Talina?'

'I think she's nodding.' Talina heard Marco Molin's voice as if through a wall. 'She's too weak to move, poor girl. Look at that blue skin. Even her eyelids ...'

'The sweetest sweets in Venice?' mused Ambrogio. 'That would have to be Golosi's at Rialto, right under here. The Ravageurs are forever raiding that shop for jam and Mostarda.'

'And what do they sell their jams in!' shouted the professor.

'Pots! Pots! Pots!' squeaked a hundred different mammalian voices, Righteous Wraiths, Penitent Hags, witches and the three Admirals.

Golosi's had suffered another Ravageur raid in the last week. The windows and doors were boarded up. Ambrogio, Tassini and the professor tore at the planks with their bare hands.

'We'll never get through in time!' Ambrogio despaired. 'Isn't there any magic you can do, Professor? Can't you just magic us inside?'

'I was just thinking the same thing, but I have none of my ingredients here. I'll hum the nails out though.'

He began to hum, and after a few notes the first nail popped like the cork of a shaken bottle of ginger beer. Then another. And another.

'Stand back!' Tassini cried. 'Take shelter!'

They cowered behind a column until the rain of nails had ceased, emerging just in time to see the entire canopy of boarding tumble to the ground. Light flooded into the looted shop.

Ambrogio was the first to rush in, his face alight. 'Now we'll find it right away!'

And then his face fell. All their faces fell.

For what they saw now were ranks of dark mahogany shelves towering up to the ceiling. Only the lower shelves had been disturbed by the Ravageur robbers: they were empty except for shattered glass pots and trickles of jam. From above the height of a Ravageur's head, the walls were solidly lined with regiments of neat glass pots, filled to their brim. The scalloped white labels announced the contents in delicate black copperplate: Strawberry Jam, Caper Jelly, Artichoke Paste, Quince Reduction and a whole wall of Golosi's Mostarda.

'There must be ten thousand pots in here!' cried Tassini. 'How can we ever find the right one?'

'We must tap them!' shouted Ambrogio. 'That's how we'll find it. The ones with jelly and jams inside sound like this!' He seized a tasting spoon from the counter and rang it against a jar of Maraschino Cherries. It tinkled richly.

'If there was sand inside, there would be completely different noise,' Ambrogio explained. 'It would be dull and muted. Get a spoon, everyone. I'll take the Sweet Jam Wall.'

A crowd of Venetians gathered on the threshold to watch the great historian, the respected professor and a curly-haired boy inexplicably engaged in the action of climbing the Golosi ladders and tapping each jam pot in turn, listening closely to the result, as if they played the world's biggest and most eccentric xylophone.

'They've all gorn mad, they have,' observed one woman. 'Too many brains. It'll get you every time.'

'Here!' screamed Tassini. 'This one sounds different!'

He held a jar aloft. 'Look, it's full of sand.'

'Empty it then, you idiot!' called Ambrogio, breaking into a radish-red blush at the realization that he'd just said these words to Venice's most famous historian.

A cascade of sand sprayed the floor with glittering fragments.

'Where's the scorpion? Is it alive?' Ambrogio slid down his ladder and began raking through the particles of sand with his bare fingers.

'Careful, boy,' urged the professor, joining him. 'Oh, here it is – a fine handsome specimen.' He flicked the scorpion free of the sand. The black insect lay inert upon the marble floor.

'It's not moving,' moaned Ambrogio. 'It's dead. And that must mean that Talina is too.'

There was a long silence. The crowd drew back, embarrassed to be caught spectating on the tragedy evidently unfolding.

'Who's died?' murmured a boy.

'Ssh,' whispered his mother.

Tassini's voice was drained of expression: 'I should have got to the jar quicker. It was in my section to search. I was too slow.'

'It wasn't your fault, old chap,' said Professor Marìn thumping his arm so hard that the historian's spectacles fell unheeded onto the floor.

'Oh yes it was. To think we've come so far, and we've lost the dear girl. Ambrogio, can you ever forgive me? I know you—'

'Wait a moment,' said the professor, bending down to pick up Tassini's spectacles from the sand. 'Where's the scorpion gone?'

'There it is, running into that mouse hole!' Ambrogio pointed. 'It must have been *playing* dead.'

Back in the Chamber of Conversation, Talina was sitting up between her parents, accepting scintillating hugs from Righteous Wraiths, damp ones from the Penitent Hags and manly handshakes from the three Admirals of the Fleet.

The small Doge smiled. 'Meanwhile, the sentence has been carried out. That cage is now empty in every way. And the Ravageur Lord is already far away. He can be a trouble to no one any more.'

'Except to anyone edible,' squeaked a rabbit.

'Listen,' said the small Doge, with a mysterious smile. 'It is more interesting than that. The Chamber of Conversation can capture conversations even many miles distant. Listen.'

Far away on the plains of northern Italy, the pack of Ravageurs had halted in its pounding gallop. In the Chamber of Conversation, their rasping breaths and howls were as audible as if the beasts were in the room. There were shuffles and snarls, a whimper, and then the sound of one set of paws running away, with howls of derision following them.

Then, surprisingly, barks of laughter echoed around the Chamber. Finally, Talina clearly heard Frimousse say to Rouquin, 'Don't you feel as if we have been in a bad dream? An itchy, irritable, unnatural sort of dream?'

'Mange and Furious Rabies'll do that to you, they say,' came the answer. 'To think Old Baldy-Chops Grignan deliberately spread those afflictions among us, so we'd serve 'is little plans.'

'Isn't it good to feel ze land under our feet and ze wind in our fur?'

'And to have fur at all! Give me another swig of the yellow juice, Frimousse. The mange is almost gone, zanks to that. The humans were kind to supply us with zis **Dandelion & Daisy**, no matter what Grignan said about it. Grignan! Boh! Miserable specimen!'

'And isn't it beeautiful to be away from swampy old Venice! I can't think why we ever wanted anything to do with zat benighted place.'

'It was ze idea of Grignan. Didn't he look ridiculous wizzout ze fur?'

'And tiny! He was all fur! All fluff! We didn't realize. But he won't be 'aving any more smart ideas on our behalf again, will 'e?'

'*Jamais*. I mean, neverrrr. We don't have to talk French any more!'

'Hooray!'

The conversation faded. The Righteous Wraiths rose to their transparent feet and saluted the small Doge. 'Justice is done,' they said, 'and seen and heard to be done.'

Then they disappeared into a pale miasma, becoming part of it.

the tower at Quintavalle, June 3rd, 1867,
Saint Clotilde's Day

'CAN YOU EVER forgive me, Talina? You must think me a monster. As bad as a Ravageur. I am surprised and delighted that you agreed to visit me. Does it ... perhaps, mean that you might forgive me?'

Talina pursed her lips. 'That depends.'

The Guardian poured Talina a steaming cup of hot chocolate and offered her a slice of jam sponge from the best *pasticceria* in Castello.

'I know you're not like a Ravageur,' Talina wiped the crumbs from her mouth, 'though I thought you were for a long time. You're not even a really terrible man. You're just a poor, weak, frightened old man who lost his family. I had a taste of what that feels like, as you know. But I do have a question ... if you once had children that you really loved, why didn't you treat me better? You were never fond of me. So why did you make provisions to get me, if something happened to my parents? Then, once you had me, you were so unkind! You exercised your rights over me, but you didn't care about me. You were remote and horrible, and you never wanted to spend time with me, unless it was to harvest my little sorrows for your books.'

'Actually, I used to come to try to talk to you when you were asleep. Sometimes I stood a long time at your door, just looking at you.'

'I remember. But I supposed you were hoping to find me weeping or foaming at the mouth in a fit brought on by awful impudence.'

'No! It was the only time I dared to come and see you. The only time I could be sure not to feel the sharp side of that tongue of yours, which can be a little beastly at times. I knew you hated the sight of me. I hoped that you might eventually grow to be fond of me, but I feared that I did not have what it takes to make a child care for me.'

'Oh my,' said Talina in a very small voice. 'I suppose I didn't do much to convince you otherwise.' Then she blustered, 'And when you came to get me at the Archives, when I was terrified and had lost my parents ... you were colder than ice!'

'How could I have acted sweetly then? For a start, my conscience was wracked. I was the cause of your parents' disappearance. To have been affectionate with you at that moment would have been hypocritical. Even I was not capable of that. Truly, would you really have wanted me to smile at you? I have always thought that a mere smile from *me* would make you run away screaming. Anyway, my smiles had grown rusty and grotesque ... since I lost my wife and babies.'

Talina nodded slowly. Then she said fiercely, 'You pulled my hair that night! Like a brute!'

'Forgive me, I *was* a brute. This may be hard for you to believe, but I was as frightened as you were. I was in a state of shock too. My instincts and habits of being a writer made me see good material in your suffering. That's the kind of writer I was: a horrible parasite. Then I suddenly realized that I had to get you safely home as quickly as possible. I did not trust the Ravageurs not to come for you too.'

'I have never been afraid of Ravageurs!' said Talina proudly.

'You have never been afraid of anything, Talina. It was *I* who was afraid of *you*. You were so determined, so aggressive . . . I never knew that a child could be so impudent. My little boys—'

'Were so little when you lost them that they hadn't had time to be impudent. They hadn't even learnt to talk. I am sorry, but it is true. All babies are angelic. It is only when they grow up a bit that they start to be a bit more lively. Or impudent, as you prefer to call it.'

'Indeed, they are a little impudent now. They simply won't come and live in the tower. They want to stay on the island of Pescatoria and they want to keep fishing, in spite of everything that I can offer them by way of comfort and luxury here! But, Talina, we were speaking of you . . . I was troubled by you, for you are such a fanciful child, to the point of being, well, ridiculous . . .'

Talina drew up to her full height indignantly. 'And your own writings are of course perfectly sensible, reflecting most accurately a high death rate among naughty children?'

'I shall never write another story like that. I shall no longer write for children. Who am I to approach such grave subjects as Goodness, Fairness and Evil? From now on, I shall simply write books for adults, about grown men talking about themselves, fighting with each other and losing their money or their hair. I shall lower my ambitions and my register. I already wrote to tell my publishers. They inform me that they shall be bankrupted.'

'I'm not sorry for them! But, Great Uncle Uberto, my fanciful and ridiculous ways were not really sufficient reason to treat me so badly, were they?'

'As I said, at first I was paralysed by the shame of what I had done to you. I saw how you grieved for your parents. All your bold and clever attempts to find them! The letters in bottles! The kites! But I was trapped: Grignan told me that he was going to deal with the situation very quickly, and yet the weeks and months dragged past. I watched you, bravely making your lonely life in the tower. And I saw that you did not expect any affection from me.'

'So you did not offer any?'

'I did not think that I was worthy of it. And anyway, I saw that you loved that cat of yours more than you could ever care for me.'

'And you hate cats. Enough to drown them!'

'Well, admittedly less so, now that I know that a cat did not kill my babies ... And to think I nearly drowned you ... because of that.'

He buried his head in his hands.

'Cats are not baby-killers,' said Talina severely. 'But, Great Uncle Uberto, do you know what one of your worst deeds was? It was the way you emptied my room in your tower after I turned into a cat. When I came back here, it felt dreadful to see how you had stripped it of everything that made that room mine. Ambrogio was quite shocked to see it. Of course, I did not own that room – a child owns no place in the whole world, really. I knew it was yours, your tower, your walls, your everything – but I had *made* it mine, my refuge, the only way I could, with my little things, my pencils, my hanging books, my pictures. I'd hardly been gone a few days and you – you – you – *expunged* me, as if I were dead. As if I had never existed. You did to me what Grignan wanted to do to Venice. What had I ever done to deserve that?'

Talina's eyes grew hot with the bitter memory.

'Is there nothing I can do to make you forgive me, child? You are very young to be so very determined not to do so. I beg you, do not spend a lifetime hating me. Hate is so corrosive ... worse than water on iron.'

This seemed like the right moment.

'There is,' Talina smiled severely, 'something you could do that would make me think the absolute world of you, Great Uncle. Something that might even make me want to give you a hug.'

Uberto Flangini blushed with hopeful pleasure, asking eagerly, 'What is that, Talina?'

'Well, you know that the Ostello delle Gattemiagole was terribly damaged in the fire, and it was so tucked away that the Runic Rain did not restore it. Poor Signorina Tiozzo has no money to hire a new place, and her landlord will not permit her to keep the cats in her little apartment. He has sent her an eviction notice.'

'So I have read. It was in the *Gazzetta*.' He pointed to the newspaper open on his desk, with its headline of '**Cat Woman Faces the Streets. "Who will help my pretties now?"**'

'Well, given that you are all alone in this tower now ... By the way, I was sorry that Razin did not survive those wounds. He was so brave and so loyal. To you, anyway.'

'Even to that poor dog, I showed lamentably little affection,' mourned Uberto Flangini. 'And now it is true. Without you and without the dogs, this tower echoes like an empty shell at night.'

'And without Drusilla, of course.'

'Drusilla, yes. How could I forget her?'

'So,' wheedled Talina, 'I was wondering if you would not like to welcome back your old maid, Signorina Tiozzo? And her cats? Some of them seem a bit rough, I grant you, but they are really very nice animals, who would prosper so in such a cultured environment. You would never be troubled by a rat again. Your sons have agreed to deliver fresh fish three days a week for the cats ... and Ambrogio says he'll come to help me empty the litter trays and Signorina Tiozzo would cook your meals again, and take care of you as well as the cats ... You would never have to buy your jam sponge in a shop again!'

During this long speech, the Guardian's expression changed a dozen times – from shock, to disbelief, to laughter, to pain and finally to a kind of wonderment. His thin lips loosened into something that might almost have been a smile.

'That is quite a big thing to ask, child,' he said.

'It is quite a big thing to say "no" to, as well,' retorted Talina. 'Especially,' – she briefly put her fingers in her mouth and whistled – 'as I had quite counted on you saying "yes". And *Ambrogio* says you cannot very well say "no".'

Albicocco and Bestard-Belou marched into the room, bearing a large dead rat between them. Talina's chest clenched with horror. It was not a rat she knew personally, she quickly ascertained. But it had been a living creature. She frowned so fiercely at the cats that a long white whisker appeared under her nose. Hastily, she plucked it out.

'Found it in the pantry, mister,' said Albicocco. 'A foin big fella too. Grown-up cat's portion.'

'This seems to me a tower wot is in serious need of *derattizzazione*,' declared Bestard-Belou.

'Yer not wrong, Bestardo,' asserted Albicocco. 'And we would do it too, disregardless of expense.'

Great Uncle Uberto actually smiled. It was not a sinister smile, or a sad one. It looked like the kind of smile that might even turn into a laugh. Seeing it, Talina clapped her hands and explained, 'The cats are showing willing. They are offering you the best rat they could find, in exchange for accommodation. I hope you will accept?'

'It appears that the deal is already done, Talina. How could I possibly destroy such a perfect scenario?'

Talina murmured suspiciously, 'Well, I hope you're not just *pretending* to be happy, because, well ... *Ambrogio* says—'

Bestard-Belou butted her ankle. 'Don't go gittin yer gussie up, girlie. Da man's fully agreeable to da notion. It's nearly a done deal.'

The Guardian insisted, 'I'm perfectly happy, Talina. If I were a poet – instead of a very bad storyteller – I would say that it was poetic justice for me to end up in a tower full of cats.'

'You'll learn to love them,' said Talina.

'Won't take a minute,' concurred Albicocco.

'The cats can have the first four floors of the tower, provided they agree – on their oaths – to leave the sparrows alone. After all, this is the tower of Our Lady of the Sparrows. The cats must live and let live.'

Albicocco growled, '"Live and let live" won't butter any chickens, but I suppose we'll be fat on rats and fish, wot is plenty toothsome in itself.'

'Not much eatin' on a sparrow, anyways,' conceded Bestard-Belou.

Talina translated from the Felish: 'The cats agree to your terms. But—'

The Guardian continued, 'Talina, I am truly happy. You mustn't worry about me. I have my sons back. Venice is saved. My family's dark history is open to the light, and our shame has been cleansed by the dishonest sale being reversed. But most of all I am happy because you came to see me, Talina, when you didn't have to. You know that I tore up the contract with your parents when I gave them the deeds to the house I bought back for them? I have no claims over you any more.'

'Ambrogio says a court would never have enforced it anyway . . .'

'Oh he does, does he? It seems that *"Ambrogio says"* comes into the conversation quite frequently.'

Blushing hotly, Talina said, 'My parents say he is a very acceptable friend and, well . . . he's a highly quotable boy.'

'Did your parents tell you that I have a present for you?'

'They didn't.'

'Good. I wanted it to be a surprise.'

Great Uncle Uberto lifted a leather volume from his desk. He showed her the title stamped in gold on the maroon leather: *Talina in the Tower Part II*.

Inside, the pages were blank.

'What the . . . ?'

'He's gonna write my bografy,' quipped Albicocco. 'Plenty to tell there!'

Bestard cuffed him. 'You ain't even worf a limerick.'

The Guardian, oblivious to the Felish that was curdling into a quarrel at his feet, smiled at Talina and handed her the book. 'This is going to be better than anything I ever wrote.'

'Really? No dead children? No mutilated ones? No mortal or disfiguring illnesses?'

'Not unless you want them.'

'What kind of book is that?' asked Talina suspiciously, fingering the cover.

'This, child, is the book *you* are going to write,' said Great Uncle Uberto.

WHAT IS TRUE AND WHAT'S MADE UP

Ravageurs – What Are They?

The Ravageurs are not, of course, exactly wolves, but they are quite like a very nasty version of those noble animals, with a bit of hyena thrown in: according to this story, they resulted from the interbreeding of migrating Siberian wolves with hyenas escaped from a circus in Marseilles.

Like wolves, Ravageurs eat meat, fruit and vegetables. A wolf can 'wolf down' twenty-two pounds of food in one sitting. But a Ravageur needs to keep eating constantly, or he dies.

Also like wolves, the Ravageurs can run, climb and swim. Wolves have been known to swim up to thirteen kilometres. As Bidet shows in this story, wolves do indeed have webbed skin between their claws.

Wolves – and Ravageurs – usually live in packs, though of no more than forty individuals. (She-wolves are not, however, locked away like the poor female Ravageurs.) Wolves are extremely territorial. They mark their territory by urinating and howling. The sound of their howls can travel for kilometres.

Like the Ravageurs, wolves suffer from tapeworms. They become infected when they ingest the eggs in the raw flesh of their prey. (The Ravageurs like their meat extremely rare, if not still twitching.) Tapeworms can grow up to seven metres long and cause intestinal blockages. European wolves get a kind of tapeworm called *Taenia crassiceps*. Wolves are also the victims of 'mange-mites' – *Sarcoptes scabiei*. Advanced mange can cause emaciation and even death. As described in this book, there are two forms of rabies, an infectious disease of the central nervous system: Dumb and Furious Rabies. The latter makes the sufferer more dangerously aggressive. Both forms are fatal.

Wolves exist in two different ways – as the living creatures that they are, and as figures in people's imagination. Humans have always projected many feelings and fears onto wolves, perhaps because they are so much like us – omnivores who have strong emotions, who like to live in communities, share their food, and train and care for their young communally. In Italy, where this novel is set, attitudes towards wolves have changed dramatically over the centuries. Once they were positive models – a wolf suckled the twin founders of Rome, Romulus and Remus. But Christian writings tended to paint the wolf as a savage, dishonest and greedy creature, and it features as an enemy in the stories of some saints. In the twelfth and thirteenth centuries, bounties were paid for wolf carcasses. Farmers hunted wolves not just to protect their animals but also for their pelts. And Italian wolves were nearly exterminated – by the late 1800s there were none left in the Alps. In 1973, it was estimated that there were no more than a hundred left in the country.

Scientific books treated wolves the same way for many years. The quote about the Ravageurs being the most useless and hated animals is adapted from real text in *The Natural History of Quadrupeds*, published in 1828.

The same book described an animal infected with rabies thus: 'The continual agitations of this restless animal render him so furious, that he frequently ends his life in madness.'

The idea of the ceremony of saluting the hindparts of the Ravageur Lord was inspired by a witchcraft trial in northern Germany in 1232. In the account of the initiation ceremonies, the novices were required to kiss the hindparts of a frog and an enormous cat.

In modern times, wolves have become quite fashionable as a symbol of a wild, free existence. There are wolf sanctuaries and centres. The children's author Michelle Paver has helped to make the wolf the object of both fascination and compassion in her award-winning series, *The Chronicles of Ancient Darkness*.

Wolves in Venice

'*Lupo*' is the Italian word for 'wolf'. In Venetian dialect, this changes to '*lovo*'. There are still plenty of traces of wolves in Venice, starting with the Bar Gelateria Ai Lupi, at 5546 Cannaregio. There's also the Farmacia al Lupo Coronato at Castello 2715 – which features in my children's novel *The Undrowned Child*. And every tourist to Venice at some point must cross over the tiny, crowded Ponte del Lovo, near Rialto.

Luprio was indeed the name of one of the lagoon islands on which humans settled in the early days. Human refugees fled from the Lombards in the sixth century, taking refuge on the island. By 774 they had a parish church, Santa Croce in Luprio. This was occupied by French monks during the twelfth century. It later became a convent for the 'Poor Clares', which was suppressed in 1810. The church was demolished at the beginning of the twentieth century, to make way for the Papadopoli Gardens, but at the time this book is set it would have been used as a warehouse.

The embankment in front of the (now demolished) church of Santa Marta used to accumulate silt carried down from the River Brenta. Eventually the silt formed a peninsula all the way to the mainland. This became overgrown with bushes, and formed a convenient passageway for wolves to enter the city. It became known as 'il Ponte dei Lovi, the Bridge of Wolves'. It was removed in 1509, when Venice was at war with the League of Cambrai: the Venetians feared a land invasion by their human enemies.

Dunking Babies

In *Venice of Today and Yesterday* (1936), Harrison Rhodes recorded that on very hot days Venetian women were known to dunk their babies in the canals, by lowering them from their windows in baskets tied with rope.

Cat Sanctuaries in Venice

A famous Italian song '*Quarantaquattro Gatti*' tells the story of forty-four cats without a home. A cartoon video of the song can be seen on YouTube: http://www.youtube.com/watch?v=-E8ucqvDVlY

These days, many visitors complain about the lack of visible cats in Venice. Once, colonies of cats were to be seen all over the city, living wild. Today, there are many Venetian cats, but most live in private homes and few are seen on the streets. A massive cull of street cats was initiated in the 1970s by an English campaigner, Helen Sanders, on the grounds that many of them were diseased and starving. Now stray cats are usually captured and taken away to sanctuaries. There are several private '*gattili*' in the historic centre. The sanctuary in *Talina in the Tower* is based on the one in San Marcuola, now sadly diminished in numbers. The biggest cat refuge is run by the charity DINGO, at Malamocco on the Lido.

There is a move afoot to set up a petting cat café, which would not only raise money for cat charities, but also provide pleasure for cat-hungry tourists.

But it is never easy to do something new in Venice.

The Funeral of Venice

On November 14th, 2009, a funeral was held for Venice. That month, for the first time in modern memory, the city's population fell below 60,000. A group of Venetians had promised to hold a funeral if that happened, because they considered the city no longer sustainable at that level. The organizers wanted to protest against the city being turned into a museum, and to show the world that behind the picture-postcard romanticism of Venice there are serious problems – particularly a shortage of housing for young families.

Like all Venetian funerals, this one was water-borne, and very theatrical. A procession rowed a pink coffin from the railway station to Ca' Farsetti, the town hall, where a funeral service was held. Some researchers from America also took swabs from the mouths of Venetian citizens, to see if they could trace the DNA of the city's population.

Unlike the Ravageurs' 'Sad Event', this funeral had a happy ending. At the close of ceremonies, the participants destroyed the pink coffin by jumping on it. From the shattered box, they drew out a flag painted with a phoenix – a bird reborn from the ashes. In a solemn oration, the death of Venice was pronounced dead.

Venetian Sweets

The names of all the sweets came from a lovely little book by A. Jarrin called *The Italian Confectioner* (1820). Golosi's at Rialto is invented. '*Golosi*' means 'The Greedy Ones'. But there is still a wonderful old-fashioned confectioner at Rialto called the Antica Drogheria Mascari. You can see its colourful piles of spices in the window in the Calle degli Spezieri (which means 'the street of the spice merchants').

Mostarda is still very popular in Venice. It's a thick mustardy chutney often served with cheese or cold meats. It is usually yellow or orange in colour.

Venice in 1866

Venice was governed by foreign powers for more than half of the nineteenth century. The city surrendered to the French troops of Napoleon in 1797, but he signed her over to the Austrians, who took possession in January of the following year. Napoleon claimed Venice back in 1805 and made her part of his new 'Kingdom of Italy'. However, after Napoleon's defeat in 1814, Venice joined the Austrian-held Kingdom of Lombardy-Venetia. Venice was liberated from more than fifty years of Austrian rule in the autumn of 1866 when citizens voted overwhelmingly to become part of the new Kingdom of Italy.

Talina's Tower and Other Towers in Venice

Once Venice boasted 103 bell-towers. Sadly, today only fifty remain, several of them decapitated, though none by Ravageurs. Some fell down through neglect; very many were demolished in the early nineteenth century after Napoleon closed down their churches. Without maintenance, they crumbled away. They were frequently struck by lightning, or collapsed because of unsteady foundations in the mud. When the *campanile* of Santa Maria della Carità collapsed in 1744, it threw some gondolas right across the Grand Canal into the square of San Vidal, an event I transposed to San Barnaba for this story.

Some towers, like that of Santo Stefano, have survived but with a dangerous lean like the tower of Pisa. The tower of San Pietro in Castello, destroyed in this book, remains safely standing today. It was last restored in 2000.

Uberto Flangini's twittering tower is invented – there was never a tower on that site. I imagined it in Quintavalle on the remote edge of Venice, looking over the lagoon, where the *vaporetto* stop of San Pietro is now situated. Even by Talina's time, the nearby towers of Sant'Anna and San Daniele had already been demolished.

In Venice, it was quite normal for bell-towers to stand apart from their churches: given the fragile structure of the city, it was considered safer that way, as the towers were the first things to fall down in fires or earthquakes.

These days, parts of some bell-towers are being used as dwellings. San Marcuola's tower is partly residential now, as is the tower of Santa Margherita (which lost its spire in 1810) and those of San Boldu and San Stae. San Vidal's lower floors are used as offices. The top floors of the abandoned towers would, of course, make wonderful studios for architects ... or writers.

Signorina Tiozzo and the Old Ladies of Venice

Tiozzo is a very common name in Chioggia.

Venice is still a town with a large population of old ladies. Some have never left the city, or even their own *sestiere* or district, in their whole lives. A few rarely leave their homes.

Instead, they lower a basket into which helpful neighbours put their groceries.

Horatio Brown, a historian who lived in Venice for many years, wrote about the old ladies of Venice in his book, *Life on the Lagoons*. He explained that it was the old ladies who kept up the traditions and superstitions of the town. There were certain families who had the reputation of breeding witches, who could perform spells to bring happiness back to those crossed in love, for example. On the more sinister side, he reported a belief that witches could steal the hair combings of babies and cause the infants to waste away and die.

Also in *Life in the Lagoons*, Brown wrote that Venetians believed that all animals could talk once a year – on the day of the Epiphany. He also mentions the Venetian belief that new witches can be created only once a year, on Christmas Eve.

Scuola del Cristo e della Buona Morte

The building belonging to the 'Company of Christ and of the Good Death' was built in around 1644. As Giuseppe Tassini tells us in his *Curiosità Veneziane*, one of the jobs entrusted to this religious and charitable company was that of taking dead bodies out of the water and giving a decent burial to those who could not be identified. You can still see the beautiful little building, near the *vaporetto* stop of San Marcuola, at Cannaregio 1750.

Quintavalle

The island of Quintavalle is also referred to as the island of San Pietro in Castello, after the church which is its landmark, and was in fact the original cathedral of Venice.

The first bishops of Venice had their palace on the island,

near the place where my invented tower stands, from the eighth till the fifteenth centuries.

There are also a *squero*, *ponte* and *fondamenta* (a boatyard, a bridge and a street) named Quintavalle.

Quintavalle probably takes its name from a noble family who made their home there from around AD 430. The Quintavalle coat of arms was a blue background, a mountain with six golden peaks, and a black eagle above.

The family were members of the Great Council, and some achieved positions of power in the church. Pietro Marturio Quintavalle was made bishop of Venice in 955. The Venetian branch of the family died out in 1328, though some members lived in Crete until 1582.

The name Quintavalle seems to have developed from an earlier one, 'Marturio', which means 'martyr'. But there is another theory that the island's name came from the word 'quinavalle', meaning 'there below', referring to the remoteness of Quintavalle from the centre of Venice. And it does still feel remote from the tourist throngs.

A map of Quintavalle in 1846 shows the single V-shaped street of this story, with buildings on the south side and orchards on the north. Behind the church of San Pietro was an old cemetery. There was also a tar factory. The island today is much more densely populated and there are buildings on the north side of the street too. A puppet-maker has a workshop in a small courtyard. The military owns part of the island.

But there are plenty of kind and chatty old ladies and their cats there still, too.

Giuseppe Tassini and his Curiosità Veneziane

Giuseppe Tassini, unlike everyone else in this book, was a real person, a Venetian who lived between 1827 and 1899.

So he was nearly forty years old at the time of this story and already very well known in the city.

Tassini was the son of a solid middle-class family. His mother was Austrian, his father Venetian. Originally he studied to be a lawyer. But he inherited a fortune large enough to enable him to leave the law and devote himself solely to his passion for Venetian history. He spent the rest of his life burrowing through public and private archives.

His most famous book is called *Curiosità Veneziane* – *Curiosities of Venice*. It was originally published in 1863, and has always stayed in print.

Curiosità Veneziane recounts the stories of the streets and squares, bridges and palaces of Tassini's beloved city, all listed in alphabetical order and meticulously cross-referenced. Tassini's charm and verve as a writer, however, blow the dust off history. The joy of the book is in its anecdotes, like the tale of the time the devil took the shape of a monkey and jumped out of a palace behind San Marco: the angel who marks the hole in the wall, like almost every other Venetian curiosity, is still there to see. Curiosità weaves hauntings, gossip, graffiti and scandal into history.

The historian himself was quite a character – a perpetual bachelor (unusual in Italy) and a great gourmand. A sketch of him shows a good-humoured-looking man with a little goatee beard and thick black-rimmed glasses. He lived in Calle dei Spechieri (San Marco 635/634).

To this day, nearly every Venetian home has a copy of his book on its shelves.

Tassini would have been able to tell you everything about the addresses of the other characters in this book and others in this series:

Professor Marìn's tall crooked house is at Santa Croce 1011. It would be hard to give the house a proper 'street' address as it lurches with contrary leanings between the

Calle del Caustico and the Calle Gradisca. Even these two street names are contrary – '*caustico*' being a corrosive substance (or something offensive) and '*gradisca*' meaning something that pleases. So in effect the professor's home is sandwiched between 'Nice Street' and 'Bitingly Nasty Street'. Small wonder, then, that it lurches.

The Gasperin bookshop is in the Calle de Fuseri. Ambrogio and his family live above the shop.

The Ostello delle Gattemiagole, Rio Terra Farsetti, Cannaregio 1839.

The Molin family live at San Marco 3070 in the Calle del Teatro, between San Samuele and Santo Stefano.

The Antonello family (Renzo from *The Undrowned Child*) live at Corte del Tagiapietra, Santa Croce 1557.

Tassini also records a Palazzo Flangini on the Grand Canal, and also a *calle* and a *campiello* (a street and a little square) called Flangini, in the San Geremia area of the city. One member of the Flangini family was a war hero in the battles against the Turks. The last of the line was a Lodovico Flangini, who died in 1804, a cardinal.

Rovigo and its Pastry-Bandits

There's an old nursery rhyme that sums up the characters of the people of Venice and nearby towns on the mainland. It starts like this:

Veneziani gran signori,
Padovani gran dottori,
Visentini magnagati,
Veronesi tuti mati ...

which means:

The Venetians – great lords
The Paduans – great scholars
The Vicentini – cat-eaters
The Veronesi – all crazies . . .

The claim that the 'Visentini' – people from Vicenza – eat cats probably originates from a historic siege in which the starving populace had to consume their beloved pets. Another version claims Venice originally lent some of her fine cats to Vicenza to help with the city's rat problem. The cats were never returned, and so the Venetians made up this horrible nickname.

As for the people of Verona being 'crazy', this probably derives from the hat-making trade in the city. Poisonous chemicals in the production of hats in the eighteenth and nineteenth centuries often had a bad effect on the workers' brain function.

The stanza ends with the town of Rovigo, and the line is:

A Rovigo, non m'intrigo!

which means

About Rovigo . . . I just don't want to know!

This reflects Rovigo's very bad – and certainly unfair – reputation as a town of roughnecks and trouble-makers.

Animal Senses

Much more research needs to be done on how animals see the world, but they definitely have a different colour sense from humans, and I have tried to reflect this in the story.

Dogs and wolves seem to be colour-blind for red and

green. But they see quite vividly in blue and yellow. They can see more shades of grey than we can. Their distance vision is not as good as humans' and they often identify things only if they move – and by the way they move. The hearing of dogs and wolves is less acute than their sense of smell.

Cats are also red-green colour-blind, it seems. Red things look dark and green things look light to a cat. So where we might see a green leafy branch with red apples, a cat would see a whitish branch with dark apples. Cats see best in low light – in the evening and early morning. Their vision is impeded by very bright sunshine. A cat can also see more out of the sides of its eyes than we can. It is also true that a cat's heart beats twice as fast as a human's – between 110 and 140 beats per minute.

Vultures probably see blues and violets much as we do. Like cats, vultures also see better out of the sides of their eyes than we can, and their frontal vision is much stronger than ours. In real life few of these birds are strong enough to carry away a child or a full-grown woman. But Restaurant has special powers.

Ravageur Words and Names

Although the Ravageurs are not French, they pretend to be. So I used many archaic French words and French slang in their conversations and vocabulary, mostly taken from Charles M. Marchard's *A Careful Selection of Parisian Slang* (1917).

'Petit Grignon' was the name of a devil said to consort with a Frenchwoman called Suzanne Gaudry, who was tried for witchcraft in 1652. A wife of a man called Nochin Quinchou was named in the same trial.

Other names have the following meanings (literal translations in brackets):

Frimousse – vicious face
Rouquin – reddish fur
Un Balluchon – (a tramp's bundle) a shabby creature, his fur all wind-tossed and standing up in spikes
Fildefer – thin
Un Croquemort – an undertaker's man
Échalas – (a lath) lanky
Un Lèche-bottes – a boot-licker
Ripopette – worthless
Une Caboche – (a hobnail) a blockhead
Une Bourrique – (a she-ass) a stupid girl
Une Bassinoire – (a warming pan) a boring female
Une Bique – (a goat) a silly girl

(If they were truly French, female Ravageurs would of course be called 'Ravageuses'.)

French expressions

Again, these are taken from old French slang and literal meanings are given in brackets.

Des navets! – (turnips!) No!
Rosbif de rat d'égout! – (roast sewer rat!) You skunk!
C'est chic – Yes, nice
La peine! – So annoying!
Ah! Malheur! – Oh no!
Ah! Zut alors! – Oh, blow it!
Milles bombes! – A thousand bombshells! Hooray!
Hommelette – puny boy

Saints

There are many relics of saints in Venice. The church of Santa Maria del Giglio has a particularly rich store of them. There is a finger of St John the Baptist at Sant'Alvise, a rib of Mary Magdalene and an arm of San Bartolomeo at San Geremia, and an arm of St Ametisto at Santi Apostoli.

Manitoba Gargling Oil

This is an invention, but there were similar products on the market in Talina's time. They were sometimes advertised using 'testimonial' letters from fictitious noblewomen or celebrities, or in almanacs. 'Merchant's Gargling Oil', manufactured from 1833 to the end of the nineteenth century, was typical of this kind of medicine in that it claimed to be able to cure myriads of illnesses. It was originally sold as a medicine for animal ills including 'foundered feet', foot rot in sheep, garget in cows, roup in poultry, and mange. But by 1875, it was also being sold to humans for use against chilblains, frostbite, bruises, toothache and many other symptoms. 'Quack' medicines of this type were often high in sugar or even alcohol, so they did induce a brief feeling of well-being. But they could also create dangerous addictions.

ACKNOWLEDGEMENTS

Despite all my years in Venice, I would probably never have explored the quiet, mysterious island of Quintavalle without the guidance of my friend, the historian Lucio Sponza, who first took me there one warm dusk in 2009. Since then, Lucio has taken me on various walking tours of the area, bringing its history to life. And it's become one of my favourite places in Venice, which is why I set this story there.

Thanks to my editor and publisher Fiona Kennedy, for her inspired suggestions, and to my agent, Sarah Molloy, for her constant kindness, attention and wonderful sense of humour. And for reading early drafts, much gratitude to the Clink Street writers' group, especially Mavis Gregson and Sarah Salway, who were generous enough to read full drafts. For their close attention to the manuscript, I'd also like to thank Mary Hoffman, Kristina Blagojevitch, Jill Foulston, Meli Pinkerton and Lily Linke. Ornella Tarantola kindly checked my Italian; Cheryl Pasquier cast a clever eye on the French. Sophie Hutton-Squire expertly ironed out the inconsistencies in her copy-edit.

Thanks to Alan Morrison for the name 'Restaurant' for the chief vulture. Tigger-Maria is named in honour of the late pet of my nephew, Miko. I'm indebted to Rosemary Wilmot for the story of the cat caught in the door-knocker, and to my Scattered Authors Society friends Kath Langrish, Leslie Wilson, Karen Bush and Nick Green for help on animal colour-blindness, French, underwear and many other important matters.